Annie Lyons decided to have a go at book writing after having worked in the worlds of bookselling and publishing. Following a creative writing course, lots of reading and an extraordinary amount of coffee, she produced *Not Quite Perfect*, which went on to become a number one bestseller. Her second book *The Secrets Between Sisters* was nominated in the best eBook category at the 2014 Festival of Romance and *Life or Something Like It* was a top ten bestseller.

Annie's most recent titles, *The Choir on Hope Street* and *The Happiness List* are uplifting stories about community, hope, friendship and cake. She tries to write books which make people laugh and cry, although hopefully not at the same time. Annie lives in a shambolic money-pit of a house with her husband and two children plus a cat, who she pretends not to like. She enjoys channelling her inner Adele as part of her own beloved community choir and trying to grow cauliflower.

You can find out more about Annie on her website at www.annielyons.com, or get in touch on Twitter @1AnnieLyons or Facebook at www.facebook.com/annielyonswriter.

Also by
Annie Lyons

The Choir on Hope Street
Life or Something Like It
The Secrets Between Sisters
Not Quite Perfect

The Happiness List

ANNIE LYONS

ONE PLACE. MANY STORIES

HQ
An imprint of HarperCollins*Publishers* Ltd
1 London Bridge Street
London SE1 9GF

This paperback edition 2018

1

First published in Great Britain by
HQ, an imprint of HarperCollins*Publishers* Ltd 2018

ISBN: 978-0-00-831001-1

For more information visit: www.harpercollins.co.uk/green

For Rich, Lil and Alf,
who are always top of my happiness list.

Chapter One

Heather

'And you're absolutely sure you're okay?'

'Gem, I'm fine. Honestly.'

'Because I know that Mother's Day can be tricky.'

'When you're an orphan?' asked Heather in a squeaky little-girl-lost voice.

'You know what I mean, Heth. Remember the year you went AWOL.'

'That was three years ago. I was in a funny place.'

'Croydon, wasn't it?' teased Gemma.

'Exactly. You were selfishly on your honeymoon…'

'I'm sorry.'

'…and so you should be. I was single, living in a dodgy flat in Thornton Heath, working at that school with the violent kids and depressed teachers. To be honest, it would have been some kind of miracle if I hadn't ended up falling-down drunk in the Wetherspoon's on George Street.'

'The police had to take you home.'

'And they were utterly charming. I'm not the first sad and

1

lonely person to dance on a bar in Croydon and I doubt I'll be the last.'

'So you're not planning to jump on a tram and head over there today?'

'Gemma, those were pre-Luke, pre-engagement, pre-job in bakery, pre-lovely house on Hope Street days. I'm happy now. H-A-P-P-Y. Plus I'm planning to make the perfect New York cheesecake to welcome my perfect fiancé home from his perfect business trip.'

'Sounds perfect.'

'You better believe it, baby.'

'So you're sure you don't want me to come over?'

'Gemma. This is your first Mother's Day as an actual mother. I appreciate you worrying about me and I love you dearly but you deserve to enjoy it with Freddy Fruitcake. How is my nutty godson by the way?'

'Absolutely bonkers,' laughed Gemma. Heather smiled as she heard the adoration in her voice. 'I meant to say, we're thinking of booking the christening for mid-May – does that sound all right?'

'Sounds great and now you need to bugger off and enjoy your family time. I'll catch up with you in the week.'

'Okay. What time's luscious Luke back?'

'Around eight. Now stop worrying and get lost, loser.'

'Love you.'

'Love you too.'

Heather knew that New York Cheesecake was a risky thing to make for Luke – the self-proclaimed world cheesecake authority and a native New Yorker to boot. She had decided to seek advice from Pamela Trott, who made cakes for Taylor-made – the café and bakery owned by Caroline and Oliver Taylor, where Heather worked. Pamela was an incredible baker, whilst also being one of the nosiest people Heather had ever met.

'I remember your nan,' Pamela had said, beaming at her when they first met six months earlier. 'Used to live two streets over from Hope Street. Lovely lady. Terrible gout. So you've decided to come back to your roots? That's wonderful. And you're engaged to that nice American fellow?'

Heather was astonished by Pamela's insight. From the look on her face she was about to explode with joy at the prospect of Heather getting married.

'Awww, your mum would be so proud if she could see you now, God rest her soul. I was very sad to hear about your parents passing away. Your mum and I used to play out together sometimes when we were little,' said Pamela fondly. 'Let me know if you need someone to bake the wedding cake – I'd be only too happy to help!'

Heather had given a polite smile and made a mental note never to tell Pamela anything she didn't want the entire Hope Street community to know. She was, however, very keen to get her advice on baking. She'd practically swooned when she tasted Pamela's mango and passion fruit cheesecake.

'The trick to the perfect New York cheesecake is patience,' said Pamela sagely. 'You have to leave it to cool in the oven for two hours with the door shut and then leave it with the door ajar for another hour before you chill it.'

Heather did as she was told and felt a thrill later that day as she peered into the oven at the pleasingly honey-coloured crust. She left the oven door open a fraction and went into the living room to distract herself with another episode of *Orange Is the New Black*.

She felt as restless as a child waiting for Christmas. Luke had been away in New York for five days now. These trips were becoming increasingly frequent but he assured her that it was a good thing. He worked for an American drinks company and the stakes were high; soda was a serious business but Luke was doing well, with two promotions in the past twelve months. If he put in the hours, he was on track for the top. Heather understood. Of course, she'd like to see more of him but she wanted him to achieve the success he deserved.

Meanwhile, she had a job she enjoyed and a house she loved – an Edwardian mid-terrace with dark wood floors, original fireplaces and self-cleaning skylights. She had bought it six months ago with money inherited from her parents – an extravagant engagement present of which they would have certainly approved.

Heather settled on the sofa and caught sight of the last photograph of her with her parents. They were sitting at a café in Cornwall during the summer, her father grinning, her mother laughing and Heather smiling at them because they were reacting to something she'd said – some silly joke or remark. She hadn't been able to look at that photo for years after her parents died, hadn't been able to accept the fact that they were no longer in the world. But now, sitting here in her beautiful house with her gorgeous fiancé on his way home, she could smile at them and say, 'Hey, Mum, Dad – I miss you but I'm okay.'

A while later, she went to the kitchen to transfer the cheesecake to the fridge and grinned. It looked perfect. She reached for her phone, ready to take a picture to post on Instagram.

The perfect New York cheesecake for my perfect New Yorker.

That should get a few likes. Unfortunately, she didn't have a tight enough grip on the tin and the whole thing toppled out of her grasp, falling upside down onto the floor. She stared in horror for a second before realizing that her phone was buzzing with a call. *Luke.* Confused, she flicked the screen to answer. 'Luke? Where are you?'

'Hey, gorgeous. Listen, I got bad news. Snow in NYC – they grounded all the flights.'

'Oh.'

'Yeah, I know. I'm sorry. We should get moving tomorrow but I've no idea what time. I'll keep you posted.'

Heather felt her cheeks burn with frustration. 'It's just disappointing, you know? I've missed you.'

'I've missed you too but it's only one more day, okay? I'll make it up to you, I promise. I love you, Heather Brown.'

'I love you too.'

'Okay, I gotta go. See you tomorrow, beautiful.'

Heather stared at the blank screen and then down at the cheesecake-covered floor. She felt a prick of tears followed by a stab of irritation.

Get a grip, Heather Brown. Everything's fine. There's nothing to cry about. It's not his fault. You're just feeling emotional because it's Mother's Day. There's no use crying over spilt cheesecake. Everything is completely fine.

Chapter Two

Fran

Fran was unloading the dishwasher when she found out that her husband had died. In fact, she was just cursing him for not rinsing the plates before stacking them so that they'd come out dirty again. Since that day, she often mused about the strangeness of the things she missed but lasagne-encrusted bowls, the carelessly dropped boxers in the corner of the bedroom, and his wallet on the side in the kitchen seemed to be right up there. They say you don't know what you've got until it's gone. They don't know the half of it.

It was Andy's best friend Sam who called her. They'd been having lunch together when it happened. One minute he was pincering a piece of tuna sashimi with his chopsticks, talking about their Easter holiday plans, and the next he was gone.

A sudden arrhythmic death or, rather ironically Fran always thought, 'SAD' for short.

Aged forty-one.

Really?

Really? Fran would scream at everything from the sky to the untidy shoe rack in the hall. *This is really happening, is it? This is really fucking happening.*

'Anger is normal and natural,' the counsellor told her. 'A completely understandable part of the grief process.'

Of course, that just made her angrier. An anger as unquenchable as a raging thirst. That was her life during the weeks and months following Andy's death. One towering rage after another. She hated it but most of all she hated herself. She could see the worry, fear and embarrassment in her children's eyes as she lost it with everything from the broken washing machine to the UKIP candidate on Croydon High Street (although he had it coming). That was why she'd signed up for the counselling.

But it didn't help. Not really. She didn't want to be the tragic widow, going through the grieving process, having her feelings validated and coaxed. She didn't want to be a widow, grieving or otherwise. Like Brexit or Donald Trump, widowhood was something she was not prepared to accept.

Fran spotted her mother parking her small white car in a huge space in front of their house, revving backwards and forwards in a futile attempt to get closer to the kerb as her father winced from the passenger seat. She was a terrible driver with an unwarranted fear of leaving her car outside Fran's house ever since Bernie from three doors down had his stolen last year.

'It was a BMW, Mum. The police said they were stealing to order. I doubt Fiat Puntos are on their wish list.'

'I'll have you know that my car is extremely nippy,' Angela retorted.

Fran did a quick scan of the living room to check that it was up to her mother's legendary standards of cleanliness. Widow or no widow, she would be the first to criticize a stray cobweb or a grubby skirting board.

In many ways Angela had been the perfect support for Fran. Her father was lovely but he would look at her with a sorrow that Fran couldn't bear. She knew exactly what he was thinking.

My poor little girl – I'm supposed to protect her from all this but I can't and I feel helpless.

Fran didn't do helpless; it was an emotion she couldn't afford.

'What can I do, Fran?' he'd pleaded.

Nothing, she wanted to shout. *There is absolutely nothing you can do so stop asking.* But this was her dad – her dear, kind dad, who just wanted to make everything all right.

'Oh for heaven's sake, Bill, stop fussing and go and play with Charlie,' Fran's mother had barked.

Bill looked wounded but nodded. 'Of course,' he said, shambling off to the living room in search of his granddaughter.

'Harsh, Mum,' remarked Fran.

Angela shrugged. 'Don't pretend you weren't thinking the same thing.'

And that was the main reason why Fran had turned to her mother for support after Andy's death. Angela Cooper took on grief like an unpleasant stain that needed attention. She refused to indulge her daughter's predicament. She was never unkind – she just didn't give Fran an opportunity to wallow.

'You're too young to be a widow,' she'd remarked almost accusingly within hours of Andy's death, as if Fran had made a disastrous life decision instead of being the walk-on part in a terrible tragedy. The flash of anger Fran had felt at this stupidly obvious comment had actually helped to distract her and probably stopped her from collapsing with sadness.

Now, satisfied that the living room was relatively dust-free, Fran went to the front door to greet her parents. 'Kids! Granny and Grandpa are here,' she called.

'Happy Mother's and Grandmother's Day!' cried Charlie, skipping down the stairs.

'Thank you, dear,' said Angela. She kissed Fran on the cheek as she stepped into the hall. 'Oh my, look at that gigantic cobweb on your hall light. Don't you ever dust?'

Fran gave a wry smile. 'What would you have to moan about if I dusted?'

'Probably the length of your hair,' retorted Angela. 'When *did* you last get it cut?'

Fran rolled her eyes as she leant over to hug her father. 'Are you all right, Dad?'

He held his daughter at arm's length, giving her his customary frown of concern. 'I'm fine, Fran, but how are *you*?'

'Right, let's open a bottle, shall we? It is Mother's Day after all,' interrupted Angela.

Fran smiled. *Praise the Lord for bossy mothers.*

Angela put an arm around Charlie's shoulder and followed Fran to the kitchen with Bill shuffling behind. 'Either I'm getting shorter or you're getting taller,' she told her granddaughter.

'And look what I can do,' said Charlie, stretching her leg straight up and pulling it to her head with one arm.

'Good heavens above, where did you learn to do that?'

'Gymnastics,' smiled Charlie proudly.

'Amazing,' said Bill.

'Such talent! You don't get that from your mum.' Angela shot a glance in Fran's direction before grinning gleefully at her granddaughter. 'She gave herself a black eye whilst attempting a headstand when she was doing her BAGA Three Award – kicked her own knee into her eye!'

'Mum!' guffawed Charlie. 'You never told me that!'

'And I never would have either if it weren't for your motor-mouth granny,' said Fran, handing her parents their wine. 'Happy Mother's Day, Mum. Cheers, Dad.'

'Cheers, darling,' replied Angela. 'Now where is that delightful grandson of mine?'

'Probably upstairs plugged into his laptop. He'll come down once he smells the roast.'

'Why don't you challenge Grandpa to a game of something,' suggested Angela to Charlie.

Fran's heart sank. She could tell that her mother wanted to 'chat', which usually involved her talking and Fran listening to a list of everything she was doing wrong.

'Okay, Grandpa, how about Connect Four? Although, you should know that I've been practising with Jude and I'm getting pre-tty good,' said Charlie.

'You're on!' cried Bill, following her in the direction of the living room.

'Come on then. Out with it,' said Fran, once they were out of earshot.

'What do you mean?' asked Angela with feigned innocence. Fran raised her eyebrows. 'Oh, very well,' said her mother. She stood up straighter and fixed Fran with a look. 'It's time you acknowledged your grief.'

Fran scowled. 'I acknowledge it every day of my sodding life.'

'No you don't, Fran, and I'm partly to blame.'

'Wow. Can I have that in writing?'

Angela cocked her head to one side and pursed her lips. 'You kept going because you had to and I encouraged that but in doing so you've never properly faced the grief.'

'Funny, because I felt as if the grief was punching me in the face on a daily basis but obviously I was skipping through meadows of wild flowers without even realizing it.'

Angela raised her eyebrows. 'This is exactly what I'm talking about.'

'What?' snapped Fran.

Angela gestured with her hands. 'This. This attitude. This sarcasm. This dark humour. You're not facing your grief. You're railing against it. And in doing so you avoid the pain instead of facing it head on.'

Fran was incredulous. 'What do you mean?'

'I mean, my darling, you replace it with all manner of things – anger, cynicism and so on – when you need to open up because that's the only way you can move on.'

'I don't want to move on,' said Fran, folding her arms

Angela's face softened. 'I don't mean forget Andy, I just mean get to a place where you can accept the world without him.'

'Thank you, Professor Freud – you should have been my counsellor. It would have saved me a lot of bother.'

'I just want you to be happy.'

Fran stared at her. She wanted to say, 'I *am* happy,' but there was no way she'd get a lie that big past Angela Cooper. She turned back to the carrot she was chopping and an uneasy silence descended. Her body stiffened as her mum placed a hand on her shoulder.

'Just think about it, Fran. That's all I ask. It's been two years. Now shall I lay the table?'

'Thanks.'

As her mother bustled round the kitchen, the same dead-end thought drifted through Fran's head like a song on repeat.

Accept a world without Andy? Why on earth would I want to do that?

Chapter Three

Pamela

It was fine. Really. Absolutely fine. Two out of three Mother's Day cards were fine. A declaration that the majority of her children were thinking of her. There were plenty worse off.

'He's a lazy, selfish bugger,' Barry declared as they sat down to Sunday lunch. 'Doesn't think about anyone but himself. He lives the nearest and does the least.'

'Oh shush, Barry. It doesn't matter,' said Pamela. But it did matter. Of course it mattered. Another moment in her life that she shrugged off, pretending she didn't mind when in actual fact it exhausted her brain every waking second. Matthew. Her middle son. A constant worry and a big mystery to her.

Her other children were getting on with their lives. Her eldest, Laura was a chef, working for a trendy chain of Mexican restaurants in the West End, living in north London with her girlfriend, Jax. Her youngest, Simon was an app designer. He had set up his own business and become quite successful with a game called *Run, Bob, Run*, in which a gigantic polar bear called Bob had to run across various different landscapes, avoiding sharks, vultures and other similar nasties. Pamela had tried to play it once and felt rather sorry for Bob but apparently it was a big hit with pre-schoolers and meant that Simon could afford a lovely Georgian semi-detached in Bristol, which he shared with his software engineer girlfriend, Skye.

Pamela's middle son Matthew, on the other hand, was a relatively unsuccessful journalist and writer, living in a flat-share in Clapham in the same place he had moved to after leaving university. He was thirty-three now and whilst the other residents had changed numerous times over the past twelve years or so, Matthew remained in situ. He made just enough money to get by, along with occasional handouts from Pamela.

'Don't mention it to Dad,' she would cluck indulgently, posting a folded wad of twenty-pound notes into his pocket following another surprise visit. She chose to ignore the fact that he only popped round when he needed something. He was her son, after all. What was the world coming to if you couldn't turn to your own mother in times of need?

Pamela stared down at her lunch – the perfect roast, with slices of tender beef, Yorkshires as light as clouds, crispy roast potatoes, veg and gravy. She glanced up at her husband, who was scoffing it with gusto.

'Belicious,' he declared through a mouthful of food. Within minutes, it was gone. Barry sat back in his chair, patting his bulging belly appreciatively. 'Are you not eating, love?' he asked, staring at her untouched food.

'I'm not that hungry,' she said.

'Maybe have it later, eh?' he ventured. Pamela nodded. 'Right, well I'd best get back to it – got to get the peas in before dark.' He hauled himself to his feet and left the room.

Pamela looked at the clock. Twenty past one on Mother's Day. When families up and down the land were sitting down to celebrate the one who had given them life, who had brought them into the world and nurtured them as best they could.

And here she sat. Alone. While her husband tended his garden and her children got on with their lives. Weren't these supposed to be her golden years – the time when she embraced her life again, like an old forgotten friend? And yet, Pamela had spent so long being a wife and mother that she felt like the last person at a party after everyone else had gone – sad that it was over and wishing she could do it all again.

She left the table and went upstairs to the box room at the front of the house where she kept her photographs. She liked to come in here, to wallow in the memories of when she'd felt really happy. She picked out a random album and flicked it open, smiling down at a photograph of the three children on holiday in Weymouth. They were sitting on the sand – Laura in the middle, Simon to her left and Matthew on her right. Laura had her arms around her brothers and they were all grinning, their faces covered with ice cream. Pamela knew their exact ages – Laura had been seven, a right little bossyboots, organizing her brothers for every activity from sandcastle building to beach cricket. Matty and Simon didn't mind, of course. They were five and two and more than happy to comply with Laura who, as their big sister, seemed to know everything. They eyed her as if she was a mystical sorceress, holding the secrets of the universe in her pudgy grasp.

Pamela longed to leap into that photograph, to be back in that time when she still had so much to offer – when she was their whole world. They were still her whole world today. It's just that she wasn't theirs. She could remember Matty on the last night of that holiday. He had wrapped his chunky little arms tightly around her neck and whispered into her ear. 'I'm never going to leave you, Mummy.'

Pamela realized that she was sitting with her arms wrapped around her chest now and felt breathless with sadness at the memory. She longed for the feel of a child's body in her arms – that vital warmth and pure essence of love. She missed it so much. She missed being needed.

Pamela jumped with surprise as the doorbell rang. She made her way downstairs, thinking it would be Barry having locked himself out. She opened the front door and was confronted by a gigantic floral bouquet and the heady perfume of lilies.

'Happy Mother's Day, Mum,' said the bouquet.

'Oh, Matty,' cried Pamela, her sadness giving way to delight.

Matthew peered around the flowers with a grin. Such a handsome boy. Although he did look a little pale. She would give him a plate of dinner. Feed him up a bit. 'Hello, Mum. Can I come in?'

'Of course, of course!' she said, accepting the flowers and taking a step back to let him over the threshold. It was then that she noticed the large rucksack leaning in the porch. Matthew's rucksack.

'Actually, Mum. There's something I need to ask you,' he said with a wrinkle-nosed grimace.

Chapter Four

Heather

'Excuse me. I ordered a flat white but this is clearly a latte.'

Heather stared into the neatly bearded man's frowning face and immediately realized her mistake. 'I am so sorry. Let me sort that out for you right away.'

'Okay, but if you could be quite quick about it please – I've got a train to catch.'

'Of course. Georg, please would you make a flat white for the gentleman? And could I offer you a complimentary cinnamon swirl by way of an apology, sir?'

'I'm gluten intolerant,' said the man.

'Of course you are,' said Heather. 'How about one of our gluten-free brownies then? They're delicious.'

'Just the correct coffee, thanks,' insisted the man irritably.

Georg held out a flat white. 'Ahh, my glamorous assistant,' joked Heather. Georg remained as stony-faced as Flat White man. 'Here you are, sir. Sorry again. Have a lovely day. Thank you, Georg.'

'Mmm,' muttered the man before he left.

'Mm,' echoed Georg.

Tough crowd, thought Heather but then the caffeine-hungry, harassed commuters always were. The trick was to be bright and efficient – inject a little cheer into their day, encourage a fleeting smile perhaps.

Georg was a different story. Despite working alongside him for over six months, Heather couldn't remember ever seeing him crack a smile. He was supremely efficient and made the best coffee in this corner of south-east London. Heather assumed that customers considered his taciturn nature a small price to pay for sublime barista skills. She in turn felt the need to overcompensate for his blank expression by smiling so hard that sometimes her face ached by the end of the day. Heather had made it her secret mission to solve the mystery that was Georg. It was proving to be a challenge.

By 8.45, the queue was thinning out as Oliver and assistant baker, Pete, appeared from the kitchen carrying trays of croissants and pains au chocolat. The air was filled with the irresistible waft of chocolate, coffee and freshly baked pastries

'Post school-run provisions,' Oliver said with a smile, plonking his tray on the counter.

'Wonderful, thank you,' said Heather.

'Busy morning so far?'

'Very,' she replied, restocking the pastry baskets by the till.

'She made mistake,' reported Georg gravely.

'Snitch,' laughed Heather.

Georg frowned. 'What is snitch?'

'A person who tells tales to the boss. It's a very serious crime, Georg,' said Pete, winking at Heather.

'Oh, sorry,' muttered Georg, looking unsure.

'Fortunately, Caroline's not in yet so you're off the hook,' said Oliver, flashing a grin at Heather.

'But you are boss too,' insisted Georg.

'Don't let Caroline hear you say that,' joked Oliver.

Heather chuckled, remembering the moment Oliver's wife, Caroline, offered her the job at Taylor-made. Heather had been in no doubt who was in charge as she issued her specific instructions with a frown.

'You'll need to scrape back your hair into a neat ponytail for hygiene and wear a minimal amount of make-up – we want you to engage with the customers, not make them fall in love with you. Please arrive at six-thirty sharp. We open at seven in time for the commuter rush. Georg is our resident barista – he'll show you the ropes. Oliver will be around but busy baking obviously.'

'Obviously,' repeated Heather feeling sick with nerves. *I am a strong, confident woman. Until I meet another woman, who is stronger and more confident. And then basically I become a jelly.*

Caroline had cast a critical eye over her newest employee. 'We've had no end of troubles finding someone suitable for this job – please don't let us down.'

'I won't,' promised Heather, praying that this was true.

'So I should tell Caroline about Heather's mistake?' asked Georg earnestly.

'Georg!' cried Heather, feigning outrage. 'How would you feel if I told Caroline about all the mistakes you make?'

Georg looked confused. 'I do not make mistakes.'

Pete patted him on the back. 'We're just joking, bro. You don't need to tell anyone anything, okay?'

'Okay,' said Georg, fixing Pete with a look of relief. 'Thank you.'

Heather grinned at Oliver. She loved working here. Despite Georg's unusual nature and the fact that she now had a mild pastry addiction, it was good fun. The place was always bustling, the customers eclectic and mostly lovely, and its location, just around the corner from where her mother had grown up, gave Heather an unexpected feeling of comfort.

'Aha, and who is this vision I see before me?' cried Oliver as

18

Pamela hurried through the door with two large cake tins in her arms.

'It is Pamela,' said Georg, confused. Heather and Oliver exchanged glances of amusement.

'Hello, my loves. How are we all today?' asked Pamela, plonking the tins on the counter.

'All the better for seeing you,' replied Oliver. 'And what delights do you have for us this fine morning?'

'Just a salted caramel layer cake and a strawberries and cream sponge.'

'Pamela, if I wasn't a happily married man, I would drop down on one knee right now,' declared Oliver.

'Oh, get away with you,' she blushed.

'These look incredible,' said Heather, lifting the lids on the tins. Pamela might have been Hope Street's resident busybody but she was the closest thing they had to Mary Berry. Credit where it was due.

'Thanks, lovey,' said Pamela with a smile. 'Oliver, would it be okay if I put up this poster on your community notice board? It's for a new course all about happiness starting tonight at Hope Street Hall.'

'Of course – be my guest.'

'Thank you. I just met the man who's running it – lovely eyes and so charming. I think I'm going to give it a go. I've always wanted to find out about that mindfulness malarkey. Anyone else fancy it?'

She fixed her gaze on Heather, who felt a flash of irritation.

Back off, lady – just because my parents died, it doesn't mean I need to go on a course.

'Pete?' asked Heather, deflecting the question.

Pete grinned. 'As an Aussie, I've pretty much got the happiness lark sorted, thanks, Pamela – it's mainly down to sport and beer. Now excuse me, lovely people, but I need to crack on with another batch of sourdough,' he said, before disappearing into the kitchen.

Pamela gave an indulgent chuckle and then looked at Oliver with eyebrows raised. He put a hand on his heart. 'I fear that if I told Caroline I was going to a happiness course, she would see it as a declaration of weakness, which, as you know, isn't allowed in our house.'

Pamela giggled before turning to Heather. 'Do you fancy it then, Heather?' she asked, holding out the poster.

Heather smiled politely as she took it from her and read out loud.

'*The Happiness List – a course led by life coach, Nikolaj Pedersen, teaching you practical skills and exercises to achieve your own version of happiness.*

Ten weeks from Wednesday, 29th of March, 7-9 p.m., Hope Street Community Hall, £8 per session including refreshments.'

She wrinkled her nose. 'Thanks, but it's not for me, Pamela. I'm about as happy as it's possible to be. Besides, Luke and I are going to be busy tonight making wedding plans.'

Pamela clapped her hands together. 'Of course – how wonderful. You deserve to be happy after losing your dear mum and dad. But you must miss them terribly, especially when you're preparing for such a happy event,' she insisted. 'I can't imagine how hard it must be organizing your big day without having them here to lend a hand and share in your joy. I mean, who will help you pick out your dress?'

Not you if that's what you're angling for, thought Heather, astonished at Pamela's tactlessness. 'My cousin, Gemma is very supportive,' she said with a curt smile. 'And it was a long time ago.'

'Oh but you never get over it, do you? I mean, I still miss my parents after all these years. I wasn't even that close to my mother but I still catch myself wondering if I should phone to check she's okay.'

'Everyone's different,' said Heather, trying to close down the discussion.

Pamela gave her a sympathetic look. 'Of course. I'm sorry. I didn't mean to upset you by dredging up the past.'

Heather was annoyed with herself because she had no right to be irritated with Pamela. She wasn't being unkind. She was just speaking the bald truth – a truth that Heather hadn't properly considered until now.

Her parents wouldn't be there for her wedding. Her mother wouldn't help her pick out her dress. Or argue over the seating plan. Or hold her hand when the day finally arrived and she felt shaky with nerves.

She caught a whiff of ginger and cinnamon from the coffee Georg was brewing and felt herself transported back to the day her parents died. She was sixteen and remembered sitting next to Gemma on the sofa at her house – a green velvet sofa with brown sagging cushions. It was November and the air smelled of cinnamon and ginger because her aunt Marian had been baking parkin. Her uncle Jim walked in and cleared his throat. Heather could see his face, grey with concern, and her aunt behind him crying. She couldn't remember her first reaction to the news but she did recall Gemma wrapping her arms around her for the longest time – an embrace so tight as if she was trying to hug away the pain.

Gemma. She was the one who had propped her up ever since it happened. She'd moved in to her aunt and uncle's house as an only child and ended up getting a ready-made family with a big sister to boot. That wasn't to say there weren't arguments and disagreements. Suddenly Gemma had to share her parents, her house, her whole world with her younger cousin. Two teenage girls living under one roof was a challenge at the best of times – the cries from Gemma of, 'Stop stealing my stuff!' and Heather's perfect storm of adolescence and grief made for some pretty epic battles. Heather couldn't remember seeing Uncle Jim in the house much during those years. He retreated to the safe haven of his garden shed, and who could blame him?

21

Still, Heather's overriding memories were of the good times – a blanket of laughter and comfort from the best friend and cousin all rolled into one, who counselled, cajoled and lent her nail varnish.

It had been Gemma who introduced her to Luke. It was the spring of 2014, months before Gemma was due to marry Ed. She and Heather had embarked on a series of nights out. Their 'Final Tour', they called it – drunken evenings where they tearfully declared how much they loved one another, drank too much vodka and danced to the Spice Girls. Heather couldn't remember the name of the club but she did recall the moment when she returned from the toilet, walking towards the blue backlit bar where Gemma was silhouetted next to a tall man. He was resting his hand on her arm and talking into her ear. Gemma was laughing and shaking her head as she turned and caught sight of Heather.

'Now this,' she slurred, grinning at the man as she gestured towards Heather, 'is the woman of your dreams.'

The stranger turned and Heather remembered feeling a jolt, not like electricity but more physical, like a lost piece of her clicking back into place. Luke Benjamin had a soft gaze and the longest eyelashes Heather had even seen on a man. Gemma had watched with smiling approval while Heather and Luke attempted a conversation over the thumping beat of the music. After a respectable amount of time, she had hugged her friend and warned Luke to 'take care of my coz or else', before heading off into the night.

Heather had spent the rest of the night walking around the streets of London with Luke, talking and laughing. Falling in love. It was as heady and romantic as it sounded and for Heather, it felt so right – her shot at happiness after so many years of fruitless searching. Heather knew that her current happiness was all down to Gemma and that even if her parents couldn't be there to share in her joy, Gemma and her parents would do all they could to fill that gap.

'It's fine,' Heather reassured Pamela. 'It will be hard but my cousin and her parents will support me.'

Pamela reached out and squeezed her arm. 'Of course. It's wonderful that you've found this lovely man. You must be so happy to have him home. Did he like the cheesecake?'

'He did,' lied Heather. She wasn't about to tell her that the cheesecake had ended up in the bin or mention the fact that she'd hardly had a chance to talk to Luke since his return from New York. Understandably he had arrived home exhausted, delighted to see her but in desperate need of his bed on the first night and on Tuesday night, after a punishing day's work, he had fallen asleep on the sofa by nine and woken full of sheepish apologies.

She'd forgiven him immediately. It wasn't his fault. He had pulled Heather into a kiss, promising to make it up to her.

So tonight was the night. She was planning a lovely dinner, a bottle of good wine and a proper discussion about the wedding. She already had a couple of venues in mind.

'I'm glad,' said Pamela. 'Well if you change your mind about the course, you know where we'll be.'

Heather nodded, safe in the knowledge that there would be no changing of minds, plans or anything else that evening. 'Thank you.'

'I will go,' said Georg with an earnest frown as if he was signing up to join the Foreign Legion. Heather stared at him in surprise.

Pamela grinned. 'Wonderful! I'll see you later then, Georg – I've baked some flapjacks for us to share. I'm looking forward to it! Right, I'll pop this flyer on the board and then I'll be off. I need to get home and make sure that Barry and Matthew aren't arguing. Again. Cheerio!'

Heather stared at Georg after she'd gone. 'A happiness course? Really?'

Georg frowned. 'Why not?'

'Surely you don't think that kind of stuff can be learnt, do you?' she scoffed.

'You do not?' asked Georg.

Heather shrugged. 'You're either happy or you're not.'

Georg fixed her with a look. 'What did you say to Pamela? Everyone is different.'

Touché, thought Heather. Clearly there was more to Georg than met the eye. 'Fair enough,' she said. 'Each to their own.'

Georg gave a satisfied nod. 'I think it will be interesting. I like to learn.'

'Good for you,' said Heather with a smile.

'Okay. You take break now. I will cover.' He handed her a cortado.

She frowned at the coffee. 'But I usually have a latte.'

'You try. You will like,' he insisted.

Heather sighed and carried her coffee to a table by the window. She took a sip. It was rich and bitter but utterly delicious. Surprised, she shot a glance at Georg, who nodded a knowing reply.

She smiled and took in her surroundings. The Taylor-made café and bakery had become something of a hub in the community since Caroline and Oliver Taylor established it eighteen months ago. It was hip but friendly with its exposed brick and soft lighting and had already won awards for its signature sourdough. Heather had been surprised at how quickly she'd settled into the job. It was a far cry from her original career plan as a teacher, but it was considerably less stressful and she decided that there was enough stress in their lives already with Luke's job. She didn't earn much but felt at home here, and besides, her inheritance more than contributed to their financial commitments. She knew how important Luke's job was to him – that he had ambitions to become a director and that there was a real chance of this happening over the next few years. She respected his desire to do well and was happy to support him because she loved him. Of course, she wished that he could switch off from work sometimes or reduce his hours a fraction but she wanted him to achieve his dream – he worked hard and he deserved it.

There was another flyer for the happiness course on the doormat when she got home later that afternoon.

'It's like you're stalking me,' she said, as she stuffed it into the recycling bin and made herself a cup of tea. She flicked her iPad into life and typed 'Chilford Park', taking in the stunning pictures of lush green lawns and the tastefully elegant ballroom. Wedding venue porn. Nothing quite like it to soothe the soul. Except wedding dress porn. That was her other current favourite.

She sipped her tea and Googled the recipe for twice-cooked chips. She was planning to cook steak with pepper sauce and chips, accompanied by a nice bottle of red. Heather stretched her arms, teasing out the tension in her aching muscles and decided that she would have a soak in the bath before getting everything ready for this evening. She wanted it to be perfect. She went upstairs and laid out the Agent Provocateur underwear that Luke had bought her last Christmas. He had been too tired for sex over the past couple of evenings so she was sure he'd be in the mood for a little seduction tonight. She ran the bath, filling it with Molton Brown bath oil, and lit some candles. Her phone rang from the bedroom and she felt a thrill of excitement as she saw that it was Luke calling.

'I was just thinking about you,' murmured Heather, tracing a finger over the lacy bra waiting on the bed. 'I've got plans for us this evening.'

'Oh, honey, I can't tell you how much I'd love that and I'm so sorry but I gotta take a rain check. The boss has dropped this last-minute dinner on me. They're important head office clients so I can't say no. I'm really sorry, Heather.'

Heather grabbed the underwear and tossed it back into the drawer. 'It's fine. It'll keep,' she said, unable to hide the disappointment from her voice.

'You're upset, aren't you?'

Heather sighed. 'A bit. You got back on Monday and you've been knackered ever since. I was planning a nice dinner so that we could talk about the wedding and catch up, you know, properly.' She winced at how desperate she sounded.

'I'll make it up to you. I promise. At the weekend – we'll talk weddings for a solid forty-eight hours and do all the catching up you want,' he said in honeyed tones.

She softened and gave an indulgent laugh. 'O-kay.'

'I love you, Heather Brown. And I'm really, really sorry.'

'I know. I love you too.'

Heather stomped around the house, feeling annoyed and then irritated at her annoyance. There was no point in getting cross with Luke. It wasn't his fault. He had to work and that was that – getting pissed off wasn't going to change the situation. And yet it niggled – the feeling that she was always taking second place somehow, second place to an American drinks company. It didn't exactly make a girl feel good about herself.

She drained the bath and went downstairs to make some toast. Somehow steak and twice-cooked chips for one didn't hold much appeal. She carried her plate into the living room and switched on the TV, flicking idly through the channels as she ate. She felt restless and irritable. Was she being unfair about this or did she have a right to be angry? She knew one person who would tell her for sure. She reached for her phone. Gemma answered after three rings.

'Hey, Heth, what's up?'

Heather could hear Freddy wailing in the background. She grimaced. These weren't exactly suitable conditions for a heart-to-heart with your bestie. 'Never mind about me – what are you doing to that baby?' she asked.

Gemma gave a weary sigh. 'I call it the baby witching hour. It's a huge conspiracy – all the babies in the world start going mental at six o'clock and don't stop until their parents are on the brink of insanity.'

'Poor you.'

'Thank you. It comes with the territory these days. Are you okay? Aren't you supposed to be talking weddings with that perfect man of yours tonight?'

Heather sighed. 'Yeah but he's got to work.'

'Again?'

'Mmm. Do you think I'm wrong to be pissed off?'

Freddy's cries intensified to a volume and pitch that sounded like something from a horror film. Heather realized that it was unfair to expect Gemma to counsel her. 'Listen, Gem, I can hear that this is a bad time. You go.'

'I'm sorry, Heth. It's difficult to concentrate on no sleep with Hitler-in-a-nappy here wailing in the background. I'm always here for you. I'll call you soon and we can talk it all through, okay?'

'Yes, of course,' said Heather breezily. 'It's fine. You go and sort Freddy Fruitcake.'

'Thank you, Heth and sorry again. Love you.'

'Love you too,' said Heather. 'And I miss you,' she told the blank screen as the call ended.

She turned and caught sight of her parents' photo and felt an urge to cry as an unexpected wave of desolation hit her. Heather turned and headed quickly for the door. 'Oh no you don't. Not tonight.' She stood in the hall for a moment, weighing up her options. 'This is ridiculous,' she muttered, as she remembered her earlier conversation with Pamela. 'You've got no right to self-pity. You moved on from that emotion a long time ago.' She exhaled.

What's it to be then, Heather Brown? Another night in alone watching Netflix? That's a sure-fire way of intensifying your self-pitying mood. Come on, there must be another option.

She glanced at her phone. 6.45. A surprising idea twitched in her brain.

Surely not? After everything you've said? You're not actually considering it, are you?

She hesitated for a fraction of a second before making a decision. 'Sod it,' she said, reaching for her bag and jacket and heading out onto Hope Street.

Chapter Five

Fran

The trees that lined Hope Street were heavy with blossom. There seemed to be no scheme to their planting – tall ones, short ones, all intermingled in a mishmash of cloud-like whites and pinks. It was that time of year when the sun shone by day but the heat soon disappeared as it got dark. There was a chilly snap to the air so that Fran wished she'd pulled on her cosy-but-smelly dog-walking coat instead of her tatty leather jacket.

She could see a glow of light pooling from the doorway to Hope Street Community Hall and a few people making their way inside. She paused just short of the pathway that led towards the door. If it wasn't for her mother, she would have quite happily turned on her heel, gone home, change into her PJs and binge-watched *Modern Family* with the dog on her lap and a family bag of Doritos by her side.

But Angela Cooper had arrived that afternoon, struggling up the garden path with the ancient carpet bag that she called her 'overnighter' and a determined look on her face. Fran knew better than to challenge that look.

'Here, Granny, let me take your bag,' Charlie had said, smiling and reaching out to her.

'Oh, thank you, Charlie dear. Gosh, I do feel old sometimes.'

'You're not old, Granny, you're young and beautiful.'

'Thank you, my treasure. Hello, Fran dear,' she said, stepping over the threshold and kissing her daughter on the cheek, while the dog ran in excited circles around them and Jude appeared on the landing. 'And who is this handsome young man I see before me?'

''llo Granny.' Jude smiled as he plodded down the stairs, leaning in to give his grandmother an awkward teenage hug. Fran marvelled at how relaxed teenagers were with other teenagers, wrapping arms around one another in an almost possessive way, but present them with someone outside their immediate friendship circle and you were lucky if they made eye contact.

'It's pizza for tea, Mum. I hope that's okay,' said Fran, leading the way to the kitchen.

'What would you say if I told you it wasn't?' retorted her mother.

Fran pursed her lips. 'I don't like to swear in front of the children.'

Charlie looked confused. 'You're always swearing, Mummy. That's why I made you this,' she said, holding up a jam jar wrapped in exercise paper with the words 'Mummy's Swear Pot' written in large purple writing.

Angela raised her eyebrows at her daughter. Fran shrugged. 'All the books on grief tell you that swearing can be a very useful form of self-expression. Plus, I'm putting the money towards a holiday.'

Angela took the jar from Charlie and weighed it in her hand. 'I'd say you've got enough for a trip to Disneyworld.'

'Hooray!' cried Charlie. Alan barked in celebration. 'Please can I go and watch TV before dinner?'

'Sure,' nodded Fran.

'Thanks, Mum. Love you.' Charlie stared at her mother, waiting for the response.

'Love you too.' Satisfied, Charlie leant over to kiss her mother and then her grandmother before disappearing to the lounge. 'Glass of wine?' asked Fran, hoping to distract her mother from Charlie's mildly obsessive behaviour.

'I was wondering when you were going to ask,' said Angela. Fran rolled her eyes and fetched a bottle from the fridge. 'So is Charlie still sleeping in your bed?' she asked, accepting the wine glass and taking a sip.

'Sometimes,' said Fran, feeling immediately defensive. 'But where's the harm? If she needs reassurance, there's nothing wrong with it – that's what the counsellor said.' After Andy died, Charlie had insisted on sleeping in Fran's bed every night for about a year. It happened less often now. Fran would never tell her mother but she relished the nights when she woke to find her long-haired, still baby-faced girl snoring softly next to her. She knew this wasn't ideal for either of them but she didn't care – whatever got you through the day and encouraged you to carry on putting one foot in front of the other was fine by her.

'It ties you down, Fran, and it's not fair on Charlie.'

'I'm not going anywhere and Charlie's still young so whatever she needs is fine by me. Now can we please change the subject? How's Dad?'

Even Angela knew when to let things go. She sniffed. 'He's got an in-grown toenail.'

'Ouch.'

'You'd think he'd broken his leg the way he goes on about it.'

'Everyone needs a hobby.'

Angela smiled. 'So are you looking forward to this course?'

Fran gave her mother an incredulous look. 'What do you think?'

'I think you should go with an open mind.'

'Says the woman who makes her mind up about people within seven seconds of meeting them,' snorted Fran.

'Except you're not like me, are you? You're younger and receptive to new ideas.'

Fran sighed. 'I'm going tonight but if it's all hygge and hot air, I won't be going again.'

Her mother fixed her with a look. 'Let's hope it brings you something unexpected, shall we?'

Fran knocked her wine glass against her mother's. 'To eternal happiness.'

Fran glanced at her watch. Five to seven. She wondered what her friend Nat was up to. She had a feeling that Wednesday might be Dan's night to have Woody so there was a chance that her friend was home alone, with a tempting bottle of wine in the fridge…

'I'm not sure whether to go in either,' said a voice behind her.

Fran turned. The woman was younger than her. Fran was terrible at guessing ages but she estimated her to be mid-twenties. She had dark brown hair, which was scraped up into a loose bun and an air of nervousness, which Fran put down to the prospect of baring her soul in front of a group of strangers. She understood completely and flashed a sympathetic smile.

'I like your jacket,' said the woman.

'Thanks. My son says I'm too old for a leather jacket, which is exactly why I wear it,' she smirked. 'And while we're on the subject, I like your scarf.'

'Thanks.' The woman grinned. 'I'm Heather by the way.'

'Fran,' she said. 'So now that we're officially best mates, shall we forget this and naff off to the Goldfinch Tavern?' She thumbed towards the direction of the local pub.

Heather laughed. 'Could do.'

Fran dismissed the idea with a flick of her hand. 'I'm just messing with you. My mother's babysitting and if I don't go home with the secrets to a happy life imprinted on my brain, she'll never speak to me or help with the kids again.'

'Shall we then?' asked Heather.

'After you,' said Fran, gesturing towards the door. 'But please be warned that I am using you as a human shield.'

Heather laughed as they walked inside.

The Happiness List

WEEK 1: Introduction
WEEK 2: Mindfulness
WEEK 3: Exercise
WEEK 4: Laughter
WEEKS 5 & 6: Keep Learning
WEEK 7: The World Outside Ourselves
WEEK 8: Resilience
WEEK 9: Contentment
WEEK 10: Review

Fran picked up the handout from one of the chairs and wondered if she could slip out now. She could probably just Google these and work it out for herself at home without the fuss of having to come along every week. She had a mindfulness colouring book somewhere, although Charlie had stolen her colouring pencils. In fact, she probably had a book covering most of these subjects. Fran bought a lot of books. It had always been her natural antidote to any life problem that arose. She loved that sense of hope when she came home with a shiny new book. Surely this would be the one to give her the answer to everything from how to tame your toddler to communicating with your monosyllabic teenager? She bought dozens of books after Andy died and friends and relatives had given her dozens more. Alas, she rarely found the time to actually read them beyond skimming the first few chapters. Now they sat abandoned and unread on her bookshelves – an archive of her failed attempts to get her life in order.

Fran sat down. The chairs had been set up in a semicircle. She nodded to Jim the postman and a couple of other people who were already seated. She identified the course leader in seconds – a tall man with George Clooney hair and an air of self-assurance and experience – he would definitely be one to encourage 'show and tell'. The very thought made her shudder with dread.

'He looks friendly enough,' whispered Heather, taking her place next to Fran and nodding towards George Clooney. 'Although of course he may have two horns underneath that magnificent hair.' Fran laughed. 'Do you know Pamela? And this is Georg,' added Heather, gesturing to her left.

'Hello.' Georg wore a blank expression.

In complete contrast, Pamela looked as if she might burst with delight. 'Hello! It's lovely to meet you. Now forgive me but I feel as we've met before. Did you used to come to the toddler group?'

Fran nodded. 'Yep, although that was a while back now. My oldest is at secondary and my youngest is in year five.'

Pamela shook her head in disbelief. 'Time flies and I've got a brain like a sieve. What was your name, lovey?'

'It's Fran,' she replied, holding her breath, ready for the moment of dreadful recognition.

It was as if a cloud descended over Pamela. She patted Fran's arm. 'Of course, Fran. How could I forget? I'm so sorry. How *are* you?'

Heather frowned with confusion.

'My husband died a couple of years ago,' explained Fran. *That's my cover blown then.*

'I'm sorry,' said Heather. 'That's terrible.'

Fran nodded because that was all you could do. It was terrible – everyone's worst fear. Over the past couple of years, she had become practised at dealing with the way people reacted when she told them – the fear in their eyes as they desperately scanned their brains for the right thing to say. It was down to her to console their shock and reassure them that they didn't need to be sorry – it was really shit but it wasn't their fault. It wasn't anyone's fault. And that was the worst thing of all.

'Heather's mum and dad passed away a few years ago,' said Pamela brightly. Fran shot a surprised glance at Heather and realized that she was trying to swallow down her mirth at this inappropriately cheerful remark.

'Best friends for life then,' said Fran with a wink. Heather chuckled.

They sat up straighter in their chairs as George Clooney clapped his hands together and called them to attention.

'Okay, everyone, let's make a start. Welcome. My name is Nikolaj Pedersen but everyone calls me Nik. So no doubt you are wondering what to expect, you may be thinking, *why am I here?* You may be doubting why you have come or thinking, *what can this Scandinavian weirdo teach me?*' The assembled group gave a nervous laugh and Nik smiled. 'That is okay. Don't worry. The point is that you are here – something has brought you here and for that you should be grateful. I don't need to know what that thing is – no one needs to know. You can share your stories of course but it is by no means obligatory. Everyone's story is different, just as everyone's version of happiness is different. My aim is to help you reframe your lives so that you can find your version. The handouts in front of you contain the list of what I see as the fundamental steps towards achieving this – it's my happiness list.' He smiled. 'These are the things I will try to teach you over the next ten weeks in order for you to find whatever it is you seek. After each session, I will set you homework based on that list item so that you can practise what we have discussed and learnt but I'll tell you more about that later.'

'Blimey, he'll be giving out detentions next,' mused Fran under her breath. Heather smirked.

Nik continued. 'I cannot promise that you will find exactly what you need but if you come to each session with an open mind, it will be possible. So, I want you to think of this hall as a drama-free space, where you leave behind your problems of everyday life – take a moment to depart from day-to-day competition and stress, a moment to be open and to open yourself up to possibility. That is all I ask. If you find this isn't for you, that is okay but I would say that you need to give yourself time – give yourself a chance.'

Fran shifted in her chair as Nik continued.

'This is also not an individual activity. We are in this together as part of a team. We will help and support one another without judgement or prejudice. We will do all we can to help others find the happiness they seek. Are we in agreement?'

There were hesitant murmurs around the room.

Nik seemed satisfied. 'Good. So, with that in mind, I am going to put you into groups.' Fran found herself in a three with Pamela and Heather. 'These are your official course buddies,' Nik told them. 'You will undertake your exercises and challenges alongside them – think of them as family.'

'Not sure that's necessarily a good thing,' murmured Fran to Heather. She laughed.

'This is going to be fun,' declared Pamela, grinning at them both.

Fun? thought Fran. *Really? Was it realistic to expect people over the age of ten to have actual fun?*

She used to watch the kids on the trampoline, bouncing with joy, laughing their heads off. One day last week, Charlie was on there so Fran decided to go out and join her because it had been a shit day and she thought, why not? Fran winced as she recalled bouncing higher and higher, encouraged by her giggling daughter, before realizing with horror that women her age really need to empty their bladders before they tried it.

Fran admired Pamela's child-like wonder but she reserved the right to remain deeply cynical about the next ten weeks being any kind of fun. She got the feeling that she might have an ally in Heather in this respect. Fran focused her attention back on Nik.

'After tea, I would like us to try a simple meditation, but, before that, I think it would be helpful if we introduced ourselves and gave one piece of information that we are happy to share – it can be anything, not necessarily to do with happiness. Something that we don't mind the world knowing – it can be funny or sad or just a fact. I'll go first to give you an idea. My name is Nik and I play the euphonium.'

Fran snorted with laughter. Nik turned to Jim, who was sitting to his left.

He looked embarrassed, running a hand over his bald head as he spoke. 'My name is Jim and I used to sing in a *Take That* tribute band.'

'Bravo, Jim, and welcome,' said Nik with an encouraging smile.

Fran felt her mouth go dry as Nik made his way around the circle. Among the group was Sue, who once appeared on *Britain's Got Talent* playing the washboard, Georg, who had won awards for his latte art and Pamela, who was a star baker. Even Heather had won a Blue Peter badge. When it was Fran's turn, she decided to play it for laughs.

'I'm Fran,' she began. 'And I have a dog called Alan.' Everyone laughed. 'Yep,' she went on. 'I thought it would be funny too but you try calling that name in the park on a Sunday afternoon. You get a lot of attention from middle-aged men and not in a good way.'

More laughter. Fran felt herself relax.

Got away with that one, Fran. You could have announced that you had a dog called Alan who saved you from the brink of insanity but maybe keep that for another time.

It was true. When her brother had turned up on the doorstep six months after Andy died, carrying a spaniel puppy under his arm, she'd wept until she felt weak. Then she punched her brother on the arm for being so bloody irresponsible. Then she hugged him and said he was the best brother ever. The children

37

were over the moon but worried that Fran wouldn't let him stay.

'Please, Mum,' Charlie begged. 'We'll help look after him.'

Jude looked at her from behind that floppy fringe, a peppering of spots just visible on his forehead above a pair of huge blue eyes. His father's eyes.

Fran felt a wave of grief – the widow's version of a hot flush she called it. It came and went and made you feel bloody terrible. The puppy waddled over and sat on her feet. Her slippers suddenly felt warm. She stared down at him in horror. He stared back at her, eyebrows raised in amazement at his own audacity.

Fran threw back her head and roared with laughter. Her brother and the kids gaped at one other with alarm. Fran knew why. It was the first time she had laughed since Andy's death and they were worried that this was the sign of her losing it properly. Ranting and raving was understandable but hysterical laughter? Not so much.

'What's so funny?' smirked Charlie, who loved a shared joke.

Fran picked up the puppy. 'Any animal who has the gall to wee on my slippers in order to gain affection, gets my vote.'

'So we can keep him?' asked Charlie, who was sometimes slow on the uptake.

'We can keep him,' laughed Fran.

'Can we call him Alan?' suggested Charlie. 'I've always liked that name. It's friendly.'

'Alan?' Fran frowned.

Jude shrugged. 'S'good name. Better than calling him something stupid like Daniel.'

Fran's brother snorted with laughter. 'Daniel the spaniel. Good one.'

Fran held up the puppy and squinted into his eyes. The puppy stared back. 'Alan,' she said. The puppy gave a cheerful bark of agreement. Fran shook her head with a grin. 'Alan it is then.'

* * *

I wish Alan was here right now, thought Fran as Nik instructed them to find a comfortable seated position after the tea break. She felt nervous and, for some reason, her daft dog always calmed her down.

'Next week we shall be focusing on mindfulness properly but today by way of an introduction, I would like us to try a simple exercise to give you an example of what it feels like to be mindful – a basic meditation based on breathing. I believe that it is a good skill to learn on the path to a happier existence and we shall be doing our best to practise it as much as possible. It can be tricky to start with so don't worry if you don't get it straight away. Now. Close your eyes and place your hands softly in your lap. Be aware of the sensations in your body as you breathe in and out. Focus on nothing but the breathing in and out.'

Fran heard a nervous fart and felt Heather's body shake with laughter next to her so that she had to bite her lip to stop herself from laughing too.

'If your thoughts start to wander, do not worry. Simply bring your mind back to your breathing. In and out. In and out.'

Shake it all about, thought Fran. Oh dear. This wasn't going very well. She tried to focus on her breathing but her overall thought was how ridiculous this was. A group of grown people sitting around in a draughty community hall waiting for it to be over. She opened one eye and looked furtively left and right. Jim's eyes were tightly shut as he mouthed the words 'in and out' to himself. Fran dared a glance at Heather and realized that she was peeking too. They both suppressed giggles as Pamela started to snore peacefully. Nik had his eyes closed so Fran pulled a face at Heather, who had to stuff a fist in her mouth to stop herself from laughing.

'Okay,' said Nik, his eyes still closed. 'Allow yourself to come back to the moment and if it didn't work for you this time…' he opened his eyes and looked directly at Fran and Heather, who exchanged sheepish smirks '…please be aware that the realization

39

that your mind has wandered is actually an integral part of meditation.'

'Gold stars for us then,' whispered Fran to Heather, who chuckled.

'Ooh, I feel so refreshed,' declared Pamela, stretching out her arms.

'That is because you sleep,' pointed out Georg with a frown. 'That is not meditation or mindfulness. That is sleep.'

'Oh. Right,' said Pamela looking disappointed.

'Don't worry, this is all good practice,' said Nik reassuringly. 'And an excellent start – well done. So, now I will set your homework. Firstly, I want you to practise mindfulness in your everyday life, find something that works for you. It could be mindful baking, Pamela or mindful dog-walking, Fran.'

'Yeah, I'm not sure Alan will go for that,' she retorted.

'Well, try things out and we can discuss it next week, when we will focus on mindfulness properly. You also have my happiness list and as you can see it is generic. I would therefore like you to come up with your own list. This week, write down one thing, relating to your happiness, that you would like to work on or achieve by the end of the course. It could be "get fitter" or "learn to paint" or something more emotional like "stop feeling guilty".' Fran felt her skin prickle. 'Try to be honest. You don't have to share it, unless you want to. I would like you to add to your list after every week as we learn together so that by the end of the course you have your own happiness list. Does this make sense?'

There were enthusiastic murmurs and nods from everyone in the room apart from Heather and Fran. They shared a knowing smile, which gave Fran an unexpected feeling of hope.

'Okay, that's enough from me,' nodded Nik. 'Feel free to ask me questions afterwards or email me in the week if you need to. Good luck and I look forward to seeing you next week.'

* * *

'A happiness list, eh?' said Fran as she followed Pamela and Heather onto the street. 'Well I don't know what Mads Mikkelsen in there is going to make of me listing "eat more KitKat Chunkies, go on a date with Idris Elba and finally clear out the loft", because that would definitely make me happy.'

Pamela chuckled before turning to Heather. 'I bet I can guess what the first item on your list is,' she said with glee before humming the tune to 'Here Comes the Bride'.

Heather shrugged. 'Maybe.'

Fran got the feeling that Heather wanted to rein in Pamela's enthusiasm. 'Any idea what you're going to focus on then, Pamela?' she asked, changing the subject.

Heather gave her a grateful smile.

Pamela sighed. 'I don't know. Try to stop my Barry and Matthew arguing all the time probably.'

'That doesn't sound much fun,' said Fran. 'I refuse to referee my kids' disagreements. Let them sort out their own arguments – make sure you do something for yourself,' she added kindly.

Pamela patted her arm and nodded. 'I'm definitely going to give that mindful baking a try. I do love my baking and I think it would calm me down if I was a bit more, you know, *in the moment.*' She smiled, making inverted commas in the air.

'Good for you,' declared Fran, keen to draw the conversation to a close before Pamela started to grill her. 'Right, I'd better get back home to Mum. Good luck,' she added, giving a hasty wave before heading off along the street.

'How was it then?' asked Angela as Fran flopped onto the sofa a while later and took a large sip of wine.

'Yeah, it was great. I've learnt all the happiness and everything is fine.'

Angela regarded her daughter for a second before shaking her head. 'Oh Fran,' she said. 'Please at least try to make some effort.'

* * *

41

The next day Fran lay back on the uncomfortable sofa and stared up at the crack in the ceiling that seemed to get bigger every week.

So are you going to give the mindfulness a go? he asked.

I think I'd rather poke myself repeatedly in the eye.

You're not really taking this seriously, are you?

When did I last take anything seriously?

True. But you need to, Fran. You know that, don't you? You can't hide behind the humour all the time.

Funny but that's pretty much what my mother said.

Well, maybe it's time to listen.

Traitor. Anyway, can't you see? My sardonic humour is all I've got to stop me from standing in the garden and howling at the moon.

You've got the kids. And Alan.

I know. And I love them.

I know you do. But you need something more, don't you? Something beyond the cynical humour and pretence that everything's okay.

So you're saying that I can't just keep hiding behind the jokes?

You know the answer to that.

Spoilsport.

Later that afternoon, Fran sat at her kitchen table staring down at the page in her notebook where she had written 'Happiness List Thing' in careless, barely legible handwriting. She had been sitting there for half an hour now, during which time she had underlined the words with a decorative curly line, drawn a doodle of some flowers and was contemplating adding a cartoon picture of Alan. She smiled down at the dog, who was, as per usual, sitting underneath the table by her feet.

'Who's a good dog, eh?' she cooed, reaching down to stroke his head. Alan stared up at her with mournful eyes. He really was the most beautiful dog – all caramel fur and velvet ears. You

42

couldn't help smiling at him. Or giving him a treat. Alan knew this, of course, and milked it to perfection. 'You're a good dog. Yes, you are.' Alan gave a gentle bark of agreement. 'Right, well you have to help me with this,' she told him, holding up the notebook, 'because I need to exceed my mother's rock-bottom expectations somehow but I don't know what to put. I am on the verge of writing "more walks with Alan", even though that would pretty much turn my life into one long dog walk.'

Alan jumped up, barking with excitement, and then to further illustrate the point, ran to the hall and began a charming chasing-his-tail dance in front of the coat rack.

'Bugger. Rookie mistake. I said the "w" word out loud, didn't I?' Another bark of affirmation. 'Right, okay. I guess we may as well head out because I'm not getting very far here.' Fran pulled on her dog-walking coat, trainers and clipped on Alan's lead. 'After you, doggy.'

They trotted along the street in the sunshine. Fran felt its warmth on her face and a sense of calm descend. Maybe this was what mindfulness felt like and she'd simply never realized. Fran wouldn't call it happiness as such but she wasn't unhappy. It was just that grief had that annoying habit of being there all the time so that these small moments of joy were a bit like licking the icing off a cupcake and finding that the cake was made of shit. Yeah. Even two years on.

Fran didn't honestly believe that people got over grief. How could they? Someone you loved more than anything was gone. For ever. How could you ever reach a point where you blithely said, 'Yeah, I'm fine with that? I'm happy again.'

Never. Gonna. Happen.

The problem was that after two years, people sort of expected you to have moved on. They weren't being unkind. She would probably do the same. You couldn't keep doing the sympathy thing for ever, the 'how *are* you?' voice.

Still, just because the rest of the world had moved on, it didn't mean that she had. In the days immediately after Andy's death, she had found herself thinking, *This time two days ago, he was here, having dinner at home with us*, and then, *This time three weeks ago, we were watching an episode of* The Sopranos *and drinking that delicious wine Sam bought us*. It then became, *This time three months ago he was here. He was alive.* But now it was ridiculous. She couldn't say to herself, *This time one hundred and four weeks ago, he was still breathing*. She knew something had to change but at this moment in time, she had no idea what it was.

As she returned home from their walk, she let Alan off his lead and made her way to the kitchen. She spied her notebook sitting on the table, open, the blank page taunting her. She grabbed her pen and started to write.

'There,' she said to Alan. 'Done.' She flicked on the kettle and gazed out at the overgrown mess of a garden. She glanced back at the book. Alan gave a quizzical whine. She stared at him. 'You're right. It *is* too soon. I'll think of something else.' She grabbed the pen and put a neat cross through what she had just written.

Chapter Six

Pamela

My Happiness List
1. Just bake

'Observe the soured cream as you gently pour it into the chocolate mixture. See how it changes the consistency of your batter. Look at the way it alters as you stir, creating swirling patterns and a light tinge to the colour.'

'Do we have any Jeyes Fluid, Pammy? That bloody fox has done his business on the front path again.'

Pamela pressed pause on the iPad. 'Barry. I am trying to do some baking here. I don't know if we've got any Jeyes. Why don't you look in the shed?'

'So-rree,' he huffed. 'I was only asking.'

Pamela closed her eyes and sighed. *Three deep breaths and bring yourself back to the moment.* That's what the nice American lady said. Satisfied that Barry was safely foraging around in the shed, she pressed 'play' on the recording.

'And now we add the vanilla essence. I recommend Madagascan

for the ultimate aromatherapy experience. Open the bottle and allow the sweet scent of vanilla to fill your nostrils.' Pamela wrestled with the cap – it was an unopened bottle, stubbornly sealed. 'Pour one teaspoon into the mixture.'

'Hang on a second, ducks,' she said, gripping at the cap and trying without success to unscrew it.

'Now mix it all together, allowing the mingled aromas of chocolate and vanilla to waft into your senses.'

Pamela tried to gnaw at the bottle top with her teeth. A loose crown flew from her mouth into the mixture. 'Bother,' she declared, fishing it out with a spoon.

'Take a moment to admire what you're creating.'

Pamela frowned at the resolutely sealed bottle of vanilla essence. 'Never mind,' she told the batter. 'You look lovely as you are.'

'Now observe the sensations in your arms and body as you mix.'

Pamela wondered if the woman meant her to dwell on the nagging pain in her wrist but decided she probably didn't.

'Once you have mixed it thoroughly, spoon evenly between the muffin cases, taking time to focus on what you're doing.'

I wonder if Barry found the Jeyes? Oh, I forgot to take the sausages out of the freezer for tea. I wonder if Matty will want to eat with us tonight? Unlikely after Barry went on at him for not having a job. How can he be so unkind to his own son? You have to support your children no matter what.

'If you find your mind wandering, just bring it back to the task in hand.'

'Sorry, lovey.' Pamela grimaced.

'And now place the cupcakes in the oven. Have a seat a safe distance away and close your eyes. Take three deep breaths. You have nothing else to do but sit here for the next fifteen minutes while they bake. Listen to the sounds around you, feel the warmth of the oven and inhale those delicious smells as they start to waft over you. If your mind wanders, don't worry. Just focus on this gentle music and bring it back with three deep breaths. Enjoy this moment in your comfortable, warm kitchen filled with its wonderful aromas.'

Pamela did exactly as she was told. She closed her eyes and began to breathe.

Oh damn, I still haven't taken the sausages out of the freezer. Never mind. I'll do it in a sec.

Breathe, Pammy.

I wonder when Matthew's going to get up. He doesn't always help himself with his dad by lying in bed until goodness knows when.

Breathe.

If only he'd find a job – something he enjoys. I might take a look in the shops on the high street to see if there are any ads.

Breathe. Keep breathing.

Mmm, those cakes do smell delicious…

It's a drizzly day – cloud-heavy and dull. Laura is splashing through the puddles on the way to school, Matthew is kicking his welly-clad feet in the pushchair. They're singing. Singing in the rain. *We're singing in the rain!* Laura glances up at her mother and gives her a gap-toothed grin. They reach the school gates and she runs off to class with her friends in a flurry of brightly coloured cagoules. 'Have a good day, my little duck – love you!' Matthew peers up at his mother, one eye obscured by the hood of his raincoat. 'Shall we go to the park and feed the ducks then, Matty?' 'Ducks! Ducks!' he cries gleefully, kicking his legs again. They reach the deserted park and head straight to the lake. There is a flock of nesting herons making a dreadful racket on the island in the middle. 'Dinosaurs!' declares Matthew happily. 'Arrrck! Arrrck!' Pamela laughs. 'Yes, Matty – they're just like dinosaurs. Now do you want to feed the ducks?' she asks, releasing him from the pushchair and holding out a slice of bread. He joyfully accepts it, pushing himself to a standing position and tottering towards the railings. He tears pieces of bread with clumsy little fingers and flings them towards the grateful ducks now gathering in front of him. Pamela smiles through the drizzle, placing a hand on her pregnant belly. She feels a surge of pure happiness as she watches her sweet little boy. How perfect life is. 'Ducks, Mummy. Quack! Quack!' he cries. 'Quack, quack, Matty,' she laughs. 'Quack, quack.'

'Mum? Are you okay? I think there might be something burning in the oven.'

'And gently come back to the moment. Open your eyes and focus on something beautiful, like a flower or a tree in the garden.'

Pamela opened her eyes and stared into her son's confused face. 'Oh bother! I must have dropped off or set the oven too high,' she cried, leaping to her feet and flinging open the oven. Twelve charred buns belched out a wave of black smoke.

'Allow the delicious aroma of your cupcakes to infuse you with positivity as you bring them out of the oven.'

'Oh, shut up you!' snapped Pamela, reaching forward to stab at the 'stop' button.

She rescued the buns and threw them straight into the bin. She never burnt her cakes. Never.

'Are you okay, Mum?' asked Matthew again with concern.

She gazed up into his worried face and felt a little restored. 'I'm fine, lovey. I must have been tired.' She noticed that he was dressed and she smelt aftershave too. That was a good sign. 'Are you off out somewhere?' she asked. 'Do you want me to make you some breakfast?'

Matthew leant forward to plant a kiss on her forehead, like a blessing. 'You're an angel, Mum, but I'm meeting someone in an hour, so thanks but I'm good.' She smiled at him. He hesitated for a second, fixing her with a troubled little-boy-lost look. Pamela knew that look. It tugged at her heart and said, *This is your child – help him.* She reached for her purse.

'Here,' she said, fishing out a twenty-pound note. 'Take this, get yourself something to eat.'

'Are you sure?' he asked, but his fingers were already closing around it.

'Of course. I know you haven't got much work at the moment so this is to help you out until you find a job.'

He hugged her then, kissing her cheek. 'Thanks, Mum. I'll pay you back – every last penny. I promise. See you later, 'kay?'

'Okay, Matty. Will you be home for tea? I'm planning sausage toad.'

Matthew grinned. 'You said the magic words – that'll be great. Thanks, Mum. Love you.'

'I love you too,' said Pamela as the door slammed shut. She felt a dip of sadness at the silence, the empty space where her son had been until a second ago. 'Sausages,' she said, rousing herself, moving towards the fridge freezer to retrieve them. She glanced at the time. Eleven o'clock. Coffee time. She flicked on the kettle and opened the fridge, frowning at the space where the milk should have been.

Unfortunately, Barry chose that moment to stick his head around the back door. 'Is it coffee time, Pammy? And will there be one of your baked goodies to go with it too?'

Pamela slammed the fridge shut. 'No! There won't be coffee or cake, Barry, because someone has used up all the milk!'

Barry frowned. 'Don't look at me – it's Matthew who eats all those night-time bowls of cereal.'

'What do you mean?'

'I mean, I saw him the other night. He was downstairs eating cereal and fiddling about on his laptop – he's up to something, mark my words.'

49

Pamela folded her arms. 'He's probably working on a new book so why don't you give him a chance, Barry!'

Barry shook his head. 'You just can't see it, can you? He takes you for a mug, Pammy. A complete mug.'

Pamela's face flushed with indignant rage. She grabbed her handbag and made for the front door.

'Where are you going?' he cried after her.

'To buy milk!' she shouted, realizing how ridiculous this sounded. She wanted to make a stand. To show Barry that she was cross. She pulled on her coat and shoes and was steeling herself to slam the door on her way out, hoping he'd get the message. Pamela wasn't really a door-slammer. She tried hard not to let life fluster her. But there was something about Barry and his attitude towards their middle son that made her blood boil. Where was the man she married? That charming, twinkly man always so full of fun and love – he used to look at her as if she were the only girl in the world and now all he cared about was Jeyes Fluid and his blessed roses.

She pulled open the door and stopped. Fran stood on the doorstep and Pamela could tell from her wincing expression that she'd heard every word.

'Fran, what a lovely surprise,' she said. 'I was just on my way out…'

'For milk?' asked Fran, pulling a pint from her shopping bag. 'If you be the coffee, I'll be the milk,' she added kindly.

Pamela smiled sheepishly. 'Well, if you're sure. Sorry if you heard me shouting.'

'Don't apologize. You should hear what goes on in my house. We've made shouting into an art form.'

Pamela laughed. 'It is nice to see you. Come on through.'

'Thank you,' said Fran. 'Is it okay to bring the dog?'

'Oh yes of course,' said Pamela, reaching down to pat Alan. 'Such a lovely boy.' Alan gave her hand an appreciative sniff in reply.

Fran followed her down the hall to the kitchen, pausing to admire the framed photographs of children at various ages – upward-grinning babies, gap-toothed schoolchildren and university-robed adults. 'You have a lot of photos.'

'My babies,' said Pamela misty-eyed. 'All grown up now but still my babies.'

Fran smiled. 'How many children do you have?'

'Three,' said Pamela. 'Laura, Matthew and Simon. All living wonderful lives.'

'Do they come home much?'

'They're very busy and all spread out around the place,' said Pamela hastily. 'Simon lives in Bristol and Laura's in north London but Matty is staying with us at the moment.' Her eyes shone at the mention of his name. 'He's a writer,' she added with pride. She loved telling people this – it made her life sound interesting.

'Wow,' said Fran. 'What kind of things does he write?'

'He's a journalist really but he's got all sorts of projects on the go. You know how it is.'

Fran nodded. 'Well if he ever needs an editor, let me know.'

Pamela smiled. 'I'll do that – thanks, Fran. How do you fit your job around your kiddies? Must be tough juggling it all.'

Fran shrugged. 'I'm lucky. I'm freelance and I've got some good contacts who trust me and get in touch whenever they need an editor. I enjoy the work, but after I had the kids, I wanted to be at home and then after Andy died, it was all a bit trickier, but I keep my hand in – I manage.'

'You have to, don't you? I really feel for you young women – so much pressure on you to do it all. In my day, you gave up your job when you got married, you didn't have a choice.'

'Sometimes the choices make it harder.'

'Don't they just?' agreed Pamela. 'Anyway, where are my manners? Let me make you that coffee.'

'How are you getting on with your happy homework?' asked Fran. 'To be honest, I'm struggling.'

Pamela flicked on the kettle and fetched three mugs from the cupboard. 'I went with the obvious.' She handed Fran her notebook. 'It's my favourite hobby but I get the feeling I could do more with it.'

'*Just bake*,' Fran read out, nodding. 'Looks good to me and, for the record, I shall do all I can to help you. I'm an excellent eater of cakes.'

Pamela laughed. 'I might have had some chocolate muffins for you today. I had a go at that mindful baking that Nik suggested but I fell asleep and they all burnt!'

'I think there's a fine line between meditating and sleeping – so easy to get the two mixed up,' joked Fran.

Pamela smiled. She liked Fran – she was easy to talk to and good fun. She felt rather protective towards her too. She was very young to be a widow and as for her poor children – Pamela's heart went out to them.

She placed a mug of coffee in front of Fran, along with milk and sugar. She opened the back door. 'Barry! Coffee!'

Moments later, Barry appeared. 'Thanks, Pammy. Did you get milk then?' he asked before spotting Fran. 'Oh sorry, I didn't realize you had company. Hello.'

Fran smiled. 'Hi, I'm Fran.'

'Fran and I are doing that course together.' Barry nodded without comment. 'Barry thinks it's a lot of old mumbo-jumbo, don't you, Barry?'

'I didn't say that.'

'You didn't need to. It's written all over your face.'

Fran looked uneasy. 'Well, I suppose some of it is a bit "out there", but I was surprised how much I enjoyed it.'

'See? Fran's enjoying it and she's a widow. No offence, Fran.'

'None taken,' laughed Fran.

'My garden gives me happiness,' declared Barry. 'So if you'll excuse me, I need to get back to the pruning. It was nice to meet you, Fran.'

'You too.'

After he'd gone, Pamela turned to Fran. 'Sorry, lovey. That man infuriates me sometimes. All he thinks about is his garden. It's as if I'm invisible.'

'Maybe you should try telling him?'

Pamela snorted. Fran made it sound so easy and maybe it was for her generation, but Barry and Pamela didn't really talk about their feelings. She would have liked to but wasn't sure where to start. 'You saw what he's like. He doesn't want to know. He can't get back to his garden quick enough.' She stole a glance at Fran and felt a pang of guilt. 'Sorry. Here I am moaning about Barry when you've got real problems.'

Fran laughed. 'Thanks for reminding me.'

Pamela looked horrified. 'Sorry, Fran, I didn't mean it like that. I get a bit carried away sometimes.'

Fran waved away her concerns. 'It's fine. Honestly. I'm joking.'

'So how is your list going?' Pamela asked, trying to cover her embarrassment.

'Not great. I need to open up but old habits die hard,' said Fran, pulling a face.

Pamela reached over and squeezed her hand. 'You've been through a lot. You stick with me and Heather – we'll help you.'

'Thanks, Pamela. So what do you think Nordic Nik's got in store for us next? Knitting big jumpers and field trips to Ikea?'

Pamela laughed. 'I don't know but I'm looking forward to it.'

Fran held her gaze for a second. 'You know what? Me too. Thanks, Pamela – you've given me the kick up the bum I needed.'

'Have I?' asked Pamela, feeling buoyed by the compliment. It was so much nicer than being taken for granted. 'Well I am glad.'

'So you should be. It's easy to be cynical, much harder to see the bright side. Right, I'd better get back. Those psychological thrillers and cupcake romances won't edit themselves.'

Pamela followed her to the front door and before Fran left, she folded her into a hug. Fran's body was rigid at first but she relaxed into the embrace. 'Thanks for popping round, Fran. I really enjoyed our chat.'

Fran smiled. 'Me too. And remember, if ever you need a guinea pig for your recipes, I'm ready and willing. See you soon.'

'Mind how you go,' said Pamela, feeling ticklish with excitement. It was lovely to have a new friend like Fran and she was determined to support her as best she could.

Pamela closed the door and walked back to the kitchen, pausing to gaze at her children's photos. Her gaze rested on Matthew's university picture. She'd been so proud as she watched him collect his degree from the Dean. But even then, Barry had been disparaging.

'What's he going to do with an English degree?' he'd scoffed. Pamela had shushed him but she saw from the dark look on Matthew's face that he'd heard. Poor Matthew. Pamela felt for him. He'd had articles published, of course, and managed to get by, but she sensed that he compared himself unfavourably to his siblings. Pamela had therefore taken on the role of chief protector. Laura and Simon seemed sorted but Matthew – her Matty – needed a bit more support. Barry might disagree but wasn't it important to feel that your mum had your back, regardless of how old you were? Pamela's maternal instinct told her that it was and Barry would just have to deal with it.

Pamela moved around the kitchen fetching the ingredients for toad in the hole. She liked to make her batter early and leave it to sit – it seemed to make for a fluffier Yorkshire. She went to the fridge and realized that she still didn't have any milk, having insisted that Fran take home the remainder of the pint she'd brought with her.

Pamela picked up her bag and made for the door. She considered telling Barry where she was going but realized that he wouldn't notice anyway. She felt as if she was punishing him somehow by just leaving the house. She knew it was childish but she was still cross with his comment about Matty earlier that morning. Didn't he understand that he would push their son away if he carried on like that?

Pamela breathed in the fresh spring air as she made her way to the end of the road to Doly and Dev's shop. She loved this time of year – the trees bursting with new life, everything beginning again.

The bell tinkled above the door as she entered the shop. Doly's head popped out from behind the shelf she was stacking. 'Pamela! How are you?' she said with a smile. Pamela felt a surge of warmth from that smile. Doly always seemed so happy and calm. She wondered what her secret was.

'I'm fine, thanks, dear. How about you? How are your lovely girls?'

'Noisy but beautiful.' Doly beamed. 'How is your son? Has he found a job yet?' Pamela shook her head. 'Well, it's not much but I may have some runs to the cash and carry if he's free. Dev and Hasan have had to go back to Bangladesh for a while as their grandmother is ill.'

'Oh, I'm sorry to hear that, Doly. Thank you for the offer, I'll talk to Matthew.'

Doly nodded. 'Tell him to come and see me if he's interested. Now what can I get you?'

'Just milk, thanks, Doly. Oh, and I'll take this too,' she said, picking up a large bar of Fruit and Nut.

'Happiness is a big bar of chocolate, right?' said a voice. Pamela turned to see Heather smiling at her.

'Oh hello, lovey. I didn't see you there. How are things?'

Heather nodded. 'Pretty good, thanks. I've just finished my shift at the bakery and popped in for this.' She held up a bottle of white wine. 'Luke and I are finally going to talk weddings tonight.'

Pamela clapped her hands together with delight. 'How exciting! Don't forget to let me know if you need a wedding cake baker.'

'Thanks.'

55

'I look forward to hearing about your plans next week.' Heather looked puzzled. 'At the next course?' prompted Pamela.

'Yeah, I'm not sure if it's for me. I mean, I'm pretty happy,' said Heather, screwing up her face.

Pamela tried and failed to hide her disappointment. 'Oh. But I thought you, Fran and I were a team.'

Heather bit her lip. 'It's only been a week, Pamela – I'm sure you'll be fine without me.'

'Of course.' Pamela nodded, embarrassed. 'I'm just being silly.' *A silly old woman getting ahead of herself. Why would this lovely young girl want to spend her Wednesday evenings with an old frump like me?*

Heather looked guilty. 'No, you're not silly. It's me. I'm just not sure I need the course.'

Pamela nodded. 'I understand. Although I did think we'd make a good trio and was looking forward to getting some tips from you bright young things. I'm sure Fran and I will manage. She's been through so much losing her Andy – I want to support her if I can. But then you understand that what with losing your parents too.'

Heather eyed Pamela for a second before shaking her head and smiling. 'All right, you win. I did enjoy it more than I thought I would. I'll come along to the next one and see how it goes, okay?'

Pamela brightened. 'Oh that's wonderful, Heather! What's your favourite cake?'

'Pardon?'

'Your favourite cake – I'll make it for next week.'

'You don't need to…'

'I'd like to.'

'Okay…lemon drizzle?'

'Perfect.' Pamela handed over her money to Doly. 'Cheerio for now and thanks again, Doly, for offering to help my Matthew,' she said before heading back on to Hope Street. Pamela felt a wave of hope as her concerns about her son and irritation with Barry were pushed to one side for a moment. She'd found Matty a job, had two new friends and was embarking on something fresh and exciting. It was as if a different door had been opened in her life. All she had to do was take a step through and see what was on the other side.

Chapter Seven

Heather

Happiness List
1. Marry Luke!

Freddy stared at Heather, a look of sheer puzzlement on his funny little old man face. It was as if he was trying to figure out a particularly difficult calculus problem. Without warning, his face reddened with exertion as he emptied his bowels to the sound of a loud wet fart.

'O-oh, somebody needs a change,' remarked Gemma. 'Heather? Do you want to take this one?'

'I'll give it a go if you want me to?' winced Heather.

Gemma laughed. 'Your face! I'm kidding. I couldn't do it to you. It's like dealing with nuclear waste. One day you'll understand that you never agree to change a baby's nappy unless that baby belongs to you. Right, come on, my boy,' she cooed, plucking Freddy from his rocker chair. 'Back in a sec.'

Heather watched Gemma go, pondering her 'one day' remark.

The thought of having a baby of her own thrilled and terrified Heather in equal measure. Seeing Gemma with Freddy had been strange at first but now, she couldn't picture a world without him and it had sparked her own maternal curiosity. Heather was used to being second in the running when it came to the milestones of life but then Gemma was two years older. She didn't mind. Gemma was her trailblazer and she loved her for it – where she went, Heather followed.

She looked around Gemma's living room now at the baby paraphernalia – you clearly needed a lot of stuff for these tiny human beings. There was a pram the size of a smart car in the hall, a fleece-lined rocker chair, which Heather decided that she wanted if they ever made scaled-up versions for adults, as well as all manner of black and white, mirrored, textured, squashy toys, which Freddy seemed to mostly ignore.

Heather tried to picture all these items in her living room. She and Luke kept a pretty tidy house. They weren't compulsive about it – no bean tins facing outwards in the cupboard or magazines kept at right angles – but it was neat and ordered. Still, maybe babies stopped you worrying about stuff like that, maybe you had to just go with it.

She tried to picture Luke with a baby. She couldn't ever remember seeing him with a child. He'd been working the last couple of times she'd met up with Gemma. They'd talked about babies in passing and she remembered him being positive – not effusively so but enough for her to feel satisfied that he would want kids one day. Maybe it was time for Luke to get to know Freddy a little better – one flash of that gummy smile and he'd be signing up for fatherhood quicker than you could say 'baby-led weaning'.

'Here we go – all clean,' said Gemma as she carried Freddy back into the living room and held him out to Heather. 'Would you like a cuddle?'

'With you or the baby?' Gemma laughed. 'Come on then, Freddy Fruitcake, let's see if I can make you cry like last time,' said Heather, reaching out her arms to take him.

'He was much smaller then, don't worry, he's a bit sturdier now. In fact, Ed reckons he could have a promising rugby career.'

'Okay, but be ready for the first sign of trouble,' warned Heather. 'I haven't had much practice.' Heather shifted Freddy so that he was sitting, cradled on her arm. They were eyeball to eyeball. Heather held her breath – this could go one of two ways. All of a sudden, Freddy's eyes brightened with recognition as if he'd spotted an old acquaintance who he hadn't seen for years. His mouth lifted into an 'o' as he bowed forwards and planted a wet, gummy greeting onto Heather's face.

'He kissed you!' cried Gemma with delight. 'He only does that to Mum and me. You should feel very honoured.'

Heather felt her throat thicken as Freddy drew back and eyed her with a look that said, *I like you.* She had a sudden glimpse into Gemma's world and it was lovely. 'Thank you, Freddy,' she laughed, kissing him on the top of his head. Freddy's smile widened even further and he kissed her again and again, relishing Heather and Gemma's delighted reactions.

'You should get one,' joked Gemma, gesturing towards her son. 'He likes you and he's a notoriously tough one to please. He screamed when this little old lady cooed at him in the supermarket the other day. Mind you, she did stink of fags and was missing a couple of teeth.'

Heather laughed. 'Well, seeing how happy he makes you,' she said, tickling Freddy under the chin, 'and given that you and I share a love of vodka-based cocktails and Justin Timberlake...'

'A round of cosmopolitans for the JT girls!' cried Gemma.

'Cheers to that, my friend!' Heather grinned, holding up an imaginary glass. 'I think it stands to reason that I would enjoy this motherhood lark as much as you do. Plus, he smells so good. Why does he smell so good?' she asked, inhaling her godson's downy head, making him giggle. 'And that laugh? Surely, that's the best sound in the world.'

Gemma regarded her for a second. 'I'm going to level with you, coz. For me, having a baby has been the most knackering experience of my life, my fanny's a car crash and my nipples are so effing sore, but honestly?' She gazed over at Freddy with a look of pure, unadulterated love. 'I wouldn't change it for the world. I mean, between ourselves, it would be good if Ed helped out a bit more, but aside from that, I've never been happier.'

Heather smiled at her cousin. 'Well here's a thought. How about Luke and I help out by having Freddy overnight one Friday so that you and Ed can go out?'

Gemma stared at her wide-eyed. 'That's a big ask. He can be a pain to settle. Are you sure you're up for it?'

Heather nodded with enthusiasm. 'Absolutely. It'd only be one night and it's win-win. You get a night out, I get time with my godson and Luke and I get to practise at being parents.'

'Let's hope he doesn't put you off for life,' laughed Gemma.

Freddy gazed up at Heather as she covered his ears. 'Mummy doesn't mean it, Freddy. You're going to have all the fun with Auntie Heather and Uncle Luke.'

'Do you think Uncle Luke will be okay with it?' Gemma frowned, doubtfully.

'Why do you say that?'

Gemma shrugged. 'Oh, I dunno. Pardon the pun but I thought he was a bit lukewarm about kids.'

Heather frowned. 'When did he say that?'

Gemma chewed her lip for a moment before dismissing Heather's concerns with a wave of her hand. 'Do you know, it's probably just my baby brain getting mixed up. I'm sure you'll have a great time. Well I'm not but I want to go out and drink gin so let's pretend, shall we?'

Heather laughed. 'Stop worrying. It's going to be brilliant, isn't it, Freddy?' Freddy squeaked in reply. She smiled and glanced at her watch. 'Blimey, I need to get going. Wednesday night is happiness night.'

'Oh yeah, your course. How's it going?' asked Gemma, reclaiming her son and following Heather into the hall.

Heather gave a positive nod. 'I only went along to the first one because I couldn't face another night in on my own, but actually, it was pretty interesting.'

'Luscious Luke still working all hours then?'

Heather sighed. 'Yeah, but at least we've had a chance to sit down and discuss the wedding. I have a shortlist of three venues.'

'That's great. Sorry, Heth – I meant to ask you about that but we got distracted by babies.'

'It's fine, Gem, he's a gorgeous distraction,' she said, leaning forwards to kiss them both.

'I'm glad you're getting the wedding sorted and remember to shout if I can help with anything.'

'Just being my chief bridesmaid and helping me choose my dress is all I need.'

'Done,' said Gemma with a grin.

Heather made for the door. 'Right. I'm off to talk mindfulness and eat lemon drizzle cake in a draughty community hall.'

'There are worse ways to spend an evening.'

'Very true. Take care and speak soon. Bye!'

Heather glanced back before she drove off, waving at Gemma standing on the doorstep with Freddy in her arms. As she focused on the road, she felt a dip of sadness in her chest, a tug of longing for when she and Gemma were growing up. Heather missed those days – Saturdays shopping in the nearby town, trying out lipstick in Boots and sitting in McDonald's nursing a strawberry milkshake for hours as boys would come and go like interview candidates. Gemma always seemed so in charge when it came to the opposite sex. Heather would watch in awe as some teenage boy, his face peppered with acne and sprouting stubble, would sidle over and try to get her attention. Gemma would flirt with the ones she liked and introduce the ones she didn't to Heather. Heather didn't mind – she received all her cousin's cast-off clothes so why not the boys as well? As the younger cousin, she was just grateful to be in Gemma's presence – she was her guiding light and her protector too. When one boy tried to persuade Heather to go for a 'walk' in the municipal gardens, Gemma tipped the rest of her milkshake over his head and told him to get lost before she told the whole restaurant that he was a pervert. Heather smiled at the memory. No one messed with Gemma Sharp.

She and Gemma were still close and they would always have that bond from growing up together but there was a distance now. It wasn't just the geography – Gemma lived less than an hour away. There was an emotional distance too – the inevitable growing apart that came with marriage and motherhood. It was normal and natural but it made Heather feel as if she was drifting and somehow losing her anchor to the past.

It made her realize how much she needed Luke, how much she loved and couldn't wait to marry him – to get on with their life, to make it something happy and wonderful, something she'd needed ever since her parents died.

'So,' said Nik, smiling as he stood before the group hours later. 'Did any of you experiment with mindfulness this week?'

'I tried mindful baking,' admitted Pamela ruefully.

'And how did it go?'

'I fell asleep.' She grimaced. 'I ended up burning my buns. I never burn my buns.'

Nik gave her a sympathetic smile.

'Sorry to say it but I don't think I have time to be mindful,' declared Fran. 'I can't be present whilst chopping up cucumber, admiring the glistening discs of translucent green or whatever. I just need to get it done and move on to the next thing.'

Nik nodded. 'The world is busy. But let me ask you this, if you go for a run, can you keep on running indefinitely?'

'Well no, obvs. You need to take a break from time to time.'

'Exactly, so mindfulness is a way of taking a moment, a break from the constant rushing, a time to reset your brain if you like – to observe what is happening. Some people learn to be mindful all the time and if you practise enough, this is possible. But I would say that perhaps this isn't realistic so you should think of it as a form of exercise to start with. And tonight we're going to try something to help us practise.' Nik took a Tupperware box from his bag and lifted the lid. 'Sultanas,' he said, walking around the circle. 'Help yourself.'

'Sorry, I'm on a diet,' joked Fran as she took one.

Nik smiled. 'I would like you to imagine that you have never seen a sultana before.' Heather and Fran exchanged amused glances. 'Take a moment to look at it properly, observe its appearance. What do you see?'

'Sorry, Nik?' said Jim.

'Yes?'

Jim looked sheepish. 'I've already eaten mine. I thought it was a snack.'

'Me too,' said Sue. 'I haven't had my dinner and I was hungry.'

Nik laughed. 'Okay, here you go,' he said, handing out replacements. 'Now, try for a moment to observe the sultana. Look at it carefully and share your thoughts if you want to.'

'Brown?' offered Pamela.

Nik nodded encouragingly.

'Shrivelled,' said Heather.

'Like old person,' observed Georg. 'My grandmother had wrinkled face like this.' Everyone laughed. Georg looked surprised. 'Is true.'

'Good,' said Nik. 'And now how does it feel in your hand – consider this for a moment with your eyes closed.'

'Soft,' said Sue after a pause.

'Sticky,' added Pamela.

'Knobbly,' said someone else.

64

'And the smell?' asked Nik. 'Take your time.'

'Sweet,' said Heather.

'Rich,' said Georg. 'Like dark sugar smell.'

'Like my mum's larder,' observed Jim with a smile. 'She did a lot of baking, like Mrs T.' Pamela grinned at him.

'And now we taste,' said Nik. 'Don't chew it at first, just let it rest on your tongue and focus on what comes to mind.'

There was a long pause before they answered.

'Liquorice,' said Pamela with a confused frown.

'Longing,' added Heather. 'I know it's sweet but I can't taste it yet.'

'Salt and sweet,' said Fran, looking at Nik. 'Sorry, I couldn't wait – I had to bite it.'

Nik smiled. 'It's okay, it's not a test. What this shows us isn't about the sultana itself. It's about our ability to focus on the present moment, to concentrate on the thing that is right in front of you. Congratulations – you all have the capacity to be mindful. I promise that if you practise, you will feel the benefits.' Fran arched a brow at him. 'Even you, Fran.'

'Cheek,' she laughed.

Nik addressed the group. 'So this week's homework is to find an activity that enables you to be mindful or present in the moment or however you would like to phrase it. Add it to your own happiness list and do your best to incorporate it into your life. Try to view it as you taking a deep breath when you need it most.'

As they left the course a while later, Fran turned to Pamela and Heather. 'Right, all that breathing and focusing on the present has made me realize that I need a drink and, as my mother is staying over again, I intend to take full advantage of the fact. Who fancies the pub?'

Heather checked her phone. No messages from Luke but as he'd been working late all week, Heather fully expected more of the same. What was the point in going home to an empty house again? 'I'm in,' she declared. 'Pamela?'

'Barry will only be glued to one of his gardening programmes and Matty's out so why not?'

'I love it when a plan comes together,' said Fran with a grin.

The Goldfinch Tavern used to be a spit-and-sawdust kind of pub with a decidedly dodgy clientele until a forward-thinking brewery took it over, replaced the sticky floor with dark wood and peeled back the Anaglytpa to expose the brick behind it. It had a cosy, shabby-chic feel and was much loved by the local community.

An open mic night was kicking off as the three women arrived, so they made a beeline for a quiet table in an adjoining room where they could hear each other speak.

'My choir often does gigs in here,' said Pamela as Fran returned from the bar carrying a bottle of Prosecco and three glasses.

'Ahh yes, the famous Hope Street community choir. My friend Nat always says it saved her after she and Dan split up,' said Fran.

'Lovely Nat, she's a treasure,' said Pamela.

'Caroline told me that she formed the choir in order to save the community hall,' remarked Heather.

'That sounds like Caroline,' observed Fran with one eyebrow raised. 'She had quite a lot of help.'

'Ahh, Caroline's got a good heart,' insisted Pamela.

'She just keeps it well hidden,' said Fran.

Pamela giggled. 'Oh, get away with you.'

'Come on then ladies, let's practise what we've learnt,' said Fran as she poured the Prosecco. 'Observe if you will, the flow of golden liquid…or does that sound as if I'm talking about wee?' She smirked.

Heather laughed. 'Watch the bubbles lift and pop on this glistening sea of gold.'

'Still sounds like wee,' grinned Fran. 'You try, Pamela.'

'Um, look at the foaming surge of liquid?' she offered, frowning with concentration.

Fran snorted with laughter. 'Okay, stop now because that sounds plain wrong.' Heather and Pamela chuckled as Fran handed them a glass each. 'So, enough with the mindfulness. Here's to my happiness buddies – cheers!'

'Cheers!' they chorused.

'So are you still singing with the choir?' said Heather to Pamela.

Pamela nodded. 'Oh yes – they're wonderful. You should both come. Choir always gives me a lift.'

Fran grimaced. 'I think you might end up with all the stray cats in the neighbourhood lining up outside the hall – I can't sing for toffee.'

Heather laughed. 'I love music but I always preferred dancing to singing.'

'Ooh, I used to love dancing as a girl – ballroom mainly but I did enjoy a bit of jive,' said Pamela.

'Go Pamela!' cried Fran. She nudged Heather. 'It's great that you decided to come along for another session of the course.'

Heather flashed a smile at Pamela. 'I'll go anywhere for a decent slice of lemon drizzle. Plus, it's good to make some friends round here. Luke's often working so...'

'You get lonely sometimes,' said Fran as if she understood.

Heather held her gaze for a second before nodding. There was something about Fran that reminded her of Gemma – both straight-talking women with teasing humour.

'It must be hard living where your mum grew up but not having her or your dad around,' added Pamela with her customary tact.

Fran and Heather exchanged glances. 'Don't feel too sorry for me, Pamela. I've got my lovely cousin, Gemma, who's supported me ever since Mum and Dad died. I moved in with her family after it happened and we've been best mates ever since.'

'Does she live nearby?' asked Pamela.

'About an hour away. She's married and had a baby six months ago. I saw them today actually.' She took out her phone and showed them a picture. 'That's Freddy, he's my godson.'

'Cute,' said Fran.

'Awww, what a poppet,' declared Pamela.

'He's lovely. I just wish I could see them a bit more but they're busy and I'm over here so it's tricky.'

'Babies ruin everything,' said Fran. 'Friendships, fannies – the whole caboodle.'

'Fran!' cried Pamela scandalized. 'Babies are wonderful!'

'In small doses,' said Fran. 'Sorry, Heather – you were saying about things being tricky?'

Heather smiled, feeling a wave of affection for them both. 'It's just lovely to make new friends over here.'

Pamela patted her hand and Fran grinned. 'Well, Pamela and I know how to get a party started,' she quipped, knocking her glass against Heather's. 'Which is more than you can say for young Georg. What is going on with him?'

Heather laughed. 'I get the feeling there's more to Georg than meets the eye.'

'He told me that his happiness goal is to find true love,' sighed Pamela. 'Bless him.'

'Now see how we all complement each other perfectly?' said Fran. 'So Pamela here is our hopeless romantic, whereas I'm the jaded cynic so that must make you…'

'The lost soul?' blurted Heather, surprising herself. 'Sorry – not sure where that came from.'

'From the heart,' said Fran. 'It's what comes with hanging out with Pamela. Don't worry, your secret's safe with us. We're a not quite perfect dream team.'

'We should have T-shirts made!' said Heather. She turned to Pamela. 'So how's Matthew getting on?'

Pamela sighed. 'Doly is going to give him some work so that

will help but he is a worry. I'm not entirely sure what he's up to half the time.'

'Well, he's a big boy, you can't watch his every move,' said Heather.

Pamela nodded. 'I know I have a tendency to mother him a bit too much but it's hard, isn't it? You just want to help your kids get what they need.'

'Don't forget what you need though,' said Heather. Pamela gave her a grateful smile.

'Poor Pamela,' said Fran. 'Makes you wish that you could keep your kids on a lead for the whole of their lives, doesn't it? I'm dreading the day I don't know where mine are. My mother makes Margaret Thatcher look weedy but at least I know my kids are safely tucked up when she's in charge.'

Heather looked distracted for a moment. 'Sorry, Fran, I am listening. I just heard that boy singing – he sounds a bit like Ed Sheeran. How old do you think he is?'

As Fran tuned in, a look of horror spread over her face. She stood up. 'Fourteen,' she said. 'He's fourteen.'

'How do you know?' asked Pamela.

Fran made for the bar. 'Because that's my bloody son and I'm going to kill him!'

The evening had fallen apart after that. Fran frogmarched a mortified Jude from the pub but not before she'd given the landlord an earful. From the thunderous look on her face, her mother was in for similar treatment.

As Heather let herself back into the house a while later, she could hear the television and peered into the lounge to find Luke asleep on the sofa. Her heart soared at the sight of him. She knelt down, watching him for a moment. He stirred and opened his eyes, smiling as he saw her. She leant over to kiss him.

'You're home,' she said.

'I'm home.' He smiled.

'You should have called me. I went for a drink with Fran and Pamela – I would have come straight home if I'd known.'

'It's okay, beautiful,' he said, stroking her cheek. 'I had a report to write. Anyway, how was your day?'

She grinned and took out her phone to show him a photograph. A Facebook notification popped up – Gemma had tagged her in a post. It was a picture of Heather and Freddy smiling at one another with the words,

Hanging out with my favourite auntie.

'Look.' She held out the phone for Luke to see.

He frowned at the picture. 'Oh wow, look at you,' he said, making no comment about the baby.

'Isn't Freddy cute?' she insisted.

Luke shrugged. 'Yeah, I guess. How was Gem? Feels like ages since I've seen her.'

Heather felt a prickle of disappointment. 'Yeah, it was great to see her – she was tired but well. She loves being a mum.'

'That's good.' She moved to snuggle next to him, wrapping his arm around her shoulder. 'Oh hello,' he said, leaning down to kiss her.

'Hello.' She smiled, pulling back slightly. 'So listen…'

'Uh-oh, sounds serious. What's up?'

Heather felt her mouth go dry. Where to start? This was a big life question. She didn't want to mess it up and she didn't want to scare off Luke either. 'Well, when I was with Gemma and Freddy today, she mentioned in passing that she didn't think you were very keen on having kids.'

'She said that?'

Heather felt a twist of panic that he wasn't flatly denying it. 'She did. And it made me realize that we'd never talked about it properly and that I'd stupidly assumed that we would just have kids one day.'

Luke sat up and ran a hand through his hair. 'O-kay, well if I'm honest, I haven't given it much thought.'

Heather turned to face him and was taken aback by his guarded expression. She reached for his hand. 'Well, maybe we should talk about it. We're about to get married – it feels pretty important.'

Luke shifted in his seat. 'O-kay.'

Heather took a deep breath. 'Well, personally, I know I'd like a family. I love the idea of miniature versions of you and me and I think we'd make great parents. What about you?'

Luke gave a faint smile. 'I don't know. I guess I still feel as if I'm too young to think about it. To be honest, I'm not about planning years into the future. I've got you, I've got my job. We're getting married and that's enough for now.'

Enough for now. That sounded reasonable. Maybe rushing into the future was wrong. Maybe it was better to live in the present. 'But you're not ruling out kids?' she asked.

He put an arm round her shoulder and kissed her cheek. 'Of course not. I think we should enjoy our lives now and see what happens.'

She stole a glance at him. 'Okay, well I've kind of offered to have Freddy overnight for Gemma.'

'Oh. Huh,' said Luke, nodding slowly.

Heather nudged him. 'Listen, it's going to be great. He's my godson and he's very cute. It might just give us some perspective on parenthood.'

Luke gave a resigned smile. 'Okay. I'm not great with babies but, you know, if you've offered and it helps out Gemma then fine.'

Heather nodded. *Enough for now.* She stood up, feeling heavy with tiredness. 'It's been a long day,' she said. 'I'm going to grab a glass of water and head up to bed.'

He caught hold of her hand. 'Okay, beautiful. I won't be long. I love you, Heather Brown.'

'I love you too.'

I really do love you, she thought as she filled a glass from the tap and stood frowning out at her reflection. And maybe that was enough for now but there was a seed of uncertainty threatening to take root in her heart. What if Luke never wanted kids? Would Heather be happy with that? What did she actually want from her life? Would enough for now be enough for ever? Maybe the truth she blurted out in the pub was just that. Maybe she really was a lost soul, still searching for what she needed and maybe, at the moment, she needed the course more than she cared to admit.

Chapter Eight

Fran

Happiness List Thing
1. Accept a world without Andy (too soon!)
2. 'Digital Detox' day with kids

On Sunday morning, Fran woke to bright sunshine and the sinking feeling that she couldn't justify yet another pyjama day. It was time to leave the house. She knew that if they stayed in, Charlie would be glued to her iPad whilst Jude shut himself in his room, playing Bob Dylan protest songs as a pointed gesture to the fact that she had taken away his phone and grounded him for a fortnight. Fran couldn't face the heavy atmosphere that would descend or the fact that she would be very likely to spend another wasted afternoon poring over Pinterest without being entirely sure what she was looking for.

She loved the idea of home improvements but since Andy died, the thought of making changes to the home they'd shared filled her with horror and sadness. The cruel irony of the situation was that she could afford to get the work done now thanks to the money from Andy's life insurance. Also, Fran's brother had had the good sense to become an independent financial advisor so their future was secure. Fran wasn't rich but she wasn't under financial pressure.

Her job as an editor had always been a constant. She'd been lucky in this respect. She'd worked for a large publisher in the years before marriage and kids. During this time, she'd had the happy fortune to acquire a little-known author, who went on to become a global phenomenon. When Fran bit the bullet after Charlie was born and decided to go freelance, the superstar author demanded to keep her as his editor. The publisher agreed because they loved Fran too. This meant that she was able to earn decent money from the author's annual bestseller and pick and choose her other projects as well.

'You're so lucky, Fran,' her former colleagues would cry. 'You've got the dream job that fits around your kids and the money's good. You've hit the jackpot.'

They stopped saying this after Andy died of course. The superstar author sent her an obscenely large bouquet. The publisher sent a tasteful one and told her to take as much time as she needed. One month later, she received a courteous and kind email from the editorial director saying that the superstar author had just delivered his latest bestseller. Should they get someone else to take over for now?

This was less than two months after Andy had died and Fran had barely left the house. She didn't care about this book or anything. How could people still be writing books, still be thinking this was important when she could barely put one foot in front of the other? She sent a short, polite reply to let him off the hook. She didn't care. It didn't matter.

Two years on, the superstar author was now the proud owner of a multimillion-pound movie franchise and Fran wished him well. He still sent her a magnum of champagne every Christmas. She was glad he hadn't turned into a rich tosser.

Fran still worked on freelance projects but her heart wasn't in it. It was just a job to her now. She used to feel deeply passionate about the written word. Now she couldn't give two hoots. She felt like this about a lot of things though. It was as if someone had pressed the 'pause' button on her life for the past two years and she couldn't imagine ever hitting 'play' again.

She looked around her bedroom now, at the faded curtains with their olive tree design. She had panic-bought them from John Lewis shortly before Jude was born, convinced that the addition of a small baby to her life would mean that she would never have time to shop again. She remembered decorating this room with Andy shortly after they moved here in pre-children days – they had spent a cheerful Saturday playing mix tapes of cheesy Eighties songs whilst they painted the walls in a shade of *Willow Tree*. Andy had wanted them to go for *Churlish Green* from the Farrow and Ball range until Fran pointed out that amusing as the name was, it probably wasn't worth spending three times the amount on the paint.

'Why don't you get a decorator in?' her mother suggested about a year after Andy died. 'Freshen up the place a bit.'

And why don't you keep your beak out, thought Fran. Some days she could take her mother's flashes of inspiration and some days, it made her want to scream with frustration. She knew what Angela was thinking, of course.

She's keeping everything just as it was, like a museum of grief.

'I'll think about it,' said Fran through gritted teeth, knowing that she wouldn't.

Her mother eyed her for a moment. She was bossy but not unkind. 'I know that your dad would be only too happy to help,' she said. Fran smiled and nodded. 'At least you had the good sense not to hang on to his clothes,' added Angela. 'I know too many women who cling on to them, like some kind of widow's comfort blanket. It isn't good for your mental health.'

'Tragic,' nodded Fran, thinking about the bags of Andy's clothes hidden in the loft.

My grief, my way.

'Right kids,' she called, standing at the top of the stairs. 'Who's up for an adventure with the added incentive of bacon rolls?'

'Meee!' cried Charlie, darting out of the living room, where she had been watching one of her American high-school comedies.

Jude's bedroom door opened a fraction enough for Fran to catch the musky whiff of teenage boy. 'Sorry, I can't – my mum's grounded me and anyway, I've become a vegetarian.'

Fran ignored him. 'Get dressed. We leave in twenty minutes,' she said, plucking her towel from the banister and heading to the bathroom.

'I love adventures,' breathed Charlie, bouncing up and down from the back seat as they sped along winding country roads. 'Where are we going?'

'To Tall Elms so that we can commune with nature,' said Fran. Alan barked his approval.

'Yay! I love nature,' cried Charlie. 'I just saw a pigeon.' Fran smiled at her in the rear-view mirror, sorely wishing that she had her daughter's talent for finding the best in everything.

'I'm so bored without my phone!' groaned Jude from the front.

'You've only got yourself to blame for being sneaky last week,' Fran told him. 'You're lucky I didn't ground you for the rest of your life.' Jude glowered at her. Fran sighed inwardly. The success of trips like these were dependent on the mood of the assembled party and given Jude's grudging presence, she feared it could easily be an out-and-out disaster. 'How about a word game?' she suggested. It was lame but if she could engage Charlie, Jude might join in too. He might be a moody adolescent but he was still a doting brother.

'I love word games,' declared Charlie. 'How about an "ABC of nature"?'

'Great idea,' said Fran, wanting to hug her daughter. 'You start.'

''Kay, erm, apple. Your go, Jude – B.'

'Badger,' said Jude flatly.

'Chestnut,' said Fran, feeling more positive.

'Oh, I love that – makes me think of Christmas,' smiled Charlie. They carried on playing the game until Jude got to 'N'.

'*No* Wi-Fi,' he said, folding his arms. 'Therefore *no* fun.'

'Personally, I think no Wi-Fi is a good thing because it means that you can enjoy being in the moment,' said Fran.

'Why are you talking so weirdly?' frowned Jude.

'I'm not. All I'm saying is that it's important to take time to just be.'

'Is this some crap you learnt on that course?'

'Jude!' giggled Charlie, scandalized.

Fran cleared her throat. 'I am merely trying to re-engage with my family in an outdoor setting instead of our usual Sunday activity of each staring at a different iPad.'

'I watch TV sometimes on a Sunday too,' pointed out Charlie.

'I know. I just thought it would be good to do something different.'

'Fine,' sighed Jude, sitting back heavily in his seat. 'But can you stop talking like a self-help manual? You're freaking me out.'

'Very well,' said Fran as they arrived at the woods. She spied a car vacating a space on the other side of the car park and was on her way round when a large black four-by-four sped in from the opposite direction and stole it.

'Bastards!' yelled Fran, sounding her horn.

'Very zen, Mum,' remarked Jude.

'There's a space just there, Mummy,' said Charlie, desperate to stop her mother from committing GBH or worse.

'Fine,' muttered Fran, pulling in to the alternative space. She gave the female driver, her family and their slobbering Rottweiler a death-stare as they walked by. Alan supported her with a bark of protest. 'Good boy, Alan.'

Sometimes your best intentions are richly rewarded. In Fran's mind, she was hoping for a relaxing stroll through the woods with her beloved children and faithful hound. Their cheeks would turn pink from gentle exertions and she would reward them all with a hearty breakfast in the café afterwards. They would chat and laugh, taking in their surroundings with studied care. Perhaps this would become a weekly pastime. They could learn the names of the trees, flora and fauna. It might inspire one of the children to become an environmentalist and possibly even save the planet.

Fifteen minutes in, Fran remembered why she liked being at home so much. She didn't have to deal with other people. It was one family, but that's all it ever takes, isn't it? One family, whose pudgy child thought it was okay to drop an empty Haribo packet on the floor, whose ugly Rottweiler chased poor Alan into some stinging nettles, whose sprout-faced matriarch threatened to break Fran's finger if she carried on pointing it in her face. The same family who'd stolen Fran's parking space. Naturally.

'Leave my mummy alone,' screamed Charlie. 'She's a widow and you have to be nice to her!'

The woman stared at Fran dumbfounded. Fran saw pity in her eyes and it made her blood simmer. She didn't want this woman's pity. She didn't want this woman's anything. 'Come on, you two,' she declared, turning on her heels and marching off towards the car park. 'This was a bad idea. A very bad idea.'

'Amen to that,' said Jude.

'Mum?'

'Yes, Charlie?' asked Fran as they reached the car.

'I think I trod in some dog poo.'

'Terrific. That's just terrific.' Fran stared up to the heavens unsure whether to laugh or cry.

Really, universe? This is what my attempt at mindfulness brings, is it? A mind-full of the desire to punch someone in the face? That would be funny if it weren't so effing tragic.

If Andy had been here, he would have caught her eye at this moment, his mouth twitching into a smile, which would have in turn caused her to laugh or at least see the funny side of her lame shot at family bonding. She felt exhausted with sad longing and had a sudden urge to lie down in the middle of the path.

'Fran?'

Fran snapped back to the present and looked round in surprise. 'Heather, hi! What are you doing here?'

Heather gestured back towards a tall, good-looking man who was pacing up and down the path, talking on his phone. 'We were about to go for breakfast and a walk – I'm trying to get Luke to do this every week. We're going to see a wedding venue later – Chilford Park. Do you know it?'

'Wow, yes I do! Chilford Park is gorgeous. I think they use it to film period dramas sometimes. How exciting! So is this Sunday routine part of your happiness homework?'

Heather pulled a face. 'Will you call me a swot if I say yes?'

'It would be a bit hypocritical. Guess what I'm doing today?' she said, nodding her head towards the children. 'I was trying to do the whole mindful thing and prise the kids away from their digital devices at the same time, but, to be honest, it's been a bit of a disaster.'

'Gold sticker for effort,' said Heather with a grin.

'Who's getting a gold sticker?' asked Charlie, bored at being ignored. 'I'm Charlie by the way.' She nudged herself towards Heather. 'And that's Jude. He's grumpy because he's had his phone confiscated but he did sneak out to play in a pub so it's hardly surprising. And this is Alan.' Alan barked a happy greeting.

'Lovely to meet you, Charlie. I've heard a lot about you. And Alan of course,' she said, patting the dog's head. 'That's my fiancé, Luke,' she added, pointing over her shoulder to where Luke was still talking on the phone. 'And I was lucky enough to be in the pub to hear you, Jude. You have an amazing voie.'

'Thank you,' muttered Jude, half smiling, a flush of pink spreading up his neck.

Luke had finished his call and was walking towards them. Fran noticed that he didn't acknowledge her or the children at first – his attention was fixed on Heather.

'Hey, babe, listen, I'm sorry but I'm going to have to bail.'

Heather's face fell. 'What? Why?'

Luke shook his head. 'It's this acquisition – we've hit a bump in the road and Mike needs some figures ASAP. I'm going to have to go home and work.'

'But, Luke, you promised! We're supposed to be going to Chilford Park – they're holding the date for us.'

Fran noticed a flicker of irritation cross his face. 'What do you want me to do, Heather? It's work and if you want your fairy-tale wedding, I've gotta work, okay?' Heather stared at him as if she'd been stung before giving a resigned nod. Luke's face softened. 'I'm sorry, baby. I know I've been busy lately and I know you want to get the wedding booked. I'll make it up to you, I promise. I'll get this report done and cook us a nice dinner later, okay?'

Heather nodded again before turning to Fran. 'We have to go,' she said, looking disappointed.

'I could give you a lift back if you want to join us for breakfast?' suggested Fran, feeling sorry for Heather. 'We were going to head home but I could murder a bacon sarnie to be honest.' She turned to Luke. 'Sorry, I don't think we've met. I'm Fran and this is Charlie and Jude.'

She noticed a frown of suspicion flicker across his face before it was replaced with a charming smile as he held out his hand. 'Luke,' he said. 'Good to meet you.'

Heather's face brightened at Fran's suggestion. 'Are you sure?'

'Of course,' said Fran with a smile.

'Okay, well I gotta shoot. Good to meet you guys,' said Luke with a quick wave before pecking Heather on the cheek and heading to the car park.

Heather watched him go with a look of discouragement. 'Come on,' said Fran reassuringly. 'I'll buy you that bacon sarnie.'

'Thanks,' said Heather.

'Erm, Mum, what shall I do about my trainers?' asked Charlie, looking worried.

'Bugger. I forgot about the dog poo incident.'

'How about we scrape off the worst on the grass and then rinse them under the tap?' suggested Jude. 'I'll help you, squirt.'

Fran stared at him in surprise. 'Thank you, Jude.'

'No worries. I'll have a bacon *and* egg sandwich, ta,' he said with a grin.

Fran smirked at Heather. 'I knew there'd be a catch. Okay, we'll see you in the café. Make sure you both wash your hands a million times.'

'Yes, ma'am!' saluted Charlie.

'They're lovely kids,' remarked Heather as they joined the queue for breakfast. The small café was busy with Sunday morning dog walkers and families, all enjoying the early spring sunshine.

'Thanks. Yeah, they're not bad,' said Fran with a smile.

'It must have been hard for you all.'

'It was. Still is. But grief sort of binds you together like superglue. I would have fallen apart without them – we're an unhappy band of survivors but survivors nonetheless. Must have been much worse for you losing both your parents at the same time.'

Heather gave a wry grin. 'Yeah, sorry, but in the grief competition, I win.'

Fran laughed. 'Congratulations.' She stole a glance at her new friend. 'It's good to talk to someone who gets it, you know?'

Heather nodded. 'I do. It's less raw for me these days but I do get it.'

81

Fran sighed. 'I worry about the kids. They seem fine but it's still there all the time.'

'I don't mind talking to them if you want me to? Not in any heavy-handed way. And only if they want to.'

'Trust me, Charlie will definitely want to. I'm not sure about Jude.'

'Well, the offer's there.' Fran gave her a grateful smile as the kids returned. 'Shall we go and find a table?' she suggested.

'Thanks.' She watched as they took their place on the decking overlooking the pond. Charlie gave Fran a wave, her face anxiously searching until she was certain that her mother had seen her.

It was completely understandable that having lost her father, Charlie had developed an innate anxiety that Fran was somehow next in line – irrational of course but entirely understandable. It was also endlessly wearing for Fran. Charlie was fine at school but at home, she needed to constantly check that her mother was a) still breathing and b) not going anywhere. Fran did her best to stay patient and cling to the hope that she would grow out of this fear whilst also trying to remain sensitive to her daughter's needs. It was a fine balance. Usually, Charlie was fine if she was left her with Fran's mother but more often than not, Fran would get a call and need to reassure Charlie that she was okay. Earlier that year, Fran had popped to the shops taking what turned out to be a rash decision to leave Jude in charge. Her biggest mistake had been to tell Jude but not Charlie that she was going out. She had returned half an hour later to find a police car parked over her drive.

'Your daughter reported you missing,' said the weary-looking policewoman. Charlie stood frowning at her mother, arms folded as Jude plodded down the stairs, apparently surprised to find all these people gathered in the hall.

'Jude! What happened?' cried Fran in exasperation.

He shrugged. 'I dunno. I was upstairs listening to music.'

'I couldn't find you,' said Charlie accusingly. 'I got worried.'

Fran turned to the policewoman. 'I'm really sorry. Her father died and she gets a little anxious.'

'I can hear you, you know,' remarked Charlie.

'Maybe it would be best not to leave them on their own in future,' said the woman.

'Righty-ho. Sorry again,' said Fran, when what she actually wanted to say was, *No shit, Sherlock.*

She gave Charlie a reassuring wave before turning back to the woman behind the counter and placing their order. She fetched cutlery and carried the tray of drinks out into the sunshine.

'Here we are. Number forty-two. I think I just heard them called thirty-five so fingers crossed.' Fran smiled, taking her place next to Jude and opposite Heather and Charlie.

'Heather's dad died too,' reported Charlie, placing a hand on her new friend's arm. 'And her mum.'

'I know, it's very sad,' said Fran nodding.

'And now she's getting married but she hasn't got anyone to give her away,' said Charlie sadly. 'Do you miss them every day? I miss my dad every day.'

'I do but they died a long time ago so I'm used to them not being around – does that make sense?' asked Heather.

'Kind of,' frowned Charlie.

'Yes,' said Jude. 'You've had to accept that they're gone so that you can get on with your life.'

Fran stared at him in surprise. *Out of the mouths of babes.*

Heather nodded. 'I think so. Of course, I miss them and I wish they were here to see me get married and know how happy I am with Luke, but they're not. And I've had to accept that. You have to find other things to fill the void and make new memories. At least that's how it's been for me.'

'Do you honestly think you can get over grief?' asked Fran with genuine interest.

Heather regarded her for a second. 'No. But you can find a way to cope so that it doesn't stop you living.'

Fran noticed Jude looking at her, his eyebrows raised as if to make a point and felt an uncomfortable truth creep through her veins. 'Three bacon and one bacon and egg sandwich?' said the waitress, approaching their table.

The mood changed as they tucked into their food. Fran wondered if she should make, 'eat more bacon' one of her happiness goals and realized how relaxed she felt sitting here in the sunshine with Heather, Alan and the kids. She could tell that Jude and Charlie liked Heather by the way Charlie leant in when she spoke and Jude seemed to have lost all traces of his earlier moodiness. Even Alan had forsaken his usual position at Fran's feet and now sat by Heather's side staring up at her with complete adoration. It may have been because she'd slipped him a piece of bacon of course, but it made Fran smile.

'He's such a gorgeous dog, aren't you, Alan?' Alan barked in the affirmative. Heather laughed.

'So, what are you going to do about Chilford Park?' asked Fran.

Heather pulled a face. 'I guess I'll have to put it on the back-burner for now as Luke's working.'

'We could come with you? If you want us to?' suggested Fran, taking a sip of coffee.

'Oh, I couldn't ask you to do that,' said Heather, looking unsure of herself.

'Nonsense. We'd love to, wouldn't we, Charlie?' Charlie gave a series of rapid excited nods. 'Look at that face – to be honest, you'd be letting her down if you said no.'

Heather looked at Charlie's expectant, ketchup-covered face and laughed. 'Well, if you're sure, but what about Alan?'

'I'll take him for a walk,' offered Jude. 'S'fine. No offence, Heather, but I'm not big into weddings.'

'None taken,' said Heather with a grin. 'Okay, thank you – that would be wonderful.'

Chilford Park Hotel was the absolute height of sophistication and elegance in the world of wedding venues. Fran and Heather smiled at one another as Charlie slid at great speed across the polished wood floor in the Empress ballroom, whilst the wedding coordinator kept her face fixed in a rictus grin.

'It's just like *Strictly* in here,' Charlie declared, gesturing up at the gigantic lavish chandeliers before galloping around the room to her own version of the theme music. 'Duh-duh-duh-duh-duh-duh-duhhhh, duh-duh-duh-duh-duh!' she sang happily.

'So we can accommodate eighty adults during the day,' said the coordinator, trying her best to ignore Charlie and remain professional. 'Plus up to forty in the evening, making a total of…'

'One hundred and twent-y!' cried Charlie like a darts commentator.

'Precisely,' said the woman with a thin smile.

Charlie grinned at her. 'Your name is Jasmine,' she said, gesturing at her badge. 'Like the princess.' She inhaled. 'You smell like a princess too and you have lovely hair.'

Fran could tell that the woman wasn't quite sure what to make of her daughter. 'Thank you,' she said slowly. 'Should we go through to the library so that I can take you through the menu options?'

'Thank you, Jasmine,' said Charlie seriously, walking alongside her. 'That would be great.'

Jasmine looked helplessly at Heather, who gave her a reassuring smile, before leading them to the library, lined with ceiling-to-floor bookcases and red velvet curtains.

'Wow, very *Downton*,' said Fran impressed, taking a seat on an elegant beige sofa.

Jasmine smiled. 'So, here's a list of all our menu options. And of course, in addition to the vegetarian option, we can offer vegan, gluten-free and dairy-free choices as well,' she said with just a hint of smugness.

'Do you have halal options?' asked Charlie earnestly. 'For Heather's Muslim friends?'

'Erm, I can check,' said Jasmine uncertainly.

'That would be kind. Thank you, Jasmine,' said Charlie.

'I'll be right back,' said Jasmine, standing up.

After she'd gone, Fran turned to her daughter. 'Charlie, you're being a little bossy. Remember that this is Heather's wedding.'

'I'm just trying to be helpful,' said Charlie. 'Heather hasn't got a mum or dad to help her with all this after all.'

Heather put her hand on her heart. 'Thank you, Charlie. I think you're being wonderful. I'm glad you're here. And I think you've got a promising career ahead of you as a wedding planner.'

'See?' said Charlie, raising her eyebrows at her mother.

Fran shrugged. 'Fine. To be honest, I think Jasmine needed to be brought down a peg or two. So are you going to book it?'

Heather sat back in her chair and sighed. 'It is lovely but I sort of wanted Luke to see it first.'

'How could he not love it if you do?' said Fran. 'Anyway, in my experience, it's always the bride who makes the final choice so I'd go with your heart.'

'You sound like Pamela.'

'Pamela Trott knows a thing or two and plus, I haven't always been a jaded cynic.'

Heather smiled. 'Where did you get married?'

Fran felt a stab of longing. 'We did the usual church and fancy reception thing. It was lovely,' she said casually.

'That overfriendly squirrel ran up your dress,' reported Charlie. 'I used to love it when Daddy told that story.' Fran shook her head in amusement. 'Apparently, Mummy went mental, flapping her arms about but she didn't spill a drop of champagne. Daddy thought that was funny. I think it's clever.'

'Me too,' said Heather, fixing Fran with a meaningful look. 'Happy memories.'

Fran nodded. She could see that Heather understood and she

appreciated it. 'Happy memories. But anyway, this is about you.'
Fran enjoyed the memories but she didn't like to linger over them
for too long. They were like expensive items of jewellery – lovely
to look at for a while but things she couldn't afford to have all
the time. 'So would you like to have your wedding here?'

'Yeah, I think it's perfect.'

Jasmine reappeared. 'We can source halal meat if required,' she
told them with a smile.

'Good,' said Charlie. 'Because we'd like to go ahead and book
please.'

Heather put an arm round Charlie's shoulder and grinned.
'My wedding planner.'

Fran lay back on the couch and tried desperately to get comfortable.

Jude's onto me, she said.

How so?

Let's just say that he made it very clear I should be moving on.

Is that what he said?

Sort of. We were discussing grief with Heather.

Heather?

*Yeah. I met her on the course. She lost her parents when she was
a teenager.*

So she knows what she's talking about.

I guess, although she's a few years further on.

What does she say then?

*Fran sighed and shifted in her seat. Reckons you need to create
new memories. Something about not letting your grief stop you from
living.*

You don't sound convinced

I'm not. I am living.

What about making new memories?

Today's bacon sandwich was very memorable.

*Mmm, don't take this the wrong way but I think you need to
aim a bit higher.*

Fran folded her arms. I'll try but I can't promise. Although I get the feeling that Jude's not going to let this go.

He is his mother's son.

'Oi, shut it, you,' she laughed. And damn your insight.

It's why you love me, he said.

Yes, said Fran. It is.

Chapter Nine

Pamela

My Happiness List
1. Just bake
2. Dinner with Matthew and Barry – be in the moment!

Pamela cast a critical eye over the dining room and felt satisfied. The table looked lovely with its crisp white linen cloth and matching napkins, along with a vase of butter-yellow narcissi and the silver candlesticks, which had been a wedding present all those years ago. She wanted everything to be perfect for Matthew's birthday dinner. She'd invited Laura but didn't get the reaction she'd hoped.

'Sorry, Mum, I'm working that night. Anyway, since when did we do family birthdays?'

She had a point. They didn't. But for once Pamela wished they were one of those families that did.

'It was just a thought, if you were free. Simon's so far away and I thought it would be nice for a change.'

'Sorry, Mum, I can't this time. I hope Matthew appreciates it.'

'He will,' said Pamela hopefully. She wasn't sure how she'd ended up with her family being spread so widely and she wished that they could get together more than once a year at Christmas but it wasn't to be. Her friend, Janet, was forever hosting birthday parties for everyone from her aged mum to her newest grand-daughter.

'I've had to bake three cakes this week,' she said, rolling her eyes as if she was exasperated when in reality she was over the moon. Pamela did her best to smile and swallow down her envy. It was foolish to wish for something that was so far out of her control – she knew this and yet, she still nurtured a vision of the dining room filled with her children and maybe a couple of grandchildren too. Ah, the thought of grandchildren was almost too much sometimes – another chance to cherish the young by showering miniature versions of your own children with pure indulgent love. What could be more wonderful than that?

She went to the kitchen to check on the lamb stew – it had always been Matthew's favourite – served with dumplings and mashed potato. Not the fussy food they liked to eat now, all vegan this and chia seeds that – no, this was proper old-fashioned food that made you happy and possibly a little overweight. She stopped in her tracks when she found Barry humming to himself whilst he cut a large slab of chocolate cake.

'Barry Trott! What on earth do you think you're doing?'

He spun round in shock. Rumbled. 'Pammy, you nearly gave me a heart attack!'

'And a heart attack's exactly what you'll get if you carry on like this. That's Matty's birthday cake for tonight. I told you that.'

Barry looked confused. 'Did you?'

'Yes, of course I did,' said Pamela, wresting the plate from his grasp and trying to slot the stolen piece back into place.'

'I'm sorry. I must have forgotten.'

'Mmm,' muttered Pamela, doing her best to smooth over the dishevelled cake.

'Do we have any biscuits?' asked Barry, opening the cupboards.

'No, we do not,' said Pamela, shooing him away with a tea towel. 'Have a piece of fruit. Honestly, I've got a big dinner planned for Matthew later so you can just wait.'

'Fine. I'll go and divide my perennials,' he said huffily.

'Make sure you leave yourself enough time to have a shower and get changed – we're eating at seven.'

'Anything else?' asked Barry. 'I mean am I allowed a cup of tea or is that forbidden too?'

'Now don't you take that tone with me, Barry Trott. I want us to have a nice dinner with Matty to celebrate his birthday – you're not to ruin it.'

'Yes, Oberstumpfenfuhrer – anything for the golden boy,' muttered Barry under his breath as he headed out the back door.

'Cheek of the man,' murmured Pamela, standing back to appraise the cake. She had managed to patch it as best she could. She might just whip up another batch of chocolate fudge icing though to be sure.

The truth was that she just wanted Matthew to feel loved. She couldn't help fearing that he was a bit lost these days. He'd been such a dear boy growing up – her 'little helper'. She could remember him at Christmas, carefully opening the dark wood canteen of cutlery that had once belonged to her grandmother and polishing each knife, fork and spoon before laying the table for her. Laura had always wanted to help her mother with the food so Matthew had been permitted to take on this role by his bossy older sister, whilst Simon would trail after his brother, laying out the Christmas crackers. She smiled to herself now as she remembered them together, all gathered in the lounge whilst she and Barry watched them open present after present.

'You spoil those children, Pamela,' her mother had remarked as she sat in the corner, sipping her gin and orange, casting judgement on everything she saw. Her mother had never been a well or happy woman. She was widowed relatively young and had no time to indulge Pamela or her younger brother, Ernie.

Pamela couldn't change this but she did make up her mind early on to follow a different path when it came to her own children. She would indulge them whenever she could and, above all, they would always know that they were loved. She was never sure if she'd been successful at this but she tried her best. Barry didn't always help, of course, particularly when it came to Matthew. It was as if he was waiting to criticize, ready to be disappointed.

She heard a key in the door shortly after six-thirty and from the length of time it took for the door to be opened it was clear that Matthew was a little worse for wear.

'Mummy, I'm home!' he cried, before chuckling at his own hilarity.

Pamela went to greet him in the hall, smiling indulgently. 'Are you all right, Matty?'

'All right?' he said. 'All right? I'm more than all right, Mummy because I have you for a mother and I can smell something delicious cooking.'

She giggled like a teenager. 'It's your favourite.'

'Is it, by jingo?' he asked, putting an arm round her shoulder and kissing her on the cheek. She could smell beer and possibly whisky but she didn't mind. He was an affable drunk.

'Can I just say that you look peachy today, Mum.'

Pamela giggled again. 'Peachy?'

'Yeah.' Matthew grinned. 'Peachy and beautiful and about seventeen years old.'

'Oh, get away with you.'

'Watch out, he's after something,' warned Barry, walking down the stairs.

Pamela felt her shoulders tighten with irritation. 'Oh for goodness' sake, Barry. Why do you have to come out with comments like that? I told you I wanted this to be a special night.'

'Dad's a fun sponge,' declared Matthew.

'A fun sponge?' Barry frowned.

'Yes, Dad – you drain all the fun out of everything.'

'I'd rather be a fun sponge than a sponger.'

'What's that supposed to mean?'

Barry fixed him with a look as he reached the bottom of the stairs. 'You know exactly what it means.' He sniffed the air. 'And you're drunk. What kind of respect does that show your mother, who's been slaving over a hot stove for you all day?'

'Enough!' shouted Pamela throwing up her hands. 'That's enough. You both need to stop arguing. I have cooked a birthday meal for Matthew today because he's going out with his friends on his actual birthday and I would like us to sit at the table and have a civilized evening. Do you think we can manage that?'

Barry and Matthew exchanged hostile glances before looking sheepishly at Pamela.

'Sorry, Mum.'

'Sorry, Pammy.'

The meal started off quite well as Pamela dished up and everyone oohed about how good it looked and then ahhed about how good it tasted, but there's only so many times you can compliment the chef on the quality of her mash.

'Shall I open a bottle of wine?' asked Matthew, standing up.

'Haven't you had enough?' muttered Barry.

Pamela shot him a warning glance. 'I'll have one,' she said. 'Thanks, Matty.'

Matthew fetched a bottle of red wine and poured two glasses. Pamela lifted hers in a toast. 'Happy birthday, Matty.'

'Don't I get one?' complained Barry.

Pamela rolled her eyes. 'Here,' she said, handing him her glass and pouring another. 'So as I was saying, happy birthday.' She smiled and tapped her glass against Matthew's.

'Cheers, Mum. Cheers, Dad,' said Matthew. 'This stew is amazing, Mum.'

'Thank you, dear. I'm glad you like it. So how's it going at Doly's shop?'

Matthew nodded. 'Yeah, good. It's just a couple of mornings but it all helps.'

'So when are you going to get a proper job?' asked Barry. Pamela frowned at him but he kept his gaze fixed on his son.

'Erm, probably when hell freezes over,' said Matthew with a shrug. 'I mean that's what you're thinking, isn't it, Dad?'

Barry adopted a look of angelic innocence. 'I never said that, Matthew. I'm just curious, seeing as we're the ones giving you board and lodging while you disappear off to God knows where and come home drunk. It would be good to know if there's a plan.'

Matthew fixed him with a look. 'Oh yeah. There's a plan, Dad, but I don't think you'd get it.'

'Try me.'

Pamela wasn't even aware that she'd thrown the plate until the meat, gravy, dumplings, mash and greens were sliding down the wall. 'You can't stop, can you?' she shouted. They stared at her in horror. 'Oh, you're quiet now, aren't you? You should listen to yourselves – all you do is argue and I'm sick of it, do you hear? Sick. Of. It.' She threw down her napkin for added drama and made for the door. 'You two can clear this lot up. Oh, and there's cake if you want it!' Pamela fled into the hall, hurrying upstairs to the box room. She slammed the door behind her and leant heavily against it, feeling her body shaking with anger.

Where had that come from? She never got angry. With anyone. She kept calm and carried on. Now she was losing the plot and chucking plates. She was surprised that she didn't cry – she didn't feel the need to dissolve into rivers of self-pitying tears. She just wanted them to stop arguing with one another and start noticing her again – to realize that she was still here and bloody well appreciate her a bit more.

She took out her albums and leafed through. Where were these people? What had they become? Why couldn't life be as it was

94

all those years ago? Look at those smiling faces. Life seemed so much simpler back then when all she had to do was wipe a face and receive a tight hug in return. She looked at the photo of her with Barry on their honeymoon – love's young dream. She was smiling out of the photograph whilst Barry gazed at her with total adoration. She couldn't remember the last time someone had looked at her like that, except Fran's dog Alan maybe.

Pamela sighed. As far as she was concerned, she was staying up here with her memories for as long as possible – the past seemed far preferable to Barry and Matthew's war zone.

A while later there was a tapping at the door. 'Who is it?' she demanded.

The door opened and Matthew's face appeared wearing a decidedly sheepish expression. 'I thought you might like a cup of tea,' he said, holding out her favourite bone china mug.

'Thank you,' she said, taking it from him.

'What are you looking at?' he asked with a tentative smile.

'Just the old photos.'

'Wow, check out those flares,' laughed Matthew, leaning over to look.

'I made those at my dressmaking class, would you believe?' said Pamela.

'You're a talent, Mum.'

'Am I?'

He stared at her. 'Of course you are, you're amazing.' Pamela kept her gaze on him. 'I'm sorry about earlier. Dad and I, well… we don't always see eye to eye.'

'You can say that again.'

Matthew laughed and sat down next to her on the bed. 'Understatement of the century, eh? Sorry, Mum. I've cleaned up downstairs.'

Pamela winced. 'Did it make a big mess?'

Matthew see-sawed his head from side to side. 'A bit. But it's fine.'

'Sorry I lost my temper.'

'No, it's okay. It was our fault.'

'What's your dad doing now?'

'Watching *Gardeners' World*, I think.'

Pamela nodded. *Same old, same old.* 'Mmm well, thanks for making me the tea.'

Matthew smiled. 'I'm just going to pop out. I realize that Doly didn't pay me today.'

Pamela glanced at her watch. 'Don't bother her now, she's got three little girls and they'll be in bed. How much do you need?'

Matthew screwed up his face. 'Are you sure? I'll pay you back.' Pamela nodded. 'Fifty should do it.' He leant over to kiss her. 'Thanks, Mum, you're the best.'

Yes, thought Pamela as she went downstairs to find her purse. *I am the best doormat in the whole world – welcoming, accommodating and happy to be trodden all over.*

'What's up?' asked Fran looking concerned as Pamela flopped down in the chair next to her when they met at the course a few days later.

'Families,' sighed Pamela.

'Happiness is having a large, loving, caring, close-knit family in another city.' Fran smiled.

Pamela snorted with laughter. 'Very true – can I quote you on that?'

Fran held up her hands. 'I can't lie, George Burns said it first but I'm sure he won't mind if you use it.'

'Evening, shiny happy people,' said Heather, taking a seat next to Pamela. 'How are we all?'

'Well,' began Fran, 'I finally persuaded the octogenarian, whose book I'm editing to tone down the sex scenes, rescued Alan from a tree after a cat chased him up there and refereed a disagreement between Jude and Charlie about…actually I'm not sure what that was about in the end, sweetcorn possibly.'

'Never let it be said that you don't lead a full and eventful life.' Heather smiled.

'Thank you,' said Fran earnestly. 'I was just consoling Pamela, who has family woes.'

'Poor Pamela – what's up?'

Pamela grimaced. 'I feel bad moaning to you, Heather.'

'What, because I'm an orphan?' Pamela gave a sheepish nod. Heather nudged her. 'Don't be daft.'

'Yeah, Pamela, don't be daft,' said Fran kindly. 'Everyone's got stuff going on – it's not a competition. We're your friends.'

Pamela felt her eyes mist. She had friends of a similar age of course, but most of them were nestled in their own lives – enjoying a second youth on cruises with their husbands or looking after their grandchildren. They were settled and often quite smug about it.

Fran and Heather were so much younger than her, still finding their way, still working out what they needed – she felt as if she was too. 'You're both very kind,' she told them. 'It's Matthew and Barry. I'm not sure if him living with us is such a good idea. I mean, I love having him around but Barry just sees the worst in him all the time. I thought it would be easier when your kids become adults but it seems harder somehow.'

'I reckon it all goes downhill once they hit the teenage years,' said Fran, shaking her head. 'Give me a five-year-old with a scabby knee and a Fruit Shoot addiction any day.'

Pamela smiled. 'I know Matty hasn't got a regular income but he is trying with his cash-and- carry runs for Doly. Anyway, I lost my temper with them the other night. I'd spent all day making this lovely dinner for Matty's birthday and then all they did was argue.'

'I don't blame you for getting angry,' said Heather outraged. 'Sounds as if they're taking you for granted.'

It was as if a light clicked on in Pamela's head. It was one thing to have these thoughts yourself but quite different when another person said it out loud. 'Do you really think so?'

'Totally,' said Fran. 'I hope you lost the plot big time – sounds like they deserved it.'

Pamela bit her lip. 'I threw my plate against the wall,' she said quietly.

Heather and Fran exchanged glances before bursting into laughter. 'A woman after my own heart,' declared Fran.

'Yeah, you go, girl,' agreed Heather.

Pamela grinned at them both, feeling unexpectedly buoyed. Maybe she had been right to read Barry and Matthew the Riot Act. Maybe it was about time they heard the truth of how she felt.

She looked up as Nik clapped his hands together. 'Good evening, my friends,' he said. 'I trust we have all had good weeks and perhaps practised our mindfulness a little more?'

'I took three hours to eat a banana on Monday,' joked Fran. Everyone laughed.

'Thank you, Fran.' Nik smiled. 'We can exchange perhaps more sensible stories during our tea break…'

'Everyone's a critic,' murmured Fran.

'…because today we have a very special guest.' He gestured towards an attractive woman with dark hair scraped back high into a ponytail, wearing a bright pink vest, leggings and a touch too much make-up. 'This is Stacey.'

'Hi, everyone,' waved Stacey, flashing an alarmingly white-toothed grin.

'Why am I getting a bad feeling about this?' whispered Fran.

'This week we are being kind to ourselves and that means we need to look after our bodies,' said Nik. 'Science has proven that exercising releases endorphins in the body and, as you no doubt know, these make us happy. So, Stacey here is going to help as we experiment with this by taking us through a Zumba routine.'

Pamela's heart sank. The nearest she came to proper exercise these days was the vigorous beating of eggs and sugar when making a sponge. She had had a deep-down fear of sport ever since her PE teacher, Miss Widdecombe, had declared, in front of the whole class, that she was too chubby to play netball. Pamela felt her ears burn with shame even now.

'Thank you, Nik,' smiled Stacey, standing before them. 'Right, let's have you all on your feet and push the chairs right back so that we have enough space. I want you to copy what I do and let yourself go. Don't worry about anyone else – this is meant to be fun and energetic. Just listen to the music and go with the flow. Okay everyone?'

Pamela hesitated. She felt old and frumpy and nothing like that young girl who used to skip round the dancefloor with Barry. Fran must have sensed her hesitation as she linked an arm through hers. 'Come on, Pamela, don't desert me. Let's face this together.' Pamela looked round at Jim, Georg and the others – everyone looked nervous as they took their places. Heather gave her an encouraging wink.

'Follow my lead.' Stacey smiled, as she pressed 'play' on her iPod and a pulsating beat pumped through the speakers.

Pamela copied Stacey as she started with straightforward side-to-side moves, before adding handclaps and shimmies. She frowned with concentration to start with but felt herself relax as some instinct from her dancing days kicked in.

'Good!' cried Stacey. 'You're all doing brilliantly. Keep going.'

The beat intensified and the pace with it. Jim was flailing around, waving his arms in the air like a drowning man but clearly having the time of his life. Pamela caught sight of Fran – she was huffing and puffing but smiling too. Even Nik was joining in. Pamela let the beat carry her, forgetting all about netball with Miss Widdecombe and remembering dancing with Barry.

'Great moves,' said Stacey, smiling at Pamela. 'You've done this before.'

Pamela felt her cheeks flush with pride as the beat intensified and she managed to keep up. She was aware that Sue and Jim had stopped but Pamela kept dancing right to the end of the track.

'Wow,' declared Stacey when they'd finished. 'That was amazing – well done, everyone. How do you feel?'

'I need oxygen,' wheezed Fran, gasping for air.

'Was fun,' said Georg, without the hint of a smile.

'I loved it!' declared Heather.

'Me too, ducks,' agreed Pamela. 'Although I could do with a sit down.'

'I thought you all did brilliantly,' declared Nik. 'I definitely think that we have released a few endorphins this evening. Thank you, Stacey.' She grinned at them all. 'So, this week, I want you to take up a new form of exercise. You can continue with Zumba if you like – I know that Stacey teaches an excellent class on a Thursday. Or try something different. Find an activity that is fun but which brings you benefits. If you couple exercise with a good diet, sleep and limited alcohol intake, you will definitely notice the benefits.'

'I mean the Zumba was fun,' declared Fran as they left the hall a while later. 'But cutting down on alcohol? It doesn't strike me as the path to everlasting joy.'

'I'm a bit nervous about going to another class on my own,' admitted Pamela.

'I've got an idea,' said Heather, grinning at them both. 'What are you two doing on Friday morning?'

'Erm, avoiding you at all costs, because from the look on your face, you're about to make me do something I don't want to?' winced Fran.

'Wrong,' said Heather. 'You're both coming with me on an adventure.'

'I'm in,' declared Pamela, feeling an unexpected urge to grab life with both hands and go for it.

'Why do I get the feeling that I'm not going to like this?' asked Fran.

'You're going to love it!' insisted Heather. 'It's going to be so much fun!'

'Fun, huh?' mused Fran. 'It's been a while but why the hell not and if Pamela's up for it then I'm in too!'

As Pamela let herself in through the front door, the house was quiet. She breathed a sigh of relief. She peered around the living room door to find Barry watching yet another gardening programme. She could remember how his face used to light up when she entered a room but that was a long time ago. Now he merely flicked his gaze in her direction before turning back to Monty Don and his herb planting. 'Hello, Pammy. How was the course?'

'Great,' she replied, 'really great. We tried this thing called Zumba – made me think of when we used to go dancing,' she added, hoping he'd take the hint.

'Sounds nice,' said Barry, only half listening.

Pamela turned away, not wanting his lack of interest to dampen her mood. 'Do you want a cup of tea?'

'No ta, love.'

'Is Matty in?'

Barry shrugged, his eyes fixed on the screen. 'No idea.'

Don't let it bother you, she told herself as she made her way to the kitchen. *Don't let the fact that you are invisible in your own home get to you.*

The kitchen door was ajar. She could hear Matthew talking in a low voice as if he didn't want anyone to hear. She leant in to listen. 'I told you that I'll get it to you by the end of the month and I will, all right?' A pause. 'Yes. I know how important it is. You'll get it on time, okay? Okay. Bye.'

She took a step back before casually pushing the door open. 'Oh sorry, Matty, I didn't realize you were in here.'

He stood up from the table and hurriedly closed his laptop with an innocent smile. 'Don't worry, Mum. I was about to go out anyway.'

'At this time?'

He grinned. 'Mum, I'm thirty-three. I'm a big boy now.' He reached over to kiss her.

'Matty, is everything okay?' she asked, her face grave with concern.

He looked into her eyes. 'Everything's fine, Mum. I promise.' She wanted to believe him. Desperately. He picked up his laptop and made for the door. 'See you in the morning. 'Night.'

''Night, lovey. Don't be late for Doly, will you?'

'Don't worry, Mum, I won't let you down.'

She looked into his eyes.

Oh Matthew, I want to believe you. I really do but I'm starting to have my doubts.

'Have a lovely evening,' she said.

He planted a kiss on her forehead. 'Don't wait up.'

She watched him go and heard the front door click shut.

Don't dwell on it, Pamela. Don't let it get to you. Your husband ignores you and you're not sure what your son's up to. But you have to focus on yourself now. Heather and Fran are right – it's time to find out what you want.

Pamela opened the cupboards, took out the ingredients for a coffee walnut sponge and started to bake.

Chapter Ten

Heather

Happiness List
1. Marry Luke!
2. Sunday walk and choose wedding venue with Luke Fran & Charlie
3. Exercise more (persuade Luke to go running?)

'Right then, young lady, where are you taking us?' demanded Fran, tapping Heather on the shoulder from the back seat. 'Because *you* promised fun and we *appear* to be stopping by a large park containing some fit-looking people wearing army fatigues. This better not be a boot camp.'

Heather winced. 'It's not exactly a boot camp – they're very nice and not at all shouty. It's just army-style exercises and lots of fun.'

Fran narrowed her eyes. 'If I throw up, you're clearing it up.'

'I don't think I can do this,' said Pamela. Fran and Heather looked over at her. She'd gone very pale.

Heather put an arm around her shoulder. She realized that she'd started to feel protective towards Pamela – she was nosier than an aardvark but she had a warmth that was hard not to love. 'Honestly, Pamela, it will be fine. You don't have to do anything you're not comfortable with. We're signed up for the beginner's taster session. I've done it before – it's just things like star jumps and tag games. You don't need to worry.'

'I'm not too old and fat, am I?' asked Pamela quietly.

Heather's heart went out to her. 'Of course not,' she said, giving her a tight squeeze.

'Anyway, I bet my muffin top is bigger than your muffin top,' declared Fran with pursed lips. Pamela laughed nervously. 'Come on – let's give it a go and if we hate it, we'll make Heather buy us cake afterwards.'

Pamela gave a brave smile. 'All right. I'll give it a whirl.'

'Attagirl.'

They climbed out of the car and made their way over to where a class of around a dozen or so people were gathering.

Heather felt a pang of nerves. What if it was a disaster? She didn't know Fran and Pamela that well. She prayed it would be as much fun as she'd remembered and that they could laugh it off if it wasn't. It would be fine. They'd try it as a one-off and then she'd find another form of regular exercise – maybe she could persuade Luke to go running in the evenings. Yeah. Maybe.

The instructor had his back to them and some of the other women in the group were gazing up at him in a slightly doe-eyed way as he talked. He was tall and broad-shouldered with pleasingly muscular arms. As they approached, he turned and smiled in surprise.

'Mrs Trott!' he cried. 'What are you doing here?'

'Trust Pamela to know the instructor,' whispered Fran, nudging Heather.

Pamela grinned up at him. 'Little Gary Walters – I haven't seen you for years! How's your mum?'

'Really well, thanks. Are you still on Hope Street? I haven't been back since Nan died.'

'We are.' Pamela nodded. 'My friend, Heather, here persuaded me to come along but I'm a bit worried that I'm too unfit.'

'Don't you fret, Mrs T. I'll look after you. You go at your own pace. Have you got any health conditions?'

'I only get a bit dizzy sometimes because of you know, the change.' Fran and Heather exchanged amused glances. 'But that seems to be much better since I've been on the HRT.'

'You'll be fine.' Gary smiled. 'If I could get you ladies to fill out these forms please, then we can make a start. So one for you, Mrs T, and here you go, Heather…and you are?'

'Fran,' she replied.

As he held her gaze for a second, Heather noticed Fran's neck flush pink. 'Here you go, Fran.'

'Thanks, Little Gary Walters.' He laughed.

'You flirt,' whispered Heather to Fran as they filled out their forms.

'Was I flirting?' asked Fran in surprise.

'Don't worry, Fran – he's a very handsome man,' said Pamela, patting her on the arm. 'And his mum's lovely – we used go to the same dances back in the day.

Gary clapped his hands together to get their attention. 'Okay, good morning, everyone. It's great to see so many new recruits today.' He flashed a grin at Pamela, who beamed. 'We're going to do a few warm-up exercises so let's start with some gentle running on the spot. Follow my lead and off we go.'

Heather watched Pamela and Fran as Gary took them through the warm-ups. Pamela's face was fixed in a frown of deep concentration whilst Fran was looking around with wry amusement. It was a promising start.

Gary offered enthusiastic encouragement as if they were competing in the Olympics instead of attempting their very best star jumps in a south-east London park. 'That's excellent. Don't overexert – keep it steady. Well done, Mrs T, great effort.'

Pamela looked as if she might burst with pride. Heather and Fran exchanged indulgent smiles.

'Right, so now if you could get into pairs. I think we're an odd number so Fran, you can be with me.'

Fran pulled a face at Heather before taking her place next to Gary. Heather felt Pamela take her hand. 'Come on, Pamela,' she said, squeezing it. 'Let's show them how it's done.' Pamela flashed her a grateful smile.

The rest of the session seemed to fly by. Heather couldn't remember the last time she'd laughed so much, especially when Fran, who had a frighteningly competitive streak, rugby-tackled Gary during a team tag game. By the end, everyone was pink-cheeked and grinning with exhilaration.

'Oh Gary, lovey, that was wonderful,' gushed Pamela, pulling the huge man into a hug as they went over to thank him.

'I'm glad you enjoyed it, Mrs T – hope to see you again,' he said with a smile. 'Oh Fran, could I have a quick word please?'

'I'll catch you up,' said Fran.

'Thanks for bringing us,' said Pamela, linking her arm through Heather's. 'I've never tried anything like that before. I reckon I've got a few of those endor-wotsits chugging round my body now.'

'Endorphins?'

'That's the stuff.' Pamela grinned. 'I feel ready for anything!'

'I'm glad,' said Heather relieved. 'So are things better at home?'

Pamela sighed. 'Not especially but I've decided not to let it get me down. From now on I'm going to do what I want.'

'Good for you. Army boot camp every week then?' asked Heather.

'You're on!'

'Did you get told off for rugby-tackling Little Gary Walters?' joked Heather as Fran caught up with them by the car.

'Not exactly,' she muttered, climbing into the back. 'He wanted my phone number.'

'Go Fran! Did you give it to him?' asked Heather.

Fran frowned. 'Do you know, I was so caught off guard, I did and now I'm wishing I hadn't.' She gazed out of the window in silence. Heather and Pamela exchanged glances.

'He's a lovely young man,' offered Pamela.

'I'm sure he is. It's just that I haven't been out with a man since Andy died.'

'Well,' said Heather after a pause, 'I know it was different for me losing my parents, but I didn't feel that I'd found a way to live with my grief until I met Luke.'

Fran folded her arms. 'Listen, don't get me wrong. I appreciate you trying to help but I do think it's different and I'm just not ready to date at the moment. But thank you.'

Heather nodded. It was the first time she'd seen Fran's serious side and could tell that she meant what she said. 'Of course. I get it completely.'

Fran gave her a grateful smile. 'Anyway, did you tell Pamela that you'd booked the wedding venue? With a little help from Charlie, I might add!'

Subject closed. Case dismissed.

Pamela smiled. 'Ooh yes, ducks. Chilford Park is beautiful – I'm so excited for you.'

'Was Luke pleased?' asked Fran.

'Yeah, yeah he was,' said Heather. *Eventually.* She'd returned home after her trip with Fran, full of excitement to find Luke still working.

'I just need half an hour more,' he told her.

Half an hour had doubled and tripled before Luke emerged looking tired and harassed. 'Sorry, baby, that took a lot longer than I anticipated. I was going to cook you something special but I'm done for – how about one of my incredible omelettes?'

He was trying to make amends and Heather didn't want an

argument so she smiled and sat down at the kitchen table, nursing a glass of wine while he made dinner.

'So how was your afternoon?' asked Luke as he chopped peppers and mushrooms. 'Sorry I had to leave you to it.'

'It's okay,' she said, because actually it did feel okay, sitting in their kitchen, chatting while he cooked. Like a regular couple. 'As it turned out, the afternoon was rather productive.'

He turned to look at her. 'Oh yeah?'

Heather couldn't hold back on the surprise. 'I booked the venue!' she blurted.

'What? You booked it?' His voice sounded flat.

'You don't sound very pleased.'

He sighed. 'I guess I'm just disappointed that you didn't wait until we could go along and decide together.'

'Well, I'm sorry but they couldn't hold the date indefinitely. I had to make a decision and Fran said…'

'Fran?'

'My friend? You met her at the woods, with her kids? And the dog?'

'Oh yeah but what was she doing there?'

'She came along with her daughter, Charlie, and we all felt that it was the right thing to do.'

'All of you? You let a stranger and a child decide our wedding venue?'

Heather folded her arms as anger rose in her chest. 'Now just wait a minute. Fran is my friend and Charlie is, well Charlie is bloody fantastic. We could have gone along together and made the decision but you had to work so they offered to come with me. End of.'

Luke ran a hand through his hair. 'Not this again.'

Heather glared at him. 'Yes. This again. I'm trying to be understanding, really I am, but you're working all the time. Of course I wanted to decide this with you but when I saw it, I thought it was perfect and Fran agreed. She's a good friend and I trust her judgement,' said Heather, feeling emboldened at the thought. 'And her daughter is wonderful. We had a brilliant time looking around and I thought that if we all loved it then you would too. Now I'm sorry if you have a problem with that but I think I did the right thing.'

Luke stared at her in amazement before his face broke into a smile. 'Wow. Sorry. You're completely right.'

It was Heather's turn to be surprised. 'I am?'

He held up his hands. 'Yeah. You did the right thing – I was out of order.'

Heather gave a cautious smile before nodding. 'Okay. I'm glad you think so.'

Luke reached for her hand. 'Sorry for being an asshole. I'm really tired but that's not an excuse – I was still an asshole.'

She laughed. 'Apology accepted.'

'And furthermore, can I say that I have never found you sexier than when you read me the Riot Act just then.' He leant forwards to kiss her.

'Oh really?'

He stood up and pulled her into his arms. 'Really,' he said, staring into her eyes. They rejected the omelettes in exchange for some pretty hot sex after that. Heather smiled as she thought about it now – Luke loved her, he wanted her and they were going to have the best wedding and the happiest life. She was determined to make sure of it.

'So, what are you plans for the weekend?' asked Fran, interrupting Heather's reverie.

'We're looking after my godson, Freddy, tonight.'

'Oh, how wonderful,' said Pamela clapping her hands together. 'All good practice for when you have your own.'

'Mmm,' said Heather vaguely. *When or if? That was the question.*

'Either that or it'll put you off for life,' joked Fran.

'Funnily enough, that's what Gemma said,' laughed Heather.

109

'A woman after my own heart,' declared Fran.

'Oh Fran,' scolded Pamela. She turned to Heather. 'Don't listen to her – the best days of my life were my wedding and when my kids were born.'

'My best day was definitely my wedding,' scoffed Fran. 'I'll take drinking champagne in a big dress over childbirth any day. Although epidurals are conclusive evidence that God is a woman.'

'But what about having those lovely babies?' clucked Pamela. 'It changes your life for ever.'

'You're not wrong there,' remarked Fran. 'They should come with a receipt.' Pamela gave an indulgent tut.

Heather smiled. She loved their banter. Fran and Pamela had been there, done that, got the T-shirts, whilst Heather was still trying to work out which T-shirt to choose. 'He's only staying for one night so how bad can it be?'

Pretty bad as it turned out, although things at least started on a positive. Heather was impressed when Luke arrived home during the early afternoon, saying that he'd decided to work from home so that he could be on hand to help out. Heather took this as a good sign.

Gemma was due to drop Freddy off at five. At half past four, Heather realized that they'd run out of milk. 'I'm just popping to the shop,' she told Luke. 'I'll be back before Gemma arrives.' He looked up from his laptop and nodded.

As she let herself back through the front door a while later, Heather could hear laughter from the living room.

'You filthy bugger!' she heard Gemma declare.

Heather appeared in the doorway. 'Who's a filthy bugger?' she laughed.

'Heather!' cried Gemma, jumping up to hug her cousin. 'I didn't hear you come in. Luke was just telling me one of his disgusting stories. It's nice to have a laugh with a grown-up for a change.'

'I'm sure,' said Heather with a smile. She glanced at Luke, who wore an oddly blank expression. She spotted the baby car seat, where Freddy was fast asleep. 'So how's the little man?'

Gemma pulled a face. 'He's teething so I'll leave you some gum gel and Calpol in case you need it. I hope he's okay for you.'

'We'll be fine, won't we, Luke?' said Heather hopefully.

Luke shrugged. 'Sure. You go and have a great time,' he said, fixing his gaze on Gemma.

There was a squeak from Freddy as his eyes opened and he took in his new surroundings. 'Well hello, mister,' said Gemma, unbuckling the strap and lifting him from his car seat. 'You're awake, are you?'

'Mamar,' confirmed Freddy.

'Oh that's too cute!' cried Heather. 'He said "mummy". Isn't that cute, Luke?'

'Yeah. Cute,' said Luke casually. 'Now if you'll excuse me, I should go back and do some work. Good to see you, Gemma,' he added, leaning forwards to kiss her. 'Remember to call me when you go for your work meeting – we can have lunch.'

Gemma smiled. 'Yeah. That would be great.'

'You should get going,' said Heather, turning to her cousin and trying to shake off the sinking feeling that Luke wasn't completely on-board with tonight's arrangement.

'Are you sure this is going to be okay, Heth?' asked Gemma, passing Freddy to her.

'It'll be great,' said Heather, hoping this was true. She made googly eyes at her godson, who giggled with delight.

'I hope you're right. He was a bit of bugger for Mum the other day.'

Heather gave Freddy an exaggerated look of horror, which he rewarded with a coo of amusement. 'Did Mummy say a bad word? Naughty Mummy – she needs to go out on the sauce with Daddy and loosen up a bit.'

Gemma grimaced. 'Sorry. I just don't want it to be a nightmare for you.'

Heather adopted a stern face. 'It will be fine, Gem. It's one night. Now go, drink champagne with your husband and have all the sex.'

'Oh God no. The only thing I'm doing in that luxurious bed with its 120 thread-count Egyptian cotton sheets is sleeping. Trust me.' She kissed Heather and then Freddy before heading for the door. 'Have fun, my darlings – I love you.'

Heather stood at the door with Freddy, waving. 'Say bye bye, Mummy. Bye bye.'

'Marmar?' asked Freddy.

'That's right. Mummy. Mummy,' said Heather, closing the door behind them as Gemma disappeared round the corner.

'Marmar? Marmar?' insisted Freddy, his brow furrowing.

'Oh, it's okay. Mama will be back tomorrow. Tonight you've got Heather. Can you say "Heather"?'

'Marmar. Marmar,' said Freddy, tears springing to his eyes.

He continued with this theme, his requests for his mother and his crying steadily increasing in volume and urgency. Heather tried everything she could to console him – food, milk, his boggle-eyed rabbit – but all were roundly rejected with determined ferocity. Eventually, Luke appeared from the dining room, a frown of frustration on his face.

Freddy seemed to calm for a second. 'Marmar?' he asked through hiccupping sobs.

'How I wish it was,' said Heather.

When Freddy saw that Luke was in fact not 'Marmar', his cries rapidly escalated again. Luke stood in the doorway, a look of disbelief on his face. 'Why is he crying like that?'

Heather rolled her eyes. 'Believe me, if I knew that, I'd make it stop. I don't suppose you want to hold him for a minute, do you? See if you've got the magic touch?'

Luke looked horrified. 'I'm no good with babies, particularly screaming ones and besides, I've really gotta work.'

Heather was annoyed. 'But I thought you said you'd lend a hand?'

Luke sighed. 'Yeah, but something's come up and I have to take a call from New York in half an hour.'

'It's Friday night,' said Heather.

'Not there it isn't. Anyway, it's not as if we're about to have a relaxing evening in, is it?'

Heather sighed. 'Probably not.'

'Actually, Heth, might you be able to take him out while I speak to New York? That wailing is kind of distracting.'

Heather was furious but staying here with a screaming baby and an unhelpful fiancé didn't feel like the right option – maybe the air would calm them both down. 'Fine. I'll see you later.'

She wrestled a squirming Freddy into his pushchair and headed out onto Hope Street. Freddy was still crying but the sound was less enclosed and intense. There was a chill to the air but the sky was a glorious peachy-pink colour and Heather felt relieved to be outside. There was something about the way that Luke had reacted to Freddy that bothered her. True, Freddy was wailing like a banshee so Luke wasn't meeting him under the best circumstances and he was clearly tired and stressed after a day at work but it made her wonder. If they did have children, what kind of father would Luke make? How would he react if he came home to find them screaming the place down? Maybe it was different with your own kids but still, that seed of doubt nestled in her brain and threatened to take root.

She hoped that the walk would calm Freddy, that he might find the motion of the buggy soothing and forget he was missing his mother. Unfortunately, the fresh air seemed to energize him again so that by the time she was outside Pamela's house, Heather was starting to lose all hope and a tiny bit of her mind. Without realizing what she was doing, she took an abrupt turn and headed up the garden path.

Heather felt an unexpected surge of relief at the sight of Pamela, who was staring at them both with an expression of kind concern. 'Oh. now then, what's going on here?' She smiled down at the baby. 'You must be Freddy! What's the matter, darling?'

'He won't stop crying,' said Heather desperately. 'I don't know what to do.'

'Ah now, come on in, both of you. Come on, Mr Freddy. Let's have a proper look at you.'

'I think he misses his mum.'

'I'm sure he does.' Pamela smiled, unbuckling his pushchair like a pro and scooping him into her arms. 'Now then, Mr Fred, what's all this noise?' said Pamela. Freddy stared at her and stopped crying for a second. Pamela saw her chance and planted a raspberry kiss on his cheek. Freddy looked astonished. Heather was sure he was about to start crying again. Pamela planted another raspberry kiss. Freddy made a sound which was half like a bark and half like a laugh. Another raspberry. Freddy gave a tentative giggle. Two more raspberries. Two more giggles.

'Pamela.'

'Yes, lovey?'

'You're my hero.'

Pamela laughed. 'I've just had a lot of practice. Have you got his milk?'

'Er, yes,' said Heather.

'Come through to the kitchen. We'll see if he wants it and I'll make us both a cuppa.'

Half an hour later, a sleeping Freddy was lying in Pamela's arms having drunk all his milk, been winded by Heather and changed by Pamela.

'We make a good team.' Pamela smiled. 'He's a beauty.'

'Thank goodness you were there to help – what would I have done without you? I'm not sure I'll ever be able to look after a baby.'

Pamela waved away her concerns. ''Course you will, ducks. You learn fast when it's your own.'

Heather nodded, feeling an unexpected sting of tears. She wiped at her eyes. 'Sorry. I don't know where that came from. It's just the thought of Mum not being here if I ever have a baby.'

Pamela reached out and took hold of her hand. 'I know it's not the same but I'll always be happy to help. I bet Fran will too.'

Heather smiled gratefully. 'This must take you back,' she said, gesturing towards Freddy.

Pamela's eyes twinkled with joy. 'Just a bit. I loved having babies. Laura was a bit of a nightmare to settle and Simon had colic but Matty was always so easy.'

'Happy memories?'

Pamela nodded ruefully. 'I wish I could go back just for one day. It was my favourite time. It's all so different once they grow up.'

Heather squeezed her hand. 'I bet it's difficult to remember the person you were before you were a mother.'

Pamela gave a surprised nod. 'Yes, that's exactly how it is.'

'Well, keep going because I get the feeling you're on your way to finding out.'

Pamela smiled. 'It's all a bit of an eye-opener, isn't it?'

Heather glanced at Freddy and nodded. 'You can say that again.'

Back home, Heather steered the pushchair in through the front door, trying to make as little sound as possible. She looked down at her godson, at the perfect curve of his lip, slightly pursed as he slept. As she listened to his gentle snuffling breath, the realization hit her.

I want a baby one day. I want the peace and the chaos and everything in between.

'Oh, you're back,' said Luke, appearing in the living-room doorway, his voice a fraction too loud. Freddy's eyes sprang open.

He stared up at Heather, his face mirroring her own expression of concern.

'Oh no,' she sighed, unbuckling the straps and lifting Freddy into her arms. Luke eyed the baby like an enemy in his midst and Heather felt her heart sink. Freddy in turn frowned at him with narrow-eyed suspicion. It was as if he could see through to Luke's soul and didn't like it one bit. The frown deepened to a scowl and then his whole face dropped as the inevitable crying started up again.

Luke looked irritated. 'Why does he keep doing that?'

Heather was exasperated. 'I don't know. He's probably just missing Gemma and doesn't like the unfamiliar surroundings.' *Or your attitude. He's definitely picking up on that.* She didn't know what to do next but she was pretty sure she wasn't about to get any help from Luke. 'I'm going to put him in the travel cot in our room and stay up there until he settles.'

Luke looked relieved. 'Okay, baby. Shall I sleep in the spare room? Give you guys some space?' He made it sound as if he was being kind.

'Fine,' said Heather flatly. The action of carrying Freddy upstairs seemed to soothe him and Heather did her best to dismiss the nagging feeling that Luke's absence was helping too. By the time she'd changed him into his sleepsuit and laid him on the bed, he was chatting happily to himself. Heather's body felt as if it was made of cement so she flopped down on the bed next to him and watched as Freddy blew raspberries and lifted his chubby little legs into the air.

'Oh, Freddy, that didn't exactly go to plan, did it?' she said. 'What if Luke decides that he never wants children? What do I do then? And why am I talking to a baby, expecting him to have all the answers?'

'Edda,' said Freddy, turning his head to look at her. She smiled. 'Edda,' he insisted, his eyes boring into her soul.

She laughed. 'You're saying my name.'

'Edda,' he repeated slowly. *Yeah, duh, lady. I'm not stupid.*

'That's right,' she said, kissing him on the cheek. 'Heather. I'm Heather and it feels as if my world is coming apart at the seams. Please will you help me?'

'Edda,' said Freddy, grasping one of her fingers and squeezing it tightly.

She smiled. 'That'll do for now,' she said.

Chapter Eleven

Fran

Happiness List Thing
1. Accept a world without Andy (too soon!)
2. 'Digital Detox' day with kids
3. Go on even more walks with Alan
4. Have dinner with a nice man (NOT a date) & laugh if appropriate

'Oh beloved children, could you come down here please? I have doughnuts!'

'Yay, I love doughnuts!' cried Charlie, bouncing down the stairs and skipping into the dining room where Fran had placed a large pitcher of peach iced tea, a plate of custard doughnuts and three plates. 'Ooh, fancy,' she added, gesturing at the plates.

'Yes well, I know we usually eat them straight from the bag but I thought we'd adopt a more civilized approach today,' said Fran.

'You're funny, Mummy,' grinned Charlie, wrapping her arms around her mother's waist.

'Thank you,' replied Fran, stroking her daughter's hair and

kissing the top of her head. She smelt of cherry-almond shampoo and sunshine. 'Now where's that brother of yours?'

'In the bathroom,' reported Charlie. 'He's been an awfully long time.'

Fran smiled at her daughter's quaint turn of phrase. She had an occasional propensity to sound like a Thirties BBC announcer. 'Jude!' shouted Fran from the bottom of the stairs. 'Are you all right?'

'Fine!' came the muffled response. 'Just washing my hair.'

'Washing his hair?' frowned Fran. Fourteen-year-old boys generally needed to be told to wash their hair and also given the shampoo and towel in order to do the job.

'He's probably dyeing it,' remarked Charlie casually. 'He's been watching loads of YouTube videos on how to do it.'

'What?' cried Fran, dashing up the stairs. 'Jude! What are you doing?'

'I told you, I'm washing my hair! I'll be out in a minute.'

'Let me in! I know you're dyeing it. I'm not cross – just let me in.'

A muttering of expletives could be heard before the lock clicked open. Fran pushed the door and stared at her son. 'Wow,' breathed Charlie from behind her mother. 'You look like your head's on fire.'

Jude frowned. 'I wanted a change. Something different.'

'Well it's certainly that. It's very—' she searched for the word '—orange.' Fran stared at him for a second before something bubbled up inside her and she started to laugh. 'You big wally – why didn't you tell me? I would have taken you to the hair-dresser's to get it done properly.'

'I wanted to do it myself, okay?' snapped Jude.

'Don't be cross with Mummy,' scolded Charlie.

'Mer mer mer mer mer mer,' mocked Jude in a squeaky voice. Charlie reached forwards and punched him on the arm. 'Ow! You little bugger!'

119

'Okay enough! Both of you,' shouted Fran. 'Jude, watch your language, get yourself tidied up and come downstairs. Can we at least sit down together for five minutes please?'

'Fine,' said Jude.

'Fine,' repeated Charlie.

Fran's mind churned as she returned to the dining room and poured out glasses of iced tea. Why was her life always like this? She had wanted to sit down with the kids, like they always used to, to talk about stuff like they always had.

Whilst there'd been a lot of gnashing of teeth and fist-shaking associated with Andy's death, it had also brought Fran closer to her children. Friends and family were there for support but she, Charlie and Jude had often preferred to stick together in the weeks and months afterwards. She remembered days when one of them would say that they couldn't face the world so they didn't. They stayed in their pyjamas, ate their body weight in ice cream and simply existed together. Sometimes they sat and talked about Andy and sometimes they didn't.

Both the children had seen bereavement counsellors and one of the suggestions was to make a memory box so that they could each share thoughts, feelings and memories. They had all been enthusiastic about this to start with. Fran suggested they each put in one thing that brought back a happy memory of Andy – hers were the ticket stubs from the Crowded House concert at which he proposed, Charlie's was a clay pipe that they had found during a mudlarking trip on the Thames and Jude's was the guitar pick that his dad gave to him, which he claimed once belonged to Eric Clapton.

In the beginning, Fran and the kids would set aside time to sit and write messages or draw pictures for Andy to go in the box – little things that struck them, moments they recalled and didn't want to forget. As time went on, the additions to the box became more ad hoc and they stopped sitting down together to write them.

Maybe it was the course or the fact that an attractive man had given her his number, which made Fran pick up the box again and look inside. It anchored her to Andy's memory like a life raft in a stormy sea.

If I just cling on to this, I won't need to consider the idea of another man who isn't my husband.

She found half a dozen of her own messages as well as the odd one from Charlie. She decided that it was time to reinstate it. Keeping Andy's memory alive was what kept them together as a family.

'So,' began Fran as Charlie and Jude joined her in the dining room, 'I realized that it was a long time since we'd sat down together and added things to Dad's memory box.' She fetched it down from the top of the dresser. 'And I thought we should make time together.'

'I love Daddy's memory box,' said Charlie, through a mouthful of doughnut. 'It makes me feel like he's here.'

Jude rolled his eyes from behind a damp curtain of orange hair. 'Fine. What do you want me to write?'

Fran felt a twitch of irritation. 'Whatever you want, Jude. Or don't you want to?'

Charlie was staring at her brother now, eyes pleading. 'Just write something for Daddy. Please Jude.'

He gave a heavy sigh. Jude found his little sister endlessly annoying but he'd also cut off his right arm and possibly his leg too if she needed it. 'Fine.'

Fran gave Charlie a reassuring smile. She grinned back at her mother through a moustache of custard and sugar. 'I'm going to draw a picture of me with Daddy at the seaside – remember when that seagull stole his ice cream?'

'I do,' laughed Fran.

'That was the day I learnt the word "bastard",' remarked Jude, his serious expression lifting at the memory.

Fran's heart soared on recalling Andy's indignant face, swearing

121

up at the scurrilous thief and then his broad beaming smile as he caught her eye and the whole family dissolved into helpless laughter. She felt almost breathless with longing – a sharp desire to go back there, right now. To experience the four of them together laughing. Was that too much to ask?

She was snapped back to reality as the doorbell rang.

'I'll go,' said Jude, standing up.

'Sit,' commanded Fran. Alan, who had been standing close to the table, hoping that someone might forget that doughnuts were bad for dogs and gift him one, sat down. Fran held out a pen to her son. 'Write.'

'This is worse than being at school!' declared Jude as Fran made her way down the hall.

'Deal with it,' said Fran. She stopped in her tracks when she spotted the broad frame of a man who almost certainly worked out, standing behind the glass. She considered retreating to the living room and hiding until Charlie shouted, 'Who is it, Mum?' and the man peered through the glass towards the sound of her voice.

Fran opened the door wearing a polite smile, doing her best to ignore the fact that Gary's face was really quite attractive. It wasn't perfect but that held its own appeal for Fran – she'd never had much truck with flawlessly chiselled men. 'Hi' she said, noticing how nervous he looked and feeling an unexpected dip of affection in the centre of her chest.

'Hi.' He smiled. 'Erm, sorry to drop round unannounced but you left this at the session.' He held out her navy-blue hoody.

'Oh. Thanks,' said Fran, accepting it. 'Kind of you to drop it back – above and beyond the call of duty.' She wondered if she was supposed to ask him in. She didn't want to. She wanted to go back to her children, to the memory box, to her oddly comforting sadness. Gary standing on her doorstep with his impossibly bulging biceps and charming smile was too real – too alive. She just wanted him to go.

He put a hand on his heart. 'The team at *Left Right Fitness* like to offer our clients the very best service.'

'You do this for all your clients, do you?' asked Fran, arching a brow.

'Of course! Although I'll admit, I was glad of the excuse to pop round.' He grinned. Fran noticed a dimple appear on his cheek and looked away. She'd always been a sucker for a dimple.

'Well, thank you,' she said, backing inside.

'Fran, listen,' he began.

Oh no, please don't do this. Please don't ask me out. You seem lovely and I'm going to feel bad turning you down face to face.

Gary continued. 'I know you told me about losing your husband and that you weren't ready to date. That's fine. I understand completely. I just felt a connection when we met and I would love to take you out some time. No strings. No pressure.'

No pressure from you maybe, thought Fran, *but the internal cogs of my mind say otherwise.*

This guy is bloody gorgeous and he likes you. What are you waiting for? Because I hate to break it to you but that dream of Idris Elba whisking you off to a Caribbean island isn't going to happen. Sorry. Harsh but true.

See what I mean? Those cogs are very opinionated.

'Mum?' called Charlie, appearing in the hall and stopping in her tracks at the sight of Gary. 'Oh hello. Who are you?'

He smiled. 'I'm Gary. Your mum came to one of my fitness classes.'

'Cool. Wow, your hands are massive!' she declared. 'I'm Charlie by the way.'

'Nice to meet you, Charlie. I won't hold you up, Fran. I'll text you so you've got my number and then just let me know, okay? No pressure.'

'Yep, okay, bye,' she said, waving him off and putting an arm round Charlie's shoulders, grateful to be saved from further awkwardness.

'He seemed nice,' remarked Charlie as they walked back to the dining room.

'Mmmm.'

'Who's nice?' asked Jude, folding his piece of paper and placing it in the memory box.

'A man called Gary,' reported Charlie.

'Who's Gary?' asked Jude.

'A man who just asked Mummy out,' declared Charlie.

Fran was incredulous. 'Were you listening at the door?' She kept a close eye on their faces. She wasn't sure what she was expecting. A flicker of anger? A hint of confusion? A sense of outrage that someone apart from their father was interested in her? She felt vague irritation that they displayed nothing of the sort.

Charlie shook her head. 'Not really. He had a big booming voice so it was difficult not to hear.'

'She was listening,' reported Jude. 'She's nosier than you.'

'I so am not!' retorted Charlie.

'Okay!' said Fran, holding up her hands. 'Okay. I'm not saying that I am but, hypothetically, how would you two feel if I did go out for dinner with someone at some stage?'

'Fine.' Jude shrugged. Charlie gave an enthusiastic nod.

Fran was stunned. 'Right. Okay. Thank you. That's interesting. Thank you. Good.'

Jude stood up. 'Can I go now?'

'Yes, of course,' said Fran, feeling dazed. She heard the sound of him stomping upstairs and the strumming of his guitar as he picked out an Ed Sheeran tune. Orange hair. Of course.

She stood watching Charlie colour her picture, her brow fixed in a frown of concentration. She peered into the memory box and lifted out Jude's folded note. Charlie glanced up at her. 'Are you going to read that?'

'Jude won't mind,' fibbed Fran with a wink. Charlie nodded and went back to her colouring. Fran unfolded the note. He had written the words in ornate arty type and clearly spent quite a bit of time on it.

Gotcha, Mother!

'Little bugger,' laughed Fran.

She stared up at the ceiling a while later. Was it her or was that crack getting bigger? How big did cracks have to be before you did something about them? Oh, never mind, it didn't matter. She shifted her weight – this sofa really was the pits.

He asked you out for dinner?

Yup.

Are you going to go? he asked.

I doubt it. Even though, rather bizarrely the kids have given me the thumbs-up.

So if they're okay with it then why aren't you?

You know why.

Guilt?

She nodded. My oldest and most reliable friend.

What do you feel guilty about?

I think it might be quicker to list all the things I don't feel guilty about.

That's quite a burden.

What can I say? I'm a regular guilt mule.

And what's the biggest cause of your guilt? The thing you can't get past?

A deep sigh. The fact that I get to live, to carry on. And that makes me angry too because I don't want to do this on my own. We still had a life to live together. I do not want this version of my life.

What do you want?

Another sigh. I don't know. That's the problem. Some things in life can be fixed but this can't. And that's all there is to it.

125

Hope Street Hall seemed very dark as Fran arrived for the course on Wednesday. She peered in through the door and was surprised but cheered to see a film projector set up in the middle of the room, shining its light onto a large white bed sheet which was hung from the ceiling.

'Good evening, Fran,' said Nik with a smile. 'Can I interest you in some popcorn?'

'Thank you,' said Fran, taking a box. 'Is it movie night?'

'Take a seat and I'll explain once everyone has arrived.'

The chairs had been set up in rows. Fran took a seat next to Georg, who was holding his popcorn as if he was afraid it might explode. 'Evening, Georg,' said Fran cheerfully. 'How are you?'

'Good. Although I do not understand what is happening.'

'Me neither,' said Fran. 'I think we have to just go with it.' She sat back in her chair and stared up at the screen. She loved the cinema but rarely went these days, unless it was to see something with Charlie. The last film had been a brightly animated, over-chirpy cartoon which Charlie had loved whilst Fran had fallen asleep halfway through.

'Isn't this wonderful?' declared Pamela, sliding into the chair next to Fran. 'I hope he shows something with Cary Grant in it. I do love him.'

'Speaking of heart-throbs, I had a visit from your friend Gary the other day.'

'Aww, lovely Gary! What did he want?'

'He was returning the hoody I left behind on Friday. And he also asked me out to dinner.'

'Ooh, are you going to go?'

'Go where?' asked Heather, taking a seat next to Pamela.

'Little Gary Walters asked her on a date!' cried Pamela with delight.

Heather smiled. 'Are you going to go?'

'My kids think I should,' admitted Fran.

'Then why not?' said Heather. 'You don't have to marry the guy – just go and have a laugh.'

Fran sighed. Heather was right of course, but was it really that simple? But then again, why did she have to make it so complicated? Plus, the endless guilt and angst was exhausting. Wouldn't it be nice to just kick up her heels and go for dinner with a charming man? No strings. No ties. Just a lovely evening out. She grinned at her friends. 'If I do go, it won't be a date – just dinner.'

'Just dinner,' repeated Heather, winking at Pamela.

Fran folded her arms. 'I'm not promising – I'm still thinking about it. Right. That's enough about that. Heather, how did the babysitting go?'

'It was eye-opening,' admitted Heather, flashing a grin at Pamela.

'Spill the beans. Did Luke weep with joyful hope at the thought of becoming a father one day?'

Heather pulled a face. 'Not exactly. I ended up de-camping to Pamela's for part of the evening because Freddy wouldn't settle and Luke had to work.'

'On a Friday night? He needs to get his priorities sorted,' declared Fran.

'Tell me about it. I don't know what I would have done without my fairy godmother,' she said, gesturing at Pamela.

'It was a pleasure.' Pamela beamed.

'Anyway, the whole thing made me realize that Luke and I aren't exactly on the same page when it comes to parenthood.'

'I think that's probably more common than you think,' offered Fran. 'For the first two years of our marriage it was Andy who wanted kids and me who needed persuading. People change.'

'Yeah. Maybe you're right,' said Heather, looking reassured.

Pamela put an arm round her shoulder. 'You'll make a lovely mum when the time comes.'

'Okay, my friends,' said Nik, standing before them. 'You are probably wondering why we are having a cinema night.'

'Yes,' frowned Georg.

Nik smiled. 'This week, we are going to consider humour and laughter and how important it is if we want to be happy. So, to illustrate my point, I thought I would present a piece of the finest comedy ever made.'

'Oh, is it the dead parrot sketch?' asked Jim. 'I love that.'

'Two soups for me,' said Sue. 'Julie Walters is brilliant.'

'No,' said Nik. 'It's a little older than those and, I must confess, that it's the film I watch whenever I need a lift in life. I hope you enjoy it.'

There was a flicker before the old-fashioned five-four-three-two-one flashed by and the titles and theme music for Laurel and Hardy's film, *The Music Box*, appeared on the screen.

'Oh, I love Laurel and Hardy!' cried Pamela.

'Who is Laurel and Hardy?' asked Georg.

'These two blokes,' whispered Fran. 'The one with the moustache is Oliver Hardy and the little guy is Stan Laurel.'

Georg frowned and nodded as he watched.

'I used to watch this with my mum,' whispered Heather. Pamela patted her hand and smiled.

Fran sat back and felt her mind relax as they watched. She had forgotten how funny they were – all the visual gags, Laurel and Hardy's nods and foibles. It was like old, forgotten treasure – something wonderful, which you never realized you'd missed until you found it again. They laughed as the two men tried time and time again to transport the piano up the mountainous flights of steps.

Fran became aware then of how natural laughter was, almost like a reflex. If you found something funny, you couldn't help but chuckle, and as this group of very different people watched the same film, they all found different aspects amusing. Jim gave a deep booming laugh at every slapstick moment, Pamela giggled sweetly whenever they dropped the piano and Heather chuckled along with the enjoyment of everyone else's laughter. Fran wanted to hug herself with delight. Laughter really was medicine and shared laughter was like a cure for all woes.

She and Andy had laughed all the time when they were first together. They loved comedy and would go to stand-up nights at local clubs or watch gigs on television. They had been dedicated fans of *Blackadder* too and could quote almost every episode verbatim. Of course, when the children had come along, things had changed – there was less adult humour and more fart jokes but still, she could remember her happiest moments as being the times in her life when she laughed so hard, she lost her breath.

'I do not get it,' said Georg after the film ended. 'Why did they not just hire a winch?'

Fran caught Heather's eye and started to laugh. Heather joined in and then Pamela, followed by the rest of the room. Nik was beaming as he stood before them all. 'I hope you enjoyed that. Laughter is a very precious but underrated tool. We tend to laugh a great deal when we are children but almost lose the ability to do it easily when we get older.'

'Life gets so serious when you're an adult,' remarked Sue.

Nik nodded. 'Very true, but see what happens when we all take time to watch a funny film? We laugh like children, we forget the seriousness and we are united in that moment. It's very powerful. So for this week's homework, I want you to find the things that make you laugh – the comedy, the people or the dog.' He flashed a smile at Fran. 'Don't force it, just enjoy it. Find the things that make you laugh and embrace them.'

'Someone's in a good mood,' remarked Fran's mother, as her daughter arrived home whistling the Laurel and Hardy theme music later that evening.

'Yeah. Tonight was fun.'

'Is it helping?' asked Angela.

Fran shrugged. 'A bit.'

Angela sat down next to her daughter on the sofa. 'Charlie told me that a man called Gary asked you on a date.'

Fran had been expecting this. 'Uh-huh.'

Angela knew her daughter well. 'I'm not going to tell you what to do – obviously I'd rather you didn't go out with a man named Gary but I'm just a hideous old snob.'

'You said it.'

Her mother blew a raspberry. 'All I'll say is give it some thought, darling. Okay? Anyway, I'm off to bed.' She kissed her daughter on the cheek. 'I do love you, you know that, don't you? And I'm proud of you.'

'Steady, Mum.' Fran smiled. 'I love you too. 'Night.'

''Night, dear.'

After she'd gone, Fran poured herself a glass of wine and sat on the sofa, clutching her phone. *Make up your mind, woman. Stop faffing and make up your mind.*

'Okay, fine,' she breathed, flicking it into life, ready to send a text.

The plan was simple.

Go for dinner with the handsome man.

Eat food, enjoy conversation, drink a little more than you possibly should but not so much that you end up snogging him.

Thank the handsome man for a lovely time but tell him that it was just a one-off, go home and never speak of it again.

Yeah. So simple. Unfortunately, Fran had never been great at sticking to the script. She started full of good intentions. She'd deliberately suggested the Spanish tapas restaurant where she had been with Andy on many occasions. That was a sure-fire way to sabotage the evening.

Perfect, she thought as they entered the restaurant (Gary, the perfect gentleman holding the door open for her). She took in her surroundings as the sad ghosts appeared before her, each with its own unique memory.

She spotted the table up on the mezzanine where they'd celebrated her birthday with her brother and his then girlfriend Melissa (she'd liked Melissa – she should try and get in touch with her again); the small table for two by the window, where she'd been grumpy because they were sitting in a draught and they'd had a row; and of course the table in the corner where they'd sung along with the Elvis impersonator, drunk two bottles of Rioja and gone home to have filthy sex on the dining-room table.

Wow, Fran, you really are some kind of weird masochist, she thought as she paused for a second to catch her breath.

The waiter led them to the argument table by the window, affording them a majestic view of the Croydon Road. Right on cue, a couple of teenagers shambled past, one of them hoicking a large gob of spit onto the pavement.

'Lovely,' joked Gary, accepting a menu from the waiter.

Fran laughed. 'Never let it be said that I don't bring you to the best places.'

'Would you like a drink?' asked the waiter.

'Sangria, please. Shall we share a jug?'

'I'm driving so I'll just have the one.'

'A jug of sangria, please,' said Fran, hoping that it didn't make her sound like an alcoholic but feeling a sense of relief that Gary was clearly intending to go home after the meal. She relaxed. It would all go to plan. They would eat dinner, drink some sangria and talk. No biggie.

Charlie had been overexcited before her mother left, skipping around like a miniature fairy godmother, full of expectation and wonder. 'Have a lovely time with Gary, Mummy! I hope you have loads of fun!'

Fran's mother was babysitting again ('Honestly, Fran, I may as well move in with you!' she had quipped, but Fran knew she relished every second with her grandchildren). Angela had been similarly encouraging but in an altogether more low-key fashion. 'Just enjoy yourself. Really. Have a good time.' She stopped short of using the words 'for once' but Fran heard them all the same.

Fran had turned to face them. 'Listen, you two, it's just dinner. No more, no less. Do you understand?'

Charlie and Angela had exchanged purse-lipped looks of amusement. 'Yes, ma'am!' saluted Charlie.

'Understood!' declared Angela, copying her granddaughter so that they fell about laughing.

It was a surprise to Fran, as the date progressed and the sangria flowed, how easy it was to be in Gary's company. They talked about his life in the army. Fran noticed that he passed over his time in Afghanistan as if it was a mere blip in his life rather than the living hell she suspected. She could relate to that kind of topic avoidance and felt an odd fondness towards him as a result. He talked about his family, how much he loved his nephews and nieces, his mum and then how he'd come to set up *Left Right Fitness* and she thought, *This is a nice man. A really nice man. Kind and funny. Lovely hazelnut eyes. I like him. I like him a lot.*

It might have been the sangria or the fact that Gary made her laugh repeatedly, but, as the evening went on, he appeared even more handsome to her; his strong jaw and kind eyes seemed ever-more appealing in the soft glow of the Spanish restaurant.

'So how about you? Tell me about your life,' he said.

She shrugged. She was onto her third glass of increasingly delicious sangria. 'There's not much to tell. I work part-time as a freelance editor, which fits around the kids and helps with the bills. And then there's the kids – Charlie, who you met briefly. She's ten and an absolute treasure. And there's Jude, who's fourteen – he's prone to teenage outbursts but basically a good kid. And Alan the dog. That's it – me, the kids and a faithful hound.'

As soon as she said this, she was aware of the fact that she was holding up her life to him like a ripped sheet, revealing the

132

screaming gap where Andy had once been. Poor guy. He'd been backed into a conversational cul-de-sac. He'd have to ask her now.

'It must be hard for you being widowed so young.'

They both looked at each other with a hint of regret as if they knew they'd have to talk about it now – the black hole of grief, unforgiving and never-ending.

They were interrupted by the whitebait and garlic prawns arriving in quick succession. Fran thanked the waiter before downing her drink and smiling gratefully at Gary as he topped it up for her.

She cleared her throat. 'It is hard. I miss him. Obviously.' Gary nodded through a mouthful of whitebait. Fran was suddenly swept along by a wave of sadness and sangria. 'I can remember sitting at this table with him actually. We had a row. I think it started as something about my mother and I wouldn't hear it so I had a go at his mother. It wasn't pretty. We were both quite stubborn when it came to arguments. I remember one time when we didn't speak for three days because neither of us would apologize and, in the end, we couldn't remember why we'd started the argument in the first place.'

Gary smiled. 'You sound like the perfect couple.'

Fran laughed. 'Yeah – stubborn and bloody-minded but then I think the best partnerships are like that, aren't they? You've got to have a bit of light and shade in your life.'

'Very true. And what was Andy like?'

The question caught Fran off guard. It had been a long time since she'd talked about him to someone who'd never met him. She was surprised how lovely it was to be asked and to answer.

'He was funny, clever – a bit too clever sometimes – not at all sporty, although he did enjoy cycling. He was a great dad…' Her voice trailed off as flashes of memories popped into her mind. Andy pushing Charlie too high on a swing, wrestling Jude on the sofa, handing her a cup of the weirdy herbal tea she liked.

'Sorry, Fran. I didn't mean to pry. It must be hard for you to talk about this stuff.'

Fran realized there were tears in her eyes. 'No, honestly, it's fine. It's actually good to talk about him but maybe a bit awkward for you?'

'Not at all,' said Gary. 'He was your husband, part of who you are, and I want to get to know you, if you'll let me.'

Fran didn't know what to say. It was one of the loveliest things she'd ever heard. 'Thank you. Really. I mean it. Now, don't worry, I'm not doing a runner but I just want to pop to the loo and check my panda eyes.'

'You look beautiful to me but then sometimes my contact lenses are a bit blurry so it's probably a good idea.'

She laughed and Gary smiled at her. *God, those dimples were sexy.*

He walked her home after the meal. They paused by his car. 'I had a lovely evening,' he said.

'Me too,' said Fran truthfully. 'Thank you.'

He smiled and held out his hand. She took it – his grasp was warm and comforting. Fran was gripped by an unexpected urge. She leant forwards and kissed him on the lips. It wasn't a lingering or even suggestive kiss but it was enough – a test to see how it made her feel.

Do I still know how to do this? Am I still capable of being an attractive woman? And what's more, do I enjoy it?

She was pleased to learn that the answer to all three questions was a resounding yes. The sangria helped but she wasn't drunk – she just felt brave, as if she was reconnecting with the woman she used to be. She knew the guilt would come as she sobered up, but for one precious moment, she felt free.

Fran noticed that Gary didn't try to kiss her again and she appreciated this. Instead, he looked at her with fond admiration.

'See you around?' she asked.

'I hope so,' he said, before climbing into his car and driving off into the night.

'I hope so too,' she murmured, heading up the garden path, wondering if she was drunk enough to face her mother's inevitable interrogation.

Chapter Twelve

Pamela

My Happiness List
1. Just bake
2. Dinner with Matthew and Barry – be in the moment!
(DISASTER)
3. Go dancing with Barry?
4. Laugh like we used to!

Pamela wasn't surprised. Why would she be? They'd been married the best part of forty years. You couldn't keep a spark going that long. Still. She'd thought he might be interested, that he might like to give it a go. For old time's sake if nothing else. And yet he'd looked almost offended when she asked him – positively mortified in fact.

He was sitting at the kitchen table eating his third slice of toast covered with far too much butter and marmalade. Oh, the horror in his eyes, as if she'd suggested something practically indecent instead of an afternoon of ballroom dancing. She did her best to ignore the smear of grease on his chin as he stared up at her agog.

'I don't think so, Pammy – not with my corns, I'd be in agony!' He picked up his mug and drained the last of his tea. 'Right, I'd best get on in the garden – those summer bulbs won't plant themselves!'

Don't let it get to you, Pamela. Keep calm and carry on.

She sniffed back her disappointment. 'Yes, all right, maybe it was a silly idea. You go, I'll clear these things.'

As he smiled at her, she spotted the trace of twenty-year-old Barry behind the double chin. She'd fallen in love with that smile – cheeky and full of charm. Where was the man behind the smile? The one who used to make her cheeks blush and her knees weaken. She missed him.

Barry reached over to kiss her on the forehead. 'Thanks, love. I'll see you later.'

Matthew was coming into the kitchen as Barry made for the door. They did an awkward dance to let the other one pass, wordless except for a surly grunt from Barry. Pamela felt her shoulders stiffen with the effort of pretending not to notice. She heard the front door slam shut as Barry left and breathed a sigh of relief.

'Can I make you some breakfast?' she asked Matthew. 'I've got bacon if you fancy a sandwich.'

Matthew squeezed her shoulder. 'You're an angel, Mum but I'm just going to grab some toast. Doly wants me to go to the cash-and-carry before lunch.'

Pamela smiled. She was pleased that he seemed to be taking this opportunity seriously and he was definitely making more of an effort at home. He'd even cooked for them the night before – a delicious chicken traybake using ingredients he'd paid for out of his own money. Pamela had been impressed and dearly hoped it would ease Barry's attitude towards his son.

'This food is delicious, Matty,' she told him, trying to ignore her husband, who was frowning quizzically at a chunk of sweet potato.

'I thought it was the least I could do after you'd helped me out,' he said, smiling at his parents. 'I do appreciate it.'

'We're happy to help, aren't we, Barry?' *Aren't we, Barry?* Pamela clenched her fists as she silently willed him to say something positive.

'Hmm,' said Barry through a mouthful of food.

'Is it all right, Dad?' asked Matthew, reminding Pamela of a little boy again – a little boy seeking his father's approval.

Barry's frown deepened. *Come on Barry*, thought Pamela. *Say the right thing for once.* She held her breath. 'Very nice, son,' he said, nodding at Matthew. 'Although I'm not sure about these orange things.'

'The sweet potatoes?'

'Mmm, but the rest of it is very nice.'

Matthew and Pamela grinned at one another and she felt herself relax.

Maybe it was possible to live with your kids after they'd grown up. Maybe it just took a bit of time to get used to one another again. Matthew and Barry still had a way to go but this was definite progress.

She smiled as she placed the plate of toast in front of Matthew and poured him a mug of tea. 'So tell me, what are you working on at the moment?' She loved to hear about his writing life – it was so exciting and far more exotic than hers.

'I'm actually working on a script for something.' He looked as if he wanted to say more but thought better of it.

'Ooh that sounds good.' Pamela smiled encouragingly.

Matthew gave a vague nod. 'And I've got a couple of freelance bits – nothing major, just stuff for weekend supplements.'

'I'm proud of you, Matty.' She stole a glance at him as he sat down at the table to butter his toast. 'You know you can always talk to me, don't you?'

He stared up at her with wide eyes. 'Of course. I love our chats.'

She slid into the chair next to him. 'I mean about stuff that

138

matters to you – work, affairs of the heart and so on. I'm always here for you, Matty.'

Matthew put an arm around his mother's shoulder. 'I know, Mum and I'm very grateful.' He took a bite of his toast. 'Actually, there was something I wanted to ask you.'

Pamela looked him in the eye. *Please don't ask me for money. Not again.* 'Oh yes?'

'Is there any chance I could borrow some cash please? I've got this opportunity and I need some money up front. I can give it back to you as soon as I get paid for the newspaper articles.'

Pamela felt her heart sink and her skin prickle with indecision. She didn't want to let him down but she was experiencing a creeping sense of uncertainty and a wearying feeling of déjà vu. Matthew saw the look in her eyes. 'I'll pay you back,' he repeated. 'I promise. Or are you starting not to trust me, like Dad?'

Guilt flooded her brain. He was a good lad. He was knuckling down now and he had made that lovely dinner. What kind of mother would she be if she turned him down? 'No. No, of course not. I trust you. How much do you need?'

'Five hundred?' said Matthew as casually as if he was asking for a fiver. Pamela inhaled sharply.

'Please, Mum? It's important,' he added, staring into her eyes. *The little boy lost. The one who needed to be rescued.*

'You're not in trouble are you, Matty?'

He reached over and squeezed her arm. 'No, of course not. I just can't tell you what it's for at the moment but I promise I will as soon as I'm able.'

She nodded. *I trust him. I have to for my own sake.* 'I'll pop to the cashpoint this morning,' she said, her shoulders sagging with defeat.

Pamela saw the relief in his eyes. 'Thank you, Mum. Thank you so much.'

She smiled, swallowing down her worry. 'Right, you'd better

get off to Doly's. I've got some baking to do for the kids' club this afternoon.'

'You're a good woman, Mum,' he said, reaching down to kiss her before he left, toast in hand.

A good woman and a complete walkover, thought Pamela, filling the sink with hot soapy water.

There was a thin drizzle in the air as Pamela walked to the hall that afternoon, carrying her bag of baked goodies. Chocolate chip cookies. The kiddies always loved them. When she thought about baking, she realized that it was the thing that underpinned her, like the foundation to her life.

She'd always baked, even as a child. Her mother hadn't been a patient woman but Pamela was a quick learner and soon she could make sponges good enough to be entered into competitions. Her mother was never impressed, of course but Pamela often heard her boasting to her friends.

'Oh yes, Pamela won first prize in the adult category – and she's only eight!' she would exclaim.

'Oh, but you must be so proud, Daphne.'

Pamela had waited for her mother to agree but she merely smiled and shrugged. A smile and a shrug. That was the best she ever got. But Pamela kept trying – she kept baking to try to please her mother and, of course, she made cakes to spoil her beloved younger brother, Ernie, too.

Her mother had been a young widow like Fran but that was where the similarity ended. She seemed to resent being left to deal with the spirited Pamela and little Ernie. Pamela gladly took it upon herself to look after her younger brother. She doted on Ernie and loved to spoil him. She would make currant buns and feed them to him like a tiny bird. He loved it, of course, but she had to be careful that her mother didn't see; she was oddly jealous of their bond so Pamela and Ernie kept themselves to themselves, happy in their own world.

Ernie died when he was twenty, from a brain tumour. Just like that. Out of the blue. Pamela returned home from a day's work at the bank and was startled when her mother met her in the hall, her face pale with shock. Pamela didn't believe her at first – she thought it was some cruel trick – but when her mother started to cry, she realized the terrible truth. She ran upstairs and vomited into the sink.

Pamela was surprised at how upset her mother was after Ernie died – maybe she was overwhelmed with guilt or maybe it was self-pity but either way she grieved, drowning her sorrows in alcohol and blaming everyone but herself.

Pamela was relieved when she met Barry a few months later, particularly as they fell in love so easily. They married the following June and she spent the next forty years throwing herself into family life.

Pamela opened up the hall and set her bag on the counter in the kitchen. She loved this toddler group – she'd been running it for years and watched generation after generation walk through these doors. Sometimes mothers who'd come here as children would bring their own toddlers. Pamela felt a great satisfaction when this happened – life renewing and repeating itself, just as it should.

She set up the tea urn and made three large jugs of squash and put them in the fridge. Then she fetched the toys from the cupboard, carefully setting up the baby mat in one corner and the ride-on toys at the opposite end to avoid accidents. Finally, she put out a table of craft activities with trays of crayons, glue, stickers and glitter.

'Afternoon, my loves, come on in. Hello, Maisy,' she said to her first customer, an adorable two-year-old with curly hair. Pamela was rewarded with a gummy grin, which made her heart soar.

The hall began to fill with children and parents, mostly mums. Pamela chatted to them as they arrived, serving drinks and smiling indulgently as small hand after small hand appeared over the hatch to take a biscuit. Pamela refilled the plate and smiled as she noticed a group of her regulars arrive. There were about five or six of them who came every week – single, young mums with cheeky boisterous children. She'd grown fond of them. They were friendly and mouthy – a breath of fresh air in Pamela's quiet world.

'All right, Mrs T?' grinned a girl of about twenty with a tattoo on her left wrist spelling the name 'Cheryl'.

'Hello, Angel dear. How are you?'

'So-so, Mrs T. So-so,' she said, helping herself to a biscuit. 'Damn, these are good. Wish I could bake like you, Mrs T.'

'You could, lovey. They're not difficult to make.'

Angel shrugged. 'I dunno how to. Cheaper to buy them cookies from Aldi, innit?'

'Not at all! Home-made is always cheaper,' cried Pamela.

'You should do cooking classes, Mrs T,' joked Angel.

The germ of an idea planted itself in Pamela's mind. 'I'll give it some thought.'

Pamela was always surprised at how refreshed she felt after toddler group. The children were full of energy and questions – they were funny, cheeky and occasionally naughty but they faced everything with pure wonder and raw emotion.

Pamela loved watching them play – a tiny world of discovery, laughter and tears. It made her think of her own children, of the times she'd cajoled, scolded and comforted and she felt that tug of longing again. She noticed one of the mothers sitting on her own while her young son, Jack, hurled himself round the room on a miniature trike. The poor woman looked exhausted so Pamela made an extra-strong mug of tea and carried it over to her.

'Are you all right, ducks?' she asked.

The woman looked up at her, eyes glazed with tiredness and gave a weary nod. 'Jack's very full-on, you know? He never stops.'

Pamela handed her the tea. 'Well, you just sit and drink this while he lets off some steam. I'm Pamela by the way.'

'Thanks, Pamela. I'm Lauren.' The woman smiled, moving her coat from the seat next to her so that Pamela could sit down. They watched the kids play in smiling silence. 'It's really good of you to run this group,' said Lauren after a while. 'Do you have any grandchildren?'

'Not at the moment,' admitted Pamela, 'but I live in hope.'

'I suppose you could say you've got thirty surrogate grandchildren right here, couldn't you?' said Lauren with a smile.

Right on cue, a small boy called Arthur with spider-like eyelashes and huge brown eyes ambled up to her. 'For you,' he insisted, pressing a crayon drawing of what looked like a dinosaur into Pamela's hands. 'T Rex – raaaaaaaar!' he added with a cheeky grin. Pamela felt her throat thicken.

'Yes,' she said to Lauren. 'Yes, I suppose you could.'

As she walked back along Hope Street later that afternoon, Pamela felt as if her world had clicked into sharper focus. She'd been running the toddler group for so many years that she'd taken for granted or perhaps never properly understood how important it was to the community. She was so deep in thought that she didn't see Fran coming towards her with Alan in tow.

'Earth to Pamela,' called Fran as she nearly walked straight past her.

'Oh, sorry, Fran, I was miles away.'

'Everything all right?' asked Fran.

Pamela smiled. 'Everything's fine. I'm just on my way back from toddler group.'

'I'm amazed you're still running it. You must be exhausted – all those tiny varmints making mess and noise.'

Pamela laughed. 'Actually, I was just thinking how much I love it and how much people value it.'

Fran gave an enthusiastic nod. 'Definitely. Nat and I always say that we wouldn't have got through those early years without your industrial-strength coffee and heavenly biscuits.'

'You don't always see what's right in front of you, do you?'

'Very true,' said Fran.

'By the way, ducks, how was your date with little Gary Walters?' she asked, raising one eyebrow.

Fran stared at her in surprise. 'How did you know about that?'

Pamela grinned. 'If you don't want to be seen going on a date with a lovely man, don't sit in the window of the local Spanish restaurant for all to see.'

Fran laughed. 'Good point. It was lovely. He's one of the good guys.'

'He is – a real treasure.' Pamela stole a glance at her friend. 'Are you going to see him again?'

Fran sighed. 'I don't know. We had a good time but I'm not sure about dating and I don't want to string him along – he's too nice.'

'Sometimes you have to let yourself fall a bit,' said Pamela.

'Maybe,' said Fran. 'Anyway, I'd better go and fetch Charlie. See you on Wednesday?'

'Wouldn't miss it for the world.'

Pamela was in high spirits as she let herself in through the front door, her mind set on cooking a family dinner so that they could sit down and share tales of their day. That was the key to building bridges between Matthew and Barry – good old-fashioned face-to-face communication. Her joy soon dissolved at the sound of angry voices flooding from the kitchen.

'You're a liar!' shouted Barry.

'I am not a liar. I'm just not going to tell you where I got it because you're always so bloody unreasonable.'

'That's because you're always lying.'

'You don't trust me.'

'No. I don't trust you.'

144

'Wonderful. What a lovely thing for a father to say to his son.'

'Well. if the cap fits…'

'Oh, piss off, Dad.'

'Don't you dare talk to me like that!'

'Why not? This is exactly why I won't tell you where I got the money. You always behave like this – so supercilious and ready to be disappointed.'

'Because you always give me cause.'

'Oh. for fuck's sake! What do I have to do? What on earth do I have to do to get you to trust me?'

'Tell me where you got the money.'

'I gave it to him,' said Pamela quietly.

Barry and Matthew turned around and gaped at her. Pamela was surprised how calm she felt, as if she was seeing things clearly for the first time in a while. They were always going to be like this, her son and her husband. They were always going to argue. It was never going to end. Unless she changed things. It was down to her.

'Pammy!' cried Barry. 'Why did you do that? What possessed you?'

She turned to face her husband. 'He's my son and he asked me. Do I need another reason?' She shot a glance at Matthew. 'And I don't believe he would let me down.' Matthew looked at the floor and Pamela felt her chest tighten with doubt. 'You wouldn't let me down, would you, Matty?'

'He does nothing but let you down, can't you see that?' shouted Barry.

Pamela's gaze flicked from her husband to her son and back again. The sight of the pair of them galvanized her into action. She spied the money on the kitchen counter and reached forwards to grab it.

'What are you doing, Mum?' asked Matthew, a look of confusion on his face.

'I'm cutting you off, Matty. It's high time you stopped seeing me as a gigantic purse!'

'I don't, Mum. How can you say that?' he began.

Pamela held up a hand to silence him. 'If whatever you need the money for is so important, you will find a way.'

'Bravo, Pammy!' cried Barry, looking pleased.

Pamela turned to him. 'I'm glad you're happy, Barry Trott, but, for the record, I am not. I can't stay in this house with you two going hell for leather so I've come to a decision.'

Barry looked scared. 'What do you mean, Pammy?'

'I'm leaving.'

'What?' cried Barry, a look of panic spreading across his face.

'You don't have to that,' insisted Matthew. 'I'll go.'

'Oh no you don't,' said Pamela. 'If you think anything of me, you will stay here and sort this out. Both of you.' Matthew stared at her. *Little boy lost being read the Riot Act by his mother.* Pamela would have felt guilty in days gone by but not today. She'd had enough.

'But Pammy!' pleaded Barry.

Pamela folded her arms and fixed him with a look. 'I've decided, Barry. I need a break.' She walked out of the kitchen and went upstairs to pack an overnight bag. When she returned downstairs, she could hear them bickering.

'This is your fault,' said Barry.

'Yeah, that's right, Dad – all my fault.'

'What's that supposed to mean?'

She walked out of the front door, along Hope Street. She had an odd feeling as if she was gliding through a dream but she knew it was the right thing to do. She'd never been surer of anything in her life.

She thought of going to Fran's but, as she reached the front gate, she remembered that she was out picking up Charlie so she kept on walking.

'Pamela! Are you okay?' cried Heather as she opened the front door.

Pamela realized that her hands were shaking and she wasn't

sure if it was from exhilaration, anger or a combination of the two. 'I've left home,' she said, surprised at how good it felt to say these words. 'Is there any chance I could stay in your spare room for a bit please?'

Heather looked at her with such kindness and concern, like a daughter to her mother. Pamela couldn't ever remember Laura looking at her like that. 'Of course, come in. You can stay as long as you need to.'

'Thank you, Heather,' said Pamela, stepping over the threshold as the full realization of what she'd done hit her. It was a scary but hopeful feeling, as if she was finally taking control of her world, inching her way towards the life she needed.

Chapter Thirteen

Heather

Happiness List
1. Marry Luke!
2. Sunday walk and choose wedding venue with Luke, Fran & Charlie
3. Exercise more (persuade Luke to go running?)
- Boot camp with Fran & Pamela
4. Go dress shopping with Gemma and laugh like we used to!

Pamela was proving to be the perfect houseguest and no one was more surprised than Heather. For a woman who could give Mr Nosey a run for his money, she was surprisingly unobtrusive. She was also wonderfully thoughtful.

'I don't want to get in your way,' she told Heather as she handed her the basket of washing she'd just ironed. 'But I saw this and had a spare half-hour so I thought why not?'

'You really don't need to but I'm very grateful that you did,' said Heather. 'And what are these beauties?' she asked, pointing at the tempting batch of cupcakes on the side.

Pamela smiled. 'It's a new recipe I'm trying. I thought you and

Luke could be my guinea pigs – they're rhubarb and custard.'

Heather picked one up and took a bite. She stared at Pamela in amazement. 'Oh my God, I am never letting you leave.'

Pamela looked delighted. 'I'm glad you like them.'

'Like them? I feel like proposing marriage to them!' declared Heather. Pamela laughed.

Initially, Heather had been concerned that having Pamela in their midst might prove awkward or uncomfortable, but as Luke was often late home, she started to relish her new friend's company. Heather loved the way that Pamela would lay out the tea things along with some delectable baked item at four o'clock and insist they have a cuppa and a catch-up. It reminded her of coming home from school when her mum was alive, sitting at the kitchen table, sharing a plate of chocolate digestives and tales of their day.

Heather felt bad that she had dismissed Pamela as a busybody when they first met. She'd never tell her anything she didn't want the whole world to know but she valued Pamela's friendship – kindness ran through her veins like writing through a stick of rock. She liked a gossip but then in all honesty, who didn't?

Even Luke seemed positive about Pamela's presence. 'It's like having a housekeeper,' he said, grinning, as she placed a plate of freshly prepared pancakes in front of him one morning before he headed off to work. He covered the pancakes in maple syrup and cut a piece. 'Oh my God,' he said as he chewed. 'These are better than my mother makes and she's a bona fide New Yorker.'

'Praise indeed,' said Heather with eyebrows raised.

'I'm pleased you like them,' said Pamela.

'Let's just say, I'm going to call them "pamcakes" from now on,' declared Luke. Pamela blushed.

Heather wasn't sure if it was Pamela's presence or if things were going well at work or if they were simply in a good place but Luke seemed more attentive these days. He made unexpected, thoughtful gestures – a bouquet of flowers, her favourite chocolate bar and Post-it notes with sweet messages hidden around the bedroom. She took heart from Fran's reassurance that he would probably come round to the idea of fatherhood and looked towards the wedding with a renewed sense of positivity.

She was using her day off later that week to go wedding-dress shopping with Gemma. She had managed to book an appointment with Caitlin Danvers, whose dresses were highly sought-after and completely stunning. Heather wasn't extravagant but she'd decided that it was practically compulsory to blow a big heap of cash on your wedding dress.

'So what are your plans for today?' she asked Pamela, picking up her bag ready to leave for work.

Pamela gestured at the ingredients on the side. 'Baking for your boss. I'm going traditional today with a Victoria sponge and a carrot cake.'

'Gets my vote,' grinned Heather. 'Have you heard from Barry?'

Pamela folded her arms, a look of determination on her face. 'He and Matthew know where I am,' she said. 'It's up to them to sort their differences rather than waiting for me to do it for them.'

Heather smiled. 'Good for you. Happy baking. I'll see you later this afternoon. Don't forget we've got the course tonight.'

'I'm looking forward to it. Have a good day, ducks.'

A bank of heavy cloud sat defiantly in the sky as Heather made her way along Hope Street. Commuters were already hurrying along the pavement, late for trains. Heather felt the first spot of rain and rummaged in her bag for an umbrella just as her phone started to buzz with a call. She glanced at the ID before answering.

'Gem?'

'Oh hey, Heth. Is this a bad time?'

'No. I'm just on my way to work. Is everything okay?'

'Yep, everything's fine. I was phoning about the wedding dress appointment – I'm really sorry, something's come up. Is there any chance we could rearrange?'

Heather's heart sank. There was a six-month wait for an appointment with Caitlin Danvers and the receptionist had made

150

it very clear when they spoke on the phone that she was 'supremely lucky that they had a last-minute cancellation and could therefore squeeze her in'.

'Erm, probably not but it doesn't matter,' said Heather with a lurch of disappointment. In the absence of her mother, Gemma was unquestionably the next best thing.

'I'm so, so sorry, Heth. You know I'd be there if I could but work need to see me about going back after my maternity leave ends. They're being a bit difficult so I can't get out of it. Will you forgive me?'

Heather could hear how sorry Gemma was and knew she couldn't give her a hard time – she loved and valued her too much to be cross with her. 'Obviously you owe me big time and I'll never let you forget it but yeah, it's fine. I can face the scary dress-design lady on my own.'

She could hear the relief in Gemma's voice. ''Course you can – you're the bravest person I know. Uh-oh, I can hear Freddy Kruger waking up – I'd better go. He's taking that demanding baby act to new levels lately. I'll give you a call on Friday to see how it went, okay?'

Heather threw her phone back into her bag as she walked into the bakery. It was daft to feel let down. She knew that. It was just that she'd always relied on her cousin, but then, Gemma had Freddy now. Her free time was limited and Heather could see that work meetings had to take precedence over days out with her cousin. She felt a burst of sympathy for Gemma – she knew how much she loved Freddy and that going back to work would be hard. She made a mental note to send her lots of encouraging, supportive texts.

'Morning, Georg,' said Heather with a smile as she took her place behind the counter.

'Morning,' he replied in his usual flat tone.

The first customers were yet to arrive so Heather decided to do a little work on unravelling the mystery of what made her work colleague tick. 'So, Georg, I haven't had a chance to ask you. How are you finding the course?'

Georg shrugged. 'Is okay.'

Something about his bald replies made Heather all the more determined to engage with him. 'Do you mind me asking what you've got on your list so far?'

He stared at her, the hint of a frown on his face. 'No.'

She raised her eyebrows and when he didn't take the hint said, 'This is the moment when you tell me what they are.'

Georg's expression lifted. 'Oh, okay. I want to find love, get married…'

'And live happily ever after?' teased Heather.

Georg looked perplexed. 'No. Win Barista of the Year Award.'

Heather smiled. 'Wow. Those are impressive goals.'

Georg shrugged. 'You must follow your dreams.'

She nodded. 'You're right. So how's it going – the finding love thing?'

'I'm working on it,' said Georg, with the flicker of a smile. Heather grinned at him. The first customers arrived and, after that, the café was pretty busy all morning. Heather noticed something different about Georg – he seemed more relaxed. They didn't talk much apart from when it came to the orders but their working relationship felt easier somehow, as if there'd been a shift towards a mutual understanding.

Pete appeared from the kitchen shortly before lunchtime carrying a tray of sourdough loaves. 'Here you go, gorgeous people.' He plonked the tray on the counter.

'Thank you, Peter,' said Georg. 'These look very good.'

'No worries, mate,' replied Pete, flashing a grin before disappearing back to the kitchen.

Heather smiled at Georg later as she and Pamela arrived at Hope Street Community Hall. He gave her a silent nod in reply.

'Ooh, this looks interesting,' remarked Pamela, gesturing

towards three tables, which Nik had set up in different corners of the room. There was a cloche-covered platter on each.

'Mmm,' agreed Fran, as they sat down together. 'Anything that involves eating gets my vote. So how's the house-sharing going?' she asked, grinning at them both.

'I'm having a lovely time,' said Pamela. 'It's like a little holiday from all the stress and nonsense.'

'I'm keeping her,' reported Heather. 'She does the ironing *and* she made pancakes.'

'Don't tell Charlie. She'll be round in a shot,' said Fran. 'Sounds as if you're well and truly living the dream. And aren't you going to do your Cinderella bit and find that dream dress tomorrow?' she asked Heather.

Heather sighed as she remembered her conversation with Gemma earlier that day. She stole a glance at Pamela and Fran as an idea struck her. 'I know it's a bit last minute but are you two doing anything tomorrow morning?'

'I'm currently editing a terrible crime novel by an established writer who should really know better so I'm up for any distractions,' declared Fran.

'I'm free!' cried Pamela.

'Okay then, how would you two like to come along and help me choose my wedding dress? Gemma's had to cancel.'

Pamela put her hand to her mouth. Fran smiled. 'Well, Pamela looks as if she's about to cry so I'm guessing she's in and it's a yes from me!'

Heather grinned at them both with relief and excitement. 'That's brilliant – thank you so much.'

'Good evening, my friends,' said Nik, taking his place in front of them. 'Welcome again. How have you all been doing with upping your laughter quota after our last session?'

'My husband and I watched every episode of *Fawlty Towers* last weekend,' reported Sue. 'We hadn't laughed together like that for years!'

153

'Excellent.' Nik smiled.

'I had a lovely evening out with a friend and laughed a lot more than I expected to,' said Fran. Pamela and Heather nudged her teasingly. She stuck out her tongue in reply.

'I'm glad,' said Nik. 'Unexpected laughter is often the best kind. And now, I'm sure you would like to know what I have in store for you this evening. You have already tried new forms of exercise so, tonight, I am building on the theme of trying new things because one of the keys to finding happiness is to keep learning and keep trying. With that in mind, I have a selection of foods that you may or may not have tried before. I would like you to work in your groups on this exercise. So each group will approach a table and you will try the food together. Each platter is different so after one group tries, we will swap around, okay? Before we start though, can I check that no one has any allergies? I have avoided nuts, of course.'

Jim raised his hand uncertainly. 'I'm allergic to cat fur.'

Fran and Heather grinned at one another. 'It's okay,' Nik told him with a wry smile. 'There is no cat fur here, but there is spice and sweet and some other surprises. So, shall we give it a try?' Everyone murmured agreement. 'And while you taste, try to use your mindfulness knowledge – taste, smell, texture and so on. I have provided water and tissues in case you don't like the taste but try to face this with open minds. I know you can.'

'Okay, you two' said Fran as they approached the first table. 'I'm just saying that if there's a kangaroo penis under there, I'm out!'

They laughed. 'Let's go for it!' said Pamela.

Heather flashed a smile at her and turned to Fran. 'You heard the lady, let's go for it! I mean, what's the worst that can happen?'

'I won't answer that,' said Fran. 'Okay, here goes.' She lifted up the cloche, raised her eyebrows when she saw what was in the dish and put it straight back down again. 'Oh. My. God.'

'What is it?' Pamela looked intrigued. Fran lifted the cloche again to show her. 'Oh. Are those...?'

'Grasshoppers,' said Nik, approaching their table. He plucked one from the platter and threw it into his mouth. 'A great source of protein and possibly the foodstuff that will stop humanity from dying out.'

'Sounds a bit extreme,' said Fran, frowning at the offending insects.

Pamela picked one up, screwed her eyes shut and put it into her mouth. Her face relaxed slightly as she started to chew thoughtfully. 'What's it like?' asked Fran, grimacing at Heather.

'Mmm,' said Pamela. 'Quite nutty and crunchy, like a nice snack. Not as bad as I thought!'

Heather and Fran looked at one another. 'I'm game if you are,' said Heather.

They picked one each and took tentative bites. 'Actually,' said Fran in surprise, 'that's not bad.'

'Mmm, unexpectedly tasty,' agreed Heather. 'If you try to forget that you're eating an insect, it's fine.'

'I guess it's not much different to a prawn,' said Fran.

'Okay, and now we swap tables,' said Nik.

'All right. Are we ready?' asked Fran, as they approached the next table. 'I don't know what you think but I wouldn't put it past Nordic Nik to serve us rancid fish.'

'Euw, get ready to barf,' said Heather, lifting the lid on the next dish.

'What is that?' asked Pamela, staring at the bowl of subterranean-looking gloop.

'Rancid cabbage.' Heather grinned. 'Or rather fermented cabbage – that's kimchi. I've had it at Wagamama – it's an acquired taste but I quite like it.' They each took a spoonful.

'Okay, bit weird,' said Fran, licking the food, which was a bright tomato-red colour. She took a tentative bite. 'Euw, that is sour!' She let the flavour develop on her tongue. 'And spicy! I don't like it.' She reached for a bottle of water, glaring accusingly at the spoon.

'I'm not sure I like this,' said Pamela, tasting a spoonful.

'It's very good for your gut,' said Nik. 'Because of all the bacteria.'

'I'll stick to yoghurt thanks,' said Fran.

'I quite like it,' said Heather, taking a spoonful.

'You're a weirdo,' teased Fran. 'Here's hoping the last dish isn't quite so insecty or rancid.'

'And now please swap again,' said Nik.

They made their way over to the last table. 'Please let it be ice cream!' she said, lifting the lid.

'You should do the lottery,' laughed Fran, as they looked down at the pea-green coloured ice cream. 'This is more like it.' She took a spoonful. 'Oh my. That is nice – quite an interesting flavour too.'

Heather tried. 'Mmm, sweet yet bitter – so delicious.'

'Ooh yes, that's lovely,' agreed Pamela. 'What flavour is that?'

'Matcha,' said Nik, smiling over at them.

'Beats grasshopper any day.' Fran picked up the bowl. 'Anyone mind if I finish this because as we all know, happiness is actually a big bowl of ice cream.'

'Amen to that,' said Heather.

'So,' said Nik at the end of the session. 'What did we think?'

'I never would have tried any of this stuff normally,' said Jim. 'But it was all right actually.'

'I like it,' observed Georg. 'I found it interesting and I think it is good to try new things.'

'I'm glad you found it useful,' said Nik. 'I want you to think about learning and how important it is for maintaining happiness. It is very easy, particularly as we get older, to stop learning new things but actually studies show that those who continue to learn, to embrace new experiences whether it be foods or cultures or knowledge, lead longer, happier lives. So this week, I would like you to think about something new you might like to try and give it a go.'

'I've never had a pickled egg,' remarked Pamela. Everyone laughed.

'It's a start,' said Nik with a smile.

The next day, Heather woke with a shiver of excitement as she remembered the day ahead. Luke had already left for work and Pamela was downstairs. As Heather entered the kitchen, she presented her with a plate of scrambled egg, toast and a mug of tea.

'Pamela, you're an angel. Thank you. How did you sleep?'

'Like a baby,' she replied. 'That bed's so comfy and I had a lovely time last night. It was fun, wasn't it?'

'Yeah, it was great – made me want to be a bit more adventurous.'

'Me too,' Pamela agreed. 'Nik has asked me to run a baking workshop next week. He wants everyone to find a new hobby.'

'Sounds good – you'll be brilliant, you're a natural.'

'Do you really think so? It's been so long since I worked or did anything like that, I'm a bit unsure of myself.'

Heather smiled. 'He wouldn't ask you if he didn't think you could do it.'

Pamela patted her hand gratefully. 'He wanted me to get Barry to do a session on gardening but I told him he'll have to go round and ask him. I'm not speaking to that man at the moment.'

'Do you think he and Matthew will have sorted things?'

Pamela shrugged. 'All I do know is that I'm sick of playing piggy-in-the-middle. They'll come and find me when they're ready.'

'You stay as long as you need, Pamela. I like having you around.'

'Are you sure, ducks? I don't want to get in your way – you youngsters need your space.'

Heather smiled. 'We're fine.' It was true. Things had been fine lately. Heather felt more determined than ever to make their relationship work and today's wedding dress fitting was another milestone on the path towards their happy-ever-after.

As they strolled to the station in the hazy spring sunshine, she linked an arm through Pamela's and they grinned at one another. Heather was glad that she and Fran were coming with her today. It was like having an older sister and mother on hand, without the complication of actually being related to them. They heard a voice behind them.

'Hang on, you two!' cried Fran, jogging to catch them up.

Heather felt a skip of happiness. Today was going to be a good day. She had checked the map and Caitlin Danvers' shop was only a short Tube ride away from Luke's offices. Heather was going to choose her wedding dress and surprise her fiancé by taking him out to lunch. Perfect.

'Heather. It's wonderful to meet you,' smiled Caitlin, shaking her hand. She was warm and friendly – the kind of creative person that Heather loved, buzzing with ideas and energy. 'And these must be your…'

'Friends,' said Heather, smiling at Pamela and Fran. 'They're my friends. My mum isn't around anymore so they're giving me moral support.'

'Very good.' Caitlin grinned.

She held out her hand to Pamela, who took it and for some strange reason, curtsied at the same time. 'Sorry. Bit nervous,' she giggled. 'I'm Pamela.'

'My mum was called Pamela,' said Caitlin kindly. 'She always used to curtsey too.'

Everyone laughed. 'I'm Fran,' said Fran, holding out her hand. 'And I won't curtsey if that's okay.'

'Feel free if you change your mind,' joked Caitlin. 'Please come through. Can I get you some tea or coffee? Then we can sit down, I'll show you some of my designs, you can try on a few dresses and tell me what you might like. Okay?'

'That sounds wonderful, thank you,' said Heather.

'Oh, she's lovely!' declared Pamela as they sat and waited for Caitlin to return with the tea.

'I can't believe you curtsied,' laughed Fran. 'Absolute classic!'

'I'm so sorry, Heather,' giggled Pamela. 'I do silly things when I get nervous!'

Heather smiled at her two friends, experiencing that rare feeling that you are in exactly the right place with the right people at the right time. 'I'm so glad you're both here,' she told them. Pamela patted her hand. 'Where did you both buy your wedding dresses?'

Pamela's eyes glittered at the memory. 'It was this lovely little shop on the high street – not there anymore, of course. I wanted to look like Grace Kelly. She was the most beautiful woman on the planet then and all the girls wanted a dress like hers.'

'Did you get it?' asked Fran.

'I did.' Pamela sighed. 'I felt like a princess. Barry said I was the most beautiful woman he'd ever seen. Of course, I was a bit slimmer then.'

'Who isn't on their wedding day?' observed Fran.

'What about you, Fran?' asked Heather.

Fran thought for a moment before answering. 'Well, as you know, I'm a jaded cynic with no time for sentiment.'

'Yeah right,' teased Heather.

Fran laughed. 'It was bloody perfect. The whole thing. And I refused to take off my dress. It had a train, which I scooped up when I danced and boy, did I dance – all night long.'

Pamela squeezed her hand and Fran nodded to show that she was okay. 'It's all good – happy memories.'

Moments later, Caitlin returned with her assistant, who delivered their drinks before disappearing again. Caitlin turned to them with a smile, her face twinkling like the fairy godmother from *Cinderella*. 'Right, ladies, shall we begin?'

The following hour was like a childhood dream for Heather.

What could be more fun than flouncing about in a big dress, pretending to be a princess?

She tried on an ivory design with a broad sweeping A-line skirt ('Of course, that skirt could double as a shelter for a whole family if it rains,' said Fran), a snugly fitted lace embroidered gown with silver thread and beading ('You look like a beautiful mermaid!' cried Pamela) and countless others. She knew she'd found the one when she slipped on a simple but beautiful lace dress and Pamela and Fran stared at her with mouths open as she walked out of the fitting room.

'Wow,' said Fran eventually.

'That's the one,' confirmed Pamela tearfully. 'You look so beautiful!'

'Do you like it?' asked Caitlin.

Heather gazed at her through misty eyes. 'I love it,' she whispered. Fran and Pamela rushed forward to hug her. 'Thank you.'

Caitlin nodded. 'Great. Don't tell anyone, but actually, this is my favourite dress. Now let's talk fabric and design. I'll come up with a rough sketch now, and if you're happy, I can take measurements and we can get the ball rolling.'

Heather watched in awe as Caitlin asked her questions whilst sketching at the same time. Within half an hour she had finished. As she held up the sketch for them to see, Heather's heart soared with joy.

'How did you do that?' she cried. 'It's absolutely perfect.'

Caitlin beamed. 'Years of practice. I think this is going to suit you perfectly. It's simple but so gorgeous – you've got the lace overlay design and I'm proposing a champagne-coloured slip.'

'It's beautiful.' Heather grinned. 'Where do I sign?'

As they prepared to leave, Fran turned to Caitlin. 'I've changed my mind,' she said. 'I am going to curtsey – you are the absolute queen of wedding dresses.'

Caitlin laughed and shook their hands before they left. 'It was good to meet you all. This job is lovely but today it felt very special.'

Pamela, Fran and Heather linked arms as they walked along the street.

My happiness buddies, thought Heather with a smile. *I never even knew I needed them and now look at us.*

'Thank you,' she said as they paused to say their goodbyes. 'This was honestly one of the best days of my life.' Pamela pulled her into a bosomy embrace.

'Trust me, this is just the warm-up for your wedding – it's going to be brilliant,' Fran told her.

'Enjoy your lunch.' cried Pamela as Heather waved them off in the direction of the station and headed down towards the Tube. Heather's renewed sense of hope about the future made her feel like dancing until she remembered that you didn't really do that in London. Still, she broke the other golden rule and smiled at all the people on the Tube. She didn't care if she looked like a crazy woman. She was getting married – it was actually happening. The pieces of her life were slotting into place. All Heather needed to do was make sure that she and Luke enjoyed more quality time together. That started today with her surprise lunch visit.

She emerged from the Tube station and made the short walk to the glass-fronted offices of Luke's building. She paused outside and her heart soared as she spotted Luke emerging from the lift. He didn't see her so she pushed through the revolving doors and called to him.

'Luke!'

He was on his way across the atrium, his smiling eyes fixed on someone who was sitting close to the reception desk. He turned and stared at Heather with a look of surprise and something else she couldn't quite read at that distance. She glanced over to where he was heading and felt an almost electric jolt as she recognized the person waiting for him.

'Gemma!' she cried, feeling nothing but joy at seeing her cousin.

Gemma's gaze flitted towards Luke and then back to Heather with an expression of joy and fleeting sheepishness. 'Hey you!' she cried, stretching out her arms ready to hug her cousin. 'This is a lovely surprise. How was the dress fitting?'

'It was great. I mean I missed you but it was great.' Heather smiled, pulling her close. 'But what are you doing here? I thought you were going to see your boss?'

Gemma nodded slowly. 'Yes, that's exactly what I was doing and then I remembered that Luke worked around the corner so I thought I would pop by and say hello and, you know, catch up about your big day. It's exciting that you've booked the venue.'

Heather grinned. 'Yeah and I've just picked my dress so I was kind of hoping to take my fiancé out for lunch to celebrate.'

Luke nodded rapidly. 'Sounds great. Where shall we go? Gemma, will you join us?'

Gemma cleared her throat. 'No, honestly, it's fine. I should get back to Mum and Freddy – he's got a bit of sniffle. But it was great to see you both.' She gave Heather a tight lingering hug.

When they pulled apart, she noticed tears in Gemma's eyes. 'Oh Gem, are you okay?'

'I'm fine. It's my stupid hormones and I miss you, you know? I'm going to come and see you again soon, okay? Bye, Luke,' she said, giving him a cursory peck on the cheek, before hurrying off through the doors.

'Poor Gem,' said Heather, watching her go. 'I hope she's okay.'

'Never mind that,' said Luke, taking her in his arms and kissing her gently. 'Let's go and get lunch. I want to hear everything about the dress fitting without you telling about the actual dress obviously.'

She smiled up at him as he leant down to kiss her again and they walked out into the sunshine.

Best. Day. Ever.

Chapter Fourteen

Fran

Happiness List Thing
1. Accept a world without Andy (too soon!)
2. 'Digital Detox' day with kids
3. Go on even more walks with Alan
4. Have dinner with a nice man (NOT a date) & laugh if appropriate
(he is nice and I did laugh)
5. Stop feeling guilty and like Gary

It had been a bad idea. A really bad idea. As soon as she'd agreed, she started to wonder if she could get out of it. But she couldn't. Not without seeming rude and, like most British people, Fran would rather make herself hopelessly miserable than enter into any potentially difficult conversations.

The problem was that it was too soon. She'd only been out with Gary once, and although it had been lovely, she needed more time to prepare for the possibility of a second encounter. So when he phoned, instead of staying calm and making up an excuse to give herself more time, she panicked.

'Hey, Fran, I was wondering what you were up to at the weekend?'

Fran heard the alarm bells go off in her head. *Why are you panicking? It's a harmless question. Now think. Do you want to go out with him or not? Take your time – no need to rush.*

'I'm taking Charlie to the National Gallery on Saturday – we go every now and then. I can remember my mum taking me to see *The Sunflowers* when I was a kid and not quite believing they were real,' she gabbled.

Gary laughed. 'I don't think I've ever seen them.'

'You should come with us.'

WHAT? Where did that come from? That is not taking your time, you idiot!

'Are you sure?'

See? Even Gary's surprised that you're inviting him on a day trip with your daughter. If anything, you're probably terrifying the poor man. Quick – retract the offer!

'Yeah, 'course! It'll be great.'

And by 'great', I presume you mean complete and utter disaster.

'In that case I'd love to,' said Gary.

'Okay, let's say eleven o'clock in the entrance hall.'

'Looking forward to it.'

Fran hung up and sank into the nearest chair. 'You're really, really bad at this thing called life,' she muttered.

The situation worsened when she told Pamela. 'Ooh, that sounds like fun. I've never been to an art gallery before.'

'You should come too,' said Fran.

For God's sake, Fran. What is the matter with you?

'Really?'

'Really.'

Really? You're going on a trip to an art gallery with Charlie, Pamela and Gary. You should ask your mother along too. Cat. Pigeons. The whole works.

* * *

The weather was bright and warm as Fran, Pamela and Charlie made their way across Trafalgar Square on Saturday morning. Charlie paused to shake hands with Yoda the street performer and read the pavement art. Fran smiled as she watched her daughter, enjoying the welcome kiss of sun on her face.

Maybe it would all be okay. Maybe something good would come out of bringing together this unusual mix of people – like when someone first put maple syrup with bacon and created a little piece of culinary heaven. Fran just prayed that it wouldn't end up being like a ham and pineapple pizza which was, regardless of Charlie's view, wrong-all-wrong.

She felt a shiver of nerves as she led them up the steps to the main entrance and spotted Gary waiting as arranged.

'Hi, Charlie,' he said, holding out his hand. Fran was oddly touched that he'd addressed her daughter first.

'Hi, Gary,' said Charlie with a grin. 'Wow, your hands are like bear paws. I'm going to call you Bear,' she declared.

Gary laughed before turning to Pamela. 'Hello, Mrs T. Fran told me you've never seen a real Picasso either,' he said, leaning over to kiss her cheek.

'No, lovey, and I'm rather excited!'

'Come on,' said Charlie, leading her by the hand. 'I know where they are. We've been here like a million times!'

Fran could feel Gary's eyes on her. 'Hello,' she said, turning to look into his face, making a deliberate decision not to kiss him. A sangria-induced peck on the lips was one thing but in the cold light of day, with your daughter and slightly gossipy friend nearby? Probably best avoided.

'It's good to see you. Shall we?' he asked, offering her his arm.

It was an unexpected but charming gesture. Fran accepted with a smile, feeling like a Jane Austen heroine as they swept up the stairs.

She loved the excited murmur of this gallery – she had often mused that every nationality in the world must pass through it each day, taking in the Picassos, the Monets, the Van Goghs. Some people barely registered the paintings, pausing only to look at them on a phone screen before taking a snap they would never look at again and moving on. Others stood or sat in quiet reflection, couples resting their heads on one another's shoulders, students looking bored, children loving the shiny dark wood floors and huge pictures. She used to come here when she worked in London, ducking in off the busy street; taking a moment to stop and break the rhythm of the chaotic everyday.

'Goodness, look at that poor girl,' cried Pamela as they stood in front of the giant painting of *The Execution of Lady Jane Grey* a while later.

'She was only sixteen,' said Charlie sadly. 'Poor Jane.'

'Why don't they help her?' asked Pamela, pointing to the other figures in the painting. 'I mean that woman's no use to anyone – she's fainted!'

'Because they can't,' said Charlie. 'That man's going to chop off her head in a minute.'

'I didn't realize art was so brutal,' commented Pamela. 'She looks like a lovely young girl.'

'Come on,' said Charlie, taking her hand. 'I'll show you *The Ambassadors* – it's Mum's favourite because of the stretchy skull.'

'Oh, okay.' Pamela smiled and let Charlie lead her by the hand.

'She's a great kid,' said Gary, as they followed on behind.

Fran nodded. 'Yeah, she is. I'm lucky.'

'They're lucky to have you too. It can't have been easy. Sorry, understatement of the year, right?'

'Just a bit.' Fran smiled. 'But we keep going.'

Gary nodded. 'Fran?'

Uh-oh. This was the part where it got tricky, where he asked her difficult questions about how she was feeling and what she thought about him. The trouble was, she didn't know. Gary was great – kind, funny, attractive and, most importantly, he understood. He got that this was difficult, that it wasn't a boy-meets-girl situation. It was a 'boy-meets-widow, who still thinks about her husband a lot' situation. Difficult didn't even come close. On paper, Gary was ideal – they liked one another, he made her laugh, he didn't put her under pressure. It was perfect. Apart from one tiny detail.

'I can't do this, Gary,' she said, turning to face him. She saw a flicker of disappointment in his eyes – it was fleeting before it was replaced with a look of kindness.

He smiled and nodded. 'I understand.'

'I'm sorry,' she told him, because she was. *Sorry to let you down. Sorry to let myself down. Sorry that things can't be different.*

'Can I ask one thing?'

'Of course.'

'Did I come on too strong? Did I scare you off?'

She stared into his eyes. 'No. Not at all. It's just that…'

'Just what?'

She gave him a sorrowful look. 'You're not Andy.'

He held her gaze for a moment before taking her hand and kissing it. 'No. But I'm here if you need me, okay?'

Fran cursed herself. He was so kind, so lovely. Why couldn't she make herself like him? And yet she knew the answer only too well. 'Thank you.' She blinked back tears. 'And I'm sorry.'

He looked into her eyes. 'You have nothing to be sorry about. Okay?' He kissed her hand again.

Nothing to be sorry about and yet why do I feel as if I'm letting the whole world down?

'But aren't you coming for lunch with us?' said Charlie after Gary told her he had to catch a train.

'Not today,' said Fran, feeling her throat go dry with guilt.

'Yeah, sorry, Charlie, I have to work.' Fran sent him a silent thank you for the lie.

'Oh, that's a shame but we'll see you soon?' she asked, reaching over to hug him, seeming tiny against his broad frame.

Gary caught Fran's eye and she looked away. 'Come on, Charlie, let Gary go.'

Yes, let him go and then we can get on with our lives and pretend that nothing has happened. It was all a big mistake.

Gary patted Charlie's head. 'Bye, lovely girl,' he said before disappearing into the crowd.

Fran felt Pamela link an arm through hers. She turned, her eyes misting with tears. 'I just can't do it at the moment,' she whispered.

Pamela squeezed her hand in reply. 'Well, I've had a lovely morning. Thank you so much for showing me those paintings, Charlie – it was all new to me but wonderful. And now I don't know about you but I'm starving. How about I treat us to lunch?'

Charlie grinned, immediately distracted by the idea of food. 'Can we get pizza or McDonald's or Pret?'

'All three if you like!' said Pamela beaming. She pulled Charlie into a hug as Fran shot her a grateful smile.

'Yay!' cried Charlie, linking arms with them both, all thoughts of Gary fading for now.

A few days later, Fran found herself in the unusual position of having a spare hour before she had to pick up Charlie. Her editing was done for the day, the washing was folded, the house was reasonably clean and so Fran was lying on the sofa with a snoring Alan beside her, nursing a mug of tea. She cast around the room feeling fidgety and then annoyed at herself for being unable to relax. This was supposed to be blissful, wasn't it? The kind of moment most mothers dreamt of – a whole hour. A *whole* hour. She stretched her aching arms behind her head and eased out her back. Alan greeted the disturbance by opening one eye and frowning quizzically at her.

'Sorry, doggy. Just trying to get comfortable,' she told him. He went back to sleep. She lay with her eyes closed and tried to take a power nap. How many times over the past fifteen years would she have relished the opportunity to indulge in a little snooze? About forty thousand times. That's how many. And yet, she was restless, her mind wandering as images of Gary's annoyingly handsome face flitted past. She snapped her eyes open. How ridiculous. Maybe she should read? Or watch TV? Or try a mindfulness exercise. She might even have some raisins in the cupboard, although they were probably out of date.

She heard a key in the front door. *Jude. Brilliant.* She would make him sit and talk to her. They could eat biscuits whilst sharing stories of their day and enjoy some quality mother–son time.

'Hey, Jude,' she sang, Beatles-style. He had always giggled at this when he was small, loving the fact that he had his own song.

'Nnnng?' he grunted, peering round the door frame, a surly textbook-teenager look on his face.

'Wow, what a treat to see my smiley, jolly son,' teased Fran.

'Don't start, Mum,' he warned.

'Sorry. I'll try to be less embarrassing by remaining silent and attempting to turn myself invisible.'

He rolled his eyes. 'I've got homework. Lots of homework,' he said, backing out of the living room and thumping up the stairs.

'Alone again,' muttered Fran. Alan let out a bored sigh. 'Don't say you've had enough of me too!' she cried, ruffling his ears.

Her phone buzzed with a call and she snatched it up gratefully, glancing at the caller ID. It was Charlie's school.

'Hello?'

'Mrs Parker? It's Phil Metcalfe from Felmingham Primary. Charlie's absolutely fine but I was wondering if you might be able to come in for a chat please?'

Fran was walking so fast that Charlie had to run to keep up with her. She needed to get home as quickly as possible without seeing anyone she knew. If she could just make it through the front door and find a random object to kick, she might be able to calm herself in order to work out how on earth she was supposed to feel. At that current moment all she felt was shame and anger – hot, burning, destructive.

'Mum, wait up!' cried Charlie, half running, half skipping along behind her mother. But Fran kept going, she didn't look back. She was furious with Charlie even though she knew she had no right to be. It wasn't her fault, really it wasn't but who else was there to blame? 'Mum, please! Ow!' Fran glanced over her shoulder to see Charlie sprawled on the pavement outside the Trotts' house. She stared up at her mother with pleading eyes. 'Ow, Mummy. I hurt my knee.' Fran was about to make her way over when she spotted Heather emerging from Pamela's house.

She saw Charlie and rushed over. 'Oh no, what's happened?'

'I fell,' explained Charlie rather obviously, starting to cry. 'It really hurts. And Mummy's cross with me because I've been telling lies at school!'

Heather glanced at Fran, who gave an exasperated nod. 'Come on, let's get you home,' she said.

'Please can Heather come in for a bit?' asked Charlie tearfully.

Heather smiled at Fran. 'I'm free if you need me. I just popped in to fetch a couple of things for Pamela,' she said, holding up a carrier bag.

Fran realized she needed someone to talk to and Charlie loved Heather. 'Sure, that'd be great.'

They helped Charlie into the house, administered first aid and sat her on the sofa with a bowl of ice cream, an alarmingly bright and noisy cartoon on the television and Alan standing guard.

'So what happened?' asked Heather, following Fran back to the kitchen. 'What's Charlie been saying?'

Fran flicked the switch on the kettle and set the biscuit tin on the table. 'It's more a case of what she hasn't been saying. She's been lying about everything. She said that she's got a new dad called Gary.' Heather winced. 'She said that we're getting married next year. And that I'm pregnant. No wonder some of the other mothers have been staring at my stomach. I should have noticed the warning signs when she drew this at the weekend.' Fran plucked a picture from the side and held it out for Heather to see. Charlie had drawn four figures and a dog, labelling them in bright felt tip – *Mummy, Gary, Jude, Charlie and Alan.*

'Bless her.'

'Bless her? I should wring her bloody neck! She can't go round saying stuff like that, she'll end up in all sorts of trouble.' Heather nodded, looking slightly cowed by the outburst. Fran sighed. 'And that's the thing – it makes me so bloody angry and I've got no right to that anger because it's mostly my fault. I mean, I shouldn't have dragged him along to the art gallery for a start. Charlie's life is confusing enough as it is and that didn't help.'

'Don't be so hard on yourself,' said Heather. 'You're doing your best. You've been through the worst thing imaginable. You need to cut yourself some slack.'

Fran placed a mug of tea in front of her, nodding wearily. 'I know what's happening. Charlie's creating a new world that she thinks will make me happy,' she said, unexpected tears springing to her eyes. 'It's not fair, Heather. It's not fucking fair…' Her voice broke off.

'I know,' said Heather, placing a hand on Fran's arm. 'Trust me. I know.'

Fran nodded. 'She's only ten, you know? She shouldn't be taking that on herself, should she?'

Heather shook her head. 'No.'

'She's trying to tell me to move on, isn't she? She's trying to help. But I just can't do it, Heather. I can't do it.' She shook her head rapidly as the tears fell.

Heather grasped her friend's hands and held them tightly. 'You don't have to do it on your own, you know? We're here. Pamela and me. Okay?' Fran gave a small nod. 'And I honestly understand – I mean losing your husband is obviously completely different to losing your parents but grief is grief, it never goes away.'

Fran stared at her in surprise. 'It doesn't, does it? I don't think

171

people understand that. They think it's something you get over, like a cold.'

Heather nodded. 'Oh yeah. And then there are the ones who tell you that time is a healer.'

Fran shivered. 'But you're allowed to punch those people, aren't you?'

'Totally. It's actually the law to punch them.'

Fran gave a weak laugh. 'Oh, Heather, I'm a bloody mess.'

Heather shook her head. 'No. You're not. You're actually facing it head on, possibly for the first time.'

Fran looked shocked. 'Am I?'

Heather nodded. 'Yeah and you're being incredibly brave about it so keep going and remember, you're not alone.'

Fran sniffed and wiped her face with a tissue. 'Shut up. You'll set me off again.'

Heather laughed. 'Seriously though, you'll get there.'

'Where?' *The eternal question.*

Heather thought for a moment. 'I can't tell you that because everyone's different but, for me, it was when I accepted that Mum and Dad were gone and I could allow myself to be happy.'

'Makes sense.' Fran nodded. 'And when did that happen?'

'Probably when I met Luke. He gave me a reason to be happy again.'

Fran smiled. 'Well, you deserve it.'

Heather fixed her with a look. 'You do too and you'll find whatever it is you need – it might be Gary or it might not but you can't live for Charlie or anyone else. You have to find your own way.'

Fran put an arm round Heather's shoulders. 'You're wise for a young 'un.' Heather laughed.

'Can Heather stay for tea?' asked Charlie, sloping into the kitchen and putting an arm around Heather's other shoulder.

'I don't know. Can Heather?' said Fran smiling at her.

'Well, Pamela is out at choir tonight and Luke's working late. Again. So yes, I'd love to – thank you.'

'Yay!' cried Charlie, punching the air.

Fran shifted her weight on the sofa and tried to get comfortable but it was impossible.

And Charlie's okay?

I think so. I've booked a few more sessions with her old bereavement counsellor so that she can talk it all through.

And what's your take on her lying?

Fran sighed. The poor kid thinks it's down to her to make me happy.

And who is it down to, Fran?

Don't be clever. You know it's down to me.

So what are you going to do?' he asked.

If I knew that, would I be lying here having this conversation with you?

A knowing laugh. I guess not.

Heather thinks I'm in the middle of facing my grief.

Do you believe her?

Yeah, I think I probably do.

So keep going then. You'll get there.

You always did have great faith in me.

You need to have faith in yourself now.

But we can still do this, can't we? I can still talk to you, can't I?

Of course, Fran. For as long as you need me, I'm here.

Chapter Fifteen

Pamela

My Happiness List
1. Just bake
2. Dinner with Matthew and Barry – be in the moment!
(DISASTER)
3. Go dancing with Barry? (Not likely)
4. Laugh like we used to! (with Heather instead)
5. Try something new – lovely trip to art gallery with Fran & Charlie
(and Gary!)

Pamela did her best to suppress the jitter of nerves she felt as she made her way to Hope Street community hall that evening. Nik had asked her and the other volunteers to arrive half an hour early. She was carrying a large bag containing all the ingredients for a batch of chocolate chip cookies. She'd chosen something easy to make because she wanted it to be fun but she also knew the recipe inside out. Pamela was anxious enough about teaching other people to bake and didn't need the extra worry of getting muddled with some complicated recipe.

Heather had tried to reassure her before she left. 'Seriously, Pamela, you've got this. All you have to do is be yourself – people love you and your bakes are amazing. It's going to be fun. Everyone on the course is on your side. Don't worry.'

'Thanks, ducks.' Pamela smiled as she gathered her ingredients. 'I'll see you in a bit.'

You've got this, you've got this, thought Pamela as she neared the hall. She knew it was silly to be worried. She could practically bake chocolate chip cookies in her sleep. It was just that she'd never done anything like this before. She'd never taught anyone anything, apart from the kids but that didn't count. Laura had seemed able to cook from the second she could hold a wooden spoon and never needed her mother's help. She had tried to teach Matthew and Simon to bake but they had always been more interested in the licking the bowl or flicking ingredients at one another. She smiled at the memory. She was missing Matthew and felt a little hurt that he hadn't been round to see her. He'd sent her the odd text to check she was okay but that was it. She tried to put it from her mind, but still, it niggled.

She was so distracted and nervy as she entered the hall that she walked straight into the person coming the other way.

'Pammy!' exclaimed Barry, unable to disguise the relief in his voice at the sight of her.

'Oh, so Nik did ask you to come,' she replied indignantly, taking a step back.

Barry eyed her sheepishly. 'Is that okay?'

Pamela shrugged. 'Makes no difference to me what you do,' she retorted, surprised at how off-hand she was being. In truth, she was glad to see Barry but she wasn't going to tell him this of course – she had to make a stand, had to make him see how she felt. It was her only hope.

Barry looked hurt but didn't have a chance to respond before Nik appeared. 'Good evening, Pamela. Are you all set?'

'I think so,' she replied, walking past Barry without a backward glance.

Keep going, Pamela. You've got to make him see.

Nik followed her to the kitchen. 'Thank you for agreeing to do this – don't forget to try out anything else that interests you. We have a dance class, Sue is going to do some paper-crafting, your friends from the choir are coming and obviously Barry is running the gardening workshop.'

'Mmm,' said Pamela, her shoulders stiffening at the mention of her husband. 'I'll probably stay in the kitchen – it's where I'm most at home.'

Nik smiled. 'I hope I haven't made things difficult for you by asking Barry along.'

Pamela folded her arms. 'Barry Trott just needs to realize a few home truths,' she said, surprised at how determined she felt.

Nik nodded. 'We all do from time to time. My wife left me because I let her down.'

'Oh dear,' said Pamela. 'What happened?'

'I ended up here,' he replied, spreading his arms. 'She is in Denmark and I am here, realizing the home truths.'

'I'm sure you'll get there,' said Pamela kindly.

Nik smiled. 'I'm sure you will too.'

Pamela felt buoyed by Nik's words as she set up in the kitchen. She was glad she'd taken a stand, not only for her sake but for Barry's and Matthew's too. She knew too many women of her age who put up with faltering marriages and unhappy families. She wasn't prepared to do that. She wanted something strong and joyful, something she remembered from her youth – an essence of that carefree time, which could carry them into the future. Surely that was possible.

Half an hour later, Pamela heard the clamour of people arriving. She felt her nerves settle a little as Jim's cheery face peered around the doorway.

176

'Evening, Mrs T. What are we baking?'

'Chocolate chip cookies. Pop on an apron and we'll get started once a few other people arrive.' She smiled as two more bakers walked in to the kitchen. She heard music pump through the speakers and the sound of the dance teacher giving instructions.

'Okay, let's make a start,' she told her three bakers. She felt her shoulders relax as they smiled back at her, ready to learn.

You've got this, Pamela.

'We need to cream the butter and the sugar together like this,' she explained, after they had measured out the first ingredients.

'I haven't got a wooden spoon at home,' said Jim sadly.

'Well you can take that one home with you, lovey,' said Pamela. 'I've got hundreds!'

'Aw thanks, Mrs T!'

She smiled. 'So we need to put a bit of elbow grease into this. I find it's a good way to get rid of your stress.'

'I'm going to do this after the school run,' said a lady called Emma. 'And then after mealtimes. And bedtimes.'

'Whereas I'm going to do it after I've spoken to my ex-husband,' joked her friend, Tasha.

Pamela laughed. 'You're all doing brilliantly. Come on, Jim, the girls are showing you up!'

Jim mopped his brow. 'This is hard, Mrs T, my arm's aching already!'

She laughed. 'Next we add the vanilla essence and egg.' Pamela watched as they followed her instructions and realized that she was enjoying this. She'd never fancied herself as a teacher but there was something very satisfying about sharing her knowledge with others, even if it was only a simple cookie recipe.

Pamela was momentarily transported back to when she was a girl and she'd taught Ernie how to bake. It made her breathless with longing as she recalled him standing at her elbow, his big eyes staring up at her in awe as she showed him what to do.

'Is this okay?' asked Jim, holding out his bowl for inspection, bringing her back to the present. She realized that Ernie would have been about the same age as Jim now.

'Looks perfect to me, Jim.' Pamela smiled, as the warmth of the memory surrounded her like a hug. Jim grinned with pride. 'So next we sift in flour, bicarbonate of soda and a pinch of salt. And then we add the chocolate chips – I like to use a mixture of white, dark and milk.'

'They look amazing!' declared Emma as Pamela lifted a tray of baked cookies onto the side a while later. 'Mine always end up burnt at the edges.'

'Try starting with a cooler oven, ducks – not hotter than 175 degrees.'

'Okay, will do. Thanks, Pamela.'

'Yeah, thanks,' agreed Tasha. 'That was great.'

'Mmm,' said Jim, who was licking his spoon. 'How long until we can try them?'

Pamela grinned. 'They'll be cool enough to eat at tea break. Well done, everyone, that was great.'

'So-o, how did it go?' asked Heather, nudging Pamela when they met at the break.

'I really enjoyed it,' admitted Pamela.

'See? I told you. You're a natural,' said Heather.

Pamela beamed. It was strange but she felt about a foot taller as a wave of newfound confidence washed over her. It was a lovely feeling – unexpected and welcome. 'How about you?'

'I did the dance thing. It was brilliant!' smiled Heather, giving a little shimmy. 'I channelled my inner Beyoncé. It made me remember how much I enjoy dancing. I might have to take it up again properly. I'd love to try a bit of ballroom.'

Heather's eyes were bright like a child's. Pamela's heart went out to her. 'I could teach you the basics. The waltz is easy – it would make a lovely first dance for your wedding.'

178

'That would be amazing!' cried Heather.

'Look what I made,' said Fran, appearing beside them, holding up an impressive hanging basket, bulging with colour.

'Wow, how gorgeous,' said Heather. 'I might give that a try after tea.'

'I know you're cross with Barry at the moment,' said Fran to Pamela. 'And rightly so, but, man, he knows his stuff. I am completely inspired to try and do something with my weed-fest of a back garden.'

Pamela pursed her lips. 'Yes well, if only he could put as much energy into being a husband and father, we wouldn't be in this mess.'

Fran put an arm around Pamela's shoulder. 'I can remember arguments with Andy that lasted for weeks because we were too stubborn to talk to each other.'

'He started it!' huffed Pamela.

Fran gave a wry smile. 'That's what I used to say.'

Pamela looked chastened. 'Oh I know, Fran, and I'm sorry. I know you'd give anything to have Andy back here to argue with.'

Fran squeezed her shoulder. 'Sorry to state the bleedin' obvious but life is short and staying angry with people is pretty much a waste of time and energy.'

'It's true,' said Heather. 'Annoying but true.'

'I know.' Pamela sighed. It made her wonder if she should speak to Barry – at least give him a chance. She noticed him stealing glances at her during the tea break and felt a tinge of regret for deliberately ignoring him.

'Anyway,' said Fran, 'sorry if you thought the baking workshop was going well because that's all about to change – you've got me next and I am blessed with a frightening ability to burn everything I put into the oven!'

Pamela laughed. 'Sounds like my kind of challenge!'

The choir had set up in the corner. Pamela waved to Nat, who was grinning at her from the front row, whilst Caroline gave a politely nodding smile. Their MD, Guy, turned to address the room. 'Good evening, everyone. We're the Hope Street Community Choir and we're going to sing a couple of songs, after which, you are cordially invited to join us for a singing workshop. We meet here fortnightly on a Thursday for singing, laughter and cake, baked by Hope Street's favourite baker – Pamela Trott.' Pamela blushed as the cheer went up. 'We're going to start with one of our favourites – "California Dreamin'' – so please join in if you'd like to!'

Pamela sang along with the choir for a while, spurred on by their energy and enthusiasm. The hall was buzzing with activity and she felt inspired by the sense of community, of belonging and being together – it was something she didn't think about very often but something she valued a great deal.

'Right, come on, Mary Berry,' said Fran, when the song ended. 'You're about to face your baking nightmare!'

'Thank you to my wonderful volunteers for showing us a veritable smorgasbord of new hobbies,' declared Nik at the end of the evening. 'Personally, I found it wholly inspiring and hope that it's given you lots of ideas. This week's homework shouldn't be a big surprise – I want you to either find something completely new to throw yourself into or immerse yourself in something you already love. This is about continuing to learn, growing confidence and enhancing our own sense of well-being. Good luck and thank you all again.'

Pamela smiled at Nik and noticed that Barry was looking over at her, like a lost soul. She shot a glare in his direction and felt a pang of guilt as he turned away sadly. She remembered Fran's words and made her way over to where he was sweeping up spilt compost with a dustpan and brush. He glanced up at the sight of her shadow.

'Oh hello, Pammy,' he said with a fearful edge to his voice, clearly worried that he was about to get shouted at.

180

'I hear you've inspired Fran,' she said.

Barry smiled as he stood up. 'She wants me to go round and give her a few suggestions.'

Pamela nodded. 'That's nice of you.'

The silence inched towards awkwardness. 'So. How have you been?' he asked.

'Fine,' she told him. 'I like staying with Heather. She's very appreciative.' Pamela hoped he might take the hint.

He didn't. 'That's good. Any idea when you might come home?'

She stared at him in amazement. 'Is that all you've got to say? *When are you coming home?* Have you even tried to work out why I left?'

Barry stared at her in desperation. 'I'm sorry, Pammy, I've never been very good at feelings. Please tell me what you want me to say.'

Pamela saw red. 'I am not about to tell you what to say. If you don't know what to say to your wife of nearly forty years, then I'm not going to write it down for you. You need to work it out for yourself. And the same goes for Matthew. But I'm guessing you haven't even tried talking to one another.'

'We have talked.'

'Oh really? Talked or argued?'

Barry looked sheepish. 'A bit of both.'

'I thought as much!'

'It's not what you think.'

'If you're arguing, it's *exactly* what I think. Well, you're in for a shock if you think I'm coming back to a war zone.'

'It's not a war zone,' insisted Barry.

'It must be with you two going hell for leather.'

Barry stared at Pamela. 'You don't know, do you?'

Pamela frowned. 'Know what?'

'Matthew's gone.'

Pamela felt her stomach drop to the floor. 'What?'

Barry frowned. 'He said he was going to email you.'

Pamela wasn't listening. Fury was rising up inside her like lava. 'You've finally done it, haven't you? You've finally driven him away!'

Barry was shaking his head rapidly. 'You don't understand, Pammy. That's not what happened.'

Pamela prodded his barrel chest. 'I understand all too well, Barry Trott. You drove him away and you're glad – admit it!'

Barry looked hurt. 'You're being very unfair, Pammy. That's not true.'

Pamela held up a hand. 'Save your breath to cool your porridge. I'm going to speak to Doly – she'll tell me the truth.' She turned on her heel and hurried to the door without a backward glance. Barry shook his head ruefully as he watched her go.

'Hey, Pamela, wait up. Are you okay?' called Heather, who had seen her storm out and was jogging to catch up.

Pamela's body shook as she stopped, all her positive energy from earlier replaced with bristling fury. 'That man! That man!' she fumed.

Heather put a hand on her arm. 'What happened?'

'Matthew's gone – driven away by his own father!'

'Matthew's gone? Gone where?'

'No idea so I'm popping round to Doly's to ask if she knows anything.'

Heather put an arm on her shoulder. 'Would you like me to come with you?'

'No, it's all right, Heather. You go home, I won't be long.'

'I'll have a glass of wine waiting for you.'

'Thanks for being so supportive – if only I could say the same about my husband!'

'He does love you, Pamela.'

Pamela knew this was true but she didn't want to hear it today. She needed to stay angry with him for now or nothing would ever change. 'I won't be long.'

Pamela rang the doorbell to the flat above the shop and took a step back. Doly's face appeared at the window of the first floor. 'Oh Pamela, hello. Wait a moment, I'll let you in.'

'Thanks, ducks,' said Pamela, pushing the door as it buzzed and walking up the narrow staircase.

'Come in,' said Doly with a smile as they met in the doorway. 'How was the workshop? I was sorry I couldn't make it.'

'It went very well,' replied Pamela. 'But we missed you.'

Two eager faces appeared behind her. 'Liza won't go to sleep,' said one of the girls. 'And Mum has confiscated her iPad,' reported the other.

Doly rolled her eyes. 'You should all be in bed. Now go!' The girls giggled before running off.

'Sorry,' said Doly. 'Bedtime always seems to get later when Dev is away – I'm a very indulgent mother.'

A mother after my own heart, thought Pamela. 'I won't keep you, lovey. I just wondered when you last saw Matthew?'

Doly looked worried. 'Yesterday. He came to get his final pay cheque. Is everything all right?'

'Not really. He's gone and I don't know where. I don't suppose he said anything to you?'

Doly looked uncomfortable. 'I'm not sure what to say. I'm surprised he didn't tell you.'

'Tell me what?'

'He's gone to America.'

'America! Whatever for?'

Doly shook her head. 'I don't know. He told me that he was going for work but he didn't say where or what. I'm sorry.'

Pamela was flabbergasted. 'Why would he go without telling me? Doesn't he realize how much I'll fret!'

Doly put an arm around Pamela's shoulders. 'I'm sure he's fine and that he'll call when he can. Try not to worry. He seemed very excited about it.'

'Did he?' asked Pamela, brightening.

'He did. And he is a good man. He worked hard for me and I know he loves you very much,' assured Doly.

Pamela patted her hand gratefully. 'Thank you. That means a lot to me. You worry so much about your children, don't you? Right from when they're born and it never stops. In fact, the older they are, the worse it gets.'

Doly nodded. 'I'm sure, but he's an adult and he'll be okay. It's hard but you have to let your children fly and make their own mistakes along the way. You are a good mother, Pamela, but your son needs his own life. And you do too.'

Doly's words echoed in Pamela's mind as she walked back along Hope Street. She knew she was right. It was just that being a mother meant you never forgot the time they fell over and scraped their knee or came home from school crying because someone had been mean to them. It was hard to shake off the feeling that they didn't need you in the same way and particularly hard with Matthew. He'd always been the one who needed her, who came back when he was in trouble. But then, Pamela had been the one who told him to stand on his own two feet, who'd finally cut the apron strings. Maybe he'd got the message but maybe she needed to as well. She felt a pang of guilt that she'd given Barry short shrift earlier. Perhaps she'd been a little harsh. Pamela wasn't quite sure where this left her but she got the feeling that she was on her way to finding out.

Chapter Sixteen

Heather

Happiness List
1. Marry Luke!
2. Sunday walk and choose wedding venue with Luke Fran & Charlie
3. Exercise more (persuade Luke to go running?)
- Boot camp with Fran & Pamela
4. Go dress shopping with Gemma and laugh like we used to!
Fran & Pamela - laughed like teenagers!
5. Surprise Luke at work
6. Ask Pamela for help with first dance for wedding!

Heather rolled over in bed and glanced at the clock: 7.30 a.m. On a Saturday. When she didn't have to work. *Slightly annoying.* From the sound of Luke's steady breathing, she could tell he was fast asleep. Heather had gone to bed before he arrived home last night so she guessed he must have been late. She decided to leave him sleeping and go downstairs to make some tea. There was no sign of Pamela so Heather padded about as quietly as she could. She switched on the radio with the volume down low. She liked the companionable hum of background noise. She'd never been a person who felt entirely at home in her own company. Some people enjoyed being on their own but it always made Heather feel uneasy.

As she carried her tea to the kitchen table, a song came on the radio that immediately transported her back to childhood. She had been eight years old and Gemma had come to stay for a sleepover. Heather could remember boasting to her school friends about this. They all knew Gemma because she was in Year Six, which was the ultimate in cool when you were in Year Four. Gemma was cool but as an only child like Heather, she loved having a younger cousin – someone to adore whilst Heather idolized her in return. Gemma had brought over her stereo and Heather remembered thinking this was the most fantastic thing she'd ever seen. It was red and silver and had a remote control. They listened to 'Wannabe' by the Spice Girls on repeat and Gemma taught Heather the dance and the Mel B rap. Heather was Baby Spice naturally whilst Gemma favoured Sporty. They recruited three of Heather's bears to play Posh, Scary and Ginger. The memory made Heather want to laugh and cry – Gemma and her upstairs in her bedroom dancing while her mum made dinner downstairs. She hadn't thought about it for the longest time.

She reached for her phone and dialled Gemma's number. Her cousin answered after three rings.

'Heth?' Her voice was heavy with weariness. 'Are you okay?'

Heather felt guilty. What was she thinking, phoning about a song on the radio? She should have just texted. 'I'm fine. Sorry. I dialled without thinking. I just heard "Wannabe" on the radio and it made me think of that time you taught me the dance moves.'

'Hm,' replied Gemma – a sound that was somewhere between a laugh and a sigh.

'Oh gawd, I feel bad now. You were sleeping, weren't you?'

'Yeah, but it's okay.'

'No. It's not okay. Here's me going on about the Spice Girls to an exhausted mother – I'm so sorry.'

'Heather, you don't have to keep apologizing. Seriously. It's fine.' Gemma's voice was curt. Heather had noticed that she'd been like this the last few times they'd spoken and it worried her.

'Gemma, are you okay? Is there anything I can do to help?'

'Unless you can think of a way to stop Ed sleeping through every single one of Freddy's bouts of crying, then not really,' said Gemma bitterly.

'Oh, hun, I'm sorry you're struggling.'

'I'm not struggling,' said Gemma defensively. 'Who said I was struggling?'

Heather drew in a sharp breath. This wasn't like Gemma. They'd argued when they were teenagers but never as adults. Her tone caught Heather off guard but then she guessed that motherhood and hormones did weird things to your body and mood. 'Sorry, I didn't mean to sound critical. You've just seemed a bit down lately.'

'Yeah well, you try painting on a happy face with no sleep,' she snapped.

'Sorry,' repeated Heather, unsure of what else to say.

Gemma sighed. 'No, Heth. I'm sorry – that was out of order. I shouldn't take it out on you. I really, really shouldn't take it out on you. You don't deserve it.'

'It's okay. You can take it out on me as much as you like if it makes you feel better,' she said kindly.

'Dear Heather. You're such a good person. You mustn't let people take advantage of that, you know?'

It was an odd thing to say but Heather put it down to more hormones. 'I don't,' she said cheerfully. 'And listen, I'm happy to have Freddy again if it gives you a break.'

'Thanks,' said Gemma in a small voice.

'Are you all set for the christening? Not long now,' asked

Heather, sensing it might be wise to change the subject.

Gemma sighed. 'Yeah, I think so. Mum's sorted a lot of stuff for me so that's a blessing.'

'Personally, I'm very much looking forward to renouncing the devil on behalf of your son,' she joked.

Gemma gave a half-hearted laugh. Heather heard a piercing shriek in the background. 'Oh great. I hear his master's voice. I'd better go. Have a good weekend.'

'You too,' said Heather, wincing slightly as she said this. It sounded as if Gemma was in for a tough one.

'Morning, beautiful,' said Luke with a grin, strolling into the kitchen. 'You're up early.'

She turned her face to kiss him. 'Yeah, I was speaking to Gemma – she sounds very fed up at the moment.'

'Oh,' said Luke vaguely. 'Poor Gemma.'

Heather smiled at him. 'Anyway. I'm glad you're up because I've got plans for us.'

'Oh yes,' he said, leaning down to kiss her neck. 'Do they involve me dragging you back to bed for a little pre-breakfast exercise?'

'Good mor-ning!' cried Pamela, breezing into the kitchen. 'How about I rustle up some eggs for my dance students? Give you a bit of energy for our lesson.'

Luke frowned. 'Dance students? What lesson?'

Heather grinned at him. 'We're heading to Hope Street Hall. Pamela is going to help us work up a routine for our first wedding dance.'

Luke's face fell. 'Oh Heth, you know I've got two left feet!'

'Don't worry, lovey.' Pamela smiled. 'Once I've finished with you, you'll be skipping round the floor like Fred Astaire!'

'That's going to be one long dance lesson,' said Luke, sinking into a chair.

Heather put her arms around him and kissed his cheek. 'At least give it a try. For me? Please?'

188

Luke regarded her for a second before shaking his head in defeat. 'How can I resist you?' he said, pulling her into his arms.

'Ooh, don't mind me,' giggled Pamela, covering her eyes. 'Young love, eh?'

'I guess I'd better go find some sweatpants,' said Luke, resigned to his fate.

'Perfect,' said Heather with a grin.

The sky was thick with cloud and the first spots of rain were falling as they made their way along Hope Street. Pamela started to hum the tune to 'Singin' in the Rain' and Heather joined in, hoping it might cheer up her surly fiancé.

'Remind me why you made me leave the house,' grumbled Luke, trying to pull his thin beige jacket over his head.

'It's going to be fun,' insisted Heather, as Pamela opened up the hall and they made their way inside.

'If you say so.'

'Come on,' she said, linking an arm through his. 'We're meant to be spending quality time together.'

'Clearly we have different definitions of quality,' he huffed, folding his arms.

'Aww, don't be grumpy. We're only going to be here for an hour and then we can do whatever you like.'

His face softened. 'That's good because I've got a surprise for you later.'

'A surprise?'

He nodded. 'To make up for all my late working and not being around.'

She looked into his eyes and smiled. 'Have I ever told you that I love you?'

'Yeah, but say it again.'

'I love you.'

He pulled her close and kissed her. 'I love you too.'

Pamela cleared her throat. They looked over to where she'd

189

stuck two squares of masking tape to the floor. 'Okay, my ducks. Let's give this a go. I hope I can remember it – I've been Googling waltz tutorials like mad!'

Heather looked at Luke. 'See? This is going to be fun.'

'Now the first thing is posture and hold. So, I want you to come and stand with your backs against the wall to make sure you're nice and straight. No hunched shoulders please!'

Luke winked at Heather as they followed Pamela's instructions. 'Excellent, now stand face to face and I want you to look at one another as if you're the only two people in the world.' Heather giggled as Luke stuck out his tongue. Pamela laughed. 'You need to hold hands so, Luke, raise your left hand and take hold of Heather's right hand. Great. And then, Luke, you cup your right hand on Heather's left shoulder blade and, Heather, place your left hand on the seam of his jumper. That's it! So then, Heather, you'll move slightly to the right of Luke so that your knees don't bash as you dance. There – you look perfect!'

Heather stared up at Luke. He was smiling down at her and she wished she could pause this moment. She had his undivided attention for once and she longed to hang on to it for as long as possible.

The problems began when they tried to start dancing. Luke's assertions that he had two left feet weren't entirely inaccurate. Pamela spent time showing them how to step around the square on the floor in a one-two-three pattern. Heather grasped it quickly but Luke was all over the place.

'This is impossible!' he declared.

They were interrupted by someone bursting through the door of Hope Street Hall. 'Pammy!' cried Barry. 'I saw the door was open and panicked. Sorry, I didn't realize you were in here.'

Pamela frowned before her face brightened with an idea. 'Actually, have you got a minute, Barry?'

'Me?' asked Barry in surprise.

'No, Barry Manilow standing behind you. Of course you!'

'Oh. Right. Well – yes.'

'Good, I need you to help me show Heather and Luke here how to do a waltz.'

Barry frowned. 'Oh right. I'm not sure. It's been a while.'

'Well, if you don't want to help,' retorted Pamela as if issuing a challenge. Luke raised an eyebrow at Heather who winced.

'No, no, of course I'll help,' said Barry, hurrying over.

'Thank you,' said Pamela. 'You dance with Heather, I'll dance with Luke and then we'll try and put it all together, okay?'

Heather smiled at Barry as he offered his hand to her and tried not to laugh when she spotted Luke pulling faces behind his head. 'All right, everyone?' said Pamela, turning on the music. 'Here we go, one-two-three, one-two-three, one-two-three, much better, Luke! Keep going.'

'You're a natural, Heather,' said Barry as they danced. 'You've got music in your bones.' Heather grinned. It didn't feel awkward dancing with Barry – it felt rather lovely. There was something very familiar about it. She realized that she was glimpsing a fleeting memory of her father dancing her round the kitchen like this. It brought an ache to her heart but comfort too.

'Thank you,' she said to Barry as the music ended. 'I enjoyed that.'

'Me too,' he replied with a gallant bow.

'Well done!' cried Pamela. 'That was a great first try.'

'Will you show us how it's done properly?' asked Heather. 'Please?'

'Oh, I'm not sure,' said Pamela with a frown, although the corners of her mouth were pulling into a smile.

'Come on, Pammy,' said Barry with a cheeky grin. 'Let's show these young 'uns how it's done.'

Pamela regarded him for a second before catching sight of Heather's eager face. 'Oh, all right then.'

Heather wanted to hug herself as she watched them dance – they looked so natural and beautiful. Pamela moved with real grace and, for a stocky man, Barry was surprisingly light on his feet. But it was the way he looked at his wife that swept Heather away – as if she *was* the only person in the world. Pamela's shoulders were stiff to begin with, but, as the two of them moved around the floor, she relaxed into the dance and her expression softened towards Barry. It was as though she was seeing an old friend again and realizing that she'd missed him.

Heather turned to Luke to share her enjoyment and was disappointed to see that he was looking at his phone, scrolling through emails, not taking the slightest notice. She turned back to watch the dancers again, a familiar feeling in the pit of her stomach. *Couldn't he switch off for one day?*

When the dance had finished, Pamela gave a curtsey and Barry bowed. Heather clapped with enthusiasm. 'That was beautiful, really beautiful.'

'Yeah – bravo,' said Luke, shoving his phone into his pocket and joining in the applause.

'Thank you.' Pamela smiled, before nodding at her husband as if dismissing him. 'Thanks, Barry.'

'My pleasure,' he said. He hesitated, looking as if he wanted to say something else but wasn't sure where to begin. 'Right, I'd best be off. Bye then.'

'Bye,' said Pamela, turning away.

Heather felt a pang of sympathy as she watched Barry leave. 'Just nipping to the loo,' she told Luke, heading towards the entrance hall. She followed Barry onto the street. 'Barry, wait!'

He stopped in his tracks. 'Everything okay, Heather?'

'Everything's fine,' she said. 'But I'm worried about you and Pamela.'

'You and me both,' he admitted.

She smiled. 'Which is why I think you should let me and Fran help you win her back.'

'Win her back?'

Heather nodded. 'You need to woo your wife, make her feel loved again.'

'But I do love her!'

'How often do you tell her?'

Barry stared at his shoes. 'You may have a point there. What do you think I should do?'

Heather winked and tapped the side of her nose. 'Leave it to me,' she said. 'I've got a plan.'

Heather stretched her arms behind her head, luxuriating in the feel of the cashmere mattress and goose-down duvet on her skin. She stared up at the blue silk canopy hanging above the four-poster bed and sighed. 'That's it – I've decided. We're moving here. I want to be the lady of Chilford Park.'

'If you promise to do that with me every Saturday afternoon, I think it would be worth the money,' grinned Luke, putting down his champagne glass and pulling her into his arms.

'Deal. And I don't know about you but I think it would be a crying shame not to make the most of this luxuriously comfortable bed,' she said, raising an eyebrow suggestively.

'If you insist,' he said, before kissing her full on the mouth and working his way to her neck.

Heather closed her eyes and allowed herself to sink into the soft, delicious moment. Now this was what she called quality time. The frustration she'd felt at Luke's long hours and endless work commitments started to drift away. Finally, Luke understood and, boy, was he making up for it by booking a surprise night at their wedding venue. Thoughtful and extravagant. Heather could get used to this.

Luke's phone buzzed from the bedside table. He glanced towards it.

'Leave it,' she urged, kissing his cheek.

He hesitated. But not for long. 'Sorry, Heather, I gotta take it – you know how it is.'

Yeah, I know how it is but I thought today was going to be different. I was actually starting to believe that you understood what was important.

193

He reached for his phone, frowning when he saw the caller ID. He jumped out of bed, pulled on a robe and made for the door as he answered. 'Hey, what's up?'

Heather gave a heavy sigh and flopped back onto the bed, trying to shake off her creeping sense of disappointment.

One day. Just one day. That's all she wanted. One day of his complete attention. Was that too much to ask?

And yet here she lay again, waiting for him to come back. Waiting for her life to start. Because that's how it had been for the longest time – ever since her parents died really. She had been waiting for someone to love her, to try to fill the gap left by their absence. Everyone needed one person in their life who loved them unconditionally, didn't they? A parent or a partner – a person who was on your side whatever, like Fran with her kids or Barry with Pamela. She'd thought it was Luke but now she was starting to question this. Had she fallen for him because she actually loved him or because he fitted her circumstances? And did he actually fit after all or was it a case of square pegs in round holes?

When Luke returned a while later, he looked shamefaced and harassed. In days gone by, Heather would have felt sorry for him, but today, she'd had enough.

'I am so sorry, Heth,' he began, ready with the excuse. 'That was Mike. He'd had a call from his boss in the States and they needed to check something with me.'

Heather folded her arms. 'Sounds as if you should be doing Mike's job for him and getting paid for it too,' she said curtly.

'Oh come on, Heth, I said sorry.' She heard his irritation – clearly he wanted to close the subject and move on. He was out of luck.

'It's Saturday, Luke,' said Heather. 'Do you know what most normal couples are doing on a Saturday?'

'Having dance lessons with their uninvited lodger?' he said in a snarky tone.

Heather glared at him. It was an unexpected blow, right below the belt. 'That is out of order. You're the one in the wrong – don't start dragging Pamela into it.'

'Yeah, but it doesn't enable us to spend "quality time" together, does it?' He made inverted commas in the air as he said this, which annoyed Heather even more. 'I mean she's a nice lady and all, but exactly how long is she planning to stay?'

Heather jutted out her chin. 'It's my house. She can stay as long as she likes.'

Luke scowled. 'Oh-ho, so it's your house now, is it?'

'Yeah, it is.' Heather was surprised at how determined she felt as she said this, as if him picking on Pamela had triggered an urge to fight back. *Bring it on.*

Luke paced the room. 'Well, that's fine. I'm working all hours to pay for your dream wedding and yet I appear to be a mere lodger in your house.'

Heather shrugged. 'I pay for the house and I could pay for the wedding too if needed. You don't have to work as hard as you do.'

'Yeah, but I want to. It's my career and I want to do well.'

'I know, but it's my life and I don't want a husband who works all the time.'

'I'm here now.'

Heather sighed. 'Yes, but what about the next time your phone rings? Luke, I get that your job is important to you but I should be too. How are we supposed to have a life together if you're working all the time? And even today, when you faithfully promised me that you wouldn't, you're answering calls from your boss. How can I trust you when you do that?'

Luke ran a hand through his hair and looked sheepish. 'Okay. You're right,' he said, holding up his hands. 'I'm sorry. That got out of hand. I shouldn't have taken the call.'

She nodded. 'And, for your information, I have a plan to get Barry and Pamela back together so we'll have *our* house back to ourselves soon, okay? And I do mean *our* house – I shouldn't have said that. Sorry.'

He pulled her into his arms. 'You're an amazing woman, Heather Brown, you know that, don't you?' She gave a small uncertain smile. 'And look.' He held up his phone and pressed the 'off' button before throwing it into the holdall on the floor. 'It's staying off for the rest of the weekend. I'm sorry – I love you and I'm here for you. Please can we try again?'

She stared into his eyes and tried to shake off the niggling feeling of frustration.

You love each other, you're getting married and he's trying to make amends. Don't cut off your nose to spite your face. Not now. You need this – this is your big chance of happiness. Don't blow it now.

'Of course. I love you too,' she said, wondering why the words felt forced all of a sudden, as if part of her was starting to question what she really felt at all.

Chapter Seventeen

Fran

Happiness List Thing
1. Accept a world without Andy (too soon!)
2. 'Digital Detox' day with kids
3. Go on even more walks with Alan
4. Have dinner with a nice man (NOT a date) & laugh if appropriate
(he is nice and I did laugh)
5. Stop feeling guilty and like Gary (EPIC fail)
6. Take up gardening again

It was her mother who galvanized her into action. 'So are you serious about the gardening or is it another of your passing fads?'

Fran chose to ignore the implied criticism because actually, it was fair. She had fancied herself as everything from a quilt-maker to a plumber in the past. When she went into hospital to have her children, she'd come home on both occasions convinced that she'd make a brilliant midwife. However, when she considered it whilst not under the influence of Entonox, she realized that she actually hated the sight of bodily fluids. As childbirth was essentially the process of excreting pretty much everything your body had to offer, she'd decided it wasn't for her.

This time, it was different. 'I am serious about it,' she insisted.

'Good. How about coming to Wisley with my friends and me next week then?'

'Wisley? The garden? With a bunch of old ladies?'

'I'm not sure I appreciate your tone or choice of words, Francesca,' said Angela, arching a brow. 'Would you like to come or not?'

'Sorry, Mum,' laughed Fran. 'Yeah, why not? It'll give me some inspiration for finally taking control of the gigantic cat toilet that is our garden. I'll see if Heather can collect Charlie from school.'

'Lovely,' said Angela.

A few days later, Fran sat with every muscle clenched as she remembered all the reasons why she hated being driven anywhere by her mother. Angela was a terrible driver, with poor spatial awareness and a scant regard for the mirror-signal-manoeuvre basics of motoring. After a near-miss on the motorway and several other blared-horn and shaken-fist incidents, Fran staggered from the car, feeling an overwhelming urge to kiss the ground with gratitude.

'We're meeting for the talk by the bird bath at eleven,' said Angela, oblivious to her daughter's terror. 'So that gives us just enough time to grab a coffee.'

Or a double vodka, thought Fran shakily as she followed her mother along the path leading towards lush green lawns and gardening nirvana.

She took in her surroundings and felt her shoulders relax. It was textbook gorgeous – nature in all its awe-inspiring beauty. She watched the chattering army of women of her mother's age strolling throughout the verdant landscape and decided that they had it sussed. There was a lot to be said for spending your retirement visiting places like these – it was food for the soul with the added bonus of delicious quiche for lunch.

They bought their coffees and made their way over to meet the others ready for the talk. Fran felt about three years old again as her mother's friends clucked and delighted in her presence but she rather liked it too. She had wondered about giving the talk a miss but their guide was so engaging and knowledgeable that Fran surprised herself by being genuinely interested in what she had to say. She took them on a guided walk along the mixed borders and Fran found herself eyeing the plants greedily, like a child in a sweet shop. She didn't understand everything the guide told them but Fran loved this. It was as if a mysterious world was being revealed to her and she longed to learn more.

The guide drew their attention to the different plants, talking about *Phlox paniculata* 'Eva Cullum' or *Helenium* 'Moerheim Beauty' and Fran felt a thrill at this exotic world. She started to recall plants from when she had gardened in the dim and distant past; verbena, cosmos, dahlias. It was like reconnecting with old friends.

When the talk was over, their group started to head back to the café for lunch.

'Coming, dear?' asked Fran's mother.

'I'm going to have another look at the borders. I'll follow you in.'

Her mother smiled. 'Okay, darling.'

Fran took her time, pausing to look at the names of the plants she liked most. She scrabbled in her bag, pulling out an old receipt and a biro and began to make a list as she walked. She brushed past one plant and was hit with a sweet fresh scent of grapefruit so familiar that it took her breath away. She glanced down at the plant, bursting with hundreds of purple-blue flowers and was transported back to her grandparents' garden – helping her grandpa pick loganberries; earning a penny for every weed she and her brother collected; being soothed as her granny pressed dock leaves onto to her stinging legs after she fell into a bed of nettles. She blinked back unexpected tears and bent down to read the description.

Salvia '*Phyllis Fancy*' – *salvia is derived from the Latin 'salvere' meaning 'to save'*.

Fran added it to the list; her shopping list of new possibilities. 'Come on then, Phyllis,' she said. 'Let's see if you can live up to your name.'

She was in a good mood when she arrived at Hope Street Hall later that week and grinned as Heather hurried over, her face guarded like a secret agent about to impart a top secret. 'We haven't got much time,' she said, glancing furtively over her shoulder to where Pamela was in conversation with Nik.

'All right, 007.' Fran grinned. 'What's up?'

'I'm hatching a plan to help Barry woo Pamela – the poor man doesn't have a clue!'

'Tell me about it. I went round there today to collect a book on roses and had to put the washing machine on for him! So what did you have in mind?'

Heather pursed her lips. 'I'm thinking flowers, candles, dinner, champagne.'

'Sounds perfect. When?'

'Friday night?'

'Sure your fiancé won't mind?'

Heather bit her lip. 'He's out on Friday.'

'Working again?'

'No, I think this is some pre-stag stag do with work colleagues.'

'Fancy.' Fran detected an air of despondency from her friend. 'Always here if you need a chat.'

Heather gave a grateful smile. 'I'm fine. Honestly. It's all good. So you're up for my master plan, Agent Parker?' she asked.

Fran grinned. 'I love it! I'll have to bring Charlie but she'll be all over this. It's a fantastic idea.'

'What's a fantastic idea?' asked Pamela, appearing next to Heather, who shot a panicked look at Fran.

'Oh, erm, my new garden plans,' said Fran, wincing. 'There's lots to do but I've got some fantastic ideas.' Heather grimaced comically.

'Well, I hope Barry is being helpful.'

'Very.' Fran nodded. 'I mean ideally we need about ten strong men to help us but we'll get there.' Pamela smiled thoughtfully.

'Good evening, my friends,' said Nik. 'I hope you're all well. How are we faring with our new hobbies?'

'I've spent a small fortune on new plants so I'm considerably poorer but I'm bloody loving it,' said Fran with a grin.

Nik smiled. 'Excellent work – who was it who said that if you have a library and a garden, you have everything you need?'

'Cicero!' declared Emma. 'What do I win?'

'Know-it-all of the week award,' said Tash. They all laughed.

'It sounds as if you're all making excellent progress,' said Nik. 'So, I've got a new topic for us tonight. This week we are considering the world outside ourselves.'

'What do you mean by that?' asked Sue, leaning forwards.

'Well essentially, to use a different quote, no man or indeed woman is an island.'

'John Donne,' said Tash, nudging Emma smugly.

'I definitely want you two on my quiz team,' joked Fran.

Nik smiled as the laughter died down. 'In truth, it's about remembering the people around us. It is very easy these days to live in a bubble, dwelling on our own problems but if we reach outside our own world say by volunteering or spending time with others who might benefit from our help, we can find great meaning and even greater satisfaction. I know that Hope Street has a wonderful community so we should be able to tap into that during our discussions and group work. I have an exercise to help us consider the other people in the room. I would like you to approach another person, not necessarily someone from your usual group but it can be. I want you to tell them something good you've noticed about them – something you think they should know. I'll give you an example. Jim?'

'Yes, Nik?' grinned Jim, jumping to his feet.

Nik put a hand on his shoulder. 'Jim, I would like you to know that I appreciate how cheerful you are when I meet you on Hope Street. It always brightens my day.'

'Really?' said Jim. 'Thanks, Nik.'

'You're welcome.' He turned back to the group with a smile. 'Get the idea? So, you can approach as many people as you like. The simple fact is that by being kind and thoughtful to others, you are also being kind to yourself. Give it a try.'

Heather turned to Fran and Pamela. 'For the record, I want to say how glad I am that I've met you two. I honestly didn't think I'd get anything out of this course, but actually, your friendship means the world to me.'

'Aww, that's nice. Shame I can't stand you,' joked Fran.

'You two are like daughters to me!' cried Pamela, pulling them both into a hug.

'Team happy!' declared Heather.

Fran pulled a face. 'I'm sorry, but you are upsetting my sensibilities as an editor by using "happy" as a noun. The word is "happiness".'

Heather laughed. 'Team happiness?'

Fran see-sawed her head from side to side. 'I can live with it.'

'Heather,' said Georg, appearing in front of them.

She stood up to face him, suppressing her amusement at his serious face. 'Yes, Georg. Are you about to tell me that I'm the most beautiful woman you've ever met?' Fran snorted with laughter. 'Shut up, you,' said Heather over her shoulder.

Georg looked confused. 'No. I wanted to tell you that I enjoy working with you – you are good company.'

Heather stared at him in surprise. 'Thank you, Georg. That means a lot.'

'Welcome,' he said before moving away.

Heather grinned at Fran and Pamela. 'How about that? Turns out Georg likes me!'

'At least someone does,' teased Fran. 'Right, I'm off to spread the love,' she said, standing up. She spotted Jim talking to Sue and was about to make her way over when Nik appeared before her.

'Fran. How are you getting on?'

'Fine,' she replied. 'I was on my way to tell Jim how much I like his bald head.'

Nik nodded. 'Can I tell *you* something?'

Fran eyed him suspiciously. 'Why do I get the feeling I'm not going to like it?'

'Sometimes we have to tell people things they don't want to hear at first and then they come to realize that we're actually being kind.'

'Cruel to be kind?' she suggested.

'If you like.'

'Go on then – hit me.'

Nik fixed her with a knowing look. 'Humour is a wonderful thing – it helps us through the toughest times but you have to be careful that you're not using it as a shield to protect yourself from the things you need to feel.'

Fran stared at him for a second before answering. 'Okay. Thanks for that,' she said, bristling with indignation. 'I'll give it some thought.' *Or alternatively, completely ignore it you bloody Scandi know-it-all.*

Nik's words rang in Fran's ears for the remainder of the evening. She knew he had a point but like a daily dose of Trump news, she didn't want to hear it.

At the end of the session, he drew them together again. 'So. I hope that you can see how much we benefit from small acts of kindness. You are all very kind people, I can see this. But it's easy to live in our own little world sometimes – to go to work, come home and simply live the day-to-day. However, if we reach out – into our community and beyond – everyone benefits. For this week's homework, I want you to find something for your list which enables you to reach outside yourself – to make that connection and make a difference if you can. I think you'll be amazed at how rewarding this can be.'

And then he accused me of using humour as a shield, reported Fran indignantly, rearranging the cushions and lying back on the sofa.

And do you think he has a point?

Probably, she shrugged. Let's just say I prefer laughing to crying.

Fair enough. And what about the gardening? Do you think it will help? he asked.

Ask me again tomorrow night. I'm going for it – Barry's going to help me start to clear ours in the morning and then I've offered to go round and tidy up a little old lady's garden in the afternoon.

Wow, you're really throwing yourself into it, aren't you?'

Oh yeah, I'm a regular Monty Don. And Alan is looking forward to taking on the role of Nigel. We're a dream team.

I hope it brings you what you need.

Fran smiled. Me too.

As she carried the tray containing coffee and a plate of ginger snap biscuits into the spring sunshine, Fran realized with a certain amount of satisfaction that today was turning out to be a very good day.

'Coffee's up!' she cried. Barry emerged grinning from the undergrowth, like David Attenborough after an astonishing new naturalist discovery.

'It's an absolute treasure trove in there!' he declared. 'Come and see!'

'What have we got?' She smiled, handing him a mug and feeling a spark of excitement.

'Just look at this hydrangea!' said Barry, making a sweeping gesture with his arm as if introducing a famous movie star. 'If we clear the ivy from round the roots, that's going to be a beauty! And I can't believe this rhododendron – it's huge!'

204

There were day lilies and roses, lavender, rosemary and vast swathes of hardy geraniums.

'Be careful of those,' said Barry, giving the geraniums a suspicious prod. 'They'll take over your garden if you let them.' Fran smiled. It was like a new world opening up and she loved it. 'All we need to do is clear the weeds to give them a bit of space and they should start to flourish within weeks. And then we can make space for your new plants.'

'It's wonderful. Thank you, Barry,' she said.

'My pleasure – I'm happy to help. Pammy always says that I spend too much time in the garden but I enjoy it – it's the place where I feel most at home.'

Fran nodded. 'I get that, I really do. I haven't had a proper chance to garden since before the kids were born. It feels as if I've been reunited with an old friend.'

Barry smiled. 'I'm always here if you need any advice. Sorry I can't give you a hand at Elsie's this afternoon.'

'Don't you worry, you've got a dream date to prepare for. Are you looking forward to it?'

'I'm a bit nervous to be honest but glad I've got you girls directing me. Heather's coming round at four.'

Fran nodded. 'And then Charlie and I will be round by half five. It's going to be wonderful. All you have to do is talk and listen.'

Barry nodded uncertainly. 'Talk and listen. Right. Well, we'd better get back to it. Lots to do!'

After Barry left, Fran made herself a sandwich and sank into the nearest chair. Her back ached, her calf muscles were sore and she had scratches up and down her arms, but she hadn't felt so positive about the world in ages. Alan's ears pricked up as the doorbell rang.

Fran hauled herself to her feet, ready with a frown for the inevitable cold caller.

'Woah, someone looks cross,' said Gary with a teasing smile.

205

Fran laughed. 'I thought you were a Jehovah's Witness,' she said, surprised at how pleased she was to see him. 'Do you want to come in? I'm just grabbing a sandwich before I head out. I could make you one too?'

'If you're sure? That would be great, thanks.'

'Aren't you meant to be shouting at poor unsuspecting boot-campers?' she asked as he followed her into the kitchen.

'The advantage of being the boss is that you can take time off whenever you like,' he said.

'Good for you. So what brings you here?' After the disastrous trip to the art gallery, Fran was pretty sure that she'd never see Gary again.

'I saw Pamela this morning.'

'Oh yes?' said Fran with an air of dread.

Gary smiled. 'It's fine. She told me that you were in need of a strapping lad to help with your garden so I thought I'd pop round and offer my services.'

Fran placed a sandwich in front of him and slid into the chair opposite. 'Gary—' she began.

He held up his hands. 'Fran, you don't need to say anything. I just want to be your friend. That's all. I like you and I want to help you, if you'll let me?'

She gazed into his kind face and felt her stomach dip with something unexpected – was it longing? She shook off the feeling before she answered. 'Just friends?'

'Just friends.'

She fixed him with a look. 'Okay. How would you like to come and help me tidy an old lady's garden this afternoon?'

Gary picked up his sandwich ready to take a bite. 'Best offer I've had all year,' he grinned.

Fran took a deep breath and grasped the plant tightly.

'Right, come on then, you bastard. You've picked the wrong woman to mess with today.'

She gave a sharp tug. As the roots emerged from the earth, she sat down hard on her backside with the tenacious weed and all its gnarly roots held aloft like a trophy. 'Yesssss! Get in! Got you, you bugger!'

'Remind me never to get on the wrong side of you!' laughed Gary, pulling at a spiky bramble that kept coming, like a line of scarves from a magician's sleeve. 'Ow! That is bloody vicious!'

'Who knew gardening could be so dangerous?' grinned Fran, rubbing her sore behind.

'Tell me about it,' said Gary.

'Well, keep going,' bossed Fran. 'We've got about another three hundred of the blighters to go.'

'Yesss, ma'am,' said Gary with a smiling salute.

They worked in companionable silence, which was broken only when one of them drew the other's attention to a particularly impressive weed or commented on how well they were doing. Fran couldn't remember the last time she'd relished such a challenge. Pruning back a chaotic buddleia may not seem a big deal to most people but she found it endlessly satisfying. She realized that the world paused while she was working, her brain stilled, the whirr of distracting thoughts quietened for a while. She also realized that Gary was the ideal gardening companion, particularly when she needed extra muscle – he managed to pull up several deep-rooted enemy weeds without breaking a sweat.

'Oh, you're doing a marvellous job!' cried Elsie, carrying a tray of drinks into the garden. 'I thought you might like a glass of squash.'

'You're an angel, Elsie,' said Fran, accepting her drink and passing one to Gary.

Elsie beamed at them both, her eyes twinkling with delight. 'It's lovely having a strong man for a husband, isn't it?' she declared. 'I do miss my Reggie – he was a big muscly man like your Gary.'

Fran opened her mouth to correct Elsie when Gary interjected.

'Feel free to call on us any time, Elsie – we're happy to help, aren't we, Fran?'

Fran stared up at him and smiled. 'Absolutely. Any time.'

Every inch of Fran's body ached as they left Elsie's house later that afternoon. 'All I can think about is sinking into a bath full of Radox,' she groaned.

'You deserve it,' said Gary.

'Thanks for your help. I enjoyed this afternoon.'

'Me too.' He smiled.

'And I'm glad you stopped me correcting Elsie when she mistook us for a couple.'

'She misses her husband – I didn't see any point in making her sadder.'

'It was a nice thing to do,' she told him.

He shrugged modestly as they reached his car. 'What can I say? I'm a nice guy.' She laughed. 'See you around, Fran Parker. Have a good weekend.'

'Bye,' said Fran, waving him off. An unexpected realization trickled into her brain as she walked up the front path. It was familiar but long forgotten – something she hadn't experienced for a while. It wasn't longing, that was too strong a word. It was something smaller – like a whispered wish, so quiet even Fran could barely hear it.

It would be nice to see him again.

She smiled to herself, like a child with a secret – a secret she would never share, but one which she treasured all the same.

Chapter Eighteen

Pamela

My Happiness List
1. Just bake
2. Dinner with Matthew and Barry – be in the moment! (DISASTER)
3. Go dancing with Barry? (Not likely)
4. Laugh like we used to! (with Heather instead)
5. Try something new – lovely trip to art gallery with Fran & Charlie (and Gary!)
6. Teach other people how to bake
7. Let Matty go and be kinder to Barry

20.28, Thursday, 14 April 2016
Hi Mum,

Just wanted to let you know that I'm okay and having a great time in sunny LA! Sorry I haven't been in touch before but I assumed Dad would have filled you in. I hope you're managing to sort things with him. He's right – I have been a waste of space but I'm sorting that, I promise. I hope to have good news for you soon but I can't say more at the moment. Thanks for believing in me and thanks also for telling me what I needed to hear. You're right – I need to stand on my own two feet instead of letting you hold me up. And I'm sorry if I haven't always told you this but I love you. You're an amazing mum and an inspiring woman – I don't think you always realize that.

I'll be in touch again soon.

Love,

Matthew x

Pamela wiped away a tear of pride as she reread the message. Los Angeles! Wait until she told Heather and Fran. She also felt a wave of guilt. It was clear that Barry and Matthew were on better terms than she'd thought. She'd accused Barry of not seeing her point of view but maybe she'd been refusing to see his too. Pamela realized that her anger had waned a little and she was definitely softening towards her husband. She'd been grateful when he'd come to her aid with Heather and Luke's dance lesson and was touched by the way he'd helped Fran with her garden. He still had a lot to learn about his own wife but he was a good man. She knew that. Her phoned buzzed with a call and she almost laughed when she saw who it was.

'Barry! How funny – I was just thinking about you.'

'Were you, Pammy? All good I hope.'

'Not all bad,' she replied. *Keep him on his toes, Pammy.* 'I've had an email from Matthew in LA.'

'Oh yes.' Barry didn't sound surprised.

'Why didn't you tell me?' she demanded.

'You wouldn't exactly let me get a word in edgeways, Pammy.'

'I was angry.'

'Yes. I got that.'

Pamela laughed. 'Good. Because you need to hear it,' she insisted before admitting, 'and maybe I do too.'

Barry cleared his throat. Pamela could tell he was nervous. 'Perhaps we could start tonight.'

'Tonight?' Pamela was caught off guard.

'Yes. I was wondering if you might like to come to dinner?'

'Are you cooking?' she teased.

'I am,' he said proudly. 'So will you come? Please?'

She hesitated. She was still cross about so many things but she could tell that Barry was trying and you had to give people a chance, particularly when you'd been married to them for nearly forty years. 'All right. What time?'

The hall was chaotic and noisy, and the kitchen felt unbearably stuffy. Pamela feared she was having a hot flush and pushed open the fire door to let in some air. She was starting to wonder if this was a good idea. She'd been so buoyed by the success of the baking workshop and inspired by the idea of doing more in the community that she'd suggested this afternoon's baking class to Angel without really thinking it through. She'd been shocked to see nine mums all with various numbers of kids in tow waiting for her to arrive. Pamela had brought out some toys that she usually used for toddler group and was now nervously sorting out her ingredients and baking equipment, wondering how on earth to make this a success.

But Pamela hadn't reckoned on Angel. As one of the older single mums, she was their unofficial leader and organizer. She appeared in the doorway of the kitchen.

'Right, Mrs T, shall we get started? How about you teach three of us at a time while the others mind the kids?'

Pamela smiled at her gratefully. 'That sounds like a good plan, Angel dear. Sorry, I'm a bit all over the place this afternoon,' she said, fanning herself with a baking tray.

'Don't sweat it, Mrs T – s'good of you to do this for us. Shall I get the first three in?'

'Please, Angel.'

Angel turned back towards the hall, put two fingers in her mouth and gave a loud, expert whistle. Everyone, children included, fell into silence.

'Oi, listen up! Leila, Dee – you're with me. Everyone else, watch the kids and try to keep it down so that we can hear what Mrs T is saying, will ya?' The hubbub lessened to a murmur. Satisfied, Angel turned back to Pamela. 'Right, Mrs T, let's do this!'

Within ten minutes, Pamela had forgotten her nerves and realized that she was enjoying every second. She taught the girls how to make banana and blueberry muffins. They listened to what she told them and followed her instructions but they also had fun too – nudging each other when they were trying to weigh out ingredients, joking and singing. Pamela had always been fond of this group of mums and she realized that it was because she admired the way they supported one another. She knew they had tough lives – she knew for a fact that most of them regularly went to the local food bank – but it didn't seem to dampen their spirits. They were always laughing, always having fun. They understood that life was about more than what you had and that if you had friends – people you loved, people who supported you – you could get by. Pamela admired that and felt pleased to be invited into their world.

'You've all done brilliantly,' she declared as they shared the muffins at the end of the session. 'Well done.'

'That was great, Mrs T, thanks.' Angel grinned. 'These muffins are sick!'

Pamela looked nonplussed.

'That's a good thing,' Leila assured her.

'I might have a go at doing some baking with the kids,' said Dee.

'I think you should,' smiled Pamela. 'And maybe next time we could get the kiddies involved?'

'Next time?' asked Angel, her eyes shining. 'Are you sure you want to sign yourself up for that, Mrs T?' Nine pairs of eyes looked at Pamela hopefully.

Pamela beamed. 'I think it would be sick!' she declared.

The girls giggled. 'Thass it, Mrs T – you got it!' laughed Angel, shaking her head in amusement. 'You got it.'

Pamela arrived back at Heather's house feeling tired but elated. She was surprised to find the house empty and decided to take a shower in preparation for the evening. As she got ready, she realized that she was excited and oddly nervous about what lay ahead. It felt strange to be going round to her own house for dinner – she'd eaten at that table with Barry hundreds of times before, after all. It was the fact that he'd invited her which made the difference. It felt like a date and that felt rather lovely too.

She put on the only dress she'd packed and brushed her hair, before applying a little make-up and dabbing her favourite perfume behind each ear and on her wrists. She checked herself in the mirror. 'Not bad for an old bird,' she said, smiling at her reflection.

The sky was a beautiful shade of peach and lemon as she walked along Hope Street – it made her feel hopeful and positive, as if the world was somehow full of promise again. As she reached her house, the door opened. Barry stood on the front step wearing a tuxedo and a nervous smile. He'd clearly been looking out for her through the lounge window.

'Pammy,' he said. 'You look beautiful.'

As Pamela walked towards him, she forgot her annoyance for a moment. It was as if the years fell away. They were teenagers again, meeting at that first dance, star-struck, nervous and excited. She reached out a hand to him and he kissed it – a small, sweet kiss that brought a lump to her throat.

Pamela allowed Barry to lead her inside. The walls and banisters were decorated with fairy lights. As he led her into the dining room, she noticed vases of fresh flowers and tea-light candles in jars on every surface. Her heart gave a skip of delight.

'This is wonderful,' she breathed, as Barry helped her out of her coat.

213

'I had a little help,' admitted Barry. 'Actually, I had a lot of help.'

'Don't listen to him,' said a voice behind them.

'Fran!' Pamela smiled, reaching forwards to hug her friend. 'And Heather!' she added, spotting her in the doorway.

'And me!' cried Charlie, bouncing into the dining room. 'I did the lights *and* the flowers,' she added proudly.

'It's wonderful,' she said, opening her arms to them. 'My happiness buddies,' murmured Pamela as they gathered into a group hug.

'We are merely the facilitators,' said Fran with a grin, plucking two glasses of champagne from a tray and handing them to Pamela and Barry. 'This evening is all about you two so take a seat, enjoy your champagne and we'll bring you your starters in a second.'

'Thank you,' said Pamela. 'I mean it, really – thank you all.' Fran, Heather and Charlie smiled with satisfaction before disappearing from the room.

Pamela felt rather overwhelmed as they sat down at the table. No one had ever done anything like this for her before and she was jittery with nerves as she sat down opposite Barry. She smoothed a hand over the linen tablecloth, noticing the way that everything had been laid with table runners and napkins. A large jar of fairy lights sat between them casting a magical glow.

'Is this all right?' asked Barry nervously. 'I tried to remember how you like it with that runner thing and the napkins but you know how cack-handed I am sometimes.'

'It's perfect.' Pamela smiled. She held up her glass. 'Cheers.'

'Cheers,' said Barry, seeming to relax a little.

Fran appeared with two plates closely followed by Heather carrying the champagne bottle and Charlie smiling behind, her face eager and excited. 'Madam, sir, may I present your starters?' said Fran. 'Smoked salmon pâté served with wholemeal bread from the esteemed Taylor-made bakery. Enjoy.'

'I buttered the bread,' said Charlie.

'Clever girl,' said Pamela, pulling her into a hug.

'And a drop more champagne for you both,' said Heather, topping up their glasses. 'Bon appétit.'

They disappeared back to the kitchen. Pamela glanced at Barry. 'Doesn't this look wonderful?' she said. He nodded. The atmosphere felt uncomfortable, all the unsaid truths buzzing above their heads like flies. Pamela took a sip of champagne and felt her body relax. 'So how have you been?' she asked as she spread some pâté on the bread.

'Oh fine, you know, busy in the garden. I'm enjoying helping Fran sort hers too – she's a natural.'

'That's good,' said Pamela. 'She's a lovely girl and she's been through so much. She deserves to be happy.'

'Yes, that's very true. She does.' Pamela took another gulp of her drink. 'And how have you been?' ventured Barry, wincing slightly at their over-polite chat.

'Fine, thank you. I've been teaching some young mums to bake today.'

'Oh yes. How did that go?' asked Barry, visibly relieved to have thought of a question.

'Very well actually – we all enjoyed it.'

'That's good.' Barry nodded, with a slight look of panic as he tried to think of what to say next.

'We made banana and blueberry muffins,' offered Pamela, realizing that he was floundering.

'Oh, those are delicious, Pammy – one of your best recipes.'

'Thank you.'

He nodded vaguely. 'Absolutely delicious.'

They had finished their starters and Pamela realized that she had also finished her champagne. She felt woozy but also discouraged. After a fortnight away from home, was this how their conversation was going to go? Was this all they had to say to one another? Maybe she'd been right to leave. Maybe you couldn't

215

stay connected to one person for your whole life. Maybe 'till death us do part' was just a big fat lie.

'All done?' asked Fran, peering around the door.

'Yes thank you, lovey,' said Pamela. 'That was delicious.'

Fran and Charlie cleared away the plates while Heather topped up the champagne. Heather was grinning at Pamela, trying to read her mind so Pamela gave her as reassuring a smile as she could muster. Moments later they returned with the main course.

'Chicken and mushroom pie with mashed potato, carrots and greens – Barry said it was your favourite,' said Fran.

'I chopped the carrots,' said Charlie.

'They look amazing,' Pamela told her.

'And some wine,' added Heather, pouring them each a glass.

Pamela glanced over at her husband who was gazing back with a look of uncertainty – like a little boy asking for a sweet. She smiled again. 'This looks amazing. Thank you, thank you all so much.'

'Like I said, we were mere helpers – this is all down to Bazza,' said Fran. 'Right, we're going to leave you to it. Barry, are you okay with the iPad or do you want me to show you again?'

'No, I'll be fine. Thank you, Fran, Heather, Charlie – you've been wonderful.'

'It's our pleasure,' said Heather with a grin. 'Have a lovely evening.'

'Yeah – have all the fun!' cried Charlie, reaching over to hug first Barry and then Pamela.

Pamela squeezed the little girl to her and looked into her eyes. 'Never change, Charlie,' she said.

'I'll try, although I would like to be a bit taller,' said Charlie earnestly.

Fran laughed and put an arm around her daughter's shoulder. 'Come on, you,' she said, leading her towards the door.

'Aww, I wish we could stay,' said Charlie.

Fran shook her head. 'Not tonight but listen, we're going to go home now, order pizza and watch a movie.'

'Yessss!' said Charlie, punching the air. 'Can Heather come too?'

'If she's got nothing better to do,' said Fran, looking at her.

'I would love that,' said Heather.

'Double yesss!' declared Charlie. They laughed. Fran paused at the door to give Pamela a big thumbs-up. She smiled in reply. There was a hubbub of Charlie's excited chatter as they left the house and then silence as the front door clicked shut behind them.

'Well,' said Pamela, wishing that Charlie was still there to fill the space with cheerful noise. 'This is all perfect.'

'Is it?' asked Barry with genuine concern. Pamela flicked her gaze towards him. 'Because things haven't exactly been perfect, have they, Pammy?'

Here it comes, thought Pamela. She was pleased at how calm she felt. She was ready for this. She stabbed a carrot with her fork. 'No, I suppose they haven't.'

'I know things got out of hand with Matthew and I am sorry.' Pamela nodded encouragement. This felt like progress and she realized she needed to listen too. 'I suppose I was just trying to protect you from being disappointed but I ended up making things worse.'

'It was like a battle zone, Barry.'

'I know. Which is why I gave Matthew the money to go to America.'

'Did you?' Pamela stared at him in surprise and saw a kind man, trying to do the right thing.

'We talked properly and he told me about his dream. It felt like the right thing to do. He's promised to pay me back and I trust him now.'

'It's important to listen and trust,' admitted Pamela. 'I'm sorry if I didn't listen to you.'

Barry nodded. 'At least we're trying now, eh? I'm so glad you came here tonight, Pammy. I want things to be how they were. I want you back.'

Pamela took a deep breath. She knew she'd jumped to the wrong conclusion about Matthew and was glad that they'd called a truce but she still needed Barry to listen to her. To hear what she needed. She looked him in the eye. 'I don't want things to be how they were, Barry. I want things to be different.' It gave her courage just saying this out loud.

'O-kay,' said Barry uncertainly. 'Is this because I wouldn't go dancing with you?'

'No!' cried Pamela. Barry looked shocked as Pamela shook her head. 'Not really, although that sort of goes to show everything that's wrong with us!'

Barry stared at her in desperation. 'Please, Pammy. Please tell me. I want to make things better – I'm sorry.'

She looked at him, hopeful that he might finally be listening. 'I've done a lot of thinking over the past few weeks about who I am. Me. Pamela. A sixty-five-year-old woman. The world writes you off when you hit my age and it's hard to work out who you are. I've spent so many years being a wife and mother. And now the kids have grown up, they don't need me anymore and I miss that – I miss being needed. I miss the small arms round my neck and the noses to wipe.' She gave a fond smile before continuing. 'But I've accepted that – I've had to. And I've found other people who need me – Angel and her friends and Heather and Fran and dear Charlie, she's become like a granddaughter to me. Do you know, I felt needed and appreciated for the first time in ages? And it made me happy, Barry, really happy.' Barry was watching her face with rapt attention, as if he was seeing his wife for the first time. 'And then there's you and me,' she went on. 'Barry and Pamela. Husband and wife. I've done a lot of thinking about us too.'

'Oh yes,' said Barry looking worried.

Pamela nodded. 'Yes. I feel as if you take me for granted, Barry. As if you've stopped seeing the woman you fell in love with. You go through the motions, eat your meals and then lose yourself in your garden. You spend more time with your roses than you do with me!' Barry's face was sad and full of regret. 'And I know I'm just a frumpy old woman. I know I'm a bit fat and wrinkly but I'm still a woman and I'm still your wife. I still need you to notice me, to need me.' She wiped away a stray tear and looked at him. 'I had to tell you the truth before it's too late.'

Barry stared at her for a second before nodding. 'Wait here,' he said, disappearing from the room.

Pamela sat for a moment wondering if this was the end. Maybe it was too late. She'd poured out her heart to him and he'd said nothing. Surely she deserved better than that. She heard the opening strains of 'Fly Me to The Moon' float through the speakers and the hairs on the back of her neck stood up.

Barry appeared before her, his face smiling. 'Remember this?'

Pamela nodded. 'Of course – it was playing the first night we met.'

He held out a hand. 'Dance with me, Pammy.'

She hesitated for a second and then smiled as she stood up. Barry gave a small bow before pulling her close and they began to dance. She wondered if she might be transported back to that night, their first dance surrounded by other dancing couples who became a blur as she and Barry lost themselves in one another. But she felt very much rooted in her house, in this moment – the thrill of being close to her husband was there but it was sixty-five-year-old Pamela experiencing it and it felt like a new kind of wonderful.

As the music finished, Barry kissed her hand. 'I'm not good with words but I'll do my best. You are the most beautiful woman I have ever known. From the moment I met you, I knew that I couldn't live without you. I love you more than my roses, crumble and custard and everything else that's good in the world.' Pamela gave a tearful laugh. 'I am sorry if I have ever made you feel less than the adored woman you are and deserve to be. Forgive me, Pammy, but don't leave me – I'm nothing without you.'

Pamela stared into his eyes. It was quite simply the loveliest thing anyone had ever said to her. 'I do love you, Barry Trott, and I will stay but there need to be changes.'

'Absolutely.' Barry nodded. 'Whatever you need.'

Pamela smiled because she believed him. He had listened and he understood. 'So what's for dessert?' she asked.

'We-ell, I did make this cake…'

'You made a cake!' she laughed.

'It didn't turn out very well.' He winced.

'Show me.'

Barry disappeared to the kitchen and came back moments later with a sponge cake that looked more like two biscuits sandwiched together with buttercream. 'It's terrible,' said Barry, shaking his head.

Pamela took his face in her hands and kissed him. 'It's wonderful. But it's not what I want for dessert – well, not yet anyway. Shall we go upstairs?'

A look of shock closely followed by delight spread across Barry's face. He put down the cake and kissed his wife again. She smiled, took his hand and led him from the room.

Chapter Nineteen

Heather

Happiness List
1. Marry Luke!
2. Sunday walk and choose wedding venue with Luke Fran & Charlie
3. Exercise more (persuade Luke to go running?)
- Boot camp with Fran & Pamela
4. Go dress shopping with Gemma and laugh like we used to!
Fran & Pamela - laughed like teenagers!
5. Surprise Luke at work
6. Ask Pamela for help with first dance for wedding!
7. Help Pamela & Barry fall in love again

'Dear friends,' said Nik, 'it pains me to break this to you but after today we only have two more sessions!' There was a collective groan of disappointment. 'So, I thought it would be helpful if we took a brief moment to review our own happiness lists to see where we are and what we can do to realize our goals. Let's take fifteen minutes to discuss with our buddies.'

'I like to think of mine as a work in progress,' declared Fran, holding out her journal for inspection.

Pamela and Heather took the book and studied it for a while, their brows furrowed with concentration. Pamela smiled. 'I think you're making great progress, lovey. You do the digital detox with the kids – Charlie has told me how much she loves that – and I always see you out with Alan.'

'And you're doing the gardening,' said Heather. 'And helping the local community by—' she read out loud '—"*working myself into an early grave by helping local elderly people get control of their overgrown gardens*".'

'Most fun I've had in ages,' admitted Fran.

'And you did try going out with Gary,' offered Pamela.

Fran winced. 'Poor Gary. I'm making progress with everything apart from men.'

'I think you need to stop giving yourself such a hard time,' Heather told her. 'Grief is ongoing, it never leaves you. You're finding a way to live around that and you're doing brilliantly. I basically hid from mine until I found Luke.'

Fran nodded. 'I wish you'd been my counsellor, would have saved me a lot of bother. And money.'

Heather laughed. 'Keep going – you'll get there.'

Fran smiled. 'Thanks, fam.'

'What about you, Heather?' asked Pamela. 'How's your list going?' Heather held open her notebook for inspection. 'Aww, Heather, you put Barry and me on there!'

'All you need to do is tick off that big "marry Luke" goal and you'll be living the dream,' said Fran with a grin.

Heather nodded. She couldn't believe how much had happened in the weeks since she'd written this at the top of her list – her ultimate happiness goal, the thing that would finally complete her. And yet, she'd had her doubts. She knew Luke loved her but she'd questioned his commitment to their relationship with all the late-working and broken promises. Still, they seemed to have turned a corner since their weekend away. Something about him had changed, as if he'd suddenly got it. He understood what she needed – what they both needed.

'And is he still working all hours, Heather?' asked Pamela, looking concerned.

Heather shook her head. 'Since our weekend away, he's been home by seven every day. It's all good.'

Pamela patted her arm. 'That's great news! I'm glad you're getting to spend a bit more time together – you need that. I expect it helps not having me under your feet.'

'Not at all – I miss your cakes and your face!' said Heather. Pamela smiled. 'Anyway, we've got Freddy's christening this weekend and I'm looking forward to it. Gemma knows Luke – she was the one who introduced us in the first place – but it will be good for him to meet my aunt and uncle properly. They're the only family I have left now.'

'Here's hoping the baby doesn't puke in the font, like Jude did at his,' remarked Fran.

Heather and Pamela laughed.

'So, tonight's topic is resilience,' said Nik a while later. 'It may seem unusual to have it as part of this course, but, in fact, resilience is a big part of maintaining happiness because without it, we aren't able to bounce back when life is tough. And if we are unable to bounce back, we're left feeling helpless and hopeless.'

'Been there, done that,' muttered Fran. Heather gave her a sympathetic nudge.

'Obviously, we have to deal with all sorts of difficult situations in life,' said Nik. 'We have big issues to cope with – money or job worries, illness or grief. But, of course, there are smaller examples – when people are unkind or rude, or we feel lonely or sad. My point is, that if something impacts you in a negative way, it is important to have the tools to be able to cope and not allow it to hold you back. So, let's have a brainstorm now where we offer

223

ideas or suggestions of things we've done which have helped to lift us when times are tough. Anyone?'

'Take Alan out for a walk,' said Fran. 'Or pull up weeds whilst swearing violently.'

Everyone laughed. 'Very good, Fran.' Nik smiled. 'Exercise or being outdoors are good ways of lifting your mood. And if the swearing works for you then go for it!'

'I phone my best friend,' said Sue. 'She lives in Devon but we speak every week and she knows me inside out. She's got me through some tough times.'

'Friends are vital when life is hard,' said Nik. 'It's good if you have someone you can count on no matter what – they can get you through the worst of times.'

Ain't that the truth, thought Heather. She couldn't imagine how she would have got through the trauma of losing her parents without Gemma and although she accepted the fact that their relationship had shifted since the arrival of Freddy, she knew that her cousin was always there for her. Heather also knew that Gemma was finding motherhood a challenge and made a vow to always be there for her too. She would talk to Luke and make sure they had Freddy to stay more often for a start. She wanted to be helpful – to support Gemma when she needed her most.

'Thank you for these ideas,' said Nik. 'I think this has given us a lot of food for thought about possible tools for dealing with life's pitfalls. Now I would like to develop the theme further because it stands to reason that there would be no happiness without unhappiness – life is about light and shade. So, in order to do this, we need to consider our unhappiest moments – the times when we felt defeated by life. This may be painful for some of us and you can opt out at any time—' Fran and Heather exchanged knowing glances '—because I want this to be a positive learning experience. If you can work out how to deal with the sadness and the darkness, to face it and not let it overwhelm you, then you will have a very powerful mindset and the ability to face anything life throws at you. I think this might be a good discussion for our individual groups and then if people want to share their thoughts afterwards, they are very welcome.'

Fran, Pamela and Heather turned to one another. Heather felt so at ease with the pair of them now – they were like a family without the petty squabbles.

'I suppose the unhappiest moments in life are always going to be when people die, aren't they?' said Pamela. 'I mean you've had it the worst, Fran – losing your Andy so young.'

'Yeah, I win,' joked Fran. 'But you're right, Pamela – dealing with grief is the pits.'

Pamela nodded. 'The unhappiest moment of my life was when my brother died.'

'I didn't know you had a brother!' cried Heather.

'Ernie.' Pamela smiled. 'My little brother. He died of a brain tumour – he was only twenty.' Heather squeezed her hand. 'You never get over it, do you? But I think you learn to live with it maybe? I married Barry not long afterwards and then threw myself into being a mother. I bet your kids have been a distraction sometimes, Fran.'

Fran nodded. 'Like you wouldn't believe. It's hard to wallow in your misery when there's an eight-year-old with her head stuck in the park railings. That actually happened by the way – Charlie was over the moon because the firemen had to use the Jaws of Life.' Pamela and Heather laughed. 'But yeah, family get you through, whether you want them to or not. And friends of course,' she added with a meaningful look.

Heather nodded. 'Gemma dragged me on every night out going after Mum and Dad died, she wouldn't let me stay in at all. She was with me the night I met Luke – she told him that I was the woman of his dreams. She's the reason we're together. I owe her everything.'

The three friends smiled at one another. 'We're lucky to have people like these in our lives, aren't we?' said Fran. 'They stop us going under. I'd have completely lost the plot if it wasn't for my kids and my mother.' She leant forwards and whispered, 'Obviously don't ever tell her I said that.'

Pamela and Heather chuckled.

'So, how have we been getting on?' asked Nik a while later. 'It's hard, isn't it sometimes, to think about the unhappy times? Much easier to box them away perhaps and not deal with them. But I promise you that if you can think in advance about what you need to do when life gets bad, you will find your resilience and be able to deal with pretty much anything. These things are never planned, are they? We never quite know how we'll react when the time comes. But, if you have the tools ready in your mind – like going for a walk in the woods or a friend you can rely on – you will find a way to cope and not allow yourself to be defeated.'

'I get by with a little help from my friends?' suggested Fran.

'Definitely. And I have to tell you that you all have some pretty strong tools in this room right now.' They looked at one another and smiled. Nik gestured around the room. 'These people are your tools – your friends, your support – don't forget that. And you will have others, outside this room and other ways of dealing with the darkness. Add these to your happiness lists this week – the people and things who get you through the difficult times. Identify them and keep them close. You never know when you'll need them.'

'Heth, do you have any idea where my silver-grey tie is?'

'Have you tried the wardrobe?'

'That was the first place I looked but it's not—oh, hang on, yeah, it's here.'

'Okay, great. We need to leave in ten minutes!'

Heather tried to shake off the prickle of irritation. For some reason, she got the feeling that Luke was trying to wriggle out of going to the christening. He woke complaining of a headache and wore a look on his face that seemed to be imploring her to let him stay at home.

She had remained largely unsympathetic. This was her godson's christening and not just her godson – he was Gemma's son. Gemma, her oldest, dearest and most valued friend. 'I'll make coffee and fetch you paracetamol and some water. You're probably dehydrated after finishing off that bottle of wine last night.'

'Oh,' said Luke sounding surprised. 'Okay. Thanks.'

'You'll feel better after a shower too. That always works for me.'

'Yeah. Probably,' he replied vaguely, watching her leave the bedroom. He had followed her instructions but now seemed to be dragging his heels, unable to find everything from an ironed shirt to his tie.

Heather placed the engraved cufflinks wrapped with gold tissue paper inside the gift bag and finished writing the card.

To Freddy.
With love on your Christening Day,
Auntie Heather
xxxxx

'Do you want to sign Freddy's card?' she called up the stairs. 'Oh, you're here, good. How are you feeling?'

Luke clutched at his neck. 'Actually, my throat is pretty sore and I'm worried about giving my germs to Freddy. Do you think I should stay home?'

Heather was surprised at how determined she felt. 'No, I do not. You're fine – just take a bottle of water with you in the car. Honestly, Luke, it's almost as if you're trying to get out of coming. Freddy is my godson and Gemma is my best friend. Now, please, can we get going?'

Luke seemed taken aback but nodded. 'Yeah, okay – let's go. I'm sure I'll be fine.'

'Great,' said Heather, stuffing the card in its envelope and grabbing the gift and her handbag.

* * *

227

There were already at least a dozen people gathered outside the church as Heather and Luke pulled up and parked in the lane. The sky was the colour of a fading bruise – yellow and purple – the threat of rain inevitable. Heather grabbed her umbrella from the back seat as the first drops of rain fell and a gust of wind took her breath away. The assembled guests were already hurrying into the church as Luke and Heather joined the back of the queue.

'I'm just nipping to the loo,' said Luke, disappearing through a side door without waiting for an answer.

'Fine,' muttered Heather. He'd barely spoken in the car, which was doing nothing to ease the irritation she'd been feeling with him all morning. He clearly didn't want to be here and she was annoyed that he was spoiling her enjoyment of the day. She spotted Gemma and Freddy, standing with Heather's aunt and felt immediately cheered by the sight of her family.

'Heather, how lovely to see you!' cried her aunt, pulling Heather into a tight hug.

'Edda,' beamed Freddy, reaching out for her.

'He says that all the time now,' said Gemma with a weary edge to her voice.

Heather noticed that Gemma looked tired – purple shadows rimmed her eyes and there was a hint of red that suggested she'd been crying. Heather kissed her cousin's cheek. 'Take the weight off and give him to me for a bit,' she said. Gemma smiled weakly and handed over her son. Heather grinned as she took Freddy into her arms. 'Hello, you,' she said, planting a raspberry-kiss on his cheek. He giggled and gave her an open-mouthed kiss in reply. Heather felt as if she'd come home. *This is my family, these are the ones who are here for me whatever.* 'So, how are you doing?' she asked, nudging Gemma's arm.

'Fine, thanks,' sighed Gemma, although she didn't sound convinced. 'Where's Luke?'

'He went to find the loo. Between you and me, I have the feeling he was trying to get out of coming today.'

'Oh really?' said Gemma, looking worried.

Heather nodded. 'I think he's still a bit unsure about babies, you know?' She kissed Freddy on the forehead. 'But I'm sure that a bit of quality time with this gorgeous dude will sort him out, right?' Gemma gave a vague nod, darting a glance towards the back of the church. Heather touched her on the arm. 'Listen, Gem, let me know when you want us to have Freddy for the night again – I want to help.'

Gemma stared at her cousin for a second before her eyes started to fill with tears. 'Oh Heth,' she cried, putting a hand to her mouth.

'Hey, Gem. Don't cry. It's okay. Everything's going to be okay. Listen, you go and take a minute. I'll keep Freddy amused.'

Gemma looked pale but nodded. 'Okay. Thank you.'

'No probs,' said Heather, squeezing her arm. She could see that Gemma wasn't herself and was determined to do all she could to help. 'Freddy and I will be fine, won't we?'

'Edda,' confirmed Freddy.

'Thanks,' said Gemma, hurrying to the back of the church.

'Where's Gemma going?' asked Heather's aunt, oblivious to her daughter's tears.

'I think she needed something from the car,' said Heather.

Marian nodded. 'So-o. How are the wedding plans going?'

'Good, thanks,' replied Heather. 'The venue's booked, the dress is ordered so we're well on the way.'

'I'm glad,' said Marian, squeezing her shoulder. 'Your mum and dad would be very proud of you.'

'Thank you.' Heather nodded. 'I feel as if I'm in a good place.' It was true. She felt as if her relationship with Luke had moved from the infatuation stage to something more open and honest. They understood one another better, had acknowledged each other's needs, and Heather felt that they were ready to make a proper commitment. Relationships took effort but it would be worth it in the end.

'You look happy,' said Marian, smiling at her niece. 'And I'm looking forward to meeting Luke properly. Ah, here's my lovely son-in-law. Everything okay, Ed?'

Ed gave a genial nod. 'Everything's fine. Hey, Heather, it's great to see you,' he said, leaning down to kiss her.

'Dadda,' insisted Freddy, reaching out for his father.

'Come here then, mister,' said Ed. 'Let's rescue Auntie Heather from the clutches of the drool monster.'

'I'm happy to be drooled on any time.'

Ed laughed. 'I'll remember that. So, did you have a good time the other night?'

Heather looked puzzled. 'What other night?'

Ed frowned. 'That Friday a week or so ago – you were out with Gemma? Or was it such a big night that you completely forgot?'

Heather shook her head. 'No, that wasn't me. Gem and I haven't been out for ages.'

'Oh,' said Ed, his frown deepening slightly. 'I must have got it wrong – I was sure Gemma said she was out in town with you. She took to her bed for most of the weekend so I assumed it was a post-girls' night out hangover. Maybe I got it wrong.'

'Yes, maybe,' said Heather, feeling a knot of unease start to curl in her stomach.

It was a beautiful service despite the storm raging outside the church. Freddy was an absolute angel and a total crowd-pleaser as he giggled his way through the whole thing.

'I've never had a baby do that before,' said the vicar, impressed.

Freddy only started to cry during the photographs afterwards. Marian was organizing them into groups. 'Right, so, Luke, you hold Freddy for this one,' she insisted.

'Erm, okay,' said Luke, accepting him from Ed's arms.

'Just let him perch on your arm, mate,' advised Ed, noticing Luke's nervous face. 'He went through a funny phase a month or so ago but he's pretty happy with anyone now.'

'Great,' said Luke, his shoulders stiffening. Freddy stared at Luke, looking deep into his eyes. His face went from one of joy to suspicion. Heather experienced an odd feeling of déjà vu as his expression dropped and he let out an anguished cry.

'What did you do?' demanded Heather.

'I'm sorry,' snapped Luke. 'I've told you before – I'm not good with babies.'

'He's probably tired,' said Gemma, reaching over and practically snatching Freddy from Luke. 'It's been a busy morning. Mum, can we go? Freddy's had enough and we can do more photos later.'

'Okay, darling.' Marian smiled. 'Let's go back to the house and celebrate!'

Luke was silent in the car on the way over to Gemma's. 'Is everything all right?' Heather asked.

He nodded. 'I'm fine. Sorry. I'm just not feeling great.'

Heather felt a twist of guilt. 'Why don't we show our faces for an hour or so and then go home?'

'Are you sure? I don't want to ruin your day.'

'No, it's fine,' she said, even though deep down she was getting the feeling that it wasn't.

Gemma's mother had laid on a fantastic spread. Everyone said so. 'Why don't you get some food?' Heather told Luke. 'It might make you feel better.'

He nodded. 'Do you want anything?'

She shook her head. 'I'm okay at the moment, thanks. I'm going to catch up with Gem – I've hardly seen her today.' She made her way up the stairs to where Gemma was putting Freddy down for a nap. She paused and smiled at the sight of the happy clown faces which decorated the wooden letters spelling 'Freddy' on the door. Heather peeked through a gap, stopping in her tracks as she saw baby and mother gazing at one another. It was a look of pure, unadulterated love, as if they were the only two people

231

in the world. Then Gemma leant down and blew a raspberry on his tummy. Freddy gurgled with joyful laughter.

Heather chuckled and Gemma looked round. 'Oh hey, Heth. Are you okay?'

Heather walked into the nursery. It was painted bright yellow and the walls were decorated with jungle animal stickers – elephants squirting water, monkeys eating bananas. The room had a sweet, unfamiliar smell to it overlaid with a whiff of baby poo and nappy cream. 'I'm fine. How are you?'

Gemma sighed. 'I'll be okay once I've got his lordship down for a nap and I'm nursing a large glass of wine.'

Heather nodded. 'Come on then, let's go and have a drink together. It feels like ages since we've done that.' She looked at her cousin feeling that twist of unease again. 'So Ed said something funny.'

'Oh yes? Doesn't sound like him – he's been severely lacking a sense of humour lately to be honest,' said Gemma, reaching down to stroke Freddy's cheek. Heather looked at her in surprise. Gemma shrugged. 'Sorry, we're both just tired and it's not all shits and giggles sometimes. Ignore me.' She turned on the baby monitor and followed Heather out of the room. 'What were you saying?'

Heather looked into Gemma's eyes, wanting to gauge her reaction as she spoke. 'So Ed thought you were out on the town with me the other night.'

Gemma stared at her for as second, her eyes narrowing as if deliberating how to answer. 'Oh I know what that was,' she said slowly, looking past Heather. 'I was out with the post-natal mums – bit of a big one as it goes, mothers released into the wild,' she joked, flicking her gaze back to her cousin. 'That's Ed not listening as per usual. He's getting quite good at that as it happens,' added Gemma bitterly.

Heather studied her face for a second. The knot of unease loosened a fraction as she felt a surge of sympathy. 'Is everything okay?' she asked.

Gemma's expression was pained. She opened her mouth as if she wanted to tell her something.

'Gemma! Where are you? The guests are waiting,' called Marian from the bottom of the stairs.

Gemma grimaced. 'Sorry, Heth. Duty calls. I'll catch up with you in a bit, okay?' she said, trudging down the stairs and disappearing into the living room.

'Okay.' Heather nodded, sensing that all was not well. She made her way to the kitchen, helping herself to a glass of juice. Something was telling her that she needed to keep a clear head today. A group of noisy, friendly women had taken up residence and looked as if they were making it their mission to drink all the wine in the house.

'We're the post-natal mums,' announced one of them with a smile.

'I'm Heather – Gemma's cousin,' said Heather.

'Oh, we've heard a lot about you – apparently you're Freddy's favourite.' The woman grinned. Heather smiled. 'I'm Claire by the way. And that's Maddy and Ali.'

'Nice to meet you all,' said Heather. They were a lovely group – full of easy banter and funny stories of motherhood. Heather started to relax, her unease about Gemma's story shrinking. She was sure Gemma was right – Ed had simply got the wrong end of the stick. She had no reason to think that Gemma would lie. It was a simple misunderstanding. Ed and Gemma were clearly having a hard time. She would make her excuses and go and find her in a minute – offer support, see if she could help.

A movement out of the corner of her eye caused her to look towards the front door, where she noticed Luke and Gemma talking. He put a hand on her arm but Gemma shrugged him off. Heather looked away and tried to focus on what the women were saying. When she glanced back towards the hall, Gemma and Luke had disappeared.

'So I said to him, if you think we're having sex a month after

233

I pushed out a baby just because it's your birthday, you've got another think coming!' said Maddy. Heather and the rest of the group laughed.

'I like you,' slurred Ali, putting an arm around Heather's shoulder. 'We're planning a big night out soon – you should come.'

Heather laughed. 'You're gluttons for punishment – didn't you go on a big night out a couple of Fridays ago?'

The mums glanced at one another and shook their heads. 'No. We were waiting for Gemma to give us a date she could do,' said Claire. 'Actually, we should pin her down today.'

Heather felt her mouth go dry as the realization hit her, like a smart slap round the face.

She's lying. You oldest, closest, most trusted friend is lying to you. You bloody, bloody fool.

Heather rushed into the living room. 'Where is she?' she demanded. 'Where's Gemma?'

The room fell silent. Gemma's father approached and put a hand on her shoulder. 'Heather, whatever's the matter?'

'We can't do this, Luke!' came an insistent voice. 'It's wrong.'

They turned as one towards the baby monitor, its red light flashing a warning.

Danger. Danger ahead.

'Who says we can't? Are you telling me you're not attracted to me? Because I was getting a completely different message the other night.'

Marian rushed towards the baby monitor. 'I think we should switch that off.'

'Leave it!' hissed Heather, taking a step forwards.

'Of course I'm attracted to you but Heather suspects. I know her. I can see it in her eyes. And I can't do it to her. She's been through enough. She's like a sister to me. This is wrong and it has to stop.'

'But I love you. I've always loved you. Since that first night in the club – I saw you first but you said you weren't interested because of Ed and then…'

'And then we made a stupid mistake – a moment of madness. But it can't go on.'

Heather looked over at Ed, who had sunk into the nearest chair – they were like a mirror to one another's hurt. 'Heather,' said Marian, reaching for her niece. 'I'm so sorry.'

'Don't touch me,' said Heather, rushing from the room. She ran up the stairs and reached the landing as Gemma and Luke emerged from Freddy's room.

'Heather!' cried Luke, trying to mask his shock. 'I've been looking for you everywhere. I was just saying bye to Gemma because we should really go – I'm starting to feel a bit rough.'

'I'm not surprised,' said Heather quietly, amazed at how calm and in control she felt. 'It must be quite a burden, carrying those lies around with you.' Luke and Gemma exchanged a look that said it all. 'Here's a piece of advice,' said Heather, pointing a finger at them both. 'If you don't want people to know about your grubby little affair, don't broadcast it over the baby monitor.'

Luke gawped at her. 'Heather, listen, I can explain. This is all a mistake.'

Heather turned to face him. 'Yeah. It is. A huge mistake. And it's cost you everything. So, here's what's going to happen. I'm going to drive myself home now. You need to find yourself a car and a place to live and I want all your stuff gone by the end of tomorrow, okay?'

'Heather, don't do this,' said Luke, trying to grab her arm.

She shook him off. 'Don't touch me. It's over.'

'Heather,' said Gemma, her face pale and misting with tears.

Heather turned to face her. 'How could you?'

'I'm so sorry, really I am. It was a stupid mistake. Please don't give up on me,' she cried as the tears fell.

Heather stared into her eyes. 'You were the one who gave up on me, Gemma – always remember that. We are through.'

Heather turned on her heels and walked down the stairs, her body shaking with anger. She hurried to the car and flung herself inside as Gemma's mother rushed out after her. 'Oh, Heather, I'm so sorry,' she cried. 'I can't believe how stupid Gemma's been. Please don't leave – where will you go?'

Heather looked up at her from the driver's seat. 'I know exactly where to go. I'll be fine,' she said, before driving away.

An hour later she parked the car outside her house and walked along Hope Street. She made her way up a familiar garden path and rang the doorbell. There was a sound of movement from inside before the door opened.

'Heather, lovey, whatever's the matter?' asked Pamela, opening her arms to her. Heather accepted the embrace with gratitude and burst into tears.

You can always find the resilience to survive life's dark times – you just need the right people on hand for support. As Heather allowed Pamela to lead her inside, she was surprised that the most overwhelming feeling consuming her was not disappointment, betrayal or even anger, although these were all bubbling under the surface, of course. The overriding emotion she felt at that precise moment, was relief – pure, mind-blowing relief.

Chapter Twenty

Fran

Happiness List Thing
1. Accept a world without Andy (too soon!)
2. 'Digital Detox' day with kids
3. Go on even more walks with Alan
4. Have dinner with a nice man (NOT a date) & laugh if appropriate
(he is nice and I did laugh)
5. Stop feeling guilty and like Gary (EPIC fail)
6. Take up gardening again (with a little help from Baz & Mum)
7. Work myself into an early grave helping local elderly people with their
gardens — most fun I've had in ages
8. Get punched in the face by grief and take it

It was Andy's birthday on Saturday and ever since he'd died, they'd marked it as a family. It felt important. They were honouring his memory, keeping it alive. They didn't do it in a ghoulish way. There was no empty chair at the table, just a meal with Andy's and Fran's parents, her brother Jack, and Andy's best friend, Sam.

Fran looked forward to and dreaded it in equal measure. It was painful to realize that her husband would have been forty-three but forever remained forty-one. It was painful to watch the children grow up without him, as she observed each new milestone alone – one more tooth lost, another prize won, even Jude's hormone-laced mood swings. They all made her catch her breath as she remembered that he was no longer there to share them.

So it was a comfort to mark the day, to get together with his parents and tell them stories of the children or laugh with Sam about how Andy would have reacted to Jude's alarmingly orange hair. It was like going to bed with a hot water bottle when you've got a stomach ache – there was pain but there was something to soothe it too.

However, Fran was starting to wonder if she was the only one who felt this way as the week progressed and the awkward phone calls began. It was Sam who phoned first.

'Hey, Fran,' he cried in a tone that she had become used to from people since Andy died. It was the 'I'm painfully aware that you're a widow,' sympathy tone.

'Hi, Sam.' When Fran first knew Sam, she'd thought that he was a tosser. He and Andy had met at university when their worlds were filled with chasing girls, drinking and behaving like arses. That was fine then but as they'd grown older, Andy had moved away from this world whilst Sam seemed to cling to his wasted youth like a sweaty T-shirt on a hot day.

When Andy and Fran were first together, she'd endured nights out with Sam and his succession of hugely vacuous and hugely breasted girlfriends all called things like Tammy or Tiggy. Eventually she told Andy that she would rather poke herself in the eye with a spork than endure another evening of Sam sharing details of his sordid love life and insisting they consume multiple Jägerbombs.

'You're such a snob, Fran. He's a very sweet guy deep down.'

'He must keep it well hidden,' she'd retorted.

Over time, Sam did change. He was still an idiot but after a failed marriage to the no-nonsense Fiona, he seemed to mellow. Fran was relieved when he only made two inappropriate jokes as best man at their wedding and surprised as he told the room how lucky Andy was to have found such a feisty, intelligent woman to be his soul mate. It was Fran who suggested him as godfather for Jude because she had mellowed too and knew how much Andy loved his friend.

'I'll take him to his first strip club,' promised Sam with a moronic grin when they asked him.

'We wouldn't expect anything less,' said Fran with a smile.

As the last one to see Andy alive, Sam became a person of even greater significance to Fran. He was very supportive to her and the kids in the weeks and months following and often took Jude and Charlie out for day trips. Unsurprisingly, they loved him because he was edgy and fun and would let them eat ice cream for lunch.

After he dropped them off following one particular day trip, Fran invited him to stay for dinner and, as they sank bottle after bottle of wine and talked about how much they loved and missed Andy, certain other truths emerged.

Sam fixed her with a steady gaze, or as steady as he could manage in his drunken state. 'I used to think you hated me when I first knew you.'

'I did,' joked Fran, before punching him playfully on the arm. 'Nah, not really. I thought you were a twat. But then I was a cow.'

'That's true,' he grinned.

'Oi! You're not supposed to agree with me.'

He laughed. 'Well, I was scared of you.'

'Quite right too,' she said, folding her arms. 'Are you still scared of me?'

He raised one eyebrow, holding her gaze. 'A bit,' he laughed. 'But I was always jealous of Andy for meeting such a smart, beautiful woman.'

She stared at him. He was a good-looking twat. She had to give him that. And he was here. And Andy wasn't. And she was drunk. And gut-twistingly, mind-blowingly sad. She lurched towards him and planted a kiss that was awkward on every single level.

Sam pulled away. 'Woah, Fran.'

Fran leapt up. 'Fuck. Sorry. Fuck. That was—fuck.'

'It's fine, really it's fine. It's just the booze and the grief and everything. Listen, it never happened, okay. And we're cool, okay? So I'm going to go. Okay?'

'Okay,' said Fran, praying for a thunderbolt to put her out of all her miseries in one fell swoop.

Sam planted a gallant kiss on the top of her head before he left. 'I'll call you in the week.'

Fran sat, staring off into nothing as she heard the front door click shut.

So, Fran Parker – who's the tosser now?

Fran had been terrified that things would be paralysingly awkward with Sam after that but they weren't at all. He took on the role of supportive, idiotic friend, filling hers and the children's lives with so many acts of kindness and fun. She realized why Andy had loved him and that now, she did too. Over the past year, Sam had been in a relationship with a girl ten years his junior in age but twenty years older in maturity. Her name was Ellen and Fran liked her a great deal. They were expecting their first child very soon.

'So-o, Fran, listen. I'm really sorry but I think Ellie and I are going to have to give it a miss on Saturday – the baby's due any day and we don't want to risk being too far away from the birth centre. I'm sorry – you know we'd love to be there.'

'It's okay,' said Fran reassuringly, because it was. What else could she say? And as excuses went, this one was solid gold. 'Wish Ellie all the love and luck for the big push.'

'I'm more nervous than her – she's amazing!' said Sam,

240

sounding awe-struck. 'We'll be thinking of you all – and Andy of course. I'll have a beer for him on the day.'

'I know. Thank you. Take care, Sam.'

'You too.'

It was fine. Absolutely fine. It didn't mean that people weren't thinking of Andy or didn't love him. Or her. They loved them very much.

Two days later she got a call from Andy's parents.

'Fran dear, we're not going to make it over on Saturday. Colin's had a bad cold and I don't think he's up to it.'

'Oh right. That's a shame,' said Fran. She'd detected Andy's parents taking a step back over the past year or so. They kept in touch for the grandchildren of course but she sensed that they found the anniversaries unrelentingly painful.

'I am sorry, dear. We'll be thinking of you and Andy of course. You know that, don't you?' There was such an edge of sadness to her voice, a desperation.

Please understand. Please don't make us come. We lost our only child – we went from being parents to being childless. It's too much for us. We simply can't take it.

Fran felt her eyes prick with tears at the thought. 'Of course. We'll make another date soon, shall we?'

'Oh yes, that would be lovely,' said Jill, sounding overwhelmed with relief. 'We adore seeing the children – do give them our love, won't you?'

'I will.'

Fran lay back on the sofa and tried to relax but something was digging into her shoulder. She turned over and attempted to knead the knotty cushion it into something more comfortable but it was useless. She flopped back down and stared at the ceiling. That crack was definitely getting bigger.

What's up? he asked.

Apart from widowhood and its resultant constant state of misery?

241

That's quite dramatic, even for you.

Thank you. No, it's Saturday – everyone's pulling out. Apparently, marking a dead person's birthday is a real drag.

But you still want to?

It feels important. And Charlie still needs to, I think – although, sometimes I worry that I'm just projecting.

But it's important for you.

You know it is. Anyway, I've defrosted the mince for the lasagne and made a cake so it's happening.

Well, I appreciate your efforts. I'm sure it will be fine, my love.

I admire your faith, I really do, but I get the feeling there's a storm coming.

Fran felt a weird kind of relief when Saturday came. She had planned a lovely breakfast with the kids and was expecting her parents and brother at midday. She had made the lasagne and Andy's favourite cake for lunch.

Fran hadn't reckoned on Jude sleeping in until eleven or Charlie having a meltdown because the card she'd made for Andy's memory box wasn't absolutely perfect.

'It's fine, Charlie, honestly. Daddy would love it.'

'But how can you know that? He's not here and it's all messy and I hate it!' she shouted, stomping up the stairs.

'Charlie! Charlie!' Upstairs, a door slammed. 'Great. Marvellous. That's just great,' said Fran, pouring herself another cup of coffee and turning on the soothing sounds of Radio 4, as Alan chose that moment to drop a dead mouse onto her slipper.

'What were you screaming about?' groaned Jude, appearing in the kitchen ten minutes later. 'You woke me up.'

'Alan brought me a rodenty present,' replied Fran. 'Thanks for coming to my rescue.'

'You're welcome,' mumbled Jude, pulling a juice carton from the fridge and taking a large gulp.

'How about a glass, Jude?' she suggested.

'How about chilling, Mum?'

Deep breaths, Fran. 'So, Granny and Grandpa should be here in about an hour.'

'Waffor?'

She stared at him, trying to ignore the grain of hurt at the centre of her chest. 'It's Dad's birthday?'

Jude sighed. 'Oh yeah.'

'Jude, it's important.'

'For you, maybe.'

'What's that supposed to mean?' demanded Fran.

He rolled his eyes. 'Forget it, Mum. It doesn't matter.' He grabbed an apple from the fruit bowl and went back upstairs. Moments later, she heard the sound of Jude's guitar and singing; his voice sweet and mournful. It made her feel heavy with sadness that she couldn't reach him. He could open his heart to the world with music but was unable to tell his own mother how he felt.

As they finished lunch later that afternoon, Charlie and Jack excused themselves to take Alan around the block for a walk. Fran gazed at the remainder of her family – her parents making polite conversation and Jude, silently brooding – the truth in their midst.

'So tell me,' she ventured after an ill-advised third glass of wine. 'Apart from Charlie and Alan, are you all simply here out of a sense of duty?' Three sets of eyes fixed on her, hesitating just a fraction too long. 'Your silence is very reassuring,' she said, taking a sip of wine.

'Fran, dear,' began her mother. 'We're here because it's important to you.'

'We want to support you,' echoed her father with a hurried nod.

Fran turned to Jude. 'You're very quiet. Is that what you think too, Jude?' She had a dangerous edge to her voice, daring him to contradict her.

'Fran,' warned her mother.

Fran kept her eyes fixed on her son's. Those blue eyes. So like his dad. But his gaze was glowering, ready to boil over. She wanted him to let rip. She needed to hear it. Like pulling a plaster off a wound. Like a slap round the face. He didn't let her down.

'Of course I'm only here out of duty. Why else would I be here? How fucking weird is it to want to mark a dead person's birthday? It's not normal!'

'Language, Jude!' scolded Angela. Fran and Jude ignored her, their eyes locked on one another – fierce and stubborn.

The truth will out and it will hurt.

'Pardon me for mentioning it but losing your father wasn't exactly normal,' snapped Fran.

Jude threw up his hands in despair. 'I know that. For God's sake, Mum, of course I know that. But he's gone and *you* have to accept that because I have. I totally get it. I'll never forget him but I won't let it stop me living my life. Like you do.'

'I do not!' Fran was on her feet now, anger rising up inside her – anger that she had no right to.

Jude held her gaze. 'Yes you do. The memory box, this creepy birthday party, the way you cling on to that bloody sofa even though you hate it!' Fran opened her mouth to protest but Jude held up a hand. 'There's no point in denying it. You've got to move on and let us move on too.' Fran could see the desperation in his face and felt her heart lurch with the realization that she'd failed him. 'I just want to be a normal kid again, instead of forever being that kid whose dad died. You *have* to accept that he's gone. I have.'

'Well I'm sorry if I've let you down, Jude,' she said quietly.

'Oh, I'm sure Jude doesn't mean that, do you, lad?' asked her dad, his face creased with worry.

Jude didn't answer. He stared at Fran. 'You have to let me move on with my life. And you have to accept that Dad's gone and move on with yours too.'

Fran felt as if the breath had been knocked out of her lungs.

You wanted the truth and there it is. In all its stripped-down, plain-speaking glory.

'I need some air,' she gasped, heading to the back door.

Her father went to follow but Angela touched his arm. 'Let her go, Bill.'

Fran walked towards her freshly cultivated flower beds, taking in the hydrangeas, whose blowsy blue and white blooms were starting to appear, and the day lilies with their fat green buds, ready to explode into life.

'This is the best time of year,' Barry had told her when she popped round to pick up some seedlings the other day. 'When the growing season gets into its stride and everything is about to burst into life – it's like Christmas!'

'He's just a big kid.' Pamela beamed indulgently. Barry leaned over and planted a kiss on her cheek.

'Look at you two,' teased Fran fondly. 'Like a couple of teenagers.'

'You're never too old for a little romance,' said Pamela with a grin. 'Which reminds me, I bumped into Elsie Loveday in the post office – she was over the moon with everything you and Gary did in her garden.'

'I'm glad we were able to help,' said Fran, refusing to take the hint.

'She thought you two were married,' added Pamela, raising her eyebrows. Barry and Fran smirked at one another. 'What?' cried Pamela indignantly. 'I'm only telling you what she said.'

Fran shook her head and laughed. 'Of course you are, Mrs Cupid.'

'You would make a lovely couple,' declared Pamela with glee. Barry gave her a meaningful look. 'What?' said Pamela. 'It's the truth.'

'Right, I'm off before Pamela books a church and a vicar,' said Fran, picking up the seedlings and heading for the door. 'Thanks for these, Barry. See you lovelies later.'

Fran glanced back towards the house now. Her father was standing at the window, peering out, a look of concern on his weary face. She glimpsed her mother behind him, hands in prayer position and Jude, in textbook-teenager pose, body slid as far down into his chair as possible, long legs stretched languidly before him. Waiting. For her. In silence. And it was this silence that hit her suddenly – a mirror to the truth. Jude's truth. Because if anything he'd said had been untrue or unjust, her mother would be setting him straight right now. Yet Fran could see that she was utterly composed and when Angela reached out to pat Jude's hand, she realized that she had a clear choice.

Ignore the truth or face it head on.

Her mother had tried to tell her numerous times but it took a taciturn fourteen-year-old to ensure that her heart heard what her head knew. After all, who listens to the people who drone on all the time? It's the ones who speak when there's something important to say that we listen to. Or at least we should.

She caught Jude's eye. His gaze was wary, fearful of having overstepped the mark. She smiled and it softened as a look of understanding passed between them.

Time to face it head on then, thought Fran, making her way indoors.

Her mother looked up as she entered the dining room. 'Fran, dear, are you all right?'

'I'm absolutely fine, thanks, Mum. But I would like to apologize to you all because Jude is right.'

'Mum, I—' began Jude. She rested a hand on his shoulder.

'It's okay. You're right.' He nodded. 'I just miss him, you know?' She saw tears mist Jude's eyes and pulled him into a tight embrace. Fran felt her mother's hand rest on one arm and her father's on the other.

We're okay. We've got each other and that's good enough. We're okay.

Fran took a deep breath and a step back. She looked into Jude's eyes and wiped away his tears. 'Thank you for telling me the truth,' she said.

'Sorry,' he whispered.

'You shouldn't be. You were right to say it. I needed to hear it.' She planted a kiss on top of his head.

'What's the matter with Jude?' asked Charlie, appearing in the doorway, her face creased with worry.

'He's just missing Dad.'

Charlie rested a hand on her brother's arm. 'I miss him too, Jude. It's completely normal.' Fran exchanged amused glances with her parents. 'Why don't we watch a movie?' she suggested. 'We could have popcorn.'

'And Maltesers?' asked Jude.

Charlie put her arm around his shoulder. 'Of course,' she said earnestly.

Fran reached for her children and pulled them close. 'I love you morons,' she said, breathing them in.

'Love you too, Mummy.' Charlie grinned. Jude smiled and nodded.

'Would you guys be okay if I popped out for a bit?' asked Fran. 'There's something I need to do.'

'Of course, darling,' said Angela.

'Thanks.' Fran fetched her handbag and coat. Moments later, she found herself sitting in the car contemplating her next move. She glanced back at the house. Charlie and Jude were waving at the window, pulling silly faces and giving her the thumbs-up. Fran stuck out her tongue before pulling out her phone and dialling a number. He answered after two rings.

'Fran. This is a nice surprise. Are you okay? Is there an over-grown bramble emergency?' Gary's voice was like two strong arms reaching out to her.

Fran laughed. 'I'm fine. No emergency. I was just wondering if you were busy this afternoon?'

'I'm supposed to be catching up on paperwork so I would welcome any distraction. What do you need?'

What do I need? Come on. The man's asking you a question. Try to answer it truthfully.

She took a deep breath. 'Okay, well I know this is going to sound weird and possibly not the most enticing offer but I need a hefty man to come to Ikea with me, please.'

Gary laughed. 'Wow. This is the ultimate test of friendship. Croydon Ikea on a Saturday afternoon.'

Friendship. Fran smiled. *That sounded good for now.* 'I know. But please be assured that you were my first choice and it is important.'

'I'm honoured.'

'You should be. I'll shout you coffee and cake as a thank you.'

'Please, Fran, that's too much,' he joked.

'Thank you. Seriously. It may be a trip to Ikea but actually, this is quite a momentous event for me.'

'Sounds intriguing – you can tell me everything when you get here. And I did say to call whenever you needed me. I'm glad you did.'

So am I, thought Fran, starting the engine. She smiled as she felt the sun on her face like a warm kiss from the future, promising something hopeful and new. All she had to do was reach for it and see what happened.

Chapter Twenty-One

Pamela

My Happiness List
1. Just bake
2. Dinner with Matthew and Barry – be in the moment!
(DISASTER)
3. Go dancing with Barry? (Not likely)
4. Laugh like we used to! (with Heather instead)
5. Try something new – lovely trip to art gallery with Fran & Charlie
(and Gary!)
6. Teach other people how to bake
7. Let Matty go and be kinder to Barry
8. Appreciate what I have & how lucky I am...

'Are you sure you want to come along tonight, lovey?'

Heather looked up at Pamela. 'I'm absolutely sure. And I've also decided to go home later. Luke should have cleared his stuff by now.'

'You don't have to rush, Heather. You know you can stay here as long as you like, can't she, Barry?'

Barry glanced up from the current edition of *Gardeners' World*. 'Absolutely. You're very welcome, Heather.'

Pamela beamed at him. She was enjoying being around this new version of her husband – he was trying to be more attentive and she appreciated it. Only last week he had surprised her with tickets to see one of her favourite *Strictly* dancers later in the year.

'I got an email from one of those ticketing places and thought you'd like to go.'

'Aww, Barry – it's not my birthday.'

'Does it need to be?' he'd said, kissing her on the cheek.

'Thank you,' said Heather. 'You're both very kind but I'm ready to go home. Really.'

'Well all right, but only if you're sure. Now, I'll just get that cottage pie in the oven and start on some veg.'

Heather sighed. 'I am going to miss your home cooking though.'

'Don't tell her that – she'll start bringing you care packages,' teased Barry.

'Cheeky!' scolded Pamela. 'You can come round for your tea whenever you like – think of it as a home from home.'

'Thank you.' Heather smiled, looking genuinely touched.

The iPad on the side began to buzz. 'Ooh, that'll be Matty – he emailed to say he'd FaceTime us today – he's got news!' cried Pamela, opening up the screen and swiping it into life. 'Hello, Matthew!' she shouted. 'Can you see us? Say hello Barry!'

'Hello, son,' said Barry, waving at the screen.

'Hi, Dad,' replied Matthew. 'I can see you.'

'You're as brown as a nut!' clucked Pamela. She was suddenly struck at how assured Matthew seemed – no more little boy lost. He looked confident and happy. It made her heart soar. 'Heather, look how brown he is!'

'Very brown,' agreed Heather.

'Hi, everyone.' Matthew grinned. 'How are you all?'

'Very good!' shouted Pamela, who hadn't quite got the hang

of FaceTime. There was a slight time delay so she asked, 'Can you hear us?'

Matthew smiled. 'Yes I can, Mum. Listen, I've got some news. You know I told you I was writing a script?'

'Oh yes?' said Pamela, leaning forwards.

'Well, the studio here wants to make it into a TV series!'

Pamela and Barry stared at one another is disbelief. 'Wow!' exclaimed Heather. 'That's amazing – congratulations!'

'Thanks.' Matthew smiled. 'So, Mum, Dad, what do you think? I didn't want to tell you before I knew it was happening for sure but it means I can pay you back, Mum – every last penny.'

'Oh, Matty, I'm so proud of you!'

Barry nodded. 'Well done, son, that's incredible news.'

'Thank you. Both of you. I know I've let you down in the past but that's all going to change – I mean it. I've got to go but we'll speak soon, okay?'

'Okay, Matty – love you and well done!' cried Pamela as he disappeared from the screen. 'Goodness!' she said to Barry. 'How about that? Our son, the Hollywood screenwriter!'

'Amazing,' agreed Barry, shaking his head. 'Truly amazing.'

'Credit where it's due, Barry Trott – you encouraged him to follow his dreams and look what's happened!'

Barry grinned up at her. 'And you cut the apron strings and let him go so let's share the credit, shall we?'

Pamela nodded happily. 'I think this calls for a celebration,' she said, walking to the fridge and taking out a bottle. 'Prosecco anyone?'

It wasn't only the Prosecco that was making Pamela feel giddy as she walked along Hope Street with Heather later that evening. It was as if she'd worked out who she was and how she wanted to be. She was Pamela the mother – devoted to her children and proud of everything they'd achieved, with Matthew's latest news the cherry on a very special cake. She was Pamela the wife –

reconnected with her beloved Barry and remembering all the reasons she'd fallen in love with him in the first place. And she was Pamela the woman – playing an important role in her community and loving every second. Maybe most women knew who they were before they reached the ripe old age of sixty-five but Pamela didn't care. Better late than never.

'Hello, my friends,' said Fran, as they met in the hall. 'I must say you look remarkably chipper for a woman whose world has imploded,' she added, turning to Heather.

'Thank you,' said Heather with a wry smile. 'I've done my fair share of weeping and wailing but I've got some good friends supporting me,' she added with meaning.

'You must give me their numbers some time,' joked Fran. 'So have you heard from the shitty bastard?'

Heather laughed. 'He's left about a zillion messages but I'm ignoring them.'

'Good girl,' said Fran. 'And what about your slutty cousin?'

'Same. And Pamela's been feeding me restorative tea and cake like it's going out of fashion so it's all good.'

'Well, I have conducted extensive scientific research over the years and can confirm that the key tools for surviving the shit storms of life are tea, cake, chocolate and gin. You're welcome.'

'We need to add, "find friend with an extra-dry sense of humour", to that list too,' laughed Heather, nudging Fran. 'Anyway, how did the birthday meal go at the weekend?'

'Really, really badly.' Fran grimaced.

'Oh no!' cried Pamela.

'But then it ended up being really, really good,' she admitted.

'Sounds promising,' said Heather. Fran tapped the side of her nose as Nik stood up to welcome them.

'Good evening, my dear friends. I am very glad to see you all but I am also sad to say that this is our penultimate session.' Everyone ahhhed. Nik nodded. 'I know, but I have the feeling that what we have started here will continue long after these sessions have ended.' There were smiles around the room. 'So, this week we are considering contentment because I hope we have all come to realize that happiness is not a constant state. Life is too full of highs and lows for this to be realistic. What we are actually aiming for is contentment which, put simply, is the art of being at ease with one's situation, body or mind. It will not surprise you to hear that I have an exercise to teach us how to be truly comfortable with who we are. We are going to undertake a character questionnaire, which will help to identify your strengths.' He handed out two stapled A4 sheets.

'Yay, I love a quiz,' joked Fran.

Nik smiled. 'You will need to spend ten to fifteen minutes filling it out and then give it to your partner, who will mark it for you.'

Pamela felt a wave of panic as she saw the questions. She'd always hated tests but as she started to fill it in, she relaxed and realized that she was enjoying being honest about what she really felt. She swapped her paper with Heather and followed Nik's instructions for marking and grading their characteristics.

'Okay,' said Nik when they had finished. 'How did we get on?'

'Apparently I'm very humble,' offered Jim.

'Aww,' said Pamela. 'I think that's true.'

'I am honest,' reported Georg.

'Least surprising outcome ever,' teased Heather. Georg laughed.

'Good,' said Nik. 'So now we need to review our strengths and in order to do this we will focus on the top five characteristics – these are your key strengths. Let's break into our groups to discuss them and then I would like you to pick one to focus on over the next week – maybe ask your happiness buddies to help you decide? Think about how you use this strength already and then note down new ways that you could use it more.'

'Okay, girls, so what have we got?' asked Fran, turning to Heather and Pamela. 'Well, that's a good start, we all share "love" as a characteristic.' She held out her arms. 'Come on, you two – group hug.' They laughed as Fran pulled them into a tight squeeze.

'No surprise that humour's in your top five, Fran,' said Heather.

'And kindness is top of Pamela's list,' said Fran with a satisfied smile.

'I think you should focus on your creativity, ducks,' said Pamela to Heather. 'It says here that you need to think of new ways of doing things.'

'Sounds about right – it feels as if my whole life needs an overhaul,' sighed Heather.

Pamela put an arm around her shoulder. 'Don't worry, lovey, we'll help you.' Heather nodded gratefully.

'What about you, Pamela?' asked Fran.

Pamela scanned her list again before a smile lit up her face. 'I'm going to focus on love and organize a surprise party for our wedding anniversary – it's our fortieth this year!'

Heather grinned. 'I love a party! What about you, Fran?'

Fran took a deep breath. 'I could focus on the humour and try stand-up comedy.' Heather laughed. 'But I should probably try to be braver.'

'Oh, Fran, you're the bravest person I know!' cried Pamela.

'Well, you're lovely but actually, I'm not – I merely pretend to be.' She gave them both reassuring smiles. 'It's okay, you don't have to pretend either – I know it's true.'

'You have to be brave when you lose someone. People give you weird looks if you walk down the street wailing all the time,' pointed out Heather.

Fran laughed. 'Sounds like the kind of pithy thing I'd say.'

'You've taught me well, oh wise one,' said Heather, taking a bow.

Pamela put an arm around Fran's shoulder. 'You know where we are if you need us. As Heather will tell you, I'm always ready with tea, cake and sympathy!'

254

Fran planted a smacker on her cheek. 'We should rename your house the Happiness Hub,' she joked.

'The Happiness Hub.' Pamela smiled as the whisper of an idea floated through her mind. 'I like it.'

They left Hope Street Hall later that evening in good spirits. It had been an interesting session and Pamela felt as if the world was full of possibility as her brain buzzed with ideas. The three friends stopped in their tracks when they saw Luke waiting outside the hall. Pamela took hold of Heather's hand as he approached.

'Heather,' he began.

'What are you doing here?' she demanded.

'I need to talk to you,' he said. He glanced at Pamela and Fran. 'Alone, if possible.'

'We're going nowhere,' declared Pamela, tightening her grip on Heather's hand.

'Yeah. What she said,' agreed Fran.

Luke sighed. 'Okay, fine. I've come to say I'm sorry.'

'I should bloody well think so,' said Fran.

Luke stared at Heather. 'I have tried to call you. I understand why you wouldn't answer but the whole thing with Gemma was a huge, huge mistake.'

'You said you saw her first in the club and that you wanted to ask her out. Not me. Those were your words.' Pamela could feel Heather's hand trembling in hers and gave it a reassuring squeeze.

'I didn't mean it. I said that because I was angry with Gemma. But I love you. I've always loved you. And I know I screwed everything up and I deserve this.'

'You can say that again, mate,' snapped Fran.

Luke tried to ignore her. 'But I mean it when I say that I'm sorry and I love you.'

'If you're about to ask for another chance, you can save your breath,' said Heather.

'Attagirl,' whispered Pamela.

'Actually, I've come to tell you that I'm leaving.'

'Oh,' said Pamela shocked.

'Where are you going?' asked Heather.

'New York. They've offered me a placement, which could end up being permanent so I thought I'd take it, unless…'

'Unless?' demanded Fran. 'Unless Heather has taken leave of her senses and suddenly stopped seeing you as an utter cock-womble? Honestly, if I was her, I would have punched your lights out.'

Luke took a step back and held up his hands. 'Okay, okay, I get it. I'm the villain here and you all want a piece of me.'

'Don't flatter yourself,' retorted Fran.

Luke turned to Heather. 'I can see that you've got some good, supportive friends here and I'm glad, but I would love to talk to you alone because I honestly believe that if you came with me to New York, we could be happy.'

'What?' chorused the three friends.

Luke held open his hands. 'Think about it, Heather – a new start, a new city. You love New York. We could get away and start over. Away from all this.'

Heather was silent for a moment. Pamela stared at her in amazement. 'You're not thinking about going, are you?'

Heather shook her head. 'No, of course not.'

'Can we at least talk?' asked Luke. 'Just the two of us? Please?'

'You don't have to,' said Fran. 'I can still punch his lights out if you want me to.'

Heather gave a weak smile. 'I'll be fine.' She turned to Luke. 'You have half an hour to talk and then you leave, understood?'

He nodded. 'Okay.'

Pamela and Fran watched them go. 'Oh Fran, I hope she'll be all right,' said Pamela feeling fiercely protective.

She'll be fine. Although I'm not so sure about Luke. Right, I'd better get back. I promised Charlie I'd kiss her goodnight before she goes to sleep.'

Give her a hug from me, won't you?'

Fran smiled. 'Will do.'

Pamela did her best to heed Fran's words and stop fretting about Heather as she made her way home. She'd become so fond of her. And Fran. They felt like family. She started to think about the anniversary party and who she would invite. She might have to hire Hope Street Hall because she'd want all the people from the course to be there as well as family, her baking mums, people from choir. Her mind was bubbling with ideas as she let herself into the house. It seemed very quiet and she was surprised to find the place in darkness.

'Barry?' she called, turning on the hall light.

No reply. That was odd. When she and Heather left earlier, he'd been about to go out into the garden on slug patrol.

'Always best to catch the little blighters when they least expect it!' he said, eyes glinting with intent.

Pamela made her way down the hall. Surely he wasn't still out there, although there had been evenings when she'd found him planting out seedlings in the greenhouse to way past nine o'clock.

'Barry!' she called again, louder this time. Pamela walked into the kitchen and turned on the light. The back door was open. She gave an exasperated shake of the head. He was still out there! At this time of night!

'Barry, what are you doing out there? You'll catch your death!' she cried, standing at the back door, peering into the gloom of the garden. It was then that she noticed the torch, shining its beam across the grass as if it had been dropped there. Pamela's mouth went dry and the panic rose up inside her like a scream as her eyes adjusted to the dark and she noticed Barry lying on the floor, face down, not moving.

Chapter Twenty-Two

Heather

Happiness List
1. Marry Luke!
2. Sunday walk and choose wedding venue with Luke Fran & Charlie
WEDDING CANCELLED
3. Exercise more (persuade Luke to go running?)
- Boot camp with Fran & Pamela
4. Go dress shopping with Gemma and laugh like we used to!
Fran & Pamela - laughed like teenagers!
DRESS SOLD ON EBAY
5. Surprise Luke at work
6. Ask Pamela for help with first dance for wedding!
7. Help Pamela & Barry fall in love again - mission accomplished!
8. Treasure my friends
9. Have the courage to take what I need from life

Heather was starting to realize that it would be a lot easier if she could simply hate Luke. She'd managed it pretty well since the christening because she hadn't seen him. Absence may make the heart grow fonder but it also keeps it pulsing with fury. Every time she felt her anger subside as the sadness threatened to take its place, she'd remind herself of all the times Luke had lied to her: the late-working, the phone calls in the evenings and at weekends, the guilt-presents and the weekend away. The list was endless – it made her skin crawl and her rage burn red hot.

And then there was Gemma; Heather's best and oldest friend – the one who'd held her like a child when her parents died, who'd always been there. A constant friend and support. Her anger almost tipped into self-pitying hurt at the thought of this so she focused on the betrayal and disappointment instead. Heather forced herself to push Freddy from her mind too because she couldn't bear to think about him. She told herself it was easier that way. She wondered if Ed might get in touch and was relieved when he didn't. All Heather could do was focus on herself and what she was going to do now.

Needless to say, she would have collapsed without Pamela and Fran to nudge her gently back onto her feet. Like a surrogate mother and teasing older sister, they surrounded her with love and told her that she would be okay. And she believed them.

So Heather was ready for Luke that evening. Ready to deflect his hand-wringing apologies with curt anger. And ready to send him packing if he continued with his ridiculous suggestion that they give their dead-in-the-water relationship another chance.

However, as she sat opposite him at the kitchen table and did her best to be standoffish and cold, Heather realized that hating someone you'd invested three years of your life in was nigh on impossible.

'Thank you for letting me come here,' Luke was saying. 'I know Pamela and Fran have got your best interests at heart but it is good to talk to you alone.'

'Why? So you can try to convince me that your affair with Gemma was all a mistake and that we should give this shambles of a relationship another go?'

Luke looked into her eyes. Heather stared back, her gaze steely and determined. Two weeks ago he could have seduced her with that gaze. 'I am really, truly sorry. I have been a complete asshole and you have every right to hate me.'

'Thank you,' she said bitterly.

'But the point is that I don't think you do hate me.'

She fixed him with a look. 'Don't be so sure of yourself.'

'Okay. Fair enough. Listen. I'm leaving for New York in two weeks and would love you to come with me.'

Heather narrowed her eyes. 'I'm surprised you're not begging Gemma to go with you. Or does the thought of playing stepdad to Freddy repel you?'

Luke sighed. 'It's all off with Gemma. To be honest, it was never really on. We didn't even sleep together.'

'Oh well, that's a blessing.'

'It was a stupid moment of madness – a fleeting attraction – we never did anything except kiss.'

'Please. Spare me the details.'

'Fine,' he said. 'I'm just going to say this and then I'll go. I screwed up and I'm sorry. I love you and I always will. I would be the happiest man alive if you came to New York and let me make amends.'

Heather's phone buzzed with a call. She frowned at the screen. *Fran.* That was odd. Heather held up a hand to silence Luke as she took the call.

'Are you phoning to check up on me?' she answered with a smile.

'Heather.' Fran sounded upset.

'What's the matter, Fran? What's happened?'

'It's Barry. He's had a heart attack. Can you come with me to the hospital?'

'I'm on my way,' said Heather, jumping to her feet and shepherding Luke towards the door.

'I hope he's okay,' said Luke as they parted. 'Think about what I said.'

She nodded gravely. 'I'll let you know.'

Heather wondered why hospital corridors always smelt like this – that sharp antiseptic tang mixed with the cabbagey whiff of yesterday's dinner. She gave a weak smile of thanks as Fran handed her a cup of tea, which was the exact same colour as old dishwater.

'I considered the Cup a Soup as a more palatable option but couldn't decide between minestrone and chicken noodle,' remarked Fran. 'Sorry. Possibly not the right time for jokes,' she added, sinking into the chair next to Heather.

'Poor Pamela,' breathed Heather. 'She was so excited about their anniversary party – she had all those plans. And she and Barry were like a couple of teenagers again.'

'I know,' sighed Fran. 'It is a truth universally acknowledged that when your world is rosy, life will usually find a way to shit on you from a great height.'

Heather nodded sadly. 'Is your mum staying the night?'

'Yeah,' said Fran. 'Thankfully, Charlie was asleep when I left. I'm dreading what will happen if I have to give her more bad news.'

'Don't think about it,' said Heather, grasping her hand. They sat in silence for a while, listening to the beeps and hisses of hospital life, each woman understanding the enormity of loss and praying that Pamela wasn't about to face it too.

The door to Barry's room opened and a weary-looking doctor emerged, closely followed by Pamela and her daughter, Laura.

'How is he?' asked Heather.

'The next twelve hours are critical,' reported the doctor. 'It was quite a large heart attack. We'll be monitoring him closely.'

'It's my fault!' cried Pamela. 'All those cakes and big dinners!'

Heather and Fran put their arms around her. 'It's not your fault. It could happen to anyone,' said Fran.

'The important thing is to get Dad better,' said Laura. 'I'll stay, Mum. You go home and rest.'

'I'm not going anywhere,' declared Pamela. 'I promised to look after him for better or for worse and that's exactly what I'm going to do.'

'I have other patients to see but the nurses will page me if anything happens,' said the doctor.

'Thank you,' said Laura. She turned to her mother. 'I'm going to call Simon with an update and try to get hold of Matthew. Will you be okay?'

'We'll look after her,' promised Heather. Laura nodded her thanks and headed down the corridor.

Fran and Heather led Pamela into Barry's room. He looked shrunken in his bed, surrounded by machines and wires. They stood together with their arms around one another. 'He looks so poorly!' cried Pamela as the tears flowed. 'What will I do if he doesn't make it?'

Fran and Heather exchanged glances and hugged Pamela tight. 'Don't think about that,' said Fran.

'Barry's strong. And so are you. Everything's going to be okay,' said Heather, hoping and praying that this was true.

Heather woke to the sound of a series of loud, repetitive beeps and panicked. Disorientated, she opened her eyes, realizing that she was in bed and the piercing noise was her alarm. She felt as if her brain was filled with glue as she rolled over and looked at her clock. 6 a.m.

On Pamela's insistence, she and Fran had left the hospital at two in the morning.

'I don't want Charlie worrying,' she said to Fran before turning to Heather like a mother hen. 'And you've got work tomorrow. Laura's here and Simon's on his way. I'll call you if there's any change.' They had hugged – a tight, heartfelt embrace which said everything.

Heather grabbed her phone and flicked it into life. No messages. That had to be a positive. She dialled Fran's number.

'Heather? Any word?'

'No, nothing. That has to be a good sign, right?'

'I live my life by the "no news is good news" mantra so yeah, I reckon. Hang on, Charlie wants to speak to you. I told her Barry was poorly.'

'Hey, Heather.' Charlie's voice was squeakier on the phone – she sounded much younger than her ten years. Heather's heart surged with fondness.

'Hi, Charlie. How are you doing?'

'I'm okay but I am worried about Barry. I like him. Do you think he'll be okay?'

What did you say to a ten-year-old who'd already lost their father and was naturally anxious about death? How did you tell the truth without upsetting them? 'I hope so, Charlie. I really do.'

'Me too. I'm going to send up lots of prayers today.'

'You do that, sweetie, and tell your mum to call me if she hears anything.'

''Kay.'

Heather felt sluggish with worry and fatigue as she dressed ready for work. She forced herself to eat some breakfast before making her way along Hope Street. The sky was the colour of a headache – yellow and oppressive. She wasn't sure how she was going to paint on a happy face for the customers today. All she could think about was Pamela and Barry. They'd only recently found one another again. She couldn't bear the thought of that being ripped apart.

Thankfully, the bakery was unrelentingly busy, so Heather had little time to dwell on her churning concerns. She was surprised at how quickly Georg picked up on her mood.

'You are sad. What is wrong? Is it Luke?'

She shook her head. 'It's Pamela. Her husband Barry had a heart attack last night. He's in a critical condition.'

Georg's face furrowed with a deep frown. 'That is terrible. Poor Pamela – she is a very kind woman.'

Heather nodded. 'Yes. Yes, she is.'

'Are you going to the hospital?'

'Probably later, after work – why?'

'I will come with you. Pamela is always very good to me – I would like to show support.'

Heather noticed something soften around his eyes. She realized that she wanted Georg to go with her – she needed his straightforward reassurance today. 'That would be great. I'm sure Pamela would be very pleased to see you and I'd be glad of the company to be honest.' He nodded before turning back to his coffee orders.

'Make sure you give Pamela our love, won't you?' said Caroline as Heather's shift ended and she got ready to leave. 'I'll organize some flowers and a card from us all.'

Heather smiled. 'Of course. Georg, shall we go? I need to pop home quickly and then we can head to the hospital.'

'Okay.' Georg nodded.

They walked back to Heather's house in silence. Usually, she would have found this uncomfortable but today, she was relieved not to have to make small talk. As Heather opened the front door to let them in, her phone rang. She grabbed it from her bag, spotting the caller ID immediately.

'Pamela? Are you okay?' Georg was studying her face, trying to read what was happening.

'Oh, Heather,' sobbed Pamela.

Heather felt tears spring to her eyes. 'What's happened? What is it?' she cried.

'He's okay, Heather. I think he's going to be okay.'

'Oh, Pamela, you had me worried there. Thank goodness.'

'Sorry, lovey – it's all a bit overwhelming. I mean he's got a way to go and he's going on a strict diet starting today but we'll get there.'

'You will. I'm so glad, Pamela. Thanks for letting me know.'

'And thank you, Heather – for everything. I mean it. I've got to go but I'll see you soon.'

'Bye,' said Heather, hanging up as an unexpected wave of old familiar grief hit her and she started to cry. 'He's okay. He's okay,' she repeated to reassure Georg, who looked worried.

I'm terrifying the poor man, she thought, but she couldn't help herself as she sobbed and sobbed. She was amazed when she felt him put his arms around her and pull her close. He didn't say anything. He didn't need to. He simply held her until she stopped crying. Eventually, Heather pulled away. 'I'm so sorry,' she said, staring up at him, noticing his clear blue eyes for the first time.

'Is okay. You were sad. You have to cry when you are sad. You don't need to be sorry.'

She smiled. 'Well, seeing as I've soaked your coat with my tears, can I at least offer to make you a cup of tea?'

'Thank you.' He nodded, following her into the kitchen. 'You have very nice house.'

'Thanks. Although it's a bit weird living here alone now.'

'I like being on my own,' said Georg.

'Do you?'

He nodded. 'Watch what you like on TV, eat what you like, go to bed when you like.'

'Don't you get lonely?'

He shrugged. 'If I do, I go out and see friends. But I like my own company.'

Heather placed a mug of tea in front of him. 'Mmm, maybe. I guess I'm a bit of a wuss. I've never really been on my own.'

Georg fixed her with a look. 'You will be fine,' he assured her. 'You have friends.' He took a sip of the tea and pulled a face. 'I am happy to come and drink your terrible tea with you any day.'

She laughed as he gave her a wonky half-smile. 'Thanks for

the offer but just as friends – I don't need another boyfriend yet.'
Georg looked horrified. 'That was a joke, by the way.'

'Good because not only do you make the worst tea but you are also not my type.'

'Please, Georg, don't spare my feelings,' chuckled Heather.

He looked into her eyes. 'I am gay.'

Heather was stunned. 'Oh. Wow. Sorry, I didn't know.'

'Not many people do. It is hard for me. You don't advertise the fact you're gay where I come from.'

She nodded. 'I'm touched that you felt able to share it with me.'

He smiled. 'I feel accepted here. People say London is unfriendly but I think people let you be who you want to be. I like that.'

'*Be who you want to be*. I like that too,' said Heather. She knocked her tea mug against his. 'Cheers to that.'

'Cheers to that and to your very terrible tea.' He grinned.

'Georg! I think you're finally getting the English sense of humour,' she laughed.

Once Heather knew that Barry was going to be all right, her thoughts turned to Luke. She knew it was ridiculous to even contemplate the idea of going to New York but in those dark middle-of-the-night periods of wakefulness, her mind flooded with irrational uncertainty. What if she never met another man? This was a chance to go to New York – the city of dreams! Could she forgive Luke and give it go? She was pretty sure that his infatuation with Gemma had been just that. Was there a world in which she could forgive him and they could start afresh?

'Are you out of your effing mind?' cried Fran when she shared her thoughts over the phone the next day. 'Stay right where you are. I'm coming round.'

Heather smiled. Sometimes in life you need a straight-talking, sweary friend to tell you the truth.

Fran arrived twenty minutes later with a bottle of wine under her arm and a look of scary determination on her face. 'Right you, get this open – we're thrashing out your future here and now and let's be clear, it doesn't involve that fuckwit Luke.'

They sat at the kitchen table and did just that. For every concern, Fran offered reassurance.

'What if I'm on my own for ever?'

'You won't be and if you are, get a dog.'

Heather laughed. 'What about having kids?'

'Overrated. Next!'

More laughter. 'But it's New York!'

'Yes and that's where Donald Trump comes from so you know, it's not all good.'

'Am I overreacting to what Gemma and Luke did?'

Fran's face grew serious. 'Abserfuckinglutely not. She is basically the nearest thing you have to a sister and sisters positively do *not* do that to one another. It is a betrayal of biblical proportions. Never forget that.'

Heather nodded as the tears fell. Fran didn't say anything for a moment. She simply topped up Heather's wine and reached for her hand. Heather stared at her with wide, sad eyes. 'Listen to me, Heather Brown. You are a beautiful, clever, funny and wonderful woman. You deserve better than you've had and you will find it. You can do this – you can be on your own, find your thing and enjoy it. Just be brave and take life one day at a time.' Heather held her gaze and nodded as fresh tears fell. Fran let her cry for a while before squeezing her hands and leaning forwards. 'Now then, you're allowed ten minutes of self-pity a day and no more. So dry those eyes and fetch some crisps, will you? I'm starving!'

Heather laughed. 'Fair enough,' she said, fetching a tube of Pringles from the cupboard. 'So, how are your attempts at being braver going?'

'Hmm, are you sure you don't want to do a bit more self-pitying?' asked Fran.

'That good?' teased Heather.

Fran shrugged. 'I'm working my way up to it, like when you go swimming in the sea and it takes you a while to get in.'

'You'll get there,' said Heather, helping herself to a crisp as the doorbell rang. 'Don't eat them all,' she warned over her shoulder.

'Sorry – can't promise that,' said Fran with a grin before stuffing two into her mouth. Heather laughed and made her way down the hall, peering towards the front door, unable to make out who it was at first.

Heather thought about slamming the door when she saw Gemma but soon realized that she was oddly pleased to see her. Despite everything that had happened, she missed her cousin. At the same time however, Heather wanted Gemma to see that she was okay. In spite of the betrayal and hurt, Heather was okay. 'What do you want?' she demanded in a voice keen with anger.

Gemma looked at the floor before flicking her gaze to her cousin. 'To apologize.'

'Is everything all right, Heather?' came Fran's voice from the kitchen doorway. 'Would you like me to go?'

Heather turned and smiled at her friend, taking courage from her presence. 'No. It's fine, Fran. Gemma has merely popped round to apologize – it won't take long,' she said casually. She turned back to Gemma with a frown. 'Come on then, get it over with.'

Gemma eyed her pleadingly and Heather felt her heart flood with sadness. 'I'm sorry.'

The sadness was shoved aside by renewed anger at these two feebly inadequate words. 'Right. Fine. You've said it. Now off you trot.'

'I miss you.'

I miss you too, whispered Heather's heart until a jolt of fury brought her to her senses. *Not today. You don't get to make me feel sorry for you today.*

'Maybe you should have thought about that before you tried to steal my fiancé,' said Heather angrily.

Gemma nodded. 'You're right but I want you to know that I didn't sleep with him and I wasn't trying to steal him.'

So Luke was telling the truth for once.

'That's a great comfort,' snapped Heather. 'I'm sure my ruined life feels reassured that your efforts to destroy it were completely unintentional.'

Gemma seemed surprised by Heather's bluntness. She hesitated before she went on. 'I completely understand your anger and I deserve all of it. I only wanted to come here to apologize and to tell you the truth.'

Heather folded her arms. 'I'm waiting.' Gemma shot a glance in Fran's direction. 'Fran is my friend,' said Heather. 'She knows everything so just get on with it.'

Gemma took a deep breath. 'I was in a weird place after Freddy was born. That's not an excuse by the way – I know what I did was unforgiveable. I just need you to know that I've not been myself. What happened with Luke was a moment of madness. Things haven't been great with Ed and then I saw Luke when I dropped off Freddy. He suggested we do lunch and we were texting and it all got a bit out of hand.'

'Understatement of the decade,' said Heather curtly. 'So what did you do?'

Gemma stared at her with sorrowful eyes. 'We met up for drinks a few times, went dancing. Kissed. It meant nothing.'

'And yet you did it anyway.'

'Yeah, I did, stupid cow that I am and now I've lost everything.'

Heather turned on her. 'Please don't expect my sympathy.'

'I don't but I would like your forgiveness.'

'Too bad.'

Gemma stared at the floor before giving a resigned, tearful nod. 'Do you think you'll ever stop hating me?' she asked.

Heather's gaze was strong and constant. 'I don't hate you. That's the problem. This would all be a lot easier if I could.'

Gemma nodded again. 'What are you going to do next?'

Heather regarded her for a second. 'That's really none of your business. And now, I think we're done here. Bye, Gemma,' she said before closing the door.

She saw her cousin linger outside the door for a second before turning slowly and walking away.

'Wow,' said Fran. 'You were bloody awesome.'

Heather pulled a face. 'Was it too much?'

Fran shook her head. 'Absolutely not – you were the bollocks.'

'Thanks, Fran. It was good to have you here. I was surprised you didn't give her a piece of your mind.'

Fran smiled. 'I was biting my tongue the whole way through but seriously, Heather? You didn't need me. You've got this.'

Heather felt a skip of confidence at her friend's reassuring words. 'Right, come on. *Carpe diem* and all that,' she said, walking towards the kitchen.

'What are we doing?' Fran grinned.

'We're writing the "get lost, loser", email to Luke,' she declared.

'Correction.' Fran smiled. 'You're writing it. I'm going to drink wine, eat crisps and keep you company.'

Heather laughed. 'I've got this?'

Fran nodded. 'You've so got this.'

Chapter Twenty-Three

Fran

Happiness List Thing
1. Accept a world without Andy (too soon!)
2. 'Digital Detox' day with kids
3. Go on even more walks with Alan
4. Have dinner with a nice man (NOT a date) & laugh if appropriate
(he is nice and I did laugh)
5. Stop feeling guilty and like Gary (EPIC fail)
6. Take up gardening again (with a little help from Baz & Mum)
7. Work myself into an early grave helping local elderly people with their
gardens — most fun I've had in ages
8. Get punched in the face by grief and take it
9. Get rid of that bloody uncomfortable sofa

Fran didn't miss sex. Not really. She'd enjoyed having it with Andy of course, but as with many couples after they become parents it was often something that got pushed down the 'to do' list, like sorting out that drawer full of spare keys and rubber bands in the kitchen. It was a school night or they were tired or a bit drunk. It didn't matter to her – they loved one another. They had sex when they could be bothered and it was always lovely.

What she did miss though was the companionship and if that made her sound like an octogenarian out of her time then so be it. She missed someone who had her back, who understood her down to her bones, who made her laugh and annoyed her like no other person in the world.

Your rock. Your soul mate. Your 'happy-ever-after'. Whatever you wanted to call the person who anchored you to life; that was what she missed.

Andy's were big, impossible shoes to fill. Fran had realized that trying to replace him was like walking up a down-escalator in custard-filled wellies – exceptionally hard work and not much fun. But she had also realized that other people – her friends and family – had begun to 'fill in' for Andy in some ways.

Her mother often co-parented in a sometimes annoying but always well-meaning fashion, her brother would rock up and horse around with the children as Andy had done, overexciting them usually right before bedtime. Nat, Pamela and Heather were the indulgent ones – giving the kids too many sweets as Andy would have and letting them stay up too late.

And now there was Gary. He had slotted into Fran's life without fuss or complication. She knew that he cared about her but he also respected Andy's memory and was happy to be the friend she needed. And because their meetings had been in Elsie Loveday's garden and on a trip to Ikea, there was no hint of romance to it – they were two people who liked each other and enjoyed one another's company. Perfect. Sort of.

One day she invited Gary along to a Sunday walk with the kids. As a friend. She made sure that Charlie and Jude understood this too.

'Just a friend. We get it, Mum,' said Charlie, rolling her eyes.

'Do I have to come?' moaned Jude.

'Yes, you do. Sunday is a digital detox day – remember?'

'Day of misery, more like.'

Fran put an arm around his shoulder. 'Aww, your life is so hard. Want me to call Childline for you?'

'I've got the number,' offered Charlie helpfully.

'I hate you all,' said Jude but she knew he didn't mind these excursions once he got there – jogging along the paths with a laughing Charlie and a happily barking Alan. There were worse ways to spend a Sunday.

'You got any crampons or Kendal Mint Cake in that bag?' teased Fran, gesturing at Gary's all-weather hiking gear and rucksack as they bundled out of the car.

He laughed. 'You may mock but I've checked the forecast and know for a fact that you'll get very wet if it rains and you're wearing those,' he remarked, gesturing at her thin summer jacket and ancient trainers.

'I'll be fine,' she said dismissively as they set off.

An hour later, Fran was soaked to the skin and shivering as the rain fell in sheets. Jude and Charlie were fine because they were both far more sensible than their mother and wore cagoules over jumpers, whilst Alan bounded along beside them, barking at the sheer joy of being outdoors in the rain.

'Bloody English weather – it's supposed to nearly be summer,' muttered Fran as she inched gingerly down a muddy slope. 'Woah!' she cried as she slipped. *Shit, that's it – I'm about to land on my arse.* Gary caught her under one elbow and steadied her. 'Thank you,' she said. He smiled.

If this was a romance novel, I'd be falling into his arms right now, thought Fran, surprised at how much the idea appealed to her.

'Isn't this the moment when you say "I told you so"?' she asked.

'I could but to be honest, it would have taken away from my knight rescuing the damsel-in-distress moment,' said Gary, his eyes glittering with amusement.

'I'm taking you down with me next time,' she retorted.

'I look forward to it,' he replied.

Nothing wrong with a little harmless flirting, thought Fran as they sat in her toasty kitchen later that afternoon, drinking mug after mug of restorative tea and eating their way through a whole packet of Jaffa Cakes. She watched Gary chatting with Jude now and smiled. She could see from Jude's face that he liked Gary, not least because he'd just told him that his brother was a music curator.

'What's a music curator?' asked Fran, looking puzzled.

Jude rolled his eyes. 'Duh, mother. It's a person who puts together playlists for hotels and stuff. He used to work for Apple.'

'Fancy,' said Fran, smiling at Gary.

'It all goes a bit over my head but he does get us tickets for gigs sometimes – your mum mentioned that you're an Ed Sheeran fan. I'll ask if he can get tickets for his tour next year,' offered Gary.

'Thanks.' Jude grinned. 'That'd be cool.'

'Praise indeed,' observed Fran. 'I don't think I've done anything cool for about five years.'

'Six actually, Mum,' quipped Jude, planting a kiss on his mother's head as he walked out of the kitchen. 'But who's counting?'

Fran and Gary laughed. 'More tea?' she asked, gesturing at his empty mug.

'No, I'm all tea-ed out, ta, and I'd better get going,' he said, standing up. 'I really enjoyed today. Thanks for asking me along – your kids are brilliant.'

Fran smiled. 'Well, I think they rather like you too.'

As do I. But I'm not going to tell him because that would make all this seem too real. Repeat the mantra after me – just friends, just friends, just friends.

And yet. You had that rather graphic dream about him the other night. You know the one. You woke feeling all sweaty and guilty, secretly longing to fall back into it. That kiss felt so deliciously real. Too real.

Just friends, just friends, just friends.

'Fran?' Gary was staring at her now. 'Did you hear me?'

'Sorry, what?' Fran hoped she wasn't blushing.

Gary smiled. 'You were miles away. I said I'll call you in the week, okay?'

She nodded and followed him down the hall. He paused in the doorway to the living room. 'Bye, Charlie,' he called.

She looked up from the chaotic American teen comedy she was watching and leapt to her feet, rushing forwards to put her arms around his middle. 'Bye, Gary. Before you go, say that thing again.'

'Marsh-mallow?' he offered.

Charlie snorted like a pig. 'Classic! Marsh-mallow! Who says that? Not even the Queen! It's marsh-mellow! Brilliant!'

'My daughter lives in a very happy place,' said Fran, 'far away from most other human beings.'

Gary laughed. 'She's a superstar. So when does the new sofa arrive?' he asked as they walked to the door.

'Tomorrow,' said Fran, thinking back to when they'd gone to buy it. She had mistakenly assumed that the new sofa would fit into her car and Gary would provide the muscle to help her bring it home but it wouldn't. Gary didn't seem to mind but Fran felt embarrassed so had stopped off at the garden centre and asked him to help her with three large bags of compost instead.

'I only want you for your muscles,' she'd joked before wincing at how inappropriate this sounded. *Shut up, woman. You're making it worse.*

'Well, obviously I feel hideously objectified but I'll live with it,' Gary had said with a grin.

Fran hadn't been able to look him in the eye after that.

'Big day then,' said Gary, fixing her with a gaze that made her stomach skip. *Get a grip, Fran.*

'Yeah, a bit.'

He paused in the doorway. 'I hope it goes okay. You know where I am if you need me.'

275

'Thank you,' she said, feeling that odd sense of regret again as she watched him drive off.

Well, that was a mightily confusing day, she thought as she folded washing later that evening. On the one hand, she relished Gary's friendship and didn't want to spoil that, but, on the other hand, she felt an urge to be brave and see what happened if she snogged his face off. It was all a tad bewildering and she wasn't entirely sure what to do about it.

Fran picked up a pile of Jude's clothes and carried them to the landing. His light was still on so she tapped on the door.

'Yeah?' She pushed it open. He was sitting on the bed, earphones clamped round his head, strumming his guitar. He smiled up at her – her beautiful boy with his shock of orange hair. She saw whispers of Andy in his face now and something else, as if he was becoming a new, different version of his dad. It used to make her cry but now it made her smile. That had to be progress, surely?

'Your laundry, sir,' she said, placing the clothes on the side.

'Thanks, Mum.'

She nodded. 'Don't stay up too much longer, okay?'

''Kay. I just want to finish this song.'

'It sounds great by the way.'

'Thanks.' She paused in the doorway. 'You okay, Mum?' he asked, glancing up at her.

She smiled. 'Yeah. So, it will be cool if Gary's brother can get you tickets for that Ed Sheeran gig next year, won't it?'

Jude nodded. 'He's a nice guy.'

'Ed Sheeran?'

'You know what I mean, Mother.'

'Yeah but it was funny, wasn't it?'

'In a slightly lame way.'

'Rude.'

276

'Seriously though, Mum, I haven't seen you as happy as this since…'

'I know.'

'You deserve to be happy.'

Fran blinked back the threat of tears and leant forwards to kiss her son on the forehead. 'Bed,' she said.

'Love you, Mummy,' he joked.

She shook her head and smiled. 'I love you too, Julian Parker.'

Fran went downstairs and poured herself a glass of wine. Carrying it into the living room, she glanced at the battered old sofa where Andy used to sit. It had been worn out when they'd got it – a second-hand offering from Sam possibly. Andy had declared it to be the most comfortable sofa in the world, whereas Fran always felt as if she was slipping down the back, like Alice into the rabbit hole. She had been on the verge of replacing it before Andy died and had even picked out a beautiful new one from John Lewis.

She plonked herself down now and lay back. It was beyond uncomfortable and yet she felt a lurch of sadness, like she did when she got rid of the kids' unwanted toys – as if the memories left with them. But of course, that wasn't true. It was just stuff. And you couldn't hang on to it for ever.

So, tomorrow's the day.

Yep.

Well, don't be sad – you've always hated this sofa.

True.

You don't sound convinced.

It's just that it feels a bit final.

It's only a sofa, Fran.

Yeah, I guess.

You heard what Jude said. And you're starting to realize it yourself, aren't you?

Maybe.

So what do you want, Fran? You've spent all this time trying to work it out. It's time to be honest. Tell the truth. It's okay.

She sighed. I'm tired, Andy. I'm tired of being sad. I want a little bit of happiness again.

Then go for it, my love. Reach out and take it. I want you to be happy again too. It's time to let go.

Fran and Heather rushed forwards to greet Pamela as they met for the final session of the course the following week.

'You made it!' cried Fran.

'I made it,' beamed Pamela, carrying a promising-looking tin under her arm.

'How's Barry?' asked Heather.

'Complaining because of his new diet but he's lost three pounds already,' smiled Pamela. 'Mind you, I had to hide these cakes from him – he's a devil.'

'Tell him I'll be round as usual for our walk tomorrow,' said Fran. Barry was under strict instructions to exercise every day and had been accompanying Fran on her daily dog walks.

'Ooh, that reminds me, he asked me to give you this,' said Pamela, pulling a leaflet from her bag and handing it to her.

'The Memory Garden,' read Fran. 'Oh yes, he was telling me about this woman who planted a garden after she lost her husband. She ended up founding a charity which uses gardening as therapy for when life gets tough – this looks very interesting.'

Nik clapped his hands to get their attention and they took their places. 'Dear friends. Here we are for the very last time. I can hardly believe how quickly these ten weeks have flown by but I also feel that we have been through a great deal together in such a short space of time.' There were murmurs and nods of agreement around the room. 'Tonight, I would like us to consider what we have learnt and I would also like it to be a celebration of where we are now. I would therefore like to invite you to share your stories if you would like to. In the true spirit of *hygge*, please think of this as a safe place, without agenda or judgement. As I am encouraging you to share, I would also like to share my story with you. For me, this has been so much more than a course where I was the teacher. You too have taught me about community, about humanity and about friendship.'

Fran felt an unexpected jolt of emotion at these words. She noticed Pamela's eyes mist with tears and took hold of her hand and smiled as Heather did the same.

Nik continued. 'Back home in Denmark, I had everything – a good job in television, the perfect wife, the beautiful family. But I lost them all because I was selfish. I drank too much and I forgot the value of what it is to be happy. So, I came to England to try and rediscover what I'd lost. I went to a course, not unlike this one, and learnt everything I have tried to teach you. I am planning to go back to Denmark to hopefully make amends with my wife and family. I want to thank you for your part in helping me to do that because I am a different man to the one who first met you and I am grateful to you for helping me.'

There was a pause before Pamela jumped to her feet and started to clap. Fran and Heather rose to join her along with the rest of the room.

'Thank you. Thank you, everyone.' Nik smiled. 'You are very kind. But tonight is about you. So please, I open the floor to whoever would like to share their story.'

The group eyed one another nervously before Sue stood up and started to speak. Everyone's story was different, but Fran was struck by how each person had managed to find something that brought them joy, whether it be starting a business or volunteering at a refuge or singing in the choir – they had all found a different slice of happiness.

When it was Fran's turn, she felt her mouth go dry. She always had something to say – a witty comment or self-deprecating remark, but this was different. It was time to get serious about happiness. Heather gave her an encouraging nod as she stood up and Pamela reached out to squeeze her hand.

Fran looked around the room, at this unlikely bunch of comrades.

'I'm getting a new sofa tomorrow,' she said.

There were nervous, uncertain glances from everyone except Pamela and Heather, who were smiling at her, their gazes steady and proud. She took a deep breath.

'Most of you know that my husband died two years ago. It was very sudden and I felt as if someone had ripped my heart out of my chest and stamped on it.' The room was pin-drop silent. 'At first, I was absolutely furious – with him, with life, with everything really. And sometimes the grief was like an ocean – I was drowning, gasping for air. I couldn't get my breath. And sometimes, it was like a shadow over my heart – dark and viscous and fucking awful. And people would say "you're so brave".' Fran shook her head. 'But I wasn't. I was scared shitless and completely helpless. So I packed the grief away. I took it out from time to time and looked at it but I didn't face up to it. And we had this sofa – it was Andy's favourite. And after he died, I would sit on it and have these imaginary conversations with him. And that was a comfort but actually after this course and all of you…' She looked towards Heather and Pamela, who were both crying and smiling, before glancing back at Nik, who was nodding with kind encouragement. Fran turned to the group. '…I don't need to do that anymore. And so my version of happiness is this – in the here and now. And tomorrow it will be gardening at Mrs Loveday's. And then dinner with my kids. And celebrating with Pamela and Barry next week. And that's enough. Because the grief will always be there and I will always miss my husband. But I am allowed to be happy. And I want to be too.'

The room seemed to hold its breath before everyone rose to their feet. As Fran found herself surrounded by tearful, kind people, embracing and praising her, one clear thought resonated in her mind.

You are loved. Give in to it.

'Oh, wasn't it wonderful tonight?' said Pamela as they strolled out onto Hope Street later that evening. '*You* were wonderful, ducks,' she added, patting Fran's arm.

'Thank you. It felt good.' Fran smiled.

'I think we should go for a celebratory drink,' said Heather. 'Who's with me?'

'Why not?' agreed Fran.

'Good idea,' said Pamela. 'Simon's staying for a few days so I'll give him a quick call to let him know what I'm doing.'

'You seem very happy, young lady,' said Fran turning to Heather with eyebrows raised.

'A wise friend told me to take things one day at a time so I'm doing just that.'

'She sounds awesome.'

'She is,' grinned Heather. 'But there's another reason why I'm feeling chipper.'

'Oh yes? Has Ryan Gosling been bombarding you with texts again?'

Heather laughed. 'Of course! But aside from that, I've decided to train as a dance teacher.'

'Oh wow. That's fantastic!' cried Fran, hugging her friend.

Heather smiled. 'It was Pamela who got me thinking about it with her ballroom brilliance. I used to run a dance club at my last school. It was the one thing about my job I loved so I decided to give it a go.'

'I'm proud of you,' said Fran. 'Put me down as your first pupil – I have zero talent but I'll be a very enthusiastic learner.'

'Well I do love a challenge,' said Heather as Pamela finished her call. 'Now come on, that Prosecco won't drink itself – to the pub without delay!'

They hadn't made it far along the street before Fran spotted Gary walking towards them.

'Good evening, ladies.'

'Hello, Gary lovey,' said Pamela with a smile.

'What are you doing here?' asked Fran, when what she actually meant was, *I'm so glad to see you.*

'I got your text.'

'Oh. Right. Well, I didn't mean for you to come over right away.'

'I know. But I wanted to.'

Fran spotted Pamela and Heather, grinning at her like couple of loons. She laughed. 'How about I catch you up?'

Heather lent forwards and whispered in Fran's ear. 'I bet you a tenner you don't make it.'

'See you later, Fran!' said Pamela with a wink as they left.

Fran shook her head in amusement before turning to face Gary. 'So. Here we are.'

Gary drew nearer and looked into her eyes. 'Here we are.'

Come on, Fran, you sent the man a bloody text inviting him on a date and here he is – your big chance. Right in front of you. Don't blow it now.

'Yeah, about that text.'

'Mhmm.' He fixed her with a look that bore into her soul. *Tell me the truth*, it said.

She swallowed. 'The thing is…' His gaze was constant, the merest smile playing on his lips. *Oh my God. I think I want to kiss him.* 'I like you,' she blurted.

He raised his eyebrows. 'You like me.'

'I like having you around,' she added. *Wow – practically a declaration of love.*

He was smiling at her now, hanging on her every, lame, insubstantial word.

'You're not making this easy for me,' she said.

She was having trouble keeping eye contact – his gaze was

282

turning her insides to honey. He stared at her for a second longer before reaching forwards and kissing her – an astonishing, wonderful, electric kiss.

'Does that make it easier?' he asked as he drew back.

She stared into his eyes and allowed herself to fall. 'Shut up and kiss me again.'

Chapter Twenty-Four

Pamela

My Happiness List
1. Just bake
2. Dinner with Matthew and Barry – be in the moment!
(DISASTER)
3. Go dancing with Barry? (Not likely)
4. Laugh like we used to! (with Heather instead)
5. Try something new – lovely trip to art gallery with Fran & Charlie
(and Gary!)
6. Teach other people how to bake
7. Let Matty go and be kinder to Barry
8. Appreciate what I have & how lucky I am…
9. Treasure the past, live for the present

Pamela glanced over to where Jim was climbing a stepladder, trailing a line of yellow, blue and red polka-dot bunting behind him.

'You be careful, ducks! I don't want any injuries today.'

'I'll be fine, Mrs T. I know exactly what I'm doing…woah!'

The ladder wobbled and Fran rushed forwards to steady it. 'Thanks, Fran,' breathed Jim.

'No problem,' she said. 'How about I stay here and hold it for you so that we avoid any unnecessary trips to A and E.'

'How many more balloons do we need to blow up?' complained Jude, looking despondently at the half-dozen pearlescent ruby and silver coloured balloons scattered at his feet.

'I love blowing up balloons,' declared Charlie.

'That's because you never actually blow them up,' pointed out Jude. 'You inflate them so far before letting go cos you like the farting noise.'

'That is totally not true,' said Charlie, half-inflating the silver balloon she was holding before releasing her grip and giggling with delight as it whizzed around the room to comical effect. 'Actually, I do like doing that,' she admitted.

'Okay, Parker children, you need to crack on,' instructed Fran. 'Have you tried using the balloon pump? I'm sure I put one in the bag.'

'Now she tells us,' said Jude, rolling his eyes at Charlie.

'Here we are,' said Pamela, bustling out of the kitchen with a tray. 'Triple chocolate muffins for my little workers.'

Charlie and Jude fell upon them with glee. 'Thanks, Pamela – these are epic,' said Jude.

'Is there a job you can do where you get paid in chocolate muffins?' asked Charlie with genuine interest as she took a large bite.

Pamela smiled at them. There was lots to do before the party this afternoon but she was loving every second. If she had learnt anything over the past few weeks it was that life was fragile and precious. It was important to enjoy the small moments – the friendship, the laughter, the farting balloons. This was the stuff of life.

People always said that health scares were wake-up calls but Pamela hadn't really understood that properly until now. As she faced the fear of losing Barry, it was as if her life was brought more sharply into focus. On the night after his heart attack, when the doctors had assured her that he was in a stable condition and Laura had begged her to get some rest, she had gone home to an empty house, thinking that she would collapse into an exhausted sleep.

It didn't happen so at two in the morning, she found herself pacing the floor, trying not to let the desolate thoughts take hold.

What if Barry has another heart attack while I'm here at home?

What if he dies and I'm not there?

What would I do then?

She phoned the hospital and spoke to the night nurse, who assured her that Barry was sleeping and that she should try to rest too. She made herself a mug of warm milk and carried it into the box room in search of comfort.

She traced a finger over the photos of Laura as a baby, then Matthew appearing a few years later and finally Simon – her three beautiful children, all doing their best at life, all working towards their own versions of happiness. Looking at these photos used to make her feel hollow with longing – desperate to go back and re-inhabit that world of small children with their sticky faces and tight fierce hugs. But things had changed. The creeping acceptance that her children had flown and would be okay was taking root.

I had that moment and I'm lucky. But it's in the past and that's where it has to stay – a treasured moment and a cherished memory. I'll always have them but I have to live in the present now.

It was her life with Barry that was most important. Pamela could see that now. They had both taken the other for granted, but after forty years of marriage, was it any wonder? All she wanted at this moment was for him to get better so that they could enjoy the rest of their lives together. She would indulge his gardening, he would encourage her baking and they could be happy.

She felt a tear drop onto her favourite photograph – the one of the three children sitting on the beach in Weymouth, their ice-cream-covered faces grinning out at her. She let herself cry as the sadness and joy mingled.

If I am lucky, there will be more moments like these – different but still wonderful as life moves forwards and we reach for the future. We have to keep reaching for the future. Please let us do that.

'Coming through!' cried Heather, entering the hall with a large tray in her arms. 'I've got focaccia, cheese twists and sausage rolls and Georg's bringing the cakes.'

'Thank you, both.' Pamela smiled. 'If you could pop them on the table, I'll lay them out in a bit.'

'Wow, you guys are doing an amazing job,' declared Heather, gazing around the room. 'It's looking lovely.'

'I've blown up three balloons,' said Charlie proudly.

'That's actually pretty lame,' observed Jude.

'Heather. Jude's being mean to me,' reported Charlie.

Heather laughed. 'I've got to get back to the bakery but I can do a couple before I go.'

'I will help too,' said Georg, who had arrived with the cakes.

'Okay. Race you.' Heather grinned. 'Three balloons each.'

Georg raised one eyebrow and fixed her with a look. 'Let's do this.'

'This, I've got to watch,' laughed Fran. 'Come on, Jim, the bunting can wait.'

Heather eyeballed Georg. 'Ready to lose?'

'In your dreams,' he replied.

'This is fun!' cried Charlie, grabbing Pamela's arm.

'Okay,' said Jude. 'Three-two-one-go!'

Heather struggled to inflate her first balloon, whilst Georg got off to a flying start. Unfortunately, he didn't have a tight enough hold on his balloon and, to Charlie's great delight, it pinged off, farting wildly around the room. Heather started to giggle but managed to blow up her balloon and tie it, whilst Georg struggled with his replacement first balloon. He regained his composure and they quickly blew up their second balloons and tied them. They both picked up their third balloons and fixed each other with a steely gaze like cowboys waiting to draw. Heather fumbled though and was too slow as Georg inflated his last balloon like a pro and dropped it to the floor before dancing on the spot, whilst everyone laughed.

'Winner, winner, chicken dinner! You lose! You lose!' he crowed.

Heather laughed. 'I have honestly never seen you so happy.'

'You're funny, Georg,' declared Charlie.

'Thank you.' Georg smiled. 'Was fun. Now we go back to work. See you later.'

Pamela reached out to hug them both. 'Thank you, my ducks. I'm very grateful for everything you've done.'

'You deserve it, Pamela – you are very kind lady,' said Georg seriously.

'What he said,' agreed Heather, leaning over to kiss her on the cheek. 'See you later, okay?'

Pamela smiled as she watched them leave. Laura arrived shortly afterwards, with Tupperware boxes full of different savoury dishes, and was soon joined by Simon and his girlfriend, Skye, who had driven up from Bristol that day. Pamela's heart swelled with love at the sight of them. She would have loved Matthew to have been there too but he was busy following his dreams in America. She understood that and it made her proud.

A few hours later, Pamela checked her appearance in the mirror, smoothing down the simple cream lace dress she'd bought especially for today.

'You look beautiful, Pammy,' said Barry, smiling at her reflection.

'You don't look too bad yourself,' she replied, reaching over to adjust his tie. 'There. Perfect.'

He kissed her on the cheek. 'I'm glad I married you,' he joked.

'Well that's a blessing!' She looked into his eyes. His face was a little drawn since he'd lost weight and his skin sagged as if the weight of being ill had dragged him down. But then he smiled and she saw that twinkle again – the spark of the man she fell in love with, still here with her, in this moment.

This is all I need. This is what I want. My husband. My Barry. We're still together and I love him more than ever.

She pulled him close and held on, feeling the warmth of him, the smell of him, the essence of him. It didn't matter what age you were – you needed that closeness with another person, the feel of a heart beating next to yours, a breath of life.

Hold on to it, Pammy. Hold on to it with all your might.

'This is nice,' murmured Barry.

Pamela rested her head against his chest. 'Yes,' she said. 'Yes, it is.'

It was a wonderful party. Even better than Pamela had dreamed. Hope Street Hall was buzzing as Barry and Pamela arrived with Laura, Simon and their partners. A cheer went up as soon as they entered and the choir began to sing. Pamela kept hold of Barry's hand as people patted them on the back, hugged and kissed them.

'Can I offer you a glass of Prosecco?' asked a voice beside them.

Pamela turned and gasped as she spotted Matthew, standing next to his siblings, his dear face tanned and smiling.

'Surprise!'

'Oh Matty – you came!' she cried, wrapping her arms around him.

'Of course I came! I couldn't miss this and I wanted to come and check that Dad was all right, obviously.' He put an arm around his father. 'I'm so glad to see you both.'

'I'm glad to see you too, son,' said Barry, gazing up at him.

Pamela felt her heart skip with love for them both but noticed that Barry was looking pale. 'Can you find a seat for your dad, please, Matthew?'

'Of course. Come on, Dad.'

'I'm all right, Pammy, don't worry. I'll just sit for a minute – maybe you could tell me about your adventures, son,' he said.

'I'd love that,' said Matthew.

Pamela squeezed his arm. 'I'm going to say hello to a few people. I'll come and find you in a bit.' She turned and noticed that Angel and her friends had arrived. She gave them a wave as Cheryl bounced over, closely followed by the others.

'We got a surprise!' cried Cheryl, her huge eyes wide with the thrill of a secret about to be shared.

'Have you? I love a surprise!' said Pamela with a smile.

Angel and her friends gathered around Pamela. 'We made this for you,' said Angel, looking uncharacteristically shy as she held out a cake tin for inspection.

Pamela lifted the lid and gasped when she saw the beautiful chocolate cake inside. Its outside was surrounded by milk and white chocolate cigarillos, its top decorated with budding pink and white roses. 'You made this for me?'

Angel sniffed and looked at her feet, while the other mums exchanged proud glances. 'Well, yeah, we wanted to get you and Mr T something so we all made it together. I hope it's okay.'

Pamela's eyes misted with tears. 'It's the most beautiful cake and the kindest surprise I've ever had – thank you. Thank you all so, so much.'

Angel flashed a nervous smile. 'For real?'

Pamela nodded. 'For real, ducks. Now put that tin down so that I can give you all a proper hug!'

'Yay, group hug!' squeaked Cheryl, wrapping her arms around their legs as they all pulled together in a huge, laughing embrace.

The choir was finishing their set as Pamela made her way back to Barry. 'How are you feeling?' she asked, noticing with relief that he had some more colour in his cheeks.

'Better, thanks Pammy. Matthew's been telling me all about LA. It sounds wonderful!'

Pamela smiled down at them both. 'Well, I look forward to hearing all about it too. Do you still want to make your speech?'

'I can do it for you if you like, Dad?' offered Mathew.

'Would you, son? I've written a few things down,' said Barry, handing Matthew a piece of paper. 'Just make sure you tell your mother how beautiful she looks,' he added, winking at Pamela.

Matthew put a hand on his shoulder. 'Of course, Dad.' He stood up. 'Could I have everyone's attention please?' The room descended into hush. 'For those of you who don't know me, I'm Pamela and Barry's middle son, Matthew. I'm going to say a few words on behalf of my dad.' He smiled at his father before unfolding the piece of paper Barry had given him. 'Pammy,' he said addressing his mother, who was sitting next to Barry now, holding his hand. 'You know I'm not much cop with words.' A ripple of affectionate laughter broke out. Matthew grinned. 'But I love you more than you will know. You are like the stake that keeps my cucumbers growing straight – constant and steady.' Pamela laughed along with the assembled company. Matthew smiled as he continued. 'You're like the fertilizer that feeds the flowers – nurturing and protecting.'

'Fertilizer?' chuckled Pamela, nudging Barry.

'Could have been worse – he could have said manure,' quipped Fran. More laughter.

'But above all, you are like a Gertrude Jekyll rose – strong and beautiful, bringing joy to everyone.' Matthew's voice faltered as he went on. 'I wouldn't be half the man I am today without you – you bring me so much happiness and I love you very, very much.'

There were sniffles from various parts of the room. Pamela's eyes were wet with tears as Barry turned and kissed her. 'It's true, Pammy,' he said.

She took his hands and kissed them before standing to

address the room. 'I would like to say a few words if I may,' she began.

'Go, Mrs T!' encouraged Angel from the back.

Pamela smiled. 'Firstly, thank you to all of you for coming today – it means the world to us.' Her gaze fell on Laura, Matthew and Simon. 'And to you three – our beautiful children – we're so proud of you and love you very much.' There were ahhhs of fondness around the room. 'Special thanks to my choir for singing so wonderfully and to my happiness course buddies for bringing me such joy. I also have to thank all my friends for helping me decorate the hall – Fran, Charlie, Jude, Heather, Georg, Jim and so many others. I'm lucky to have you in my life. And special thanks to Angel and her friends for the beautiful cake – I'm very touched and I love teaching you girls.'

'You rock, Mrs T!' cried Dee.

Pamela smiled, before turning to Barry. 'But most of all, I have to thank you, Barry – my dear husband of forty years. While I was thinking about what to say today, I found this Apache blessing on the internet. It sums up perfectly what I feel so I would like to read it to you all.' Pamela rummaged in her handbag and pulled out a piece of paper. She put on her reading glasses and cleared her throat.

'*Treat yourselves and each other with respect, and remind yourselves often of what brought you together. Give the highest priority to the tenderness, gentleness and kindness that your connection deserves. When frustration, difficulties and fear assail your relationship, as they threaten all relationships at one time or another, remember to focus on what is right between you, not only the part which seems wrong. In this way, you can ride out the storms when clouds hide the face of the sun in your lives – remembering that even if you lose sight of it for a moment, the sun is still there. And if each of you takes responsibility for the quality of your life together, it will be marked by abundance and delight.*'

She turned to Barry, who was smiling and nodding. 'It's easy after nearly forty years of marriage to lose sight of one another. But I remember the first second I met you, Barry Trott, like it was yesterday. We were at a dance and all your friends had partnered off with other girls. You came up to me, grinning and said, "I can't believe my luck – the most beautiful girl in the room and no one has asked her to dance yet."' Ahhhs of approval echoed round the room. Pamela smiled. 'And then you offered me your hand and said, "Would you make me the happiest man in the world?" and we danced and the rest of the room fell away and it was just you and me.' Barry wiped away a tear as Pamela took his hand. 'And it's still you and me, Barry Trott. I remind myself every day of that moment and how lucky I am. And even though we lost sight of each other for a while and I nearly lost you, the thing that brought us together is still here. The sun is still shining. We are blessed, we are lucky and I love you.'

People wiped away tears as the room gave way to cheers and some particularly enthusiastic whoops and whistles from Angel and her friends. Pamela smiled and hugged Barry.

'Beautiful speech,' said Fran, approaching Pamela and kissing her on the cheek. 'How does it feel to be universally celebrated and adored?'

'It feels wonderful.' Pamela beamed. 'And how are things with that lovely man?' she added, gesturing over to where Gary and Charlie were playing tag with balloons.

'Lovely,' said Fran. 'We're taking it one day at a time. But it's lovely.'

'I'm so glad, Fran,' said Pamela, patting her arm.

'I spy empty glasses!' cried Heather, topping them up from the bottle she was carrying. 'Cheers!'

'Cheers,' echoed Pamela and Fran.

'Don't you wish you could do this every week?' asked Heather, gazing round the room.

'What? Have a party?' Fran frowned.

'No-o, I mean bring all these different groups of people

together – people who wouldn't normally meet. It's lovely. Look at how well they get along.'

Pamela gazed around the room. It was true. Angel and her friends were laughing with some mums from the choir, Elsie Loveday was talking to Doly, whilst children aged between two and fourteen played and giggled together. Different generations, races, religions all mixed together. Call it community or call it life – it was noisy, lively, colourful, cheerful and utterly wonderful.

'I've had an idea,' said Pamela, her eyes glittering with excitement. Fran and Heather smiled at one another as Pamela put an arm around each of their shoulders. 'But I'm going to need your help.'

Chapter Twenty-Five

Six months later…

Heather

Happiness List
1. Marry Luke!
2. Sunday walk and choose wedding venue with Luke Fran & Charlie
WEDDING CANCELLED
3. Exercise more (persuade Luke to go running?)
- Boot camp with Fran & Pamela
4. Go dress shopping with Gemma and laugh like we used to!
Fran & Pamela - laughed like teenagers!
DRESS SOLD ON EBAY
5. Surprise Luke at work
6. Ask Pamela for help with first dance for wedding!
7. Help Pamela & Barry fall in love again
- mission accomplished!
8. Treasure my friends
9. Have the courage to take what I need from life
10. Trust my instincts and value my own company

Hope Street Hall was buzzing with excitement. Heather, Fran and Pamela stood at one end of the hall while the camera crew prepared to start filming. The journalist smiled at the three friends. 'Okay, ladies, are we ready?'

They grinned at one another. 'Ready when you are, ducks,' said Pamela.

'Great. Okay, Dave? Have you got the banner in shot?' She gestured to the large 'Happiness Hub' sign which was stretched across the far wall.

'Yep – all good and ready to go, Anita.'

'Can we have a bit of hush please?' called the sound man.

There was a loud whistle from one corner of the room. 'All right, listen up people,' cried Angel. 'Mrs T is about to be on telly so zip it, yeah?' Silence descended.

'Thank you.' Anita smiled as she gave Dave the signal to start filming. She spoke to the camera. 'I'm here today at Hope Street Community Hall. You may remember hearing about Hope Street a year or two ago. This was the community that formed a choir in order to save this very hall and I'm back here today to meet three members of the community who have decided to start a rather special project.' She turned to address the women.

'Heather, could you tell us what the Happiness Hub is all about and how you got involved?'

Heather smiled. 'Well, it all started with a course, which the three of us attended – it was about finding your own version of happiness. I have to say I was pretty sceptical when I went along.'

'How so?' asked Anita.

Heather shot a glance at her friends. 'I thought I was happy. I was planning my wedding and looking to the future with my fiancé.'

Anita nodded. 'But things didn't go quite to plan, did they?'

You can say that again, thought Heather. 'No,' she admitted. 'We broke it off, but actually, it was for the best. I know that now.'

'And so why did the three of you set up this project?'

'Well, it all stemmed from what we learnt on the course – we realized that everyone is searching for their own piece of happiness and that we could perhaps help with that.'

'So what is the Happiness Hub?'

'It's like a community club. We run forums on different topics – everything from mindfulness to taking up a new exercise. I'm running a "dance like there's no one watching" club. We like to channel our inner Beyoncé during that session. But we're evolving it to be whatever the community wants and needs to be happy.'

'It sounds like a fantastic idea.'

Heather grinned. 'It was Pamela's idea and I'm proud to be part of it. It's a project born out of friendship and that's very important to me.' Pamela reached over and squeezed her hand.

Heather knew that she wouldn't have got through the last six months without her friends. It wasn't merely their support that she valued but also the courage they'd given her to rebuild her life without Luke. Fran was predictably straight-talking but always kind, Pamela was reliably overindulgent and Georg was a refreshingly unemotional constant. They were the ideal combination and Heather felt safe in the knowledge that she always had someone to call on.

Over the months after her split from Luke, she settled into a new life on her own and found that, as Georg predicted, she enjoyed her own company. However, there was one friend that she missed every day. Her parting with Gemma remained a tangle of regret in her mind. She didn't miss Luke at all but she did miss Freddy and she desperately missed Gemma – their chats, their stupid banter, their deep-rooted sisterly love.

She woke on one of her days off looking forward to a lazy morning when she caught sight of the newly framed happiness list, hanging beside her bed. Her gaze lingered on 'treasure your friends', and at that moment she realized that it was time to visit Gemma. No word of warning, no call or text. She simply got in the car and drove over. It was mid-morning when she arrived. She rang the doorbell and held her breath.

The first thing she noticed when Gemma answered was how much weight she'd lost. A lot of women lose their post-baby pounds but Gemma looked pinched and worn down by life. The second thing she noticed was the look of surprised hope on her face – it was guarded but there nonetheless.

Are you here to forgive me? Please tell me you are.

'Heather, this is a surprise. How are you?' she asked with real feeling.

'Hedda, Hedda, Hedda,' squeaked a voice as Freddy crawled down the hall at great speed.

'He's crawling! Oh my God, you're crawling!' she cried, holding out her arms to him. 'And you remember me, don't you?'

'Hedda!' he confirmed as Gemma moved to one side and Heather scooped him into her arms. 'Mwah!' he added, planting a gummy kiss on her face.

'He remembers me,' said Heather, her throat scratchy with the threat of tears.

'You're his godmother,' said Gemma. 'He's got your picture in his nursery. We talk about you all the time. He misses you.' *I miss you.* She didn't say the words but Heather felt them in the air all the same.

'I've missed him too. Can I come in?'

'Of course. Sorry. Would you like a coffee?'

'Please.'

'Still just milk?'

'Still just milk.'

'Hedda, Hedda. Bricks. Bricks,' insisted Freddy, pointing towards the lounge.

'He's obsessed with building bricks at the moment,' called Gemma from the kitchen.

'Shall we go and have a play with your bricks, Freddy?' asked Heather.

'Bricks, bricks,' said Freddy, as she set him on the floor and sat down next to him. They made walls and houses and bridges, all of which Freddy eyed with delight as they went up and knocked down with glee as soon as they were built.

'Well, he's either going to be an architect or a wrecking ball operative,' joked Heather as her cousin brought in the coffee.

Gemma laughed. 'So how have you been?' It was casually uttered but loaded with meaning.

Heather nodded. 'I'm okay. I feel as if I've come through a storm to a calm and better place.'

'I'm glad,' said Gemma with genuine relief. 'I've been worried about you.'

Heather rested her gaze on her cousin and saw the regret and sadness in her eyes. She remembered that look from the last time they'd met except, today, Heather felt a wave of sympathy. 'When I saw you last, I was angry.'

Gemma nodded. 'I deserved it. I still do.'

'Maybe. But there's only so long you can hang on to anger before it eats away at you. And, in truth, splitting up with Luke has been the best thing that's ever happened to me.'

'Honestly?' asked Gemma.

'Honestly,' said Heather. 'I needed to be on my own, to stop relying on another person to define how I was feeling. And that's what I'm doing. It was scary at first but now it's good, really good. I'm living my life, my way.'

Gemma studied her face. 'You seem happy.'

Heather nodded. 'I am and I'm done with being angry. I've moved on. Oh, and I've got a new lodger to help with the bills.'

'Oh yes?'

'Mhmm. He's a guy I work with – Georg – very serious but actually very nice.'

'Nice?'

Heather shook her head. 'He's gay and he's started seeing someone from the bakery where we work – it's rather sweet actually. I'm happy to be on my own for a change. I went from grieving for Mum and Dad to leaning on you, to my relationship with Luke. I never allowed myself time to just be Heather. I thought that Luke, marriage, babies, all that stuff were what I needed but actually I need time to be me, to find out what I want from life. And if that includes a husband or a baby one day then great but if it doesn't, I've always got Freddy.' She kissed her godson on the head.

'I'm proud of you,' said Gemma, tears brimming her eyes.

Heather smiled. 'I'm proud of me too. And what about you? How are things with Ed?'

Gemma stared at the floor. 'We're going for counselling. It's going to take time.'

Heather sat down next to Gemma and nudged her on the arm. 'You'll get there. Everyone deserves a second chance.'

'Even me?' asked Gemma, scanning Heather's face for the truth.

Heather put her arms around her friend and pulled her into a hug. 'Especially you.'

Gemma sobbed and Heather held her, just as her friend had done all those years ago when she needed her most. She'd come to realize that happiness is fleeting, life is short and often peppered with sadness but it's true friendship that endures and carries you forwards to a bright and brave future.

Fran

Happiness List Thing
1. Accept a world without Andy (too soon!)
2. 'Digital Detox' day with kids
3. Go on even more walks with Alan
4. Have dinner with a nice man (NOT a date) & laugh if appropriate
(he is nice and I did laugh)
5. Stop feeling guilty and like Gary (EPIC fail)
6. Take up gardening again (with a little help from Baz & Mum)
7. Work myself into an early grave helping local elderly people with their
gardens — most fun I've had in ages
8. Get punched in the face by grief and take it
9. Get rid of that bloody uncomfortable sofa
10. Accept a world without Andy and love my world with Gary

'Now Fran, if I can turn to you, you've become involved in this project as a result of losing your husband. It must have been tough to face that at such a young age.'

Fran smiled. 'It was, although can I just say that I love you for calling me young.'

Anita laughed. 'You can. So tell us about your part in this project. I believe that Pamela's husband is also helping you.'

Fran nodded. 'We're using the outside space around the hall to create a well-being garden. It started when I rediscovered my love of gardening. Pamela's husband, Barry, encouraged me to give it a go. I found it really therapeutic. It gave me a break from my grief in a way but I also enjoyed helping other people with their gardens too.'

'Tell us about the garden.'

'It's open to anyone who needs it. Barry and I run sessions where we plan, design, plant – the whole caboodle. We've got a vegetable plot and some fruit trees. It's evolving all the time and it's bloody wonderful! Sorry, am I allowed to say "bloody"?'

'I think you just did,' laughed Anita. 'Now tell us about this sofa at the centre of the garden. What's the story there?'

'Ahh yes, the sofa. Well, it was my husband's and we decided to use it as a centrepiece because, well, I think it's comforting and also pretty cool.' Fran smiled. 'The point of the garden is to promote well-being, so it's for people suffering from stress or anxiety and that may be caused by grief. But above all, it's a haven for the community to help, heal and nurture.'

It had actually been Gary's idea.

The new sofa arrived as planned. It was everything Fran wanted a sofa to be – lush, plump, comfy without lumps or kinks or feathers poking in her back. She was so pleased with it, she kept going into the living room for an admiring glance and shooing Alan away whenever he slunk towards it.

'No doggies on the sofa,' she told him, doing her best to ignore his adorably plaintive stare.

'What about teenagers?' asked Jude, lying on it, dangling his smelly Converse-trainered feet dangerously close to the fabric.

'Don't you dare, Julian Parker,' warned Fran.

'Uh-oh, Mum's doing her threatening voice,' said Charlie, wandering in with a pot of yoghurt.

'And you can take that right back to the kitchen,' declared

Fran, putting her hands on her daughter's shoulders and marching her in the opposite direction.

'S'like a Gulag in this house,' said Jude.

'I think you need to look up the definition of Gulag again,' observed Fran. She spotted her scruffy happiness list, now pinned to the fridge with a magnet and smiled. The doorbell rang. Fran's smile broadened as she walked down the hall to let Gary in.

'Hello, gorgeous,' he said, wrapping her in his arms and kissing her in a way that made her insides turn to liquid. She had decided that allowing herself to fall for this utterly charming man was possibly one of the best decisions she'd ever made.

'And hello to you,' she murmured, pulling away with a smile and leading him down the hall. 'Now can you please talk to these children about respecting my new sofa.'

'Right.' Gary nodded. 'Kids, respect your mum's new sofa. Or else.'

'Or else what?' asked Charlie, standing in the kitchen doorway, eating her yoghurt.

Gary frowned. 'Or else we'll bring the old one back in.'

'And then we'll have two sofas?' asked Jude puzzled.

'Mmm, yeah, I possibly haven't thought this through.'

'That reminds me,' said Fran. 'I need to get in touch with the council to take the old sofa away. Although the idea of sending it to a landfill floods me with all kinds of middle-class guilt.'

'You could use it in the garden,' said Gary, his eyes lighting up with the idea.

Fran shook her head. 'Crazy fool. How would I use it in the garden?'

He fixed her with a look that made her stomach skip with longing. 'Mock not, young lady. I saw a thing on the Chelsea Flower Show a few years back where they re-upholstered this sofa in moss – it was amazing. That would look fantastic as a centre-piece in your well-being garden and keep a memory of Andy there too.'

'I love that,' said Charlie.

'Yeah – could be really cool, Mum,' said Jude with a smile.

Fran blinked back tears as she wrapped her arms around Gary's neck and kissed him. Jude disappeared into the living room. Charlie covered her eyes but peeked through her fingers with delight. 'You watch the Chelsea Flower Show?' she teased, arching a brow.

He laughed. 'What can I say? I really am the perfect guy.'

Fran smiled and kissed him again.

Yeah, and how lucky am I to have met two of them in my life?

Pamela

My Happiness List
1. Just bake
2. Dinner with Matthew and Barry – be in the moment!
(DISASTER)
3. Go dancing with Barry? (Not likely)
4. Laugh like we used to! (with Heather instead)
5. Try something new – lovely trip to art gallery with Fran & Charlie
(and Gary!)
6. Teach other people how to bake
7. Let Matty go and be kinder to Barry
8. Appreciate what I have & how lucky I am...
9. Treasure the past, live for the present
10. Just love

'And finally, Pamela, if I could turn to you.'

'Of course, Anita, lovey – I'm a huge fan of yours.'

'Thank you,' laughed Anita. 'Tell me, what gave you the idea for the Happiness Hub?'

Pamela smiled. 'It was something Fran said that got me thinking – she told me that my house was like a Happiness Hub. And then we were at the party for mine and Barry's wedding anniversary, and Heather pointed out how wonderful it was to have the whole community – all different people from different walks of life – in one place and I thought, yes, this is wonderful. We should try to bring everyone together more often.'

'And this was shortly after your husband had a serious heart attack?'

'It was, Anita. I thought I was going to lose him. It was terrifying. But I tell you what. It made me realize what is important in life.'

'And what is important to you, Pamela?'

Pamela looked into the camera. 'Well, it's love, isn't it? It's family and friends and being kind to one another. It's about looking after each other in the community and spreading a bit of happiness where you can.'

There were whoops and cheers from Angel and her friends. 'You said it, Mrs T. You said it!'

Anita smiled. 'It sounds as if you've already struck a chord in your community.'

Pamela grinned. 'That's Angel and her mum friends. I've been teaching them how to bake and they've been teaching me about life. They're a wonderful group of women – often ignored and unheard by the powers that be. But I'm listening and I'm trying to help if I can.'

'And what would be your message to anyone who's interested in what you've had to say?'

Pamela patted the notebook by her side. 'Start your own happiness list. Come along to the hub. Get involved! If you don't try, you'll never know.'

'That's great advice. You must have a lot of energy to organize all this for the community,' said Anita.

'Well, I've got my helpers,' said Pamela, winking at Fran and Heather. 'And Barry and I are a good team too. Now if you'll excuse me, Anita, I must get ready for my next baking class.' Pamela smiled as she made her way to the kitchen. She thought back to the previous week when she'd returned home from the hall feeling worn out to her bones.

As she opened the front door, Pamela was surprised to hear the sound of water running upstairs and the smell of something delicious wafting from the kitchen.

'Barry? What are you up to?'

He appeared at the top of the stairs, looking pleased with himself. 'I have taken the liberty of drawing a bath for madam,' he reported in a mock-butler's voice.

'Oh, don't mind if I do,' laughed Pamela, walking up the stairs.

'I didn't have any rose petals but I did use my best Radox,' he said with a grin.

Pamela walked into the bathroom and smiled as she noticed the lit candles. 'Oh, Barry, it's wonderful,' she told him, planting a kiss on his cheek.

'Right, well. I'll let you enjoy. Dinner will be served in half an hour. Would you like a glass of something?'

Pamela screwed up her nose. 'I could murder a cup of tea.'

'Coming right up.' He smiled, heading for the stairs.

'And Barry?'

'Yes, love?'

'I'm glad I married you.'

'Well, that's a blessing,' he said with a wink.

Yes, thought Pamela, as got ready to sink into her bath. *Yes. It really is.*

'As you can see,' said Anita, smiling and gesturing around Hope Street Hall. 'The Happiness Hub has become something very special in this community. You can probably hear the music from Heather's dance lesson and Pamela is now in the kitchen with her bakers – I have to tell you that the smell is incredible. I'm still here with Fran, who will shortly be going out to run a session in the Memory Garden. Fran, could you give the final word on this project – how would you, Pamela and Heather like people to view it?'

Fran smiled. 'As a place for everyone. It's somewhere for people to come and find their own version of happiness – whether it be through baking, singing or just being. I think the three of us came to realize how fleeting happiness really is. Life isn't all puppies and rainbows – it's hard and sad sometimes, but everything is a moment too. There are dark times but bright ones as well. I know Pamela, Heather and I all agree – you've got to reach out for those moments of joy, embrace them and hold them close because they carry you through life. We all need to recognize the things that bring us happiness and try to fill our worlds with them. Life isn't perfect but if the happiness outweighs the sadness then I reckon you've got it sussed.'

Acknowledgements

Many thanks to Victoria Oundjian for encouraging me to start this story and to my editor, Charlotte Mursell, for helping me to finish it. Thank you to Lisa Milton, Nia Beynon and the rest of the team HQ for their enthusiasm and support.

Huge thanks to my best book buddies – Sarah Livingston, Helen Abbott, Melissa Khan and Becs Little – for their sage advice, kind words and gin/Prosecco/coffee/wine-based support.

Endless thanks to my fellow writers, particularly the HQ authors past and present and the wonderful RNA bods, who are always so generous and supportive – you know who you are and I love you very much.

To the incredible bloggers and online community who read, review and share the love for my books – your support means everything to me.

Special thanks to Rebecca Minton, who has raved about my writing since day one – you're a diamond and a good friend.

Finally, love and thanks to Lil, Alf and Rich for everything else.

Books

The following books were particularly useful to me while I was researching this book:

Happy: Why more or less everything is absolutely fine by Derren Brown

Grief Works by Julia Samuel

Websites

The VIA Institute kindly gave me permission to use parts of their fascinating free character surveys in chapter twenty-one of this book – you can try them yourself by following this link: http://www.viacharacter.org/www

A Letter From The Author

Dear Reader,

Firstly, congratulations. You are now one of my favourite people in the world. You have taken the time to purchase and read this book and have therefore immediately secured a place on my own happiness list in between 'looking at pictures of pandas playing in the snow' and 'thinking you've run out of Double Deckers before finding one at the back of the cupboard.' Exciting times indeed.

Secondly, I hope you enjoyed this book. People often ask me what the best thing is about being a writer and although 'never having to brush your hair properly' and 'Googling George Clooney for research purposes' are right up there, the thing I love most is when a reader gets in touch and tells me how much they've enjoyed one of my stories. Writers spend a lot of time in their own heads (mine is particularly chaotic) so it's not until your book is unleashed on the world that you truly know if it has had the desired effect. I try to write stories that make people laugh and cry (sorry about that) – that give voice to what readers might be feeling and offer a view of life that is real and true.

With *The Happiness List*, I wanted to bring together three very different women to see if happiness can be learnt, whilst also considering what the three generations can learn from one another. I hope I've managed it.

So if you did enjoy Heather, Fran and Pamela's story, I'd love to hear from you. You can get in touch via Twitter (@1AnnieLyons) or Facebook (www.facebook.com/annielyonswriter) and please spare a moment to post a review – they're catnip to authors and readers alike.

Thank you for reading and sharing, and well done for making my happiness list – you are lovely.

Much love,
Annie x

Turn the page for an exclusive extract from *The Choir on Hope Street*, another gorgeously uplifting story from Annie Lyons!

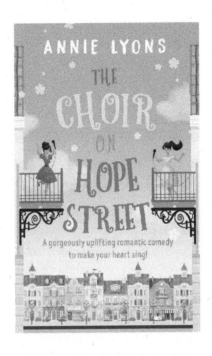

Turn the page for an exclusive extract from *The Choir on Hope Street*, another gorgeously uplifting story from Annie Lyons!

Chapter One

Natalie

'I don't love you anymore.'

That was it. Five words delivered so simply, as if he were reading the news.

'*Good evening and here is the news. The marriage of Natalie and Daniel Garfield, which lasted for fifteen years, is over. In a statement today, Mr Garfield said, "I don't love you anymore." Mrs Garfield responded by punching him in the face and trashing the house.*'

At least that's what I wished I'd done later but at the time an odd sensation of calm descended. It was as if this wasn't really happening to me. It was at best some kind of joke and at worst, something that could be sorted.

This wasn't in the plan. This kind of thing was never going to happen to us. Other people split up, their marriages disintegrating like a swiftly disappearing desert island, but that was never going to happen to us. We were rock solid – a steady ship; Nat and Dan, Dan and Nat. It had the ring of one of those American teen shows that Woody loved to watch on Nick Junior; all jazz hands and sparkly teeth.

We were a great couple. Everyone said so. We were the kind of couple that others looked at with awe and secret envy. Everybody loved Dan. He's just one of those men that people like – old ladies, babies, men, women, children have all told me over the course of our marriage, what a really great guy he is.

I would go on nights out with my female friends as they ripped apart their partners and husbands, picking over their faults like vultures feasting on carrion. I would nod with sympathy but never really had anything to add. They would often turn their sleepy, drunken gaze to me, pat me on the shoulder and slur, ''Course you're lucky, Nat. You've got Dan. He's such a lovely guy.'

And he was. Possibly still is.

Dan was my husband, my soul mate. Of course he had his faults. The underpants on the floor and the toilet seat in the perpetual 'up' position were an irritation, but not exactly a major crime against domesticity. He was, *is* a good man – a good husband and father. He was my happy ever after.

Naturally, we had disagreements and wobbles. Who doesn't? We didn't spend as much time together on our own as we would like but that's to be expected. We're busy with work, Woody and life. Obviously it would be lovely to go on the odd date-night or even have sex but frankly, we were usually too knackered. I'd always thought that the shared bottle of wine on Friday night with a movie was good enough. Clearly I have been labouring under a major misapprehension.

Initially, I went into full-on denial mode when he dropped the bombshell. I wondered later if my body had actually gone into shock in a bid to protect myself from the truth. Certainly at the time, my brain sent me a quick succession of messages to counter his statement: *he didn't mean it* (he did), *he'd been drinking* (he hadn't), *he was tired* (true) *and angry* (not true). It wasn't until I'd picked over the remnants of that evening with various friends (my turn to be the vulture now) that I'd fully taken in the order of events.

It was a Tuesday evening. I hate Tuesdays. They make me feel restless and impatient. Monday is supposed to be the worst day but for me, it has always been Tuesday. I can deal with the post-weekend slump and Monday is usually my most productive day but by Tuesday, I am longing for the week to move 'over the hump' towards the downhill joy of Thursday. I often long for a glass of wine on Tuesday evenings but on this particular day I was disappointingly sober because I was having a so-called healthy week. At least I was before he said it.

It was around 8.30 and we had just finished dinner. Woody was reading in his room before lights-out and I had been about to go and tuck him in. I normally love this part of the day; the feeling that another episode of motherhood is successfully complete; no one died. Everyone is safe.

If I had been paying attention, I would have noticed that Dan was particularly uncommunicative during dinner. Again, it wasn't until later that I recalled the details; his downward gaze and hands fidgeting with the cutlery, his water glass, the pepper mill.

I had been telling him about a problem with my latest book. I am a children's picture-book writer and have enjoyed some success with my series of books about 'Ned Bobbin – the small boy with the big imagination', as my publisher tags it. There have been three books so far and my editor wants another three but I was struggling with ideas and wondering whether to take him down the super-hero route.

When I recalled the conversation later, I realized that I had done all the talking; posing and answering my own questions with just the odd 'mhmm' or nod from Dan. That was the problem with being a writer – you spent too much time at home on your own with no one to talk to.

I talk to myself all the time when I'm working. I read back what I've just written, talk to the radio or hold imaginary conversations with all manner of people, including Ned. I read somewhere that adults have a certain number of words they need to say in a day and that the word quota for a woman is higher than a man's. I believe this. It isn't unusual, therefore, for me to unpack my day to Dan when he gets home. I thought he liked it. Maybe I was wrong about that too.

I had finished my dinner; an unimaginative stir-fry containing any vaguely vegetable-like item I'd found in the fridge on opening it at 7.30. Woody had eaten earlier. He was eight years old and always starving when he returned home from school so I tended to feed him straight away and then either Dan or I cooked our dinner later.

I stood up to clear the plates, reaching out for Dan's. He looked up at me and only then did I notice how pale he looked – that handsome face, slightly pinched with age, but still handsome. He stared at me, unsmiling, and I realized he was nervous.

'What?' I asked with an encouraging smile.

He swallowed and bit his lip. Then he said it.

At first I assumed he was joking.

'Yeah right, and I'm having an affair with James McAvoy.' I shook my head and made for the door.

'Nat.'

I paused, turning to look back at him. He was crying and that was when I knew it wasn't a joke. It was the first rumble of a threatening storm. Still, my brain told me to keep going, carry the plates out, kiss Woody goodnight, come down and sort this out. It was just another thing to be sorted, like pairing the socks in a basket of washing.

I could hear my heart beating in my ears as I padded upstairs, pausing outside my son's bedroom door. I focused for a moment on the wooden letters stuck to the upper panel, spelling 'WOODY'. Each letter was represented by an animal with the same corresponding first letter and I reached out a hand to stroke the wombat's cheery face. *I will sort this out. I'm good at sorting. All will be well.*

I pushed the door open, blinking into the half-light, feeling immediately reassured by the sight of my son. He was sitting up in bed reading by the light of the twisty snake-lamp we had given him last birthday, propped up by the patchwork cushion my mum had made him when he was born. His chin was resting on his chest, that customary frown creasing his perfect face. He flicked his gaze in my direction and then back down at his book.

'How's Mr Fox doing?' I asked, as if nothing had happened, as if my world was still intact.

Woody sighed. 'Not good. Boggis, Bunce and Bean shot him.'

'Ooh, that's *not* good.'

Woody shook his head in agreement but kept reading, his eyes darting left and right. I looked around his room at the dog-eared football posters, the framed prints of scenes from some of my books, the Lego models and the shelves stacked with books. Woody was a bookworm. He had learnt to read at the age of three and not really stopped since. He had probably read *Fantastic Mr Fox* at least fifty times. I felt a sense of calm descend. It would have been the easiest thing in the world to nestle down at the end of Woody's bed, to pretend Dan hadn't said what he had just said and hope that it all went away. I felt safe there.

'Time for lights-out, fella,' said Dan's voice from the doorway. I jumped, jolted back to reality. I couldn't see his face properly but his voice was throaty from crying.

Woody glanced at him and then me. 'Can I just finish this chapter, please?' His expression was wide-eyed and impossible to resist.

Dan stepped forwards and ruffled his hair. 'Okay, but then straight to sleep.'

''Kay,' replied Woody. ''Night, Mum.'

I leant down and kissed him. ''Night, darling boy. Love you. Sleep well.'

'Love you. Sleep well,' repeated Woody like a robot. ''Night, Dad.'

''Night,' said Dan. He turned towards the door and paused, looking back over his shoulder at me. 'Coming?'

319

I stared down at my son as if he might offer a solution. He sensed my hesitation and looked up. "*Night*, Mum,' he said again with a trace of impatience.

"Night,' I answered, turning and following Dan out of the room and down the stairs. We didn't speak again until we reached the dining room.

'I'm going to get a glass of wine,' I said. 'Want one?'

'No,' sighed Dan, 'thanks. We do need to talk, Nat.'

'And that's why I need a glass of wine,' I said, making my way to the kitchen. I poured a polite helping and then doubled it. Taking a large gulp, I refilled it and carried the glass into the dining room. Dan was sitting at the table, his hands in prayer position.

I slid into the chair opposite. 'So,' I began, trying to stay calm and matter-of-fact. 'What's this all about?'

Dan ran a hand through his neatly parted hair and stared up at the ceiling. 'I'm leaving.'

I was surprised to learn that two gulps of wine could inflame immediate righteous anger. 'Because you don't love me anymore?' I almost spat the words.

'I think so.'

'You think so?' I snapped. 'Because that's a fucking big statement if you're not sure. Do you love me or not? Simple question.' My voice was increasing in volume and it unnerved me. My childhood had been punctuated by anger between my father and mother. As an adult I had made a monumental effort to keep mine under control but all bets were off now. Red was the new black.

Dan stared at his hands, unable to look me in the eye. 'No, I don't and I'm sorry.'

The sarcasm devil took control of my brain. 'Well that's all right then. If you're sorry then I forgive you. That makes it all just fine.' I folded my arms and stared at him.

I couldn't get a grip on my brain somehow, couldn't work out what I was supposed to say or how I was supposed to feel. I had no point of reference for this moment. It felt like somebody else's life.

Dan tried to be reasonable. That was one of his greatest strengths. He was eternally reasonable and always took other people's opinions seriously. We rarely argued and this was largely down to Dan. He was able to defuse a situation like the most practised of bomb-disposal experts. 'I understand that you're angry, Nat, and you have every right to be, but if you'll let me, I'll try to explain.'

I took another deep gulp of wine before holding up my glass as if proposing a toast and saying, 'Please. Be my fucking guest.'

Dan swallowed. 'It's nothing you've done or said. You have always been the perfect wife.'

'If you're about to use the words, *it's not you, it's me,* I will get violent,' I retorted.

Dan looked at me, tears brimming in his eyes. 'I have tried to stay in love with you but I just don't have those feelings for you anymore. I love you but I'm not in love with you.'

My head was spinning from a combination of wine and fury. I stood up. 'So you're planning to leave?'

Dan nodded. 'I want to speak to Woody first.'

'Very decent of you, but you'll have to come back to do that another time because I want you gone.'

'Nat.'

People talk about a red mist and others talk about an out-of-body experience but for me it was neither. I thought nothing and felt nothing but pure white-hot fury as I smashed the wine glass to the floor and screamed. 'GO! NOW! I WANT YOU FUCKING GONE!'

Whether out of self-preservation or respect for my feelings, Dan left the room. Moments later he reappeared with a bag, which I realized he must have been hiding in the back of his wardrobe for goodness knows how long. Waiting for the right moment. He had clearly been waiting for the right moment for a while.

He didn't try to speak to me again before he left and I was oddly grateful to him for this. I heard the front door close like a full stop to my life so far. I looked around the room, numb with anger, unable to cry. I looked at the shards of broken glass and swore.

The annoying thing about a burst of righteous anger is that you have to clear up afterwards. I went to fetch the dust-pan and another glass of wine.

If you enjoyed *The Happiness List*, then why not try another feel-good story from HQ Digital?

www.ingramcontent.com/pod-product-compliance
Ingram Content Group UK Ltd.
Pitfield, Milton Keynes, MK11 3LW, UK
UKHW022331250325
456726UK00004B/190